FEEL NO EVIL

ROSEMARIE AQUILINA

Sabieha
PRESS

FEEL NO EVIL

ROSEMARIE AQUILINA

*This book is lovingly
Dedicated to the best people I know:
David, Jennifer, Johanna, Marissa, and Michael,
My children,
My inspiration,
My reasons for reaching my goals, and
Without whom I would be lost.*

ACKNOWLEDGMENTS

There were times when I thought I would never finish *Feel No Evil*. The encouragement I received from my children, family, and friends must be acknowledged with a special thanks to the readers of the first edition who enjoyed it and were very verbal about wanting more.

This Second Edition is an updated version of the First Edition. A sequel is under consideration because of loyal readers who are demanding more works with these characters.

A special thank you to my editor and friend Teresa Crumpton, who not only helped in the revision and edits but prompted me to publish a second edition, revised.

Thank you to Carey Aquilina, the first and loudest cheerleader of *Feel No Evil*.

Thank you, Morgan Cole, for being the greatest proponent of *Feel No Evil* and keeping the story moving forward. Your friendship and words of encouragement mean more than you know.

You are all appreciated more than you know.

CHAPTER 1

At counsel table next to her attorney, Samantha sat limply—reliving the terror she'd felt when they'd arrested her for murder.

It had started further back than the murder though. Almost a year ago, now. The Prosecutor played the recordings of messages copied from her phone. She shut the ugly noise out. She shut the whole courtroom out. She shut everything out. Because when she didn't, she remembered it all.

Except who she used to be.

Samantha couldn't identify with any of her childhood memories. She couldn't recall the last time she felt that anything she said or did mattered. He'd taken it all. After the worst thing that could ever happen, he took her identity, too.

But she was wrong. *He* was the worst thing that had happened to her.

Something on the edge of her field of vision moved, and she turned to look at it. It was the courtroom artist shifting in his seat. He sat behind the bar that separated the well of the court and the visitors' seats. Samantha stared at the emerging picture. It was a drawing of the once-friendly face she had grown to despise. And it made her feel sick.

The artist had given Skyler more gray hair than she'd remembered and darker circles and lines around his eyes. How was it she never saw those things? Could fear have blinded her and made her see only his savage strengths?

Now emotions flooded in.

Just over a year ago, she'd been walking home from the library. Taking the alley would cut the walk in half.

But alone in the alley, the creepy silence and pervasive darkness put her whole body on alert. She sensed she wasn't alone. She turned, listened for footsteps. Turned the other way, suddenly, intuitively.

A face. Right there.

It was a familiar face, and it surprised her. She smiled, acknowledged him. *How silly of her.*

But he grabbed her, his grip hard and cold against her flesh. His aloof expression blasted her with instant terror.

Samantha struggled to pull away. She tried to calm herself, to take control, but she couldn't connect his actions with what she knew about him.

Ever since she could remember, she had called him Uncle Greg. She always teased and called him "Geggy," even after she had mastered language and could pronounce the "r." He'd taught her to ride her two-wheeler and to play basketball. He helped her with her math when her father was away on business. He wasn't really related, but he'd been an employee and old college roommate of her father's, and she'd grown up with him in her life.

She blinked into his face—she'd never seen that expression. His coarse beard chafed against her skin, the stench of his alcoholic breath, his immense body bearing down. He clawed at her clothes until her skin was exposed in the clammy night air. He unbuckled and ripped the leather belt from his trousers, held it firm against her neck, pinned her into breathless silence.

She couldn't scream. She tried to scratch at his eyes, but couldn't. With all her might she tried to keep her body stiff and together, but it was no use. He pried open her legs.

She could do nothing. She looked for weapons. Her nails tore into his flesh as he pierced her body. His blood dripped on her, but his intensity didn't lessen.

Pain pulsed through her. Her most private flesh ripped, and the warm wetness sickened her. She couldn't tell if it was blood or him or both. She wasn't sure she was breathing. But then he was done.

He dropped her like something disgusting and fled. The dull thud of the pavement didn't hurt. She felt paralyzed. But she rolled and vomited. She had to stand. To leave. To get home.

* * * *

The next hours blurred, but she made it home. Her parents' enormous house was comforting—safe, but empty. Her parents were in Washington. Her father was handling some confidential legal matters and negotiations for the Governor. Her mother, the perfect hostess, would keep the wives occupied.

Her room looked the same as she had left it. She locked the door and staggered into her shower. Dazed, she turned the knobs, used scalding water and lots of soap. She scrubbed until the water turned cold. She watched the bloodied water go down the drain. A little whirlpool.

The shock of the temperature change sent her, still dazed, out of the shower. Samantha stood there, momentarily confused about what to do next. She was shaking and couldn't stop. She pulled the familiar terry robe over her wet body. She couldn't look in the mirror. She didn't brush her long dark tangle of dripping hair. Instead she drifted around the room, as if she were a visiting spirit. Finally, she lay on her bed and pulled over herself the feather-filled quilt. Clenching her fists, she rocked herself slowly until her mind succumbed to blackness.

When she awoke, she felt heavy. She wasn't sure where she was, and then she remembered, and cold sweat ran down the backs of her calves. What should she do? Who should she tell? Who could she tell?

The doorbell interrupted the kaleidoscope of thoughts. Who would be calling on her at this hour of the morning? Everyone knew her parents were away. It had been highly publicized. Had he come back for more?

She went down the staircase and peered through the sheers. A man. Skyler Marks. She could trust him. Fate had brought him, the youngest attorney and partner in her father's law firm. He would know what to do.

In a frenzy, she opened the door and hugged him. His broad shoulders felt comfortable and familiar. His cologne eased her spirit. Samantha watched Skyler's gaze as he took her in. He was obviously taken aback. She shouldn't have let him see her so unkempt, so panicked, so needy.

"Calm down, Samantha. What's wrong? What happened?" Skyler grasped her shoulders and held her gently away from him.

"I'm in terrible trouble. I need to talk to you. I don't know what to do," Samantha whimpered.

"Let's sit in the living room. Can I make you some tea?"

"I really shouldn't bother you, but... I'm sorry... Something happened. Something horrible."

"We'll fix it–whatever it is." Skyler's voice was warm, rich, and gentle.

She told him why she'd taken the shortcut and what had happened. "I couldn't stop him," she wailed.

"Couldn't stop who?" Skyler sat on the couch and

moved closer to her.

Her breathing was unsteady. "Uncle Greg."

Skyler looked at Samantha. "Greg Maston?"

She saw the disbelief in his eyes. "Uncle Greg raped me." It didn't sound like her voice at all.

Skyler looked scared. "Are you all right? Did you see a doctor? Did you report it?" He leaned forward as if to inspect the scrapes and bruises on her neck, face, and hands. Could he guess how many more there were under her tightly wrapped robe?

"No. I didn't report it. I didn't know what to do. I feel so bad. I should've stopped it."

"If you'd tried, you might not be alive. Trust me, it's better to be alive. I can help you. You did the right thing in telling me." His voice was soothing, hypnotic.

Samantha couldn't speak.

Skyler wrapped his arms around her, but she stiffened into corpselike coldness and pushed away from him. She took a deep cleansing breath and looked squarely at Skyler. His actions unthreatening, she felt secure again. She could trust him.

"I want to help you," Skyler said. "I can help you, if you let me."

"I can't tell my parents; they won't understand. Maybe they won't even believe me."

"They're back from Washington Thursday. You'll have four days to recover. If you're not feeling better tomorrow, stay home from school. Tell people you fell off your bike. You have some scratches and bruises that may be difficult to cover." He talked as if he handled stuff like this every day.

Now she would have to look in the mirror. It didn't occur to her that her outsides might be hurt, just as her insides had been.

Samantha felt embarrassed he'd seen her fear and her shame.

He said, "You'll heal in a few days. Makeup will cover the rest. Don't worry, although, you should see a doctor."

"I told you I can't do that. My doctor would talk to my parents. I know he would." Samantha's voice spewed determination.

"As an attorney, I can tell you that you should've gone to the police right after it happened, and you should've been seen by a physician. You've showered all the evidence off. Without witnesses, it will be your word against his. But, if you want to pursue it and put him behind bars, I'll help you. I believe you." He was still talking like he was trying to hypnotize her. But compassionate.

Samantha felt awkward. She was taller than other girls her age and felt self-conscious about her height. Even now. Even with Skyler.

"There are other factors that need to be considered—like sexually transmitted diseases and a pregnancy test. I can help you with all of those things, if you want me to."

"I don't think I can go through it, explain it to strangers. I can't face anyone. I want to forget it. I want to feel normal. I want to erase him from my life," Samantha said.

"If you pursue it, you'll have to face him. If you tell your parents, and he denies it—" He paused. "There's the media. If they find out, they'll have a field day with all of you."

Samantha looked up, stunned. She hadn't even thought of that. "I can't have that. Forget it happened. Promise me you won't tell." Samantha said. "Please."

Skyler nodded.

Samantha stared at him, and then added, "Thanks … for talking … for everything. I, I have to go." She fled up the stairs and to the safety of her locked bedroom.

* * * *

Skyler could do no more. It was time to leave. He pulled the door shut behind himself and stepped into the fresh air, and then clicked off the microcassette he always kept hidden in his breast pocket, proudly patting it. Down to the driveway. He whistled softly and climbed into his emerald-green Jaguar. He could hardly believe his good luck. It was good to be prepared. Just like a Boy Scout, he laughed to himself. This tape would give him the two things he most desired in the world: power and Samantha Armstrong.

And what about that old lush, Greg? He'd guzzled one bottle too many and gone off his horny rocker. Had he, too, been lustfully watching beautiful Samantha grow up all these years? Or did he have a psychotic hobby of randomly assaulting women in alleyways? Maybe Samantha was wrong; maybe the rapist was someone who only resembled Greg Maston. But if not, Skyler had a double dose of power in his pocket. Skyler smiled; he loved secrets.

* * * *

Days passed, and Samantha tried to put the rape behind her. But her dreams kept the rage and fear alive. Every night she prayed she'd forget. But she didn't. She couldn't. She tried to think of happier times and to focus on good things, but they were all so meaningless. She felt distanced from her family, her friends, even herself. She knew she'd survive. She had to. But how? And how long would it take?

Skyler called regularly to support her and to see if there was anything she needed. He suggested counseling, but she resisted, not trusting her secret would be kept confidential. Besides, she knew she could always talk to Skyler. He seemed to understand, and she took his interest in her problem at face value. He was a good friend to her and her family. He had everyone's interest in mind, and he knew how to keep her family protected. He'd tried to reassure her, said eventually she'd forget. Soon, someone would come into her life to help her forget. It would just be an ancient bad dream.

She tried hard to believe him, but she worried

constantly about being pregnant. She didn't believe in abortion. She was a good Southern Christian, who believed in waiting until marriage to have sex. But all that changed. She could no longer laugh with her friends about their sexual adventures. In romance novels, when she got to the sexual scenes, she skipped them. If she did go to a movie, and there was a sex scene, she suddenly had to go to the restroom. She moved away from any man, who stood too close to her or tried to touch her—even in friendship. Worst of all, she no longer liked her father kissing her good night and treating her as his "little girl."

And now, some weeks later, her period missed, she might be pregnant. She lay in bed each night certain she could feel her body swell. She rubbed a small hardening in her taut flat belly. She wasn't sure if it was real or imagined. Was she just caving into her own fear, or was she really pregnant? She had to do something. Skyler would help her.

Several weeks passed, and she awoke every night uttering her mantra: Skyler will help me. Resolving to go to his office was another issue.

It took eight weeks before she had the courage to go downtown and into her father's law building. The overly adorned building intimidated her. Through the foresight of her great grandfather—and a winning poker hand— her father's family had acquired this historic building.

It seemed like hours before Skyler, briefcase in hand,

appeared in the office waiting room.

He apologized for the divorce clients who'd made him late and steered her by the elbow out to parking lot and into his Jaguar. Steaks at MacArthur Station. That's what they needed.

Samantha needed cooked meat like she needed the flat of a shovel upside the head, but she didn't speak up. She just studied him: his deep bronze skin made his shirt look whiter, and she liked the diamond-cut cufflinks under the double-breasted, pin-striped navy suit. His clothing made him seem older than his thirty-two years. She even liked the way his face creased when he smiled.

It didn't feel right to burden Skyler, or anyone else, with her problems. She was losing her nerve. She had to tell someone, though. She needed help. Skyler was the only one she could tell. She'd find a way.

The restaurant was nice. Her father had brought her here many times. She liked the food and the atmosphere, but she wasn't comfortable so close to her father's office. She hoped no one recognized her here with Skyler. She knew Dad wouldn't like it; he wouldn't understand. But Skyler put them in the back. Maybe she didn't have to worry about being seen, after all.

Once they ordered, she said, "I'm wondering what I'll say to my father if we're seen together. You know how he is."

"You leave that up to me. I'll tell your father I ran into

you, and I invited you to lunch. I'm giving you the inside scoop about college. He'll be fine with that. Trust me," he said, and then placed his hand over hers.

Samantha had no choice but to trust Skyler. She was already in too deep. She needed his help.

"So how's school going? What are you seniors doing for your graduation party? I remember my graduation night. We all drove to Lakewood and spent the night on the beach. Some of us were even brave enough to go skinny-dipping. It was great fun." He paused. "Ever been skinny-dipping?" he asked lightly.

"I couldn't. I wouldn't want to."

"Come now, a pretty thing like you? You must have all the boys asking you out."

"I've been focusing on my grades for college. Father says there's plenty of time for boys. You know how strict he is," Samantha said. "Besides, being the youngest and the only girl, my parents are overprotective. Really, I don't mind. I'll miss them when I go to college."

"Aren't you going to stay close to home?"

"I want to be a vet," Samantha said, relieved the conversation had shifted. "And Michigan State has an excellent school."

"You've applied?"

"They've accepted me into the school, but I haven't heard whether I've been accepted into the pre-vet program. From the photos in the brochures, their campus is beautiful like Arkansas in spring."

"I didn't know you wanted to be a veterinarian. That's quite an ambition," Skyler said. "Now, why don't you tell me what's on your mind? Do you need a letter for the pre-vet program? Because I'd be happy to support you, to send a letter, make a phone call."

"I'm all set with my college plans, but thank you." Samantha decided to go for it. "I wanted to thank you for all of your support and help over the past few weeks. Your phone calls and advice really helped me. But now, well honestly, I need more help." Samantha's voice quivered, and she avoided his gaze.

Taking her hand in his, Skyler said, "I'm here, whatever it is."

"I haven't been feeling well. I thought it was the flu. I thought I was just upset from what happened. But it's not. It's awful." Samantha tried to anticipate his response from his face, but his law training clearly taught him to mask his expression.

"Continue, please. You can trust me. I will help. I promise," Skyler said softly, his emerald eyes compassionate, urging.

Samantha moved closer to him on the seat of the round leather booth. "I skipped out of my Friday classes and went to the clinic in Sherwood for verification. I was tested for AIDS."

Skyler's eyes grew wide. "You didn't use your real name, did you? I told you I would help you with all that. I could have protected you from anyone finding out,"

Skyler said. "Do you have AIDS?"

"I'm smart enough not to use my real name. I put my hair up and teased it a lot, wore tons of makeup, and changed into ragged clothes. I even traded cars with Sally, telling her I felt like driving a convertible for the day. It was easy. I temporarily became someone else."

"Good," Skyler said.

"The clinic was very impersonal. I paid cash for the exam and tests. I told them I didn't have insurance. I waited three days and called. I don't have AIDS." Samantha paused. "I'm pregnant."

"Is that all?" Skyler sounded sympathetic. "I know people who will help you. You're only about, what, seven or eight weeks, right?"

Surprised at his cavalier response, Samantha listened numbly to his solution.

"No problem," Skyler said, with his boyish grin, as if he'd heard this kind of news every day. "I'll set it up. I know a doctor, who deals with these things. He'll give you an abortion without even asking your name."

"Is it safe?"

"Perfectly. You just leave it all up to me," Skyler said, washing down his last bite of steak.

Samantha felt uneasy, but couldn't think of any other options. Skyler was right. She'd already disgraced her family by being raped, and now she needed an abortion. Okay, she told herself, and she played in the mashed potatoes on her plate. She had no choice.

Skyler outlined the plan.

Samantha felt as if her body was being paralyzed from the inside out. The numbness encapsulated her, but her mind absorbed the information she needed.

Skyler told her to skip her Friday afternoon classes and tell her parents she was spending the night with a friend to study for exams. She'd be home Saturday afternoon. Skyler would take her to a clinic about two-hundred miles away.

Was that far enough?

Skyler explained how safe it was and how no one would ever know, how it was the right thing to do, the only thing to do.

His words became like a chant that she recited over and over until it became a refrain, until she believed it was true.

On the ride back to his office, Skyler reminded her she needed to repeat the AIDS test in six weeks, and then at three months, six months, and twelve months. He reminded her to use another fake name, to be careful, and to keep her actions as normal as possible, so her parents wouldn't be suspicious. Samantha knew she should be grateful, but she felt apprehensive. For now, she had to follow Skyler's directions. They were all she had.

CHAPTER 2

The next few weeks passed slowly, and Samantha withdrew into a self-imposed cocoon. She felt everyone could see through her, even though she tried to act normal. She had a hard time forcing herself out of the house and turned down several invitations from her friends, using studying for finals as her excuse.

Samantha stopped eating breakfast with her parents. She wanted to be alone. She needed to be alone. Her parents wouldn't leave her alone. She didn't want them to worry; she just couldn't be with them right now. She had to be alone.

A few days after Samantha met with Skyler, her mother walked into her room without knocking and turned off the music. Samantha decided not to speak up about it. She tried to act casual, but when her mother demanded to look at Samantha's naked body to make sure she wasn't "one of those girls who were anorexic or bulimic, or worse yet, on drugs," Samantha was floored.

After several strained minutes, Samantha convinced her mother it was just exams, graduation, and her friends going to different schools. When Samantha promised she'd be there for breakfast from then on, her mother acted so relieved, Samantha knew she could never tell her the truth.

Samantha's thoughts ran rampant as she carefully applied her makeup, trying to hide the dark circles under her eyes. It was important for her to show her parents everything was all right. She couldn't risk them asking any more questions or forcing her to see a doctor.

Breakfast with her parents was the last thing she wanted. She hated the tenderness in her breasts and wondered how long it took before her belly would show. Most of all, she feared the morning sickness that had become part of her before-school routine. How could she fool her parents when they sat inches from her at the breakfast table? If she got sick in front of them, her worst fears would materialize. Samantha, filled with anxiety, put on as cheerful a face as she could muster, all the while biting her inner lip, so she wouldn't break down and cry.

"That new Liz outfit we bought looks wonderful with that creamy complexion of yours," her mother said. "You're very lucky to have such clear smooth skin at your age. I was such a sight when I was young. My skin didn't clear up until after I had children."

Her father smiled behind his newspaper, as if knowing his husbandly duty. "Anne, you have always been beautiful. Never an unsightly mark on your face at any age."

"You are sweet, Travis dear, and I'm glad you don't remember them. But they were there."

Dad just kept reading his morning paper.

"Really, Samantha, those walking shorts and jacket are very practical. Those pastels give your face some color. You look like you're feeling much better," Mother said.

"I am. But I always feel good in new clothes. The outfit is really comfortable. Thank you for shopping with me." Samantha shifted the eggs around on her plate.

Mother beamed. "What are your plans after school? Can we go on another shopping excursion? I need a new dress for the Bar Association cocktail party and dinner. I do so value your opinion."

"I was planning to study. I'll join you for a few hours after school. I need to be back early, okay?"

"Anne, Samantha's school work must come first if she's going to *stay* accepted in college. Michigan State University will still review her final grades." Dad focused continuously on the *New York Times*. "If, however, you insist on shopping, why don't we all meet for dinner at Pete and Mickey's. They have a new chef, who trained in Paris. He's the talk of the inner circle. About seven?"

"Spectacular idea," Anne said.

Samantha had to go. She grabbed her backpack and said goodbye.

* * * *

Travis Armstrong was a powerful man when it came

to his clients and his own needs. He was confident and charismatic and very respected. Most of those he knew admired his directness and his ability to cut through red tape and get things done. He had taken over his father's law firm at thirty, and now, at fifty, his was the most prestigious law firm, and he the most influential attorney in the county, maybe even in all of Arkansas. He'd hired twenty-five of the best attorneys he could find, and together they had a cartel that could crush even the most carefully calculating enterprise—attorney, business, or Mafia.

Everyone thought twice before they crossed him, and everyone who asked for favors from him knew they owed him. Travis Armstrong took nothing for granted, trusted no one except his wife and children, and talked about personal issues with only a select few. Women enjoyed his company. He could easily choose among the finest beauties Arkansas had to offer, but he declined each offer. Few of his male friends believed in his self-proclaimed sexual virtue.

Somehow, the white accents in his formerly jet-black hair and his receding hairline made him even more attractive. He was grateful that he'd remained faithful to Anne Bommerito, the Italian beauty in his English class, his wife of thirty years. She was still as vibrant as the first day they'd met in college. In fact, his love for her continued to grow. They melded and had formed an alliance stronger than any he had known. She was always there for him, and he would do nothing to endanger their bond. His biggest regret was not spending enough quality time with his children.

His twin sons, Taylor and Tad, were in their first year of law school at Georgetown University. He was proud they were following in his footsteps; someday the firm would be theirs. Samantha was beautiful, with a petite bone structure, pale skin, and long curly brunette hair. She had his eyes—eyes that at times looked as stormy as the deep blue sea—but her mother's beauty was duplicated in Samantha's fine features. While Samantha believed she was too tall at 5-foot-8, with her high cheekbones, long legs, and tiny waist, she could easily find a career in modeling. Travis thanked God her shyness and self-motivation kept her feet planted firmly in the direction of college.

He worried about his children, but concerns about his only daughter raced around his head while he drove to work.

Initially, Travis thought he was worrying about nothing; it was his tendency to be overprotective. But he noticed she'd stopped going out on dates and didn't spend much time with her friends. They hadn't fought over her curfew in weeks.

Her grades were remarkable, she had lots of friends, and she had ambition. Maybe there wasn't anything to worry about; maybe she was finally maturing.

He rounded the corner, engulfed in thoughts about

Samantha, and then he slipped his silver Mercedes into reserved parking. Reaching for his briefcase, he left his concerns in the convertible. Travis Armstrong made it a rule to keep separate his business and family problems. The car door slammed, and his brain switched gears, prioritizing work on an upcoming trial.

CHAPTER 3

Samantha hardly noticed the drive. It wasn't really happening, so in her mind's eye there was nothing to remember. Her fluttering thoughts kept her occupied. Fear kept her still. The mounting lies kept her alert. It was dark now. She hadn't had anything to eat for days. Skyler said it was better to eat later. After it was all over.

She followed his orders. She couldn't think clearly. When she tried to focus, her thoughts cut too deeply. They hurt.

Skyler's directions seemed rational. She trusted they made sense. She believed everything was taken care of. This was a bad dream that she would wake up from and leave behind.

The back entrance to the building was unlocked. It was still. Sterile smelling. The doctor's office door was open. He sat behind a large desk filled with stacks of files and x-rays. His grayed temples matched the overstuffed leather chair, where he sat, quietly observing them enter. Introductions were made. He motioned her to a chair and ordered Skyler out of the room. The medical history was easy. She'd always been healthy.

Skyler had briefed her on the necessity of claiming she'd commit suicide if she didn't have the abortion. The doctor believed her. She didn't have to act that part. She already felt dead.

The next steps made her feel as if she were reliving her first pap smear: The unisex gown, a vacant green color; the cold stirrups; the rubber gloves; the large instruments; and finally, the pain. More pain than she remembered from a pap smear. And then the blood. It seemed it would never end.

And then it did.

She stood to get dressed. She felt herself drift. When she awoke, Skyler was bending over her, trying to get her dressed, and the doctor was not in the room.

"You fainted," Skyler said. He was holding two pill bottles.

Moments later, they were walking through dark hallways and doors until they were finally outside. Samantha noticed how calmly Skyler maneuvered her. She wondered what kind of work he'd brought that was locked inside the briefcase he held. How could he be calm enough to work while she committed murder?

She wasn't thinking clearly, she decided. After all, he was a lawyer, trained to handle difficult situations. Why not work while he waited? She should be grateful. The pills he'd given her began to work. Her body numbed. She fell into a deep sleep under the soft cotton blanket in the tiny back seat.

* * * *

Skyler drove slowly. In his thirty-two years, he'd never felt so content. His plan was working better than expected. He admired his own cleverness. He'd always been confident. It's what helped make him a very successful attorney; but now he'd have real success. Total control of another human being, someone he'd thought about being with since she was fourteen years old.

It was a long drive home. He'd reserved a room in a small motel not far from the doctor's office, with two beds, so he could watch her and make sure she was comfortable. He had the home number of the doctor and a few other prescriptions—in his name—she might need. He couldn't afford any mistakes or problems. He needed his investment to pay-off as planned. Five more months to go, and he would have his prize.

In the rearview mirror, he could see her sleeping peacefully. He hoped the whole night was peaceful, and the double dose of pain pills he gave her would help.

Samantha didn't weigh much. He cradled her in his arms and carried her to the room, placed her in the bed, and gently slipped off her jeans, shirt, and bra. Opening the travel bag, he'd packed, he pulled out his old college jersey that would be soft against her skin and keep her warm. The doctor warned him of chills and bleeding. He would change her pads throughout the night. He hoped the one box he bought would be enough.

He was in awe of her youthful beauty. She lay pale in semi-comatose sleep, dark curls framing her delicate face. The drugs induced such a deep sleep, he couldn't verify she was breathing, except for the occasional tiny hint of movement under her eyelids. What was she dreaming?

Soon the drugs would wear off, and she'd be in agony.

The doctor had advised him the first twenty-four hours would be the worst, and the bleeding, although initially heavy, would subside in a few days. Skyler remembered the sullen look on the doctor's face during his explanation that she shouldn't have intercourse for two weeks, her own family physician should check her, and she may need psychological treatment due to her immaturity. Both of them knew his warnings were to cover himself and to warn Skyler against touching her until after that time.

Skyler arranged the year's supply of birth-control-pill samples the doctor had given him at the bottom of his travel bag. She had to decide to take them on her own; but she'd take them, one way or another.

Skyler prepared himself for a few hours of sleep and collected a bottle of water, a drinking glass, the medicine, pads, and towels, situating them carefully on the nightstand. He had referred many clients to the "Extermidoctor, or Dr. Cide." Local attorneys used those names to protect his identity.

After Arkansas blocked medication abortions mid-2018, some clients refused to set foot inside an abortion clinic. Other clients were in terror of being recognized. Skyler never directly participated in an abortion, other than making a simple phone call. Attending with Samantha was new to him. He never received any complaints, and all of the women he referred had moved past that event in their life, which helped him feel guiltless. After all, he rationalized, if he didn't help these women, they would go to some butcher, who only wanted the cash and would ruin them for life—or worse, kill them. The way Skyler saw it, the bottom line was he was doing all of them a favor, and he and Dr. Cide were able to obtain tax-free play money. Instead of sheep, he counted the increasing number of crisp bills that lined his wall safe.

* * * *

Samantha, groggy, and disoriented, couldn't focus her eyes. She was too weak to make a sound. Her throat was dry. She shifted under the sheets and felt the heavy packing and the wetness between her legs. Her abdomen hurt, and her attempt to reach for the lamp switch failed.

She remembered the daytime nightmare—the abortion. She looked around, and her eyes adjusted to the night shadows. Skyler slept soundly in the bed across from hers. She pulled herself from the bed soundlessly stepping onto the carpet toward what looked to be a door. She prayed it was the bathroom.

She needed a shower. She had to cleanse herself from that awful doctor touching her insides, ripping something away from her.

She wrapped her arms tightly around her waist and walked one painful baby step at a time. She didn't feel like she was inside her own skin. Her body seemed old and unfamiliar. She didn't like the feel of the unknown shirt around her. It was big and bulky. Where had it come from? Why didn't she remember? Tearing the shirt off, it fell onto the floor. She pulled her soiled underpants off and dropped them with the soaked bulky pads into the garbage pail. There were so many pads. She'd lost a lot of blood.

Sitting on the stool, she watched fresh blood trickling down her legs, and bit her lip. Small clots flooded into the toilet as she urinated. The mother of all periods, she thought. Mother, what a funny word; she was anything but that. The doctor and Skyler had seen to that.

In the shower, the water felt good. She turned the shower knob so high, the pulsing water burned her skin. She didn't care. She felt weak, and the water made her feel weaker.

She didn't want to feel anything ever again. Soon, she'd be back in her own clothes and her own bed. Soon, she'd be the good Christian girl her parents had raised. Soon, she could put all of this behind her. Maybe even learn to forget and learn to feel again; but not now. Now, she had to get through the next few hours. Grim, she focused on the drain—the water, now pooled around her feet, reflected a transparent red. A sudden ringing in her ears caught her by surprise, and she faded into nothingness.

* * * *

Skyler heard the dull thud. He leapt out of bed and saw Samantha wasn't there. Hearing the shower, he dashed into the steamy bathroom. She'd collapsed inside the tub. Turning off the water and grabbing a large white towel, he scooped her up in his arms and lay her on the terry bath mat.

He listened for the sound of her heartbeat. Finally, hearing her breathing, he felt relieved.

Hoping she'd wake, Skyler moved her onto her bed. But she didn't wake. A bruise appeared on her right temple, and he knew he needed to apply pressure and ice. Opening the room's small refrigerator, he found a white tray half filled with ice. Quickly, he popped out the little cubes and wrapped them in a wet washcloth. Touching the bruise slowly, he saw Samantha's brilliant blue eyes open, blink, and try to focus.

"What happened?" she asked in a low voice. "What are you doing in my shower?" she mumbled, looking around.

"I told you I was here to help you. If you wanted a shower, I would've helped you. You're too weak. The medicine the doctor prescribed is very strong and you took it on an empty stomach. You must stay in bed for a few more hours. Trust me, you'll feel better soon." Trying to be both strong and sympathetic, he was nevertheless irritated she hadn't followed his instructions.

"I've lost so much blood," she said.

"The doctor said that's normal and will stop in a few days. We just have to make sure it keeps decreasing. You'll let me know if it gets worse, won't you?"

* * * *

Samantha nodded in embarrassment.

"Do you need help getting dressed? I've got extra clothes and pads for you."

"No, I'll be fine," she said, pulling the towel closer to her and the sheets over her half-naked body. "Could you just put a shirt and the pads on my bed and bring me my purse; I have extra underwear in it."

"Tell you what, I'll go into the bathroom for a few minutes, so you can get dressed in private. Let me know when I can come out. I can help you get dressed—if you're too weak, I mean."

Samantha tried to smile. "I'm fine. If I need help, I'll let you know."

"I've left your pain medication and a sleeping pill for you. I think it would be a good idea if you took them. You could use a few good hours of quiet rest. Please eat at least a few of these crackers with the medicine."

"Thanks. I'm fine," Samantha said. She just wanted him to leave her alone. She wanted to get dressed, be alone, and sleep in her own bed. Just a few more hours, she thought, and quickly dressed.

The dry wheat crackers were just what her stomach needed. Almost instantly she felt better. Her exhausted, hollow-feeling body couldn't help but welcome the sleep—a desirable escape from Skyler's annoying willingness to care for her. She swallowed the pills and called him back from behind the bathroom door.

* * * *

Morning moved quickly into afternoon, and Skyler woke Samantha and fed her a hearty breakfast. He refused to take her home until she cleaned her plate.

Samantha said she was grateful for the food, and that it tasted better than any other breakfast she remembered.

Skyler watched her carefully. Color returned to her face. He loved to watch her eat. Her long dainty fingers fed her porcelain-like body with precise movement. She was a delicate beauty, and he was tantalized by her.

Skyler was sure Samantha remained unaware of his desire for her. He knew, for the moment, he'd have to curb his appetite. He collected their things for the ride home and smiled at the briefcase beside his overnight bag.

* * * *

The ride home was uneventful. The bleeding had slowed, and Samantha was gaining her strength. The drugs made her queasy, but that too would pass. Samantha's parents wouldn't be home until early evening. It was their day to play doubles at the club. They loved playing golf, and most of her life she'd heard stories of their adventures at the most famous golf courses in the world.

Golf and piano. Two forced interests, both of which she hated.

Now, she had a third. Sex.

Was her life to be guided by events and other people, rather than by what she wanted? She fell into another drug-induced slumber, despite the loud roar of the engine and the bright sunlight.

When she woke, Samantha saw the familiar surroundings: streets, buildings, trees. She knew they were the same. They couldn't have changed overnight, but somehow they were different, and she wasn't sure why.

She kept repeating the story she'd tell her parents about what she did last night, until in her mind's eye she began to believe it.

Skyler repeated the story, asking her every possible question her parents could come up with. He didn't want to take any chances, for which she was thankful. He was a fine attorney. He hadn't forgotten anything.

Privately, Samantha decided what she really needed to tell her parents, if they asked what was wrong with her, was that she felt like she was coming down with the flu. That would keep her father from asking a lot of questions and would keep her mother occupied making her chicken soup. That would ensure she didn't make a mistake in answering any questions, and she could delay conversation until her mind was clear. She wished she were home right now. The thought of her mother's chicken soup made her feel homesick, even though they were only a few miles away.

Samantha looked down the street toward her house. It had never looked so good to her. She was grateful to Skyler, but ecstatic their allegiance was over. She couldn't bear anymore lies. She didn't want to think about it; she only wanted to put it behind her. Skyler had been helpful; she wasn't sure what she should say or how to properly thank him as she gingerly climbed out of the car.

Relieved, Samantha simply smiled and said, "Thanks, thanks for everything."

* * * *

Once she entered the sanctuary of her home and the refuge of her own room, Samantha breathed deeply, relieved it was over. She would put everything behind her.

She unpacked her clothes and placed the bag of prescriptions Skyler gave her deep in the back bottom of her underwear drawer, confident no one would find them. Soon she could throw them out. Before covering the bag of prescriptions, she decided to inspect its contents, not remembering it having been so bulky. Immediately her eyes spied a folded note. She opened it and read the fine printing.

Samantha,

The doctor thought it was a good idea you take birth-control pills. He gave me a year's supply and said when you go to college the health center on campus would refill it. No one need know, and you should only take them if you want to. If they make you sick in any way, you need to see a doctor—remember what is between you and your doctor is confidential. I would have talked to you about this, but it is your decision, and you have had enough to deal with.

Feel better—S.

Samantha stared at the note and then at the contents of the bag. She was uncertain why he would give this to her, but she was too numb to think about it further. She quickly stuffed all of the contents back into the bag, carefully covering it with an array of old underwear, nylons and socks.

Her parents weren't home yet. Good. She needed time to sort it all out. Uninterrupted time. She suddenly craved a shower, not sleep, as she had desired moments ago. She looked at the Minnie Mouse clock, its innocent face, which had been on the shelf for over a decade.

Samantha had time to shower, change, and apply some makeup. They would never suspect anything.

When her parents arrived home, they were obviously tipsy, and Samantha was grateful for their festive mood. They had gone to eat dinner at the club with their golfing partners.

"Samantha, we missed seeing you last night at dinner. How was your evening with Emily?" her father asked.

"It was great, Dad. We have the same taste in music and exchanged some Pandora stations. We talked about college. She hasn't heard from any of the universities she applied to. I tried to talk her into going to Michigan State with me, but I think she wants to stay closer to home. You know, being an only child."

Samantha smiled at her father. She knew he couldn't tell she was lying. Really, she wasn't lying; she simply explained what happened, not last night, but two weeks ago, when she'd spent the night with Emily Osborne, her best friend. She prayed she could keep the sequence of her stories straight and catalogued them internally.

"That's nice, dear," her mother said. "You two must have stayed up too late though. You look so tired. Maybe you should go to bed early."

"I do feel tired, but I think it may be the flu creeping up on me. I felt feverish a few hours ago, so I did take a nap, and some Tylenol. I'm feeling a bit better," Samantha said. A chill surged through her body, and she shrugged it off.

"Well then, I'm not taking any chances. I'll make some chicken soup for you. You know when one of us gets sick, we all get it. Your father and I have a busy week ahead. Why don't you go up and lie down? I'll make it with noodles and an egg, just how you like it, and when it's done, I'll bring you a bowl. Okay?"

Samantha's mother, smelling of too many martinis, still appeared morning-fresh. She smiled and kissed Samantha on the cheek. She didn't discharge Samantha to her room without first feeling her forehead.

Samantha, grateful the inspection was over, said, "Love you, Dad." She retreated to her bedroom.

CHAPTER 4

The phone. Samantha hated the phone. It had become an intruder into her sanctuary. People wanting her to do things. Her parents checking up on her. Skyler, wanting to talk, to remain her confidant. She wanted silence. She wanted time and the safety of her room and her house. She wanted no surprises until she could go to Michigan and remake herself.

Reading novels took her to faraway places and make-believe people—the only people she wanted to deal with. But the phone kept ringing. Her iPhone was on silent. The house phone couldn't be silenced.

It was the housekeeper's day to go to the farmers' market for fresh fruits and vegetables. There was no one to answer the phone. Samantha was alone in the house, and there was no one to lie and say she wasn't there.

The ringing mesmerized her. She had to answer it. "Hello," Samantha said into the ivory receiver.

"Samantha?"

"Yes. Oh, Skyler. Hello. I didn't recognize your voice. The connection is really bad; it's hard to hear you,"

Samantha lied.

"I'm on my cell phone. I'm just driving back from court. How about meeting me for lunch?"

"How'd you know I was home?"

"Your dad mentioned you had a half-day and then a four-day Memorial weekend, so I got to thinking I should check in on you. We should get together."

"I've already made plans for the weekend. I'm going with Emily to her family's beach house. Maybe another time?" Samantha was relieved she had come up with an excuse so effortlessly.

"No problem. I'll call again. Have a great weekend."

* * * *

Clenching his teeth, Skyler hung up the phone. She wasn't going to get away from him that easily. He'd left her alone for weeks. She'd had her space. Now he wanted her to see him in a different light, not associated with the past.

But now, he'd fix it so she had to spend some time with him. She owed him, and he would collect. His jaw line relaxed and he smiled. Payback would be fun. He pictured her luscious curves and grinned.

* * * *

Samantha had planned to decline Emily's invitation, but now she felt compelled to accept it. She had to get away from Skyler. He had become too concerned about her. She wanted the whole incident to go away, but he wouldn't let it drop. Her appreciative feelings toward him were being systematically eradicated by his constant invitations, phone calls and so-called friendly concern.

She was increasingly frightened of being with him, but she wasn't sure why. He never touched her. He had been only friendly, helpful, and supportive of her predicament. Yet each time she heard his voice, she winced. She wasn't keen on the voice of any man, except her father and brothers.

She knew what they would be discussing. He wouldn't let her forget. His voice haunted her to the depths of her being. Unconsciously, she had tucked Skyler away in the same secret place in her mind she had exiled the rapist. The rapist was no longer someone she thought of as Uncle Greg. It was difficult to believe the Greg she knew was the rapist she feared, so she tried to forget them both. But Skyler's overbearing and continual concern for her made it impossible. They had formed an irrevocable contract. There was no one she could turn to. The calls had let up a little, and she thought he'd almost forgotten her. But now this.

Reluctantly, she dialed Emily's number and hoped for forgiveness. When Emily had mentioned the long weekend at her family's beach house, Samantha had been a little rude. But Emily was her lifelong friend.

Samantha's parents were glad, too. They were doing

the long holiday weekend at the Osbornes. As usual, they shared the chauffeur-driven journey to the beach house in silence, each consumed with their own musings.

Karen Carpenter's words rang in Samantha's head, song after song. Samantha identified with Karen. She wished she could talk to her. For the moment, Karen was the only woman she could identify with. The songs were ancient by today's standards. And Karen Carpenter was dead.

More frequently than not, Samantha wished she could die; that she would die. It would be easier. No one would ever know what had happened. No one would ever be able to tell her how stupid it was to take the shortcut home from the library. Or how stupid it was to have stayed out so late. Or how stupid she was to have ever trusted anyone.

Death would be better. Easier. But she couldn't do that to her parents or her brothers.

All she wanted was to get out of this town and go to Michigan. Michigan State would be her place to heal, her place to study hard and spend time with animals. She'd find a veterinarian who would hire her, even if it meant cleaning cages. It would help her forget. Animals didn't have the capacity to hurt someone like people did.

She knew she'd find serenity in solitude. She remembered her grandmother often saying those three words to her when she asked her Nana to come downstairs to the sitting room with everyone else.

When Nana was alive, Samantha enjoyed being with her. Her first memories were of her smooth, powder-soft skin. She often wondered how such wrinkled skin could feel so soft and smooth. She loved the fresh scent of lilac-scented soap nestled in the grooves of her Nana's skin.

Samantha remembered feeling cheated when she was taken off to school. On the first day of nursery school, Nana promised if Samantha were really good and brave, they would have their time alone. Nana said she'd tell her a special story about proper southern ladies and how they used to go to etiquette school. They kept their ritual time together on most days, and whenever Nana couldn't see Samantha, she'd tearfully apologize. Nana always kissed her, gave her a big hug, and said, "Dear child, I'll miss you, but there is serenity in solitude."

Samantha missed Nana more than she had ever missed anyone, especially now. She hadn't truly understood Nana's words, or why she enjoyed the quiet and the aloneness so much, until now. If Nana were alive, Samantha could have confided in her without worry, without fear. Nana would have known what to do.

When they finally rounded the last corner, the limousine crawled up the long driveway leading to the large Victorian summer house. Its white pillars were stretched up, tall and proud, almost boastful as they led to a second-story veranda, outlined in clay pots filled with pastel flowers of every shade. It looked so peaceful.

The front grounds were full of vivacious colors in

cheerful bloom. Stepping out of the car, Samantha took in the house as if she were seeing it for the first time, quickly assimilating the layout.

Her gaze fell on their limo as it slowly moved away. The spacious parking area had several cars, looking freshly washed, and parked neatly in a row.

"Mom, why are there so many cars here?"

"The whole firm has been invited."

"No one told me; I thought it would just be us, like it used to be."

"Since our summerhouse is being renovated, your father asked Mr. Osborne if he wouldn't mind hosting the firm. He wanted to reward everyone for doing so well the first half of the year, and he has some announcements to make that are cause for celebration. Wasn't it a lovely idea?"

Samantha, aghast, could utter no response. She tried to smile. Her mother needed a positive response, or Samantha would have no peace, no quiet, no serenity in solitude.

"Yes, it'll be great," Samantha murmured and then added, "I just wish I would have known."

* * * *

Watching from behind sun-yellowed mesh shears as people pulled in and out of the drive, Emily sat nestled in the window seat of her massive room. Patiently, she waited for Samantha to arrive. Emily was disappointed her father had agreed to the retreat, but she hoped this one would, at least, be less formal than the previous retreats. She wanted her last long weekend before leaving for Europe to be private and fun.

Emily wanted some adventure, a last bit of freedom, without any worry of having to act like an adult or a proper lady. Now she was eighteen, they would be too visible; and she and Samantha would be expected to be dressed for meals and make appearances at the evening parties.

Samantha wasn't in the mood for parties these days, and Emily, genuinely concerned, had hoped over these next four days, she could help Samantha with whatever was bothering her. She had been so moody over the phone lately, and she never wanted to do anything. Samantha had assured her everything was okay, and she wasn't mad or upset with her. Emily believed her, but she also knew her well enough to know Samantha was genuinely upset about something—something that wasn't going away easily. Emily slicked her unruly curls behind her ears.

Emily hated that she was going off to Europe for most of the summer and leaving Samantha behind.

* * * *

Samantha tapped meekly on her door.

"Hey, come on in. What are you doing knocking? This is practically your room," Emily said, pushing back her tears with relief at the interruption.

"Hey, yourself." Samantha smiled, too. "You know I always knock. What are you doing sitting there all curled up? You look too comfortable compared to the rest of the people around here." Samantha felt relieved to be in the comfort of a room she'd been a part of as long as she could remember. It felt impenetrable, isolated from the rest of the world.

"Yes, I know. It seems we've been preparing for days, instead of only hours, for everyone's arrival. So far, only five of the partners are here. Most brought their wives; you and I are the only kids."

"That's fine by me. I hope it stays that way," Samantha said, put at ease by Emily's announcement.

"It probably will. Mom told me not everyone is staying the whole four days because of other commitments, but everyone is staying at least until Sunday-morning brunch."

"Great. That means there will be some free time away from 'the great charade,'" Samantha said.

Emily nodded, and Samantha was comforted by Emily's unquestioning acceptance. For the first time in weeks, she didn't feel the pressure to act—to be something she no longer was. She didn't feel like she had to prepare her answers in advance and pretend. She wished she could explain everything to her. She knew her best friend must wonder why she had been so different lately.

But—at Skyler's insistence—she had decided not to

tell Emily anything. She wondered if maybe she should confide in her anyway. She knew Emily was trustworthy and would help her. Samantha needed to confide in someone other than Skyler. Most days she felt as if she'd explode. She needed to relieve some of the pressure, some of the guilt. She needed to feel normal again.

Suddenly Samantha felt tired, as if she hadn't slept in days. She probably hadn't. She couldn't remember a night since the rape that she hadn't woken in a cold sweat. She longed for one good night's sleep.

"Sam? Sam? Are you all right?" Emily asked.

"What? Yes, yes, I'm fine." Her cheeks warmed a bit. "I was just thinking about how many things will change after graduation. On one hand, I'm not sure I want to graduate, to have everything change. On the other hand, I'm excited, and sometimes think I need change now, more than ever. Know what I mean?" Samantha hoped Emily believed her, even though that had not been exactly what she had been thinking.

"You know, I do know what you mean. Sometimes I feel the same way," Emily said, looking squarely at Samantha. "I can't believe we'll be graduating in a few days. We'll always be more like sisters, not just best friends. I'm really going to miss you, Sam."

"Me too. I don't know what I'll do without you."

"Remember when we were about nine, and we decided the grown-ups played more 'pretend' than we did?" Emily asked.

"It's amazing how perceptive we were," Samantha said. "I wish I would, wish I could." Samantha suddenly stopped.

"Come on, you what?" Emily said, coaxing.

"I don't know. I'm not sure I want to grow up. I know what I want, but I look around me, at all of the so-called adult role-models, and I know I don't want to be like them. I want to be able to say what I want, and what I feel, and not worry about what anyone else will think, or how they'll react," Samantha said.

"Yeah, I know what you mean. I know my mother doesn't like half of the people in the firm, but you'd never know it by watching her. You're more independent thinking," Emily said confidently. "That's why you're going all the way to Michigan State University. You'll probably come back a totally different person."

"I hope so," Samantha said, crossing her fingers, hoping those words would come true.

"You won't change so much you'll forget me, will you?" Emily said. "Who else could I talk to like this?"

Samantha spent the next hour with Emily, unloading her clothes from the heavy wardrobe bag the butler had brought up. Showing off the new wardrobe her mother happily bought for her on their latest shopping spree allowed Samantha to temporarily forget her problems. For the moment, her tortured thoughts were replaced with fashion ideas from Emily and her latest issues of *People, Cosmopolitan, Seventeen, Vanity Fair, Vogue,* and

Glamour magazines.

Guests continued to arrive. One by one, they got into the spirit of being on a retreat at a home away from home. The Osborne estate was comfortable and spacious. Each couple had the privacy they needed.

As the dinner bell sounded, the group collected around six glass-topped, antiqued green, cast-iron tables decorated with geraniums and place cards. The smell of barbecued steaks, chicken, and ribs filled the air. Mountains of vegetables, salads, fruits, and breads were lined up in silver dishes, held in the outstretched hands of servants, tidily dressed in nurse-white starched uniforms, black aprons, and ties.

Samantha and Emily sat next to each other in comfortable silence, watching as the adults—sheep-like—followed each other to their seats, cocktails in hand. Each of the women, dressed in simple, but obviously designer, dresses and heels, were adorned with gold, silver, or pearls. The men were more relaxed with open-collar golf shirts and casual slacks. The scene looked more like a private country-club dinner than a relaxed retreat and cookout.

The meal progressed into trays of desserts and after-dinner liqueurs. Travis began the highly anticipated speech regarding the success of the firm and the financial balance sheet that had been presented to him earlier in the week by Greg Maston, lifelong friend and accountant to the firm. The figures were so good that, in addition to the usual salary and bonuses, each would receive 10,000 shares in one of five stocks of their choice. Samantha had heard her father practice his speech and couldn't bear to hear him say and praise Greg's name.

She had to leave and asked Emily to join her. They were almost out of earshot, cutting through the sliding-glass door to the breakfast nook, when they heard Skyler's familiar voice.

"So, girls, what'd I miss?"

A shudder passed through Samantha's spine.

"Mr. Marks, I thought Daddy said you weren't able to join us?" Emily said. "You haven't missed much," she continued. "Mr. Armstrong just began his announcements. Everyone is still working on dessert. Would you like me to tell Cook to bring you a plate of food?"

"No, thanks. That's very nice of you to offer. Dessert is all I need. I'd better get out there. See you two." Skyler winked at them and briskly walked out to the patio.

"See you later," Emily said, not noticing Samantha's choked back surprise and sudden self-consciousness.

"So, what do you want to do?" Emily asked. "It's early; we could drive into town and see what's playing or go to the beach, and see who's hanging out. I heard Tommy Snyder is getting a group together for a bonfire."

"Either is fine. I'm really tired, though. I don't want to stay out late."

"Sam, it would be great for you to get out. You never want to go out anymore. People have been asking about you." Emily stopped as they climbed the wide, rounded stairs. "You're not sick or anything are you? You'd tell me if something were wrong, wouldn't you?"

"Why would you say that? I'm fine. I'm just tired from the long drive. Come on, let's get our stuff and go."

"Okay, just remember you can tell me anything. You know that, don't you?"

"Don't be a goof," Samantha said. Then, suddenly putting her hand over her mouth, she made an urgent rush toward the bathroom.

Samantha vomited violently in the powder room, and Emily stood outside the door. Quietly knocking and gently pushing the door open, Emily entered. Samantha was rinsing her mouth and face in the cool water flowing from the gold faucets on the marbleized gray and burgundy sink.

"Are you okay? Can I get you anything? Should I get your mom?" Emily asked, wide-eyed.

"I must have eaten something that didn't agree with my stomach. I think you better go ahead without me. I really want to take a shower and get into bed. Tomorrow we can do something," Samantha said, apologetically, her arms clenched around her middle as she walked to Emily's room.

"No problem. I think I'll go watch TV and stay in tonight, too. I'll check on you later. Do you have everything you need?"

Samantha nodded and moved toward the pullout

couch on the wall opposite Emily's bed. Fortunately, the maids had the bed already made up and the crisp grape-colored sheets looked inviting. Samantha grabbed her nightclothes and toiletries from her bag. She needed a shower before she entered those sheets. Thankfully, Emily's bathroom was attached to her room, and Samantha could listen to her own music and have a private shower. She slipped into the wet cocoon.

After her shower, Samantha crept between the sheets in relief at the solitude and safety of her best friend's room. It was hard to get rid of the buried thoughts that had pushed forward since Skyler showed up.

Sleep wasn't coming as easily as she thought it would, and she was relieved she had packed her sleeping pills. She had become accustomed to using them when her mind wouldn't stop reeling. The pills gave her a few hours of peace.

Suicide she couldn't do, but escaping into a deep sleep, even for a few hours, was easy. And no one got hurt. Within minutes after swallowing three of the pills, she fell into a numbing sleep while counting the hand-painted floral porcelain beads on the brass head and footboard of Emily's queen-sized bed.

* * * *

Samantha awoke to sunlight, the sound of birds, and a cool breeze. Emily was a late riser.

Familiar breakfast noises—trays delivered to the

various rooms—sounded from the long corridor. Samantha decided she'd wait until brunch and eat with Emily. The men would be on the golf course, most of the women would join them, and the rest would be by the pool. The next gathering would be formal dinner, and on Sunday, brunch with everyone. Then some of the team would leave. Samantha would find a way through it. She'd have to talk to Skyler without being seen. Without being overheard. He'd bring up everything; he always did. Around him, she felt disturbed, but she did owe him.

She didn't know what to do. She didn't want this weekend to be trashed. She didn't want her time with Emily to be swept in with the horror she kept burying in her mind's dim parts. Those parts grew every day and crept into her consciousness like weeds.

Thoughts of Skyler suffocated her. Samantha had to have a shower to clear her mind.

* * * *

The sound of running water woke Emily. It seemed it had been running for hours. She hated being woken up early, especially on a holiday weekend. Samantha couldn't need another shower. Samantha had been preoccupied—like forever. What was she thinking? Emily hated to mess in anybody's personal stuff, and she and Samantha had always given each other room. But this was going on too long. Emily had to get it out of her today.

Emily crossed the room, cracked the bathroom door, and yelled, "Hey Sam, save me some hot water." The bathroom was a mess. Emily waited for a response.

But none came.

She inched the door open. Sam was whimpering. "Sam, are you all right?" Emily asked loudly. *Don't panic, Em.* "I'm coming in there, Sam."

"No! I'll be out in a minute," Samantha said.

Emily gathered her courage and strode in.

Samantha clambered up from the tile floor. "Em. Are you nuts?" She pulled on the pink robe and pushed Emily out the door.

Emily stumbled back into her room. "What's wrong with you?"

But when Samantha appeared, and Emily looked straight into her eyes, they looked clear. Her face wasn't puffy, as if she had been crying. Maybe she was humming some weird song, and Emily had mistaken it for whimpering. After all, Samantha didn't usually sing, and she claimed she couldn't hold a tune. That must be it, Emily rationalized.

"I can't wait to eat; the shower made me hungry," Samantha said.

Was Samantha kidding? Sitting naked on the bathroom floor, an hour goes by, and now she acts like nothing happened? Emily didn't know what to do.

* * * *

The girls went about their day as they'd always done on the many long summer days they spent at their respective summer houses. They swam and ate and lay in the sun until their fair skin turned to a pale shrimp color. They pulled on their woven straw hats and took out the small paddleboat Emily's father had given her for her twelfth birthday. They talked about boys, clothes, college, their future dreams. Eventually, it was time to come in. The adults pulled up, and the servants put away the mass of golf clubs.

Another shower, carefully applied makeup, and then they dressed for dinner. They both wore sundresses with sweaters covering their bare shoulders. Bare shoulders in the dining room were forbidden. They agreed they would make an appearance and then leave the table as dessert was being served.

Tonight was Saturday. They were anxious to throw off their sweaters and head for the bonfire at the beach down the cove, where some of their classmates gathered nightly. Samantha, although privately reluctant, had promised Emily she'd go with her to the beach. She was relieved it would take her away from any possible confrontation or discussion with Skyler, whose gaze followed her from a distance. With each passing hour, she felt his presence get stronger, but of course she didn't see him.

Dinner was uneventful, and Samantha was thankful. Although Skyler was a successful attorney, he was still one of the youngest and newest partners, so he was virtually at the opposite end of the long dining table. It was easy to avoid eye contact and conversation with him. The girls' plan to disappear early worked, and when dessert and coffee were served, they were excused. Into the night they happily fled into Emily's blood-red graduation present, top down.

Samantha felt her soul release into the wind with each gust that blew through her long loose curls. She breathed deeply, feeling her lungs fill up and out. She felt a freedom she hadn't known in months. She prayed it would last. She looked at Emily, innocently driving while tuning the radio. She wished they could drive for days without turning back.

* * * *

Emily parked the car on a stony patch. Several familiar teens were roasting marshmallows, and Samantha and Emily climbed out and quickly joined in. Bags of chips and pretzels and a cooler of buns, hot dogs, and beer lay open in the sand.

The night went quickly, and before they knew it, people started to disperse, either in couples to remote parts of the beach or into their cars. Beers in hand, Emily and Samantha made a toast to their friendship, said their good-byes, and headed for the car. They were not used to drinking, and they each felt the quiet tiredness the beer left them with. Thankfully, they only had a few miles to go.

Returning to the house, they found most of the lights off and retreated to their room. Emily opted to use the bathroom first, knowing she'd never get in once Samantha entered it.

Samantha felt a headache come on and wanted something fizzy to drink. She got some aspirin from her purse and crept down the long stairwell to the kitchen for a cola. There, in the dark, she saw the tip of a lighted cigarette and smelled its repugnant smoke. Not seeing the face behind the cigarette, she excused herself for intruding.

"Oh, I'm sorry. I won't be but a minute. I just want to grab a soda." Samantha opened the refrigerator door.

"Samantha, it's just me." Skyler chuckled. "I startled you. I'm sorry. I couldn't sleep. I came to the kitchen for a glass of wine and a cigarette."

"I didn't recognize you in the dark."

"Listen, I'm restless. Would you take a walk with me?"

"I have a headache."

"The fresh air will do you good. Swallow your aspirin, and you can take the soda with you. We won't be gone long," Skyler said. "I promise."

There was no way out. "Just let me get my sweater."

"If you get cold, I'll give you my jacket."

"But I've got to tell Emily I'm going. She'll wonder if I'm not back in the room."

"She's sleeping." He wrinkled his nose. "You've been drinking."

"A bit." There was nothing more to say. She simply followed him through the servants' entrance off the kitchen and into the dark.

"I haven't heard from you for a few weeks, so I figured you were getting on with your life." Skyler sounded sincere.

But she didn't want him thinking about her. Why the hell couldn't he leave her alone? "I'm not a champion liar. This is new for me. And I'm afraid of seeing Uncle Greg. I haven't seen him since—"

"Since the rape. Samantha, once you can say it, you can forget it, and move on," Skyler said.

"I need to figure the rest out on my own. Really. I appreciate everything you've done, but I'm anxious to go away to college and start over—by myself. Then I'll put it all behind me. On my own."

"Change will do you good. Just remember, I'll always be there."

She cringed.

Skyler pointed. "Look over there. The door on the boat house is ajar. Let's go have a look, make sure it hasn't been broken into."

Samantha instinctively paused.

"You're cold." Skyler shrugged out of his jacket and tried to drape it around her shoulders.

She stepped out of his reach. "No." She had to get away from him. "We should head back."

"In a minute." Skyler grasped Samantha's wrist

and—with his foot—pushed the boathouse door open. He stepped in and brought her with him. It was clear they were the only ones in the building, and Skyler kicked the door shut behind them. It was dark, except for the stream of moonlight coming from the panes of thick uncovered glass.

"Samantha, there is something we need to talk about." He pivoted her in an about-face, placing both of his hands on her shoulders.

Samantha cringed. But he gripped her so tightly she couldn't pull free.

"You are such an innocent."

She hadn't been innocent for six months.

"You couldn't know—" He stroked her cheek with one finger. "—but I've become very attracted to you."

Samantha stared into the dark distance. She had no answer. Nothing to say. Greg Maston's face flashed in front of her. It was like the alley. Not again. God, not again. Her pulse raced, her body beaded with sweat, her mind tried to steady her. The instinct to run seized her.

Samantha tried to push Skyler away, but he lunged at her.

Smashed her close against his chest.

She didn't want this to happen. Samantha hugged herself.

He held her in front of him so he could get at her and rubbed her throat.

She tried to hold her body taut.

His fingers slowly pressed in, while he outlined her collar bone, searching like a blind man.

Samantha gasped, tried to escape. She couldn't. Skyler grabbed her body whole. He pushed her down on the boat covers and wool blankets, which lay in the corner behind the door.

"Skyler. No. Don't. No. This can't happen." Samantha's voice was scratchy and high and fast.

He pinned her and explored her body.

"Why? Why are you doing this?"

"Just follow my lead, everything will be great. Trust me," Skyler whispered.

She should never have trusted him that first night.

He kissed her ears, her neck, and the crevice leading to her breasts.

Samantha felt blood trickling down her throat. She wasn't sure where the blood came from. It scared her. It was difficult to move. She felt dizzy and nauseous. She saw shadows in the boathouse moving slowly, dancing in the walls. She wasn't sure of reality.

The face assaulting her faded in and out: seemed to be Greg, seemed to be Skyler. She wasn't sure. Why wasn't she sure? Samantha tried again to free herself. Her mind questioned what was happening. Was it real, was she dreaming again?

The beer had made her mind tired and her body limp. It seemed to her they were moving in slow motion; this might even be a dream. She wasn't sure of anything. The taste of blood in her mouth faded into a taste of sweaty salt in what now felt like a desert-parched throat.

* * * *

Skyler stopped and looked at the petite girl in front of him. She was beautiful in the moonlight—more attractive than any woman he'd ever known. When he was with her, he felt miles high, absolutely powerful. She was too immature to understand her effect on him. He would help her understand what he had really done for her, for them. She owed him, and it was time to make that known.

His anticipation of having her beneath him was no longer to be suspended, no longer to be held in abeyance. She was here now, and he had a need for her, with a sense of urgency so deep within him he couldn't control himself. He found himself reaching for her with such an eruption of limitless desire, it was as if he were someone else. He had never known such raw unabated want. He didn't notice her horror. He didn't notice her grimacing face or her contorted body. He didn't feel her pushing away. Her sounds fell on his deaf ears. He didn't notice when the sounds stopped. He only noticed when her body became compliant to his—finally giving in with cool casual indifference.

* * * *

Samantha knew she had to comply, just as she knew she'd had no choice when Uncle Greg had held her down with the belt. To her horror, she felt her body bowing with Skyler's, as his sweaty hands reached into her bra, fiercely pushing it up, yanked it off and unbuttoning her sundress. He removed her dress and panties.

She felt exposed.

He cupped her breasts, moving from one to the other, first his hand, and then his mouth, swallowing her whole.

She gagged. She stiffened. She wanted to scream. She tried. She tried again. As if she were in slow motion. Her voice no longer worked at her mind's command. She had lost control. Finally, she let go. She screamed an internal scream so loud and so deep it numbed her entirely. It no longer mattered that no one else could hear her scream. Nothing mattered.

He probed and pried at all of her.

She could feel his swell against her. He was hot, and breathing heavy. She unconsciously searched his body as he searched hers. Together they became impostors, and Skyler became the art collector buying with an untrained eye, as she feigned her pleasure, arching her back, moving her body with his to rhythmic crescendo.

When he finished, Skyler was genuinely enraptured with her performance. He believed it, and Samantha knew she had pleased him. Her slow deliberate movements had fooled him.

He held her and his breathing became more even.

Finally, stroking her breasts, he spoke in a soft thick voice. "That was wonderful. I'm so glad you understand. It has been you all along I have wanted. I know you feel the same way. We are two of a kind, you and me," he said into the sudden dead air.

It was over, and he had believed her. He lay still, sprawled on her with his eyes closed, seemed to be waiting for a response. But Samantha couldn't speak. Warm, uncontrollable tears spilled down the sides of her face, raining on her ears. She nodded.

Samantha felt like an intruder in her own body. She felt her mind sinking and knew she couldn't let it shut down, or she'd never find her way back. She had to find her voice—to erase this horror—to fill it with strength, so she could find a way out. She studied the boathouse.

Her mental transformation made it impossible for him to penetrate her soul like he'd penetrated her body. She'd been on the sidelines watching. She wasn't really the woman who had matched him movement for movement.

Samantha had grown to know Skyler well enough to know she had to keep him in a friendly mood, so she could leave and find a safe harbor to figure things out. Her voice came, soft, clear, and deliberate.

"Skyler, I am thankful to you for all you have done for me, but this cannot happen again. It was just the alcohol I had. I shouldn't have had any. I'm sorry. It was my fault," Samantha said carefully. Her voice broke, cutting sharply into the silence.

"No. You don't understand. This is the way it is to be. This is the way it has to be," Skyler said. He held her arms so tightly she couldn't move again. "You owe me. Why do you think I've kept all your little secrets?"

Samantha quivered in the darkness. "You said you would help me because you were my friend, my father's friend."

"Yes, but everyone has their price, and you are old enough to learn that. My price for my silence is you. I want you. And if you think I won't tell, or I have no proof, you just try me. I have all the medical documents and records from our little trip. Do you remember that?" Skyler reached for a small envelope from his wrinkled pants, which lay in a tan pool next to their still-naked bodies, he handed it to her.

"What's this?" Samantha held the manila envelope, afraid to open it.

"Just my insurance. Don't open it now. Wait until you go home. The envelope contains a thumb-drive you'll want to listen to on your computer. You'll see just how serious I am. I have other copies, so I suggest you destroy this one to ensure it doesn't fall into the wrong hands." Skyler stroked her hair. She hated for him to touch any part of her.

"You wouldn't do anything to hurt me," Samantha said, unsure of herself. "You're my friend. I confided in you. You promised to help me. You wouldn't do anything that would hurt my parents."

"Sure I would. I work hard for your father, and I have made him a lot of money over the years. I don't owe him anything. Besides, he would probably be grateful I helped out his daughter in her time of need. He won't believe Greg raped you, and I'll get a dozen guys to say they slept with you. And then there's the recording. You shouldn't make any hasty decisions until you've listened to it."

"You wouldn't. You couldn't do that." Samantha held back her tears though she was crying inside. Deep down she knew he could, and he would. Samantha looked around for something to fight with. She saw nothing. She wished she could kill him and end it all; her whole nightmare could die with him. She had been a fool to trust him, and it was too late to do anything.

She looked at him squarely and shrugged.

"I have a lot to teach you. It will be the best summer you've ever had." Skyler was jovial, almost laughing. "You'll go off to college a real woman."

And then he did it again.

CHAPTER 5

The next morning, Samantha awoke, slowly removed the covers from her buried face and blinked the sleep from her eyes, trying to focus and remember where she was. She had been in a trancelike dream. Her mouth was parched and stale. She ran her swollen tongue over her teeth, counting to ensure they were all there. Her cheeks still tasted of blood as she traced the coarse ridges inside them where she had bitten down.

Thankfully, nothing visible was missing or injured. Her body felt stiff, sore, and bruised from her insides out. She ached. Her head hurt. Faint pictures flashed from within her.

She remembered.

It wasn't a dream. What was she to do now? Where could she go? Who could she tell? Suddenly, she remembered the envelope he'd given her. Where had she put it? She got up and quietly moved around the room, so she didn't disturb Emily. Samantha grabbed her pink robe and reached deep into the large pocket where the envelope lay hidden.

She had to find a computer and listen. What could it contain? Pulling open Emily's desk drawers, she discovered a laptop. She turned it on. It had some charge. Quietly she removed it before slipping into the safety of the bathroom. This time she remembered to lock the door.

Turning the shower on to muffle any sound, Samantha sat on the toilet, placed earphones on she'd grabbed from her purse, and put the flash-drive into the slot. Hesitantly, she clicked on it.

To her shock, she heard her own timid voice, explaining tearfully to Skyler how Uncle Greg had raped her. She listened for a few minutes and then heard Skyler's voice replying. She was reliving that awful morning after the rape. She couldn't listen. She pulled the flash-drive out and held it with shaking hands and trembling body. How had he recorded their conversation? She didn't recall his cell phone or Dictaphone like her father used. Had someone else been in the room? Would she have noticed?

Samantha wanted to destroy the flash-drive. She couldn't do it here though; someone might find it. She placed it back into the deep pocket of her robe. She walked into the shower and numbly slumped over.

* * * *

"Samantha, what's going on?" Emily said. "My God, you're blue. Did you fall asleep in the shower? Are you sick? Put this blanket on you. Scoot further onto the bed."

"I'm fine. I did. I fell asleep in the shower; can you believe it? What a dumb thing to do. That beer last night really made me sick, and I took a few aspirins before I fell asleep. I guess they must not have mixed well. Uh, here." She handed Emily the computer. "I was going to check my email. My cell isn't charged."

Emily grabbed the computer but looked unconvinced.

"Please don't say anything. I'll be fine," Samantha said, compounding her lies. She felt sorry for Emily, who looked at her with genuine concern.

"Fine. But you and I are getting ready, and we are going downstairs for some food. There is an extra phone charger if you need it. It's in the same drawer where you found my computer."

"Thank you," Samantha said.

"You probably threw up everything you ate last night. You better eat something this morning before we see everyone and say good-bye to people. You can't let any-one see you looking like this. Our parents will kill us both if they find out we were drinking," Emily whispered, and she rubbed Samantha's arms through the blanket.

Samantha was happy to take orders and to feel a kind hand warming her, caring for her. There wasn't anything she could do for the moment. She just hoped she didn't run into Skyler.

Surely, she must have misunderstood him. After all,

Samantha reasoned, she had been drinking, and she had mixed medicine and alcohol. She knew there were side effects to mixing drugs and alcohol; maybe that's what happened. Samantha had heard her father call Skyler the most eligible man in the county. So why did he want her?

As she cautiously walked down the staircase with Emily to eat breakfast, Samantha was well aware Emily was watching her closely. As they entered the breakfast room, they could see the table just being set for brunch.

The girls agreed to sit in the kitchen and eat while Cook prepared brunch for the others. The smell of fresh cinnamon rolls and lemon muffins filled the air. Cook smiled at them. She put plates in front of them, so they could help themselves to anything they wanted. Fortunately, the girls were not expected to join everyone for the final meal together before most of the group departed. Sunday was relaxing, and the girls were on their own until dinner.

The rest of the day was routine. The girls spent the day on the paddleboat and played a game of croquet with the house rules they'd made up on Emily's tenth birthday. They had wanted to prove the boys who'd been invited couldn't meet the girls' course. They placed the wires in challenging positions: in the midst of flowers, rocks, and roots. They still liked to play that course and, even now, the challenge of it gave them a sense of control, accomplishment, and sheer relaxation.

Neither of them questioned why, but they knew they would play croquet until they were so old they could no longer hold the mallets. They laughed with ease and felt like small children again. This time together was precious, and they were determined to enjoy it to the fullest. Without discussing it, they knew their time together was growing short before Europe and college interfered.

Samantha remained introspective most of the time, but Emily attributed her silence to last night's beer and the fact things were changing.

The girls went to join the remaining guests for dinner, only to find a comfortable place setting for six. Samantha was relieved that everyone else, including Skyler, had gone. Samantha and her parents would leave with the Osbornes tomorrow.

As the evening progressed, Samantha rigidly controlled her face and answered each question with an instinctive delicacy that carefully mimicked happiness. Everyone who'd worried about her, including Emily, quietly marveled at her sudden transformation.

Samantha was mastering her world. Her world as she now knew and understood it. Her quiet manipulation of those closest to her reinforced what little strength she had remaining. She couldn't control what was happening to her, but she could control her own behavior. Her first and most important goal was to reassure her family and friends she was okay. She'd deal with the rest later. She had no choice. Her silent determination left her with more fortitude than she'd had in months.

"Dinner on the patio was a marvelous idea, Stephanie," Mom said lightly. "It's such a beautiful evening and the perfect way to spend our last night."

"Thank you. Really, though, I must confess it was Oren's idea. He said he has a surprise for us all." Emily's mom beamed, looking around the table at the faces now turned toward Emily's dad.

"Later dear. Later. I don't want to spoil it," Oren said, chuckling, as he raised his wine glass. "I'd like to make a toast," he said, now standing. "A toast to good friends and time well spent. A toast to Travis for his kindness and fairness to the firm. And, finally, a toast to the future, to our safe journeys home and continued good health, safety, and prosperity until we can meet again."

Everyone raised their glasses, clinking them in unison.

Then Travis, beaming, spoke in a boisterous tone, "I couldn't have said it better, and we would like to thank you for your kind words and your hospitality." Travis raised his glass, and again the six glasses clanked.

Samantha and Emily remained silent watching their parents repeat kind gestures back and forth, as they had on so many other occasions. Samantha wished this meal would end, so she and Em could enjoy their last night together.

Finally, dessert was cleared. Emily spoke up first, asking that they be excused to pack for tomorrow and to go for a walk. Samantha remained silent, but nodded as she heard Emily's explanations and apologies for being too tired to stay at the table any longer. Both sets of parents instantaneously agreed as they moved to the garden gazebo to sit and sip their after-dinner drinks.

* * * *

"So give, Samantha," Emily said, as the girls walked barefoot on the shoreline, their shoes tied and slung over their shoulders.

"Give?" Samantha said. "What do you mean?"

"Come on, you know. You're holding something back. You were too quiet at dinner. For God's sake, you haven't been yourself all week. I know something's up."

"Okay, you're right. Everything is changing. It's depressing me. I don't want to lose you, and even though I know you'll always be there, things will be different. I can't bear it."

"Come on, Samantha, you're lying to me. We already discussed all of that. What's really going on?" Emily said. "Remember me? I know you. The real you. You are not acting like you."

"I—" Samantha started.

"No, Sam. I want the truth."

"I can't tell you right now. I swear I will. But right now, I just can't. There is something, something awful, but I have to work some things out before I can tell you," Samantha said, tears streaming. "I'm going to be fine. I haven't told you because I don't want you to worry."

"Sam, I'm your best friend. If you can't tell me, then who can you tell? Whatever it is, you know you can trust me; you know I can keep a secret. I'll help you no matter what."

"That's just it. I can't tell you. I can't tell anyone. I haven't told anyone. I will, when I'm ready. Then you'll understand why. Please don't be mad at me." Samantha's voice was shaking, her breathing uneven. She felt sweat on her brow and under her arms. Her whole body was warm and faint, but talking with Emily gave her inner strength and calmed her rampant thoughts. "Trust me, please, just trust me. You know in your heart I would tell you, if I could. I just need some time."

"Okay, I'll trust you. I'll give you that time, not because I want to, but because you've asked me to. Even if you just need me to listen, I'll be there," Emily said, with a strength in her voice Samantha never knew she had. "I'll call you from wherever I am in Europe, too. You'll have all my numbers. Then you can call me if you need to. Anytime."

"I know I can count on you," Samantha said, locking Emily into a sisterly hug.

CHAPTER 6

Graduation came and went without incident. After a week, Samantha still hadn't heard from Skyler, except for eighteen beautiful pink roses sent from the entire firm and accompanied by an oversized card with many signatures, including his.

Samantha opted not to have a graduation party and had been presented with a check from her parents for $25,000 in lieu of a car and party. Undergraduates couldn't drive a car on campus at MSU. Since she was living in a dorm and shopping was close by, it didn't make sense to have a brand-new car that sat at home. Her parents, surprised at her maturity, decided she could handle a large check and could take her time to decide what she wanted to use it for later. Touched at their undeserved trust in her, Samantha decided to put the money away and forget about it.

As each day passed, she became more certain everything was fine, and her involvement with Skyler was just a bad mistake, a misunderstanding. Samantha was convinced Skyler must think so, too. Otherwise he would've called her; he would be pursuing his threat of blackmail.

She was grateful she had been taking her birth-control pills since the abortion. She wasn't sure why she had decided to take them, except she had followed Skyler's instructions to the letter. At least she didn't have to worry about going through another abortion, another murder. Her short pregnancy and constant thoughts and nightmares about the abortion held her mind hostage with guilt that kept her body thin and undernourished.

The abortion involved an innocent victim she'd never know or touch or hold, but she'd always remember. She had no explanation for it to herself, for her family, or for God. And though she longed for one, none came.

Samantha regretted not talking with Emily, not telling her when she had the chance. Emily could have been her reality check. Maybe she could've helped.

But it was too late. Emily was gone to Europe for the summer to learn German and gather bits of culture she'd share with the future husband she intended to find at college. That was her plan; that was the antiquated plan of her parents. Soon Emily's name would be found on the society pages, and she'd be pictured on the arm of an up-and-coming man from a well-known family.

Samantha was glad her parents allowed her to pursue her dream of becoming a veterinarian before thinking about finding a husband and being a proper southern lady, like her mother and her mother before her. Thankfully, her parents were having too much fun with their own lives to seriously interfere with Samantha's.

Still, she wished she could talk to someone. Her thoughts were driving her crazy, and she was sleeping less and less.

Two more weeks passed. The house phone rang, and Samantha answered it.

"Samantha, it's so nice to hear your voice," Skyler's deep voice came. It might as well have been a knife.

"Uh, yes." Samantha went numb. She felt dizzy, and her knees buckled and she sank onto the carpet. "What can I do for you? Do you want to leave a message for my father?"

"I want to talk to you. You know what I want. You need to meet me for dinner at seven."

Samantha froze. She couldn't respond. She felt flushed and faint and couldn't find her voice.

But Skyler's voice continued to echo in the receiver. He didn't care that she hadn't responded to his question. "I'll pick you up. Wear a dress," he commanded.

"But, I—"

The dial tone.

The clock moved slowly, but not slowly enough for Samantha. She dreaded the evening. She loathed Skyler's voice and everything else about him. He was just an object of pain.

Her first mission, above all else, was to find any recordings or other evidence he had and destroy everything. She also had to figure out how he'd recorded her and how many conversations. It was too easy to record on cell phones. What if he had other evidence? He'd told her he did. She didn't believe him, but she had to behave as if she did, so she could find out the truth.

* * * *

At exactly seven, the doorbell rang. Samantha opened the door. She had her hair wrapped in a tight French twist secured by two Chinese sticks and wore a long-sleeved, high-collared dress, despite the heat.

"Hi there. You look great," Skyler said, looking her up and down. "You'll be a bit warm in that dress."

"I always freeze in restaurants," Samantha said.

"Well then, let's go. Your carriage awaits." Skyler held out his arm for her as if she were his princess.

Samantha ignored his arm and comment. Quietly she climbed into the front seat of his shiny green Jaguar, keeping close to the door. After Skyler locked them in, she unlocked it.

"You can keep the door unlocked. You can even get out any time you wish. I'm in the habit of locking my car doors," Skyler said.

Samantha said nothing. Fear filled her with silence. Fear made her alert. Fear made her spend this time with him.

Skyler made small talk about Memorial Day weekend at the Osborne estate. He rambled on and on about how great it was being part of a firm that liked to be together, that handled things as a large family. He made several comments about how much respect he had for each of the partners, especially her father. He said nothing about the boathouse. He said nothing about the recording or the blackmail. And, for the first time, he said nothing about the rape or the abortion.

He seemed so normal. He seemed to forget what had happened between them. But she knew better than to believe him.

The moment Skyler turned the engine off, Samantha opened her car door. She'd be damned if he'd treat her like they were a couple, when she was there under protest. Clutching her purse, she waited for him a few feet from the car. She was glad he hadn't used the valet parking. She needed these few moments walking in the fresh air.

Dinner was a diversion from the discomfort of being alone with Skyler. She had admirable restraint considering the resentment and hate that was quietly seething beneath her calm composure.

* * * *

Samantha was a desirable break from Skyler's heavy caseload. He knew she was there only under threat, but he would change that. She needed him, whether she knew it or not. She'd eventually want him, once she realized all the female desires stirring within her.

Skyler carefully studied her, feeling an undercurrent

of agitation. It had to be his way. It wouldn't take long for his labor to bear fruit. Looking across the table at her, he was absolutely convinced she'd be his.

Already he felt her mounting confusion about his change from wearing the white hat to the black one. Skyler was a watcher of women, a connoisseur. He knew women. All women were, for the most part, the same. Women were naturally curious creatures, who liked to nurture and control, yet they liked to be taken care of and needed. They liked challenge and strength. Women lived for paradoxes. He lived to create them. Skyler, like the puppeteer, planned, carefully plotted to pull each string just right.

"What would you like to drink? Champagne or perhaps some wine?" Skyler asked.

✳ ✳ ✳ ✳

Samantha ordered lemonade and Skyler had dark German beer, and nobody talked about the last time Samantha had beer. Samantha ordered an appetizer instead of a main course. But Skyler changed it to the entree and added a soup and salad for her, over her protests, and then he ordered the same for himself, with prime rib as his main course. He directed her to eat everything in front of her, no matter how long they had to stay there. Skyler would see to it that she ate a decent meal, and the experience would be enjoyable. She'd gotten almost too thin. Samantha ate to avoid conversation.

She wished she could sink into the floor. She hated feeling his eyes burning through her.

"Come now, it can't be that bad. Am I such boring company you have to scowl?"

Samantha looked surprised. She didn't realize she had let go of her feelings, so he could read her expressions. She'd not let that happen again.

"I, we, shouldn't be here at all," Samantha whispered.

"The food is superb. We'll relax together. You'll see I'm not the ogre you think I am." Skyler's tone was serious. "You just need to give me the benefit of the doubt, like I gave you when you needed me."

"And, if I don't?"

"Samantha, you're intelligent enough to know that if you said anything, no one would believe you. And I'll be happy to testify you got drunk and you wanted me." Skyler paused.

"You seduced me."

"Emily witnessed your drinking, did she not?" Brutally, Skyler forced his point. "In this town, your family and your reputation would be permanently scarred."

"I was raped."

"You have no proof; you didn't report it. No one will believe you."

"You told me not to report it."

"No, I told you that you had washed away the proof by taking a shower, and it would be difficult to prove. I told you the media would get a kick out of putting your family in all of the newspapers. All of those things are true. Are you telling me they're not? That the facts are somehow different?"

"No, but—"

"In court, there is no 'but.' It's either 'yes' or 'no.' 'Maybe' doesn't count."

"I'm not in court. We're not in court."

"You will be if you report the rape. You'd be put on the witness stand against Greg. You'd have to answer a lot of personal questions."

"And you would have to do the same. You helped me. You found the doctor and set up the abortion. You took care of everything. And then you raped me."

"The way I remember it, you demanded my help and my silence, for your own protection. I'll be happy to testify to that. Of course, you could try to use alcohol as your defense, maybe even incapacity or insanity. Is that what you want? If so, be my guest. And by the way, you should think about the fact that abortion, for someone your age, without parental or judicial consent, is illegal in our state. It's a crime."

"Against the doctor. Against you for arranging it. Not against me. That's not possible. I'm the victim." Samantha felt like jumping up and hitting him. Her flushed skin was hot, and she felt as if spiders were crawling over her flesh.

"There's no evidence except what I have in my possession, locked up for safe keeping. As far as anyone will know, you did it yourself. Any physician will be able to testify you've had an abortion. You may not go to jail, but jail would be easier than what you'll be faced with in the media and within our small community. You'll find people love to gossip." Skyler seemed merciless. "As to the issue of rape, men will believe you wanted it, you even enjoyed it. They'll seek you out."

Samantha turned cold. She couldn't think. He'd thought well beyond what she'd even considered. She'd been too wrapped up in the individual acts to see the whole picture. He was right. Everyone would look at her and see *guilt*.

* * * *

"What evidence do you have from the doctor?" she asked, her eyes like round blue pools, the calm before the storm.

"The file. The medical file on you. Your history: the procedure, medication, instructions, everything."

"He gave that to you? That's confidential; that's mine."

"Sorry. The file is missing. Of course, no one knows it even exists, at this point. Even if someone were to find out, no one will know where the file is, or what happened to it," Skyler said quietly.

"Except you," she said indignantly.

"You're such a smart girl," Skyler said.

Samantha shifted the tri-color fettuccine noodles under the grilled garlic shrimp back and forth, artfully separating the colors in piles. Silence descended over their table.

Skyler needed Samantha healthy and strong to keep up with him. It wasn't just sex he wanted. He wanted her companionship. He wanted to take her sailing, hiking, skiing. He wanted to teach her to love him, the same way he'd grown to care for her.

Skyler could see she was distraught and hiding tears. In the momentary silence, he decided he'd better ease up on her before she fell apart.

"Are you all right? I truly am sorry. I had no intention of bringing all this up. But it is better you know the facts."

* * * *

"I've gotten myself into quite a situation. I should probably thank you," she lied, riddled with guilt and anger. Samantha was anxious to find some time alone, so she could sort out what he'd said. And to look in her father's law books to see if any of his statements were true. What did he want with her? Why her? He had so many other women available to him.

"Things will be better from now on. I promise," Skyler said, now smiling, gently patting Samantha's hand across the table.

Samantha smiled, too, just enough to remove any sign of doubt or disapproval from her expression.

Dinner finally cleared, and Skyler ordered dessert

and cappuccino to end the evening. As she slid a delicate spoonful of chocolate mousse, she mentally braced herself for the evening that lay ahead of them.

* * * *

Skyler was impressed with himself. He had pulled it off. She trusted him. She understood his rules and his reasoning. She'd play along. She'd be his.

The couple left the restaurant side by side. Skyler, watching her closely, felt her anxiety about the rest of the evening. Neither spoke about it. Skyler made small talk. When he exited the ramp leading to her home, Samantha looked even more tired.

"Where are we going?" she asked him.

"Home," he said. "Where else would you like to go?"

"Not here. You're not going to—I can't—" Samantha was reduced to stuttering.

"I have an early day tomorrow. I have to make it an early evening," Skyler said gently, looking at her with apologetic eyes. "How about Friday? I'll pick you up on Friday, say six? Dinner and a movie?" Skyler's tone was one of adolescent friendship, sincere and unsure of her willingness.

"I—Well, okay," Samantha said. She sounded confused and was stuttering again.

* * * *

Samantha was shocked he hadn't touched her. He was almost a perfect date. Something had to be wrong. What happened? Had she done something wrong? From the driveway, she watched him slowly drive away, a playful grin on his handsome face.

Contemplating the evening, Samantha climbed the staircase of the dark, still house. She felt grimy in her dress. Taking it off, she carelessly flung it over the velvet loveseat. Her only thought, at this moment, was the deep cleansing of a shower.

* * * *

Samantha awoke in a sweat. She oriented herself to her dusky room and then again looked at Minnie Mouse, whose hands were not moving quickly: 4:17 a.m. At first, she was afraid to close her eyes again and see the faces. To dream. But then morning came quickly.

Rummaging through her clothes, sorting what she was giving away, what she was leaving home, and what she was taking to school in the fall, she focused on moving away to college. She created checklist after checklist of the things she needed to do and the items she needed to buy. The lists would keep her busy, both mind and body.

She was more and more anxious to leave and begin her new life in Michigan. She was determined to do one thing in preparation for her departure every day until she left. From this day forward, she vowed, she'd live one day at a time and fill her days with positive accomplishments, even if they were small.

She had to use every ounce of energy she had to focus on the positive. Then, maybe, she'd find the strength to put her struggles behind her. After last night, she knew she had to rely on herself and trust herself, at least for now. There was no one else. They were uncomfortable thoughts, but in an odd way, they gave her strength.

Samantha had two days until she had to see Skyler. She decided to ask the housekeeper to tell everyone who called *she was out*. When no one else was available to answer the phone, she'd leave the answering machine on and screen the calls. She left her cell on silent. She didn't want to talk with Skyler before he picked her up on Friday. She needed this time to search her father's study for any law books that might answer her questions. So she waited until everyone was out, and went into his home office. She couldn't risk going to the office-office, but she could go to the State's law library if she had to.

Samantha could tell people, if they asked about her sudden interest in law, she might consider law school after, or instead of, veterinarian school. Given her family, no one would question that. In fact, that would give her an opening to ask her father and brothers questions about hypothetical situations. Of course, she decided, she'd only do that as a last resort.

Samantha didn't trust lawyers, not even the ones she was related to. Growing up, she'd seen and heard too many unpleasant things. Lawyers thought differently. They examined every word and phrase too closely. They noticed reactions and asked questions that led you to say the wrong thing or too much of the right thing.

Black's Law Dictionary would explain to her the legal words she didn't understand. Then she could go from there. She flipped the crisp pages until she reached the Bs. Expectantly, she ran her finger down the margin, finding the second word on the page, just under *Black Lung Benefit's Act* was *Blackmail.* She read the passage carefully, scrutinizing every word, every line, every sentence. She reread the part that could pertain to her and said the words out loud as if they would mean more to her that way.

> *Blackmail. Unlawful demand of money or property under threat to do bodily harm, to injure property, to accuse of crime, or to expose disgraceful defects...
> See Extortion; Shakedown.*

Nothing. Blackmail for sex. There was nothing about blackmail for sex in the definition. Skyler wasn't demanding money or property. He had all the money and personal possessions he could ever use.

She couldn't let herself panic. She tried hard not to, but the words in the thick book turned blurry. She forged ahead, flipping crisp pages until she found *Extortion.*

> *Extortion. The obtaining of property from another induced by wrongful use of actual or threatened*

force, violence, or fear, or under color of official right. 18 U.S.C.A. Sec. 871 et. seq.; Sec. 1951. A person is guilty of theft by extortion if he purposely obtains property of another by threatening to . . .

Samantha grew frustrated. She skimmed the itemized list.

. . . (1) inflict bodily injury . . .; or (2) accuse anyone of a criminal offense; or (3) expose any secret tending to subject the person to hatred, contempt or ridicule . . .; or (4) take or withhold action as an official . . .; or (5) bring about or continue a strike . . .; or (6) testify . . . ; or (7) inflict any other harm which wouldn't benefit the actor. Model Penal Code, Sec. 223.4. See also Blackmail; Hobbs Act; Loan Sharking; Shakedown. With respect to "Larceny by extortion," see Larceny.

The words blurred into a whirlpool of letters, jumbled into foreign lines, led to infinite ramblings. So many more words to look up. She had counted on an exhaustive list, but she hadn't counted on so many words— so many she didn't understand within the definitions. Samantha had been taught the dictionary was to clarify words and their meanings, not to confuse them.

Relentlessly she pursued each word, which led to more references and more bewilderment. Her inner turmoil grew deeper and deeper. None of the definitions fit. Not one definition talked about sex, about rape, or about blackmail of any kind relating to those things.

Blackmail and extortion led her to the Hobbs Act and racketeering, which were totally off the track. Larceny and larceny by extortion seemed to help her, but again, neither mentioned sex.

Could it be it was legal to blackmail for sex? It was illegal to blackmail for money or to threaten someone.

There were dollar amounts on larceny, and the definition mentioned property, but not stealing a person by rape or forced sex. Samantha was baffled. It was legal, she surmised with deep dismay. Skyler was smart. Her father always said he enjoyed trying cases with Skyler because, "If there was a loophole in the law, Skyler was the one who had the nose to find it or the way around it." Well, she reluctantly concluded, he had found the loophole, and it was she who would pay.

Although Samantha continued turning pages, she'd lost hope. She needed time to digest the words. She decided to use her father's copy machine to collect every possible definition she needed.

Carefully, Samantha clipped from the copied pages only the necessary definitions and pasted them on one page, making a final copy. Then, gathering even the tiniest scrap, she shredded all of the remains, except for one legal-sized sheet, which she folded and placed in her pocket. She'd read it later. She'd read and ask questions until she learned what it all meant. She'd find out why she seemed to be a loophole in the law. She'd uncover the hidden meaning in the words. She vowed she had to save herself, and this would be the start. It was up to her. She felt stronger than she had in days.

Samantha inspected her father's office to ensure everything was in place. Her father was particular about his office, and even her mother dared not enter.

Climbing the staircase to her bedroom, with a sandwich and soda in hand, she felt confident the folded paper in her shirt pocket was the first clue to her solution. For the first time, she felt like she was fighting back, taking back what she had lost. She sat in the comfort of her room, pulled out the words, and began to study them.

* * * *

Early the next morning, Samantha felt like a mummy opening her eyes for the first time in years. She'd had the same floating dreams, but this time she was less frightened. Although she still couldn't speak, this time she was able to bring her hand up to her throat and rub it, smoothing it gently, as if to heal and coax her voice.

Listening to the birds chirp, she focused on her white ceiling. She still felt like she was dreaming, and yet her mind told her she was alive and awake and well.

And then she remembered, and reality came flooding in. Today was her last full day before she had to see Skyler again.

She had to go back to the library to find more clues and reread the definitions. Maybe she'd missed something. Maybe she forgot to look up a word. She got into the shower, where the water felt good, splashing and spraying over every part of her thinning body. The water gave her life.

Later, wrapped in a comfortable navy sweatshirt with matching overstretched sweat pants, Samantha walked into the kitchen and grabbed a large mug of creamed coffee and a piece of dry toast. Silently, she made her way into her father's study and the arms of the burgundy leather chair planted at the head of his desk. Again, she grabbed Black's Law Dictionary. She needed a new angle, different words, maybe a different book.

She thought of Skyler. Fretfully, she brushed her fingers through her curls, still damp from the shower. She remembered how she used to look up to him. She remembered his caring selfless tone when he'd first befriended her. She remembered his cruel impatient tone when he raped her.

Samantha knew she had to find a way to help herself. She had to find someone to help her. But who and how? She couldn't trust anyone. She couldn't risk any questions. She couldn't act suspicious. She needed to think. She needed a nap.

For now, she'd concentrate and learn and fill herself with the words. The words would wrap a protective shield around her, inside her. If she kept the words in her head, Skyler couldn't reach her core, her soul. She could hide behind the words, and they would protect her. No one could touch her. No one would.

CHAPTER 7

Samantha decided she'd dress creatively each time Skyler forced her to go out with him. She'd hide her body under clothing that wasn't easily removed. Surely that would deter him. She didn't want to give Skyler any reason to believe she was agreeing to his desires.

The bell chimed, and Samantha inspected herself for the last time in the hallway mirror. Purse slung over her shoulder, she opened the door.

"Hello," Samantha said blandly, avoiding Skyler's eyes.

"Aren't you going to invite me in?"

"No." She stepped out, slamming the heavy white door behind her.

"Okay. There's no need to go inside. I just thought we could talk for a few minutes. I thought the show started at seven, but it begins at half past," Skyler said cheerfully, opening Samantha's door.

Samantha remained silent. She wasn't sure what might set him off, so she decided to give the illusion of her best behavior.

Skyler turned on the engine, then reached into the back seat and his arm brushed her shoulder.

Samantha bristled.

"For you. I hope you like it," Skyler said, smiling.

Samantha eyed the yellow cellophane. It held a perfect yellow rose surrounded with babies' breath and greenery. She wished it would disappear. The rose was beautiful and under any other circumstance, Samantha would have been thrilled. "Thanks."

"Look at me, Samantha." With two fingers, Skyler turned her face toward him. "Come on, look at me," he coaxed playfully.

Samantha stared at him shyly, quizzically.

"Yellow. One perfect yellow rose. For you. A symbol for us," Skyler said. His voice oozed sincerity. "Yellow is the color for friendship. I want us to be friends. Close friends. Best friends. You'll see—we are perfect for each other. I'll give you all the time you need. Promise."

Samantha held Skyler's eyes. She was mute with disbelief.

"Don't worry, it'll be great," Skyler said. With one finger, he touched her knee for a second and pulled out of the driveway onto the road. "Fifty Shades of Grey is playing."

"I don't prefer to see that," Samantha said coldly, looking out her window at the rows of houses they passed, trying to occupy her mind, wondering about all the other lives in those houses.

Skyler didn't say anything about the movie, but asked a lot of questions about upcoming school and friends. Samantha spoke in short answers until he shifted the subject to previous boyfriends.

"I'm not dating," she said. "If I go out at all it's in a group. I'm not interested. I'm leaving for college."

"But you had a boyfriend. Jason. That was his name, wasn't it?"

"Ages ago."

"You dated him for more than two years. You must still like him."

"No. It's over, and I'm glad," Samantha said, for the first time taking her eyes off the window, looking directly at Skyler's profile. "I don't want to talk about him, and I don't want you to bring him up ever again."

"I'll bring up whatever I want to bring up, and you'll answer me. That's what friends do. That's what we'll do. Do you understand?" Skyler said, clenching his teeth, speaking in a low- but-fierce tone.

"Yes." Samantha followed his lead and responded through clenched teeth.

"So, did you have sex with him?"

Samantha remained silent, seething at the invasion of privacy and the inference of the question.

"It's okay. You can tell me. I won't be mad. I want to hear about it. Just pretend I'm one of the girls."

"We didn't have sex. He wanted to; I wouldn't. We broke up. End of story."

"That's a shame. For him, I mean. I can understand how he wouldn't be able to resist you. But I can also understand you wouldn't want him. A boy, I mean. Why have a boy when you can have Superman?" Skyler flashed his too-white teeth.

Nauseated, Samantha said, "It wasn't like that."

"It doesn't really matter. I'm happy it's over. I don't want you to have any distractions from our relationship."

"We don't have a relationship." Her voice was sarcastic.

"Oh, but we do," Skyler said, reaching over, stroking her forearm, patting her hands.

Samantha didn't want to aggravate him.

✶ ✶ ✶ ✶

When they finally arrived at the theater, the prospect of two hours of silence was a relief.

All through the movie, Samantha waited for his hand to creep over to her in the darkness. It didn't.

The anger and apprehension she'd felt earlier receded. She enjoyed the movie, finished a large bucket of buttered popcorn, and a large diet soda.

"Great movie," Skyler said. He lifted himself from the uncomfortable pop-up seat, standing closely behind Samantha, while waiting for their row to clear.

"Mmm," she agreed.

"What? You didn't like it?"

"I didn't say that. It was okay. I'm tired."

"It's too early. We'll eat and then go to Riba's to dance."

"I'm full from the popcorn, and I can't get into Riba's. I'm underage, remember?"

"You can get in with me. I just won't let you drink." Skyler winked.

Shrinking back, Samantha said, "Maybe a burger or chicken fingers."

"Whitney's it is. They have great food, and we can dance in the back room after dinner. Have you ever been there?"

"I've heard about it." Her curiosity overshadowed her fear for the moment. She'd always wanted to go to Whitney's. Maybe she could salvage something positive from the evening. "Do you think we can get in on a Friday night?"

"They know me."

The crosstown drive was filled with Skyler's pretentious insights into the movie. Samantha nodded as if she cared.

"So what'd you think about the movie?" he asked.

"Listen, I've been thinking," Samantha began. It wasn't the kind of movie she was comfortable discussing with a man. "What if we're seen together? What do I tell people? What do I tell my parents?"

"You were keeping me company. There's nothing more to tell."

"What if they want more?"

"Trust me."

She knew how far she could trust him. "But—"

"Trust me."

When they reached Whitney's, there was a wait of over an hour. But Skyler tipped the host a fifty-dollar bill, which solved everything.

"Great timing." Skyler winked.

"Great tipping," Samantha said sarcastically. She hated that pompous wink.

"So what's your pleasure? Everything on the menu is grand," Skyler said in a gallant tone.

"Veggie burger, if they have one." Samantha ignored the menu, let him know she was unimpressed.

"Whatever you want is yours."

"Again, veggie burger." She lifted the glass of ice water and chugged it.

"As you wish. It's called a garden burger," Skyler said.

The waiter appeared, and he ordered for both of them.

Samantha made mental notes of topics she could raise to prevent the subject being her. "Do you come here often? It seems like a fun place," she said.

"I've been known to frequent this place. What about you? Where do you go for fun?"

"Nowhere. I spend my time getting ready for school."

"That can't be all you do."

"How do you have time to take me out with your workload? Dad says right now you have the heaviest caseload in the office."

"I want to be more than just the youngest partner. I want to be the best. I want the firm to recognize me as the best."

"Dad says you are one of the best."

"I want to be the best—not in a pool of the best. I want a raise and a bonus that says I'm the best. I deserve that. I always get what I deserve," Skyler said with such intensity Samantha dared not challenge his words.

Moments later, plates were placed in front of them and their drinks refilled.

"This garden burger, as you call it, is the best I've had," Samantha said, relieved to change the subject.

"Good. I'm glad you like it here," Skyler said, wide-grinned.

"I should get home. My parents will worry if I'm not there when they call. I didn't tell them I was going out."

"Why didn't you tell them? You knew in plenty of time."

"I didn't want to lie. I've lied enough to them. I couldn't tell them I was going out with you. You know they wouldn't like it."

"Sure they would. You could tell them I offered to take you out to keep you company while they're gone. Your dad would thank me," Skyler said, winking at her again.

Samantha hated his wink, his tone, and his comments. She hated him. She had to get out. She grabbed her purse, knowing every man knew that meant his date was ready to leave. But, Skyler didn't move. He wanted her to ask.

Exasperated, Samantha took a deep breath. "Really,

Mr. Marks, we have to go. I can't worry my parents. If I'm not home when they call, they'll ground me for life."

"Mr. Marks, is it?" Skyler waited.

Samantha read laughter in his green eyes. "Okay, Skyler. Take me home, or I Uber it." Samantha kept her voice soft. "It's almost midnight. I don't want to upset my parents. They'll ring that phone until I'm home."

"That wasn't so difficult was it? Your wish is my command, my dear lady," Skyler said, slightly bowing, as if he were her Prince Charming. Then looking up at her he added, "Next time we come, we're going to Whitney's Back Stage. You'll love it. The music, the dancing—you'll be queen of the dance floor." He stood and then added, "My queen."

Samantha cringed, but remained silent. She didn't want to think about any other dates with Skyler, and refused to give him any hope that she'd look forward to a date, to a dance, to anything.

* * * *

Samantha's silence didn't bother Skyler. He enjoyed her company regardless of her mood. In time she'd see. In time she'd want him as much as she hated him. Her confusion was already apparent and right on schedule. Skyler smiled to himself, proudly.

The ride home was peaceful. Neither spoke, each in their own quiet and separate worlds. Again, Skyler dropped Samantha off, walking her to the door. She fumbled with her key, trying to put it in the lock and get quickly inside.

"Don't worry, Samantha, I'm not coming in. I don't want you to miss your phone call, so I'll talk to you later. And here, your rose. You wouldn't want to forget it, would you, friend?"

"See you," Samantha said.

"Save next Friday night. I'll pick you up at eight. Wear something casual. Jeans and tennis shoes."

"Whatever." She shut the door.

* * * *

In the morning, Samantha awoke, startled by a nightmare of floating faces. The faces were in pieces and without ears. This time they were wearing armor and bowing and rhyming in deep sullen voices. She couldn't make out what they were saying. The only thing she was sure of in her dreams, was she wanted to go home, and she would, in fact, get there. There was warmth in her dreams, despite her confusion. They deeply scared her. She needed to decipher them and dispose of them.

Samantha felt exhausted. She climbed into her morning shower closing her eyes tightly while the hot water pounded.

"Samantha. Samantha?" Her mother banged on the bathroom door. "Are you in there, dear?"

"Yes, Mom, I'll be out soon."

"Where is everyone? Why is there no one to take our

bags? And I don't see Cook anywhere. What have you done with them?"

"Mom, really? Let me finish my shower. I told the staff to be back by noon today. I didn't expect you till later this afternoon. I cleared it with Dad. Didn't he tell you?" Samantha stepped out of the shower, wrapped herself in a towel, and opened the door.

"I forgot," Anne said.

"I brought the bags up," Travis said, behind his wife. "Is everything okay?"

"Shutting the door," Samantha said and then locked it.

"Samantha." Her mom pounded on the door again. "We'll expect you on the veranda for lunch."

"Yes, Mother," Samantha yelled through the door.

✶ ✶ ✶ ✶

Samantha flipped through a stack of magazines on the nightstand next to her bed. She didn't want to leave her room until the very last minute. She needed time to think. Her mind, racing in all directions, categorized and catalogued the questions she wanted to ask her father about the law books in his study. She'd carefully hidden her dictionary list of words with the damning thumb-drive Skyler had given her. She wanted to learn the legal terminology that puzzled her. She had to unlock the mystery and free herself.

Hearing the luncheon bell ring, Samantha bounded

down the stairs, through the house and out onto the back veranda. She sat with her parents. An array of club sandwiches, salads, and fresh fruits were set around a bouquet of freshly cut roses from the garden. Samantha detoured the conversation to college, explaining that she'd received her dorm assignment and planned to contact her new roommates.

Sipping his tall glass of iced tea, Samantha's dad read the *New York Times*. He appeared to have not heard a word she said.

"Dad. Dad?"

"Yes, Samantha?" He peered at her over his bifocals.

"I'm wondering if there's some work I can do in your office this summer."

"A job? Why not enjoy your last summer before college? You don't need to work."

"I thought, well I wondered—what if I decide to be a lawyer, instead of a vet, or do both? I've considered the area of animal rights. I might want to go into law to protect animals, so I thought—"

"You thought you might like to learn a little bit to see if you're interested in the field? That's smart thinking, Samantha. I'm proud of you. You know we only hire third-year students to clerk."

"You don't have to pay me. I just want to learn. Hang out. Watch some of your trials, and you could explain what happened later? Kind of a father-daughter project?"

"I suppose that would be all right."

"I need a new computer for college. I'm hoping you could teach me a few programs I might need. I mean research programs."

"Legal research?" He set down his newspaper. "You're getting a little ahead of yourself, aren't you?"

Samantha filled her plate with salad. "If I learned how, maybe I could do legal research for you. And, I need to decide what kind of computer I want to take to school. We use Macintosh at school, but yours is a PC."

"Learning new things is never a waste of time. How about this? I'll ask an intern to come over and help you. Unless you'd like to stop by the firm some morning."

"Actually, I'd prefer it be here," Samantha said, beaming at her father. "Thanks, Dad."

"Anything for my girl. And yes, we are buying you a computer for college. Let us know what you prefer. I understand most colleges prefer Macintosh."

"Will do," Samantha said.

As the conversation progressed and lemon meringue pie and coffee were served, Samantha's mind focused on the next part of her plan. She had to make sure the court cases she saw were ones Skyler wasn't assisting in. She didn't want to ask who was working on the case with her father. She was fearful to even mention Skyler's name. But for the first time in weeks, Samantha felt things were in her favor. She had made a plan and had followed it. It would be her salvation. Even if it didn't work, it would keep her mind occupied. Her spirits were lifted for the moment, and nothing could break her serenity.

Again, in the solitude of her room, she retrieved her list of dictionary words and definitions confident she would be able to determine if Skyler had found a loophole. Knowledge would be her weapon. It would shield her from Skyler's evil.

CHAPTER 8

Every night around midnight, Skyler called Samantha's cell phone to make sure she was home and in bed. Even when she tried to sleep through the ring, she waited for the call or text. She muted her phone, but checked it regularly out of fear he'd call the home line. Skyler had been the only person she had talked to, other than her parents, since their last date almost a week ago.

The conversations started out small. Samantha listened to his comments and his wishes for her to have a wonderful sleep. She didn't say much. After several phone calls, she began to respond to his questions. She told herself she didn't want to upset him, and talking to him on the phone was better than being subjected to more dates with him. Samantha still hadn't told her father they'd gone out. She feared it was only a matter of time. Their town was too small and gossipy for her parents not to find out.

Her cell phone vibrated on cue, like an alarm. "Hello."

"Well, you're still up."

"Just barely."

"How was your day? What did you do?"

"Mom and I shopped for college. Bought things for my dorm room and priced computers."

"Sounds like fun. Did you see anyone?"

"Like who?"

"Anyone, anyone at all."

"No one. I keep telling you, most of my friends are gone, working, or busy. I've been busy, too. I haven't seen or talked to anyone except my family."

"Well then, what's new with your family?"

"My brothers won't be home until August. My mom is planning a combination welcome home/good-luck-at-college/birthday party. It'll be just family and close friends," Samantha said. "I really miss the twins."

"Sounds like fun. Whose birthday will it be?"

Suddenly sorry she had mentioned it, she said, "My eighteenth."

"Eighteen is a big birthday. It must be celebrated differently from those you've had up until now. It marks the sign of many wonderful things to come."

"I've never enjoyed celebrating my birthdays," Samantha lied and feigned a yawn.

"Every year is special and must be celebrated."

Samantha wanted to hang up, but she knew the end of the conversation was up to Skyler. She punctuated the silence with another yawn. This one was real. She could hardly keep her eyes open.

"All right, get some sleep. But first, tell me when your

birthday is."

Samantha hesitated. She didn't want him to know, but she couldn't lie. He would find out. "August twenty-third," she said.

"Sweet dreams," Skyler said, his tone seductive. He clicked off.

Fatigue overcame Samantha, but she couldn't ease into sleep. She hadn't told Skyler she was going with her dad to the courthouse in the morning. Wednesdays were motion days. He said she'd probably be bored, but she could sit in the courtroom and watch attorneys called, case by case, to argue their motions and oral arguments. Her father called it 'a good beginning' for her. Her father couldn't sit with her; he had two pretrial conferences. She preferred it that way. There wouldn't be anyone to monitor her reactions or read her notetaking.

Crawling out from her warm soft sheets, she entered her bathroom and found a half empty bottle of sleeping pills in the medicine cabinet. She swallowed three and slipped back into the solitude of the covers and the depths of sleep so cavernous, no dreams crept in.

But an hour before the alarm sounded, she was wide-eyed and disappointed that even with sleeping pills, she couldn't sleep a full eight hours. She showered and then chose a simple navy dress, sheer stockings, and navy pumps. Gold knot earrings and a plain gold chain with a locket completed the outfit. Samantha pictured the navy suits her father usually wore to court and knew her attire was appropriate.

She slid a fresh notepad into its leather cover and the long chain of her purse over her shoulder. She'd appear at breakfast like she imagined any enthusiastic pre-law student would. No one would guess she was on a mission to solve a mystery.

* * * *

Samantha loved the smell of her father's car: cologne and leather. The music was always soft and relaxing. But she clutched her leather notepad so tightly her knuckles turned white.

"Samantha, there's nothing to be nervous about. You're only watching. Honestly, you look the way I feel just before trial," her father said, revving the engine.

"You still get nervous?"

"Trial work is difficult. I have to be prepared. I over-prepare. I have to anticipate and be able to counter any argument from the other side and answer questions from the judge. I always have to be able to justify to the client what I'm doing."

"I didn't know that."

"The case is always about the client. Everything I present has to comply with the law and be understood and believable by a jury. Very intense work. That's why I'm so happy you've taken an interest. Your career is your decision. It's wise to explore options. It shows maturity. I'm proud of you for that."

Samantha remained still as her father spoke. He was finally talking to her as an adult—something she'd always wanted. She wanted to revel in it for just a few seconds, all the more because she felt unworthy of his trust, of being treated as an adult. She was a liar. She was a murderer. She was imprisoned in an impossible situation she couldn't talk about. She didn't want to hurt her family. Silence was better than the lies. Easier to keep track of.

"Here we are. I'll show you around quickly. After you're seated in the courtroom, I'll go to my pre-trials. When I'm finished, I'll find you. If I'm not out by noon, or by the time the judge takes a recess, please wait in the courtroom. If anyone questions you, tell them you're my daughter, and you're waiting for me."

Samantha nodded. "I'll be fine, Dad. I won't get lost in here. It's not that big."

"You're right."

"I remember when I was a little girl, meeting you here with Mom. I thought it was so huge. It scared me then."

He laughed. "You don't have to be a little girl to be scared of this building. Whatever size it appears to be, believe me, there are many adults who fear it."

"Oh Dad, you know what I mean."

He placed an arm on her shoulder. "Sometimes I miss those days. Here's the courtroom. You're okay?"

"I'm not five years old." Samantha squeezed her father's arm. She did appreciate him. She wouldn't admit that today she did feel as if she were five.

"Have fun, dear. We'll make you a member of the Bar yet. See you soon."

Seated on a hard-wooden pew in the second row, Samantha looked around the courtroom at the oil paintings of the justices, the long oak attorney tables, and the cushioned wooden jury chairs, the witness stand, the podium centered in front of the oversized judge's bench. She pictured herself there in the judge's large black leather chair. She wished she could control lives and make important decisions. Most of all, she wished she could pass judgment on Greg and on Skyler.

"All rise," the deep voice boomed announcing entry of the white-haired man in a long black robe.

"You may be seated." The judge sat.

Samantha marveled. She knew she wasn't in church. He was a judge not a priest, but this courtroom was powerful.

"Booth versus Zimmer, docket number ..."

Samantha watched intently as attorneys rose. Some argued motions and answered the judge's questions; other attorneys were there for pleas and sentencings. No one got upset at the judge's decision. She watched attorneys argue like they didn't get along, and then leave the courtroom friends. They made lawyering seem so easy.

Everyone knew what was going on—everyone but her. She refused to get discouraged. She watched case after case. Much of what she saw looked familiar from court television. Still, she really didn't learn anything.

The cases were interesting, but not one gave her information she needed. Samantha convinced herself it would get easier, and her search would produce something that would help her. She'd find a way.

Someone slid in beside her. Her sense of smell recognized him first—his cologne, his warm breath.

"Samantha, how beautiful you look," he whispered.

Samantha turned, surprised. "Skyler?"

"Your father told me you were here. Thought I'd stop by and see how you're doing."

Great. "I thought it would be fun to watch what lawyers really do. I may decide to go to law school."

"So you do listen to me."

"My father taught me to listen to all views before I make my decisions."

"I'm impressed you listened to me," Skyler whispered, so close to her ear she felt his soft, warm lips brushing against her.

She gagged. Maybe Skyler would leave if she ignored him. She remained intent upon the attorneys before the bench.

The row got more crowded. Skyler moved even closer to her. She was about to tell him not to sit so close to her, when she noticed he'd moved closer because her father sat in their row.

Samantha watched as her father unknowingly betrayed her by shaking Skyler's hand. The men whispered for a few minutes, moving papers back and forth. Finally, she heard her father's voice as he leaned forward over Skyler toward her.

"Ready for lunch?"

"I'm not hungry. You can take me home if you want."

"You need to eat. Besides, I want to hear all your thoughts about court," Dad said. "Skyler has agreed to join us."

Her belly churned.

Turning to Skyler, her dad handed him a file and said, "These need to be filed downstairs with the clerks. Call the office, and let them know where we'll be. We'll go on ahead and get a table before a crowd gets there. Meet us at Bernie's."

Skyler grabbed the files and placed them in his brief-case. He nodded. "See you there."

✳ ✳ ✳ ✳

Samantha followed her father through the long marble corridors, down the steps into the parking lot.

Her dad didn't notice she felt awful. She turned her face away from him while he unlocked the passenger door.

Climbing into the car, Samantha said, "Dad, really. I'm not hungry. Would you mind dropping me off at home?"

"Yes, I would mind. Is there a problem? Or, is it that you don't want to be seen with your old dad?"

She hesitated. "I'll be bored while you and Skyler discuss work."

"I promise we won't talk too much about work. I thought you liked Skyler. He told me he entertained you while we were away last week. A movie? It's a way to thank him for taking such good care of you in our absence."

Samantha was stunned. Skyler had told her father they'd gone out, and he hadn't told her. Now she really felt like a liar. "Okay, Dad. I'm sorry. Of course, I want to go."

"So did you have a nice time at the movie?"

"The movie was just something to do, Dad. It was nice of Skyler to call and offer to take me."

"Oh, I thought you two ran into each other at the mall, and that's when he offered to take you."

"Oh, yes. I was in shorts. I thought I would be too cold at the theater, and Mom would've had a fit if I went into a theater dressed in shorts, so I told him I needed to change and I'd meet him there, but he offered to pick me up," Samantha said. How was she going to keep all these lies straight? What would her parents think of her if they ever found out what a liar she was?

"That's nice," her dad said.

Bernie's Pub & Grill was getting crowded as they sat down. Samantha looked around. She recognized some of the other attorneys her father greeted. She felt almost grown-up sitting in a restaurant where most of the people, including her, were dressed in business attire. She wished she didn't have to be here waiting for Skyler, but she'd handle it. She had no choice.

"Well dear, did you learn anything?"

"It was really interesting. You and Mom were right; once I sat down, I felt comfortable. Everyone ignored me. For the most part, what the attorneys were doing was repetitive: different cases, similar arguments. I'm not sure if I were a judge I could sit and listen to it all day. Judge Stanley seemed to ignore some of what was said, but then all of a sudden he'd ask a question or announce a decision, and it made sense."

"You have to understand he's been on the bench for almost twenty years. He's heard it all, and most of the motions you heard were probably routine points of law. But you're right; from a non-attorney point of view, it probably seemed redundant and like he didn't pay attention."

"I was thinking I'd really like to watch a trial and more criminal motions. Criminal work is interesting."

"It's not like what you see on TV, but I'll check the criminal court docket and see what's on the calendar that you might find interesting. Maybe Skyler would take you and explain what's going on."

Samantha gasped inwardly. "No, please. I've bothered him enough."

"I'm sure he'd be happy to do it. He seems to have adopted you, like a sister. There's no harm in asking."

"I want to go on my own. If he goes with me, I'm not going. Please, don't even mention my interest to him." Samantha panicked. Her face warmed. She took a deep breath. "I want to make an independent judgment about whether I want to be a lawyer, or whether I'm just curious because it's what you and Taylor and Tad are doing. You've always said Skyler is made for the law. I don't want that kind of influence—"

"Calm down. It was just a thought."

Their conversation lagged for only a few seconds before Skyler showed up and joined them. "What have I missed? You two seem awfully quiet."

"I was just telling my father about the Michigan State campus and how beautiful it is. I'm hoping he'll find the time to come and visit me."

"You know your mother and I will visit you."

"I've been to Michigan State," Skyler said. "My younger brother went there two years before transferring to Michigan Tech. Then he transferred back to Michigan State for his Master's Degree. He has another term or two before he finishes. I don't know what the draw is to Michigan. The sky has been gray every time I've been there, and the winters there can be nasty. I prefer our beautiful blue cloudless skies and southern sun."

"I didn't know you had family that went to MSU," Samantha said. "I don't know anyone who went there. I chose it for the pre-vet program."

"Would you like me to ask my brother to give you a

call? He might have some pointers."

"That would be great. Wouldn't it, Sam?" Her dad beamed at Skyler and then nodded at Samantha.

"I don't want any expectations. I just want to be surprised."

"How could Skyler's brother ruin your expectations? He could help you adjust to the enormous campus."

Samantha couldn't win against both her father and Skyler. She decided to agree now and deal with it later. Skyler's brother couldn't be like him. Or could he?

"Okay," she said. "Would he know what I need to buy?"

"Not everything." Skyler chuckled. "But I bet Tom's girlfriend, Darcey, could direct you. She'll be a junior this fall. I'll call you later with their cell numbers or give them to your dad. Let's plan on meeting with them during summer break."

"When is that?" Samantha asked, genuinely interested.

"Not sure. He'll have to use vacation time. He works— something in engineering, as a student intern. That pays for most of his tuition."

"Hard work leads to success," Samantha's father said. His beaming face could be on a billboard.

"Tom says there are ski slopes in Michigan. Enrolling in a ski class is a great way to meet people," Skyler said.

"I could buy you your own skis for Christmas." Her dad leaned back in his chair. One big happy—whatever they were. "How about a family vacation in Colorado?

You could show off what you've learned."

Samantha called a halt to the mapping of her future and asked her dad if he'd mind taking her home. She still had a list to get through. Dad agreed, and Skyler said he didn't mind.

But just then Samantha realized one of her earrings was gone. She always wore them—even in the shower. "Oh no," she said. "My earring—" She checked the table, the floor, and under her chair. Samantha was religious about wearing them and twisted one when stressed, which had become more frequent.

* * * *

Skyler stood and helped check the area. A cloth napkin fell from his lap onto the floor. He reached for it and noticed the earring. He scooped it up inconspicuously into the napkin, and then into his pocket like an expert thief. Thank God he had done enough criminal defense to have learned the tricks of the trade.

Unable to locate it, Travis said. "Choose a new pair, I'll pay for it."

"Thanks dad. But it's not the same," Samantha said.

"I'll leave my card with the hostess in case they find it," Skyler said. He never looked more sympathetic.

* * * *

Samantha stared at the ceiling waiting for sleep to come.

Minnie's arms moved to midnight and then to one. No call from Skyler. Why hadn't he called? It wasn't like him. Had she offended him? Why would he be upset with her? She was upset with him.

Sleep was what she needed. Sleep was what she wanted. The bottle in the cabinet. That would bring her sleep. Pills would tune her out, turn her mind off. She didn't use sleeping pills too often, she told herself. Just when she needed them.

Sleep. She faded into sleep and into the boundless mirage of faces. The kaleidoscope of immeasurable pieces, undefined parts, interchangeable features. The ears were still missing, the eyes unblinking, staring at her waiting for an answer. She couldn't respond; her voice was lost. She watched pieces floating all around her.

It was sleep, but somewhere from the depths, the dark places in her mind where the faces loomed, a small voice whispered, "You should've taken more. More pills would've kept us from creeping in."

CHAPTER 9

Two days and nights passed without a call from Skyler. What was he up to now? Samantha worried. He was too quiet. She couldn't sleep when he called, and she couldn't sleep when he didn't. What was she to do? Tired of thinking about it, she reached into the medicine cabinet and pulled out four sleeping pills. Surely, she'd sleep soundly with four. Two or three were just not enough.

She looked at herself in the mirror as she swallowed the pills. She used to spend hours sitting on the sink, inches from the mirror, investigating her face, her hair, her body. Now she only stole glances at herself. That's all she could handle. She repulsed herself. Her face, her body, her hair—they held fingerprints. She could feel them. They held lies. She had made all of those lies real by lying more every day. She had crime to report and failed to. Even her silence was a lie.

Samantha didn't want to see, to feel, or to think. She was about to fall into a deep and wonderful sleep, a dead sleep. Her dripping hair made her pillow cold and wet. She didn't care. She wanted to hide in a deep sleep and never wake up.

She turned toward the phone. She was numbing, almost unconscious, when she heard her cell vibrate, and then vibrate again against the wood of her nightstand. Her limbs were weighted; it was difficult to move. Finally, from a will that reached far within, she reached for the cell phone.

She clicked. "Hello?" she mumbled, eyes still closed.

"Samantha? Did I wake you?"

"Uh huh."

"You don't sound well," Skyler said, and then added, "You weren't drinking again, were you?"

"Mmm, no. I'm tired." She tried to sound normal, but she recognized she was slurring her words.

"I don't call for two days, and you don't even miss me? You should've waited for my call. You know I can't stay away for long," Skyler said. His voice was playful, but stern.

Samantha tried to focus, but she couldn't move her mouth to form words. She could barely hold her phone. She didn't care what he was saying. She agreed with everything he said. That was all he wanted. "Mmm."

"I'll see you tomorrow. Sweet dreams, baby," Skyler said.

Samantha drifted into sleep, and the cell fell next to her. She was numb. No dreams. No tossing or turning. No movement.

The pills wore off, and she started to dream. Samantha's

eyes fluttered open into the darkness. She snapped them closed. She couldn't get up. It wasn't time yet. In a dream, she saw the pieces again; the faces. No longer above her, they aligned in front of her face and then encircled her.

She saw herself reaching up, higher and higher, to a lever jutting out from the piece that resembled her own face. She pulled the lever. The circle turned and spun. Pieces passed her while she stood still, watching, unafraid. The pieces were familiar. Hair. Long hair, short hair, thinning hair, scalps. White hair, black hair, brown hair, blonde. Eyes, almond-shaped, round, brown, blue, green. They stared at her as they passed her. The faces were familiar.

She had to piece them together. She knew the game. She had to build the faces: piece by piece, part by part. Eyebrows, cheeks, mouths. No ears. Where were they? How could she complete the faces in the time allotted? She heard the ticking of a timer.

She began to perspire, her hands shook, and she pulled the lever again. Around it went, and when it stopped, she collected one piece, and then another. She collected them all. But they didn't fit together. Like an uncoordinated child, she forced them. She tensed; she'd lose if she didn't finish. She didn't want to give up her time. She heard the buzzer. Time was up.

The parts all disappeared. She looked up. A mirror. Heavy and gilded. An antique. She stared into it. Was she to step through it? Why was it here? She walked closer, toward the reflective glass. She reached out and placed her palms on the mirror. She saw no reflection. The mirror disappeared. Her eyes shot open.

Startled awake, her mind sputtered. Where was she? What was wrapped around her? She tugged at the sheets. What had happened? The phone. Slowly she focused, she remembered. She had a vague recollection of the phone call, of Skyler's words. She was supposed to see him today. Where were they going? She didn't remember.

She blotted out the world by placing her pillow over her face. She groaned. It wasn't even a temporary fix. She heard her mother at the door. First a polite rap, but not for long. Then she was knuckle-pounding Samantha's door. "Are you up?"

"Yes, Mother." She felt exasperated. "I'm just lying here for a minute."

"Just wanted to check on you. I'm meeting your father for golf and lunch at the club." Her mom paused, but then she barged into Samantha's room and whipped open the drapes. "It's time you got out of bed. Skyler called and said something about needing a golf partner today, since your father and I are already playing with the Pumerfords. He wondered if you'd like to join him. Apparently, your father told him you wanted to practice."

"With him? Mr. Marks? How boring, Mother. What did you say?"

"I told him you'd call him at the office when you got up."

"Gee, thanks." Samantha didn't hide her sarcasm, but smacked the pillow back over her face.

"Come now, Samantha. It will be fun. Besides, your father tells me he offered to introduce you to his brother in Michigan. It wouldn't hurt to be nice to him. Anyway, Skyler is an excellent golfer."

Samantha blasted the pillow across the room at nothing in particular.

"Aren't we mature?" Mom said. "You need to spend some time with quality people."

Couldn't her parents see what Skyler was doing? Why weren't they their usual overprotective selves? Why did they choose to meddle in her life now and throw Skyler Marks at her? He'd fooled them, just like everyone else. No one would ever take her side or believe her against him. It was impossible. She had to go along—for now.

"Okay. You're right, Mom. It'll be nice to get outside in the sun."

"You'll have to dust off your clubs and shoes. Remember the ones we gave you for Christmas last year? The ones you haven't used," Anne said teasingly.

"I get the hint already. I'll get in the shower and get ready, and then I'll call him."

"Maybe we'll see you two at the club for lunch?"

"I doubt it, Mother," Samantha said, now out of bed, closing the bathroom door behind her.

* * * *

Wet hair still dripping, Samantha dialed the office number. After the fourth ring she almost hung up. Then she heard his voice. "How may I help you?"

"Mr. Marks, please," Samantha said, not wanting him to know she recognized his voice.

"Well, well, the sleepyhead wakes up. I'm so glad you finally called me. I thought you'd forgotten me."

"Skyler? Why are you answering the phones?"

"Because your father and I are the only ones here. It's so nice to hear your voice this early in the morning."

Samantha didn't want to talk with him any more than she had to. Every time she opened her mouth, she accidentally told him things she didn't want him to know. It was difficult for her to act. To try to be someone she wasn't.

"Mmm," She finally said to fill the emptiness.

"Did your Mom tell you about golfing? Would you like to go?"

"I guess. Whatever."

"We don't have to. I'm just here to please you. We can do whatever your little heart desires."

"Really, I don't care. Golfing is fine."

"I'll pick you up at ten. Bring your clubs, a change of clothes, and be dressed ready to golf. See you then," Skyler said in a soft, deep voice and hung up.

* * * *

Skyler pressed on his bandaged shoulder—the wound

from last night's encounter with the waitress with the inviting legs and fiery hair. He hadn't been rough, but she had irritated him. He'd bought her drinks and a late dinner. She had no reason not to go along. Or to scratch him. He'd been with her before, and she'd said she liked him. She was old enough to know what he was about— old enough to have experienced the raw sex his body ached for, the passion of the animal inside.

Samantha would make him feel better. He was sure of it. He packed up his briefcase to make an exit for the day. Destiny was with him today, and having an insurance policy didn't hurt. He chuckled and pushed the elevator buttons.

* * * *

When Samantha saw the hall mirror, she remembered her dream. She didn't look at the full view of herself, but glanced at herself from a distance, making sure her attire was in order. She smoothed her hand over the buttons of the polo shirt, verifying each tiny button was securely fastened. She'd give no hint of flesh that didn't need to be exposed. Her long khaki pants, acceptable for golf, loose on her since her weight loss, no longer flattered her slight body. In an oversized bag, she tossed jeans, a t-shirt, and a sweatshirt for later. He said casual. She kept it very casual. She refused to make any extra effort; it was not a date. Samantha was skeptical she'd ever date again.

The doorbell rang, she grabbed her bag. She didn't want the scent of his cologne lingering in her house, her sanctuary. She stepped out and closed the door behind her.

* * * *

"Good morning," Skyler said, taking a sidelong glance at Samantha. "You are beautiful."

"Thanks."

"Did you decide what you want to do?"

"I told you I'd do whatever you wanted. You said golf." Samantha paused. "What else did you have in mind?"

"A hike. I have a loaded picnic basket in the back seat. There's a great trail that leads to a magnificent sandy point and private cove. Not many people know about it. It's the most peaceful place on Earth."

Samantha was acting friendly for a change. She must like the idea of a picnic with him. Who wouldn't?

But when they passed the exit to the club, she acted surprised. "You missed the turn."

"I thought by the expression on your face you'd rather see the cove. Shall I go back?"

"Oh. No. That's fine. Whatever."

Skyler, a seasoned man, had enough dealings with women to know that there, in the silence, was a sudden wordless quarrel between them. He wouldn't give in to her emotionally tangled mind. Soon she'd figure it all out and succumb to him without question. She'd find the emotional battlefield a desolate place. She'd learn not to harbor such negative emotions. Skyler turned up the radio, and for the next several minutes, they listened to the top forty hits.

Samantha hated listening to her favorite radio station and her favorite songs with Skyler. How dare he invade the music she liked best? How could she bear to associate those songs with him and this captive un-date?

She felt claustrophobic. Her life was out of control. Her body had been invaded, her soul cornered. Her parents were being brainwashed into believing Skyler had good intentions toward her. And now this: her music. The music she marked time with. The music she listened to in the solitude of her room. The music she'd now remember him with.

* * * *

The countdown was close to revealing the number one song. Skyler turned off the highway onto a service drive that led to a dirt road and an orchard-like area. Dust and small rocks sputtered around the car, but Skyler didn't mind. He drove slowly, enjoying his private thoughts. The music put him in a positive mood. The mood for good company, fine champagne, and exquisite food. Everything was perfect. Skyler didn't care what kind of mood Samantha was in. He'd fix it, whatever it was.

That's what he did best—or so his women told him. He smiled, looking at the pale youthful beauty next to him.

He smelled her clean scent. She didn't wear perfume. Its absence suited her innocence. She was unlike the others he had been with, and she'd learn to appreciate him just as they had. He wanted to smell her and only her. Her warm soap-clean skin, soft against his own.

* * * *

Samantha watched, her eyes alert, filled with the majestic view of the trees. Small ones, tall ones, broad and tangled ones. They all looked so happy staring into the sun. She looked beyond their green peaks to the blueness of the sky and the marshmallow-like clouds suspended beyond. Was God up there? Would he help her?

"Too much thought for such a beautiful girl." Skyler turned off the radio. "We're almost there. Just beyond those trees."

"Where?" Samantha didn't see any water.

"Patience. It's a virtue," Skyler said.

"I've got plenty of patience. You're pointing to air expecting me to see something."

"And see you will. It's an exquisite sight. Ours to share for the afternoon."

Samantha suddenly felt more uncomfortable. Surely, he wouldn't touch her out here in the open? He couldn't. Someone would see them. There would be others that would be there on a day such as this. There had to be, she convinced herself.

"Here we are." Skyler parked the Jag facing a wall of

large boulders at the end of the road. "We walk from here."

"Let me get my sneakers out of my bag."

"Sure. I'll grab the picnic basket," Skyler said. He gathered up a large blanket, a cooler, and a picnic basket and slammed the car door.

Samantha took in a deep cleansing breath and the scent of running water and fish. "Where are we?"

"I can't tell you. You can try to find this place on your own, but it's difficult. Even with a GPS and an excellent sense of direction, you could drive around in circles for hours."

"How'd you find it?" If he abandoned her, would she ever be found?

"I was a good little Boy Scout," Skyler said. He took her hand into his, steadying her down the rocky path, like some long-forgotten primitive road. Samantha lost her footing several times, and Skyler saved her from tumbling down the steep incline and into the water.

When the bottom came full into view, it captured Samantha's breath. A clear blue expanse of water met the sky. There must be land where the water met the sky, but at their angle and distance, it wasn't visible. It was truly stunning. Picturesque, like the Renoir above the baby grand piano in their living room. She and Skyler strolled into the painting. Nothing like this really existed, at least not so close to home, and yet, here she was with Skyler. She felt a chill despite the heat—uncertain if it was from fear or excitement.

Samantha helped Skyler spread an oversized picnic cloth. Mesmerized, she watched him meticulously arrange each item he pulled from the basket. After he pinned the corners of the cloth down against the breeze, he invited her to sit.

Rubbing her hands together, Samantha muttered to herself over and over in her mind: You're fine, you're okay. Everything will be fine. You can do this. But she didn't sit.

Birds squawked and fled. Samantha gazed in awe at the flock, wishing she could be one of them. She kneeled on the side of the blanket.

"Kick off your sneakers, and sit down. Get comfortable. Can I pour you some champagne?"

He knew she wouldn't drink with him. "I don't drink alcohol."

"So you've said." Skyler poured her a glass. "I've brought soda for you as well, but we need to have a toast. Chilled to perfection, this champagne has a special taste under this sweltering sun."

Compliantly, Samantha accepted the glass. She sipped it. She liked it. It tickled her nose as it went down, yet it cooled and warmed her insides. She sipped again, not thinking of Skyler, but of her own sensations, trying to divert herself from what she worried was the inevitable. She emptied her glass, casually looked around for the view she wanted to see most—people, just one person, but they were truly alone.

"I see you like champagne." Skyler chuckled. He refilled the tall glass. "We still have our toast to make."

"Oh? And what are we toasting?" Samantha asked blandly, masking her curiosity.

"To youth, beauty, and an everlasting summer." Skyler clinked his glass against hers. "Just you and me, babe."

Samantha didn't sip. She couldn't. She felt like running away, like when she was a little girl playing hide and seek. But she wasn't little, she couldn't run, and she was frozen. She saw no place to hide.

"Drink it down, or it won't come true. The toast is for you. Don't you understand how lucky you are? Most girls would be thankful to be here with me."

"What's not to understand? Toast, make a wish, take a sip, it comes true—like magic," Samantha said sarcastically, her eyes downcast into the champagne. Then, shrugging her shoulders, she drank it all down in one gulp wishing it were poison, and her nightmare would end. She needed the alcohol to drown her feelings, her pain. But it didn't.

"Hey, slow down. There's plenty more," Skyler said, laughing. He refilled both their glasses.

"Whatever," Samantha said, raising the glass in a toasting motion toward him. Then lifting it to her lips, she prayed her pain would drown in the sweet taste of the champagne.

"Don't behave like a lush," Skyler said. "I want you

sober. I want you to remember our time together."

Samantha gulped the champagne until the glass was empty.

Skyler took the glass from her.

"Hey, refill. What are you doing with my glass?"

"You'll not get drunk with me. Your parents wouldn't like that." Skyler sounded angry.

"Speaking of my parents, why did you tell my father you took me to the movies last time we went out? I'm sure my surprise at the mention of it gave me away. Why you would do that to me? Tell him, I mean, when you promised you wouldn't say anything."

"Samantha, no one tells me what to do. I thought it best to mention it in passing. Trust me, your father thought it very gallant of me to rescue you from another night at home alone." Skyler paused. "In fact, he tells me you spend too many nights alone at home."

Samantha couldn't speak.

"I assured him I'd help you not be such a hermit." He lifted a long curl from behind her right ear and twirled it round and round his finger.

"You don't care that I feel like a liar to my parents, do you?" She was angry with him. "You should've told me."

"Fine. Next time I'll make it a point to tell you, to warn you of every move I make with your family." Skyler's voice mocked her.

"Now you're making fun of me. You're being mean. Why?" Samantha knew he didn't really care about her, but he was cutting through her, just like when he raped her.

Skyler snickered, placed a hand on each of her shoulders and pressed his fingers into her. "That's what I love about you: your complete innocence."

Samantha thought about this for a minute. She didn't understand. She didn't want to understand. She wanted to go home. She thought of the safety and serenity of her room. Despite being with him, she put her mind in that room. It was safe there. He couldn't enter.

"Let's eat." He began to uncover the carefully placed plates and containers. "Ripe brie and crackers, a variety of mini-sandwiches, grapes—green and red—pasta salad, and specially prepared for you: a raspberry mousse torte, with a whole can of whipping cream."

"I'm hungry," Samantha said. She was. And eating would take time, and maybe she could think of a reason he needed to take her home. Besides, the meal did look as wonderful as their surroundings. She loved eating outdoors in the fresh air. She always had. Food tasted better outside. Had this been under any other circumstance, this would've been a very romantic date, Samantha thought with dismay.

She ate slower than she'd ever eaten. The longer she spent eating, the more likely she could make the excuse it was getting late, and her parents expected her home. That was the only plausible excuse she'd found.

Samantha considered the array of food. She'd eaten

more than she had in weeks. She didn't want to become so full that she became tired or ill. Therefore, her only option for delay was to talk companionably with Skyler.

She began making a mental list of subjects she could raise to keep him talking. Finally, she broke the silence. "I'm about ready to go into a food coma."

Skyler laughed.

"Have you been working on anything interesting?"

Skyler grinned. "I've got a case set for trial in a few weeks. Have you heard your father mention the name Johnny Castriano?" Skyler said, obviously proud.

"No, but that name seems familiar to me. Isn't he the guy they always talk about with big Mafia connections?"

"Very good. So your father has mentioned it," Skyler said, his compelling green eyes prideful.

"No. I've read the name in the papers and heard it on the news. I do read," Samantha said. She sensed somehow she'd given him the wrong answer. "My father made it a rule many years ago not to bring his work home with him. That's why I joined him at the courthouse, to learn."

Samantha could see that Skyler believed her. Samantha continued to make idle chatter about her father, the courthouse cases she saw, anything that ran through her mind.

* * * *

Skyler nodded pretending to be attentive and interested in Samantha's words. Her words held no information for him. He was on his own mission. If this little girl thought she could outsmart him by yacking, he'd let her think that. His anger at Travis Armstrong would be quelled by having his daughter. Travis hadn't recognized Skyler for landing such a big client. If he won the case the state had against Johnny Castriano and kept him out of jail, his client list would grow immeasurably within months, maybe even weeks.

And there was the $180,000 retainer his client had paid the firm. Samantha was his cut, the money would come later. And if it didn't, well then there was much to tell. He nodded, laughed, even gave one of her stories a small applaud and a thumbs up. He was so good. Women were his specialty.

Skyler didn't believe what Samantha said about Travis not bringing work at home and not talking about it. With two sons in law school, and now Samantha showing up at the courthouse, it must be quite the opposite. The fact his children wanted to become lawyers must have been from Travis's influence. He even bet Travis talked about him. Travis must mention the attorneys in his firm and the cases they handled. Even if Travis didn't regularly speak about work, Skyler never underestimated the power of pillow talk. There was no way he didn't talk about the firm to Anne. She was too involved in his life not to know what went on at the firm. There had to be conversation beyond the bedroom.

Why would she withhold information about what her father talked about at home? Her lying further demonstrated that Travis Armstrong, in his discussions at home, continued to fail to recognize Skyler's importance and his contribution to the firm. He bet Travis boasted and took credit for the things Skyler had accomplished. Skyler swallowed his mounting anger. Its taste was bittersweet. He knew his time would come. He tuned back in to Samantha's jabber.

* * * *

Samantha watched a flush spread up from Skyler's neck to the tip of his ears. "Are you all right?"

"I'm too warm in these clothes," Skyler said. He flashed perfect white teeth and quickly tossed off his shirt. "That feels much better. You should try it."

Samantha darted a look at his bare muscular chest. It looked like something right out of the muscle-man contest her father and brothers liked to watch on weekends. She cast her gaze downward onto the blanket, but she noticed a white bandage taped to his back and shoulder. Had he had surgery? Samantha averted her eyes from the stark white gauze. "What happened? Were you in an accident?"

"I got scratched up pretty badly doing yard work, clearing bushes. It'll heal in a few days," Skyler said casually. "Thanks for asking. You really do care. It's great to see you're concerned about me." He sounded playful.

He was playing her. "Just curious, that's all," Samantha said blandly. She focused on searching the grass for a four-leaf clover.

"Swimming now or later? The exercise will bring you out of your food coma," Skyler said.

"I didn't know we were coming here. I didn't pack a suit."

"Bathing suits don't matter here. There's no one for miles." Skyler chuckled.

"Besides, if anyone else is around here, they're not paying attention to us."

"I think I'd like some of that dessert you said you packed. Where is it?" Samantha asked. She focused her attention on the cooler next to the wicker picnic basket. "Can I rescue it from the cooler?"

"It's all for you, babe."

Samantha slid her body carefully toward the cooler, which placed her several inches farther from Skyler.

"Don't bother serving it. Just bring it here with two forks," he said. "We'll dig into it whole. In my estimation, some foods—and all desserts—should be eaten just for the fun of it, without ceremony."

Samantha wasn't sure what to make of his peculiar editorial, but she knew better than to ask for further commentary. She followed instructions, carefully unwrapping the raspberry mousse torte, and placed it between them. Avoiding his eyes, Samantha handed Skyler a fork. She could feel him staring at her.

Skyler sprayed whipped cream over the torte. He lifted his fork and clinked it with hers. "Here's to tasting all things sweet." Skyler plunged his fork in and removed a huge bite. He forked another and balanced the forkful up to Samantha's lips.

She compliantly opened her mouth, removed half the mound, and then watched him devour what remained on the fork.

"Mmm, mmm, I'm not sure which is sweeter—you or this wonderful torte," Skyler said.

Saw that one coming.

He paused for just a second and then continued in a soft, sensuous voice. "I think it's you Sam—all you. You are the sweetener I need in my life."

Samantha felt embarrassed. Scared. Her breathing shallowed. What was he doing now? She focused on forking food to her mouth and keeping it full. She had to delay him. She had to get home. She needed the safety of her room, the room where he couldn't touch her. Stay focused. I am in my room. No one can touch me.

"Champagne?"

Samantha looked at him, purposefully not responding as he filled their glasses.

"We've just about finished the bottle. Almost time to return to reality."

Skyler seemed to be studying her like moving cells under a microscope. Nothing escaped him. "I told my parents we'd be home early," she said, and then added, "They'll wonder why they didn't see us at the club."

"No they won't. I told your father we'd likely go to the

driving range. And that is what you are to tell them," Skyler said in a stern voice. "So you see, I've got things covered."

Samantha sipped her champagne. She liked the way it made her feel. She allowed her mind to drift in and out of her room: her safe harbor, where he couldn't be. Skyler removed the torte from its place between them.

"Turn around, Samantha. You're so uptight. I brought you here to relax. All this pent-up tension is not good for you."

Samantha froze. But Skyler helped her turn around, positioning her by placing a hand on her shoulder.

"That's it, now relax," Skyler said. He rubbed her shoulders, working gently down her neck to her back, and then up to her temples. Skyler whispered over and over, "Relax. Let yourself go. You are floating now. Can you see yourself? Relax. Relax. That's it; your body is floating."

Samantha felt distressed when he touched her. But his hands were kind, warm, and gentle. Not the hands that had assaulted her. Not the hands of the man she loathed. They felt good; they released tension. Samantha felt her body loosen. This wasn't the man she despised. She began to float. No. That wasn't what she wanted. She couldn't let herself relax. She had to stay alert, but she began to feel very tired, very limp, almost comatose. She wanted to close her eyes, but she refused to. She tried hard not to blink, for fear of slipping away. Despite her well-intentioned efforts, she felt herself detached, relaxing. No, she couldn't let go. She couldn't release herself into any sleeplike state with this evil man. She shouldn't have had the champagne.

"Relax. You're safe. You're with me. You'll always be safe with me. Relax. Relax. Release yourself from all tension. Relax. Let yourself float," Skyler chanted over and over.

And, for a few moments, Samantha's mind continued to drift in and out of her room. She felt herself back in the safety of Nana's arms. Back in the safety of her room.

Serenity in solitude. Nana's words kept repeating in the waves of relaxation. For a moment, the current of the chant was so strong, Samantha thought she actually saw Nana; she knew she felt her presence. She felt safe in her illusion. She felt unsafe with reality.

She knew Nana wasn't there really, but she lived each day on the brink, wanting to believe wishful thinking would come true. And yet, she knew it wouldn't. As her waves of hope crested, she had to sail her mind back to reality, which meant she had to get Skyler's hands off of her. She was clear about that, but she found herself fighting Skyler's words.

"You're floating; release your tension; release your pain," Skyler repeated.

Samantha floated on a riverboat, relaxing, dozing in the sun. Suddenly she awoke, startled she had let herself mellow so deeply, escaping into the shelter of her imagination.

"Hey. Remember me?" Skyler whispered into her ear. "You should get massaged regularly. You take to it so well."

Samantha shuddered internally. Her head was heavy. Her mouth dry. She wanted to take a nap, away from Skyler.

"Time to go," Skyler said, his hands on her shoulders, his head so close to hers she could hear his even breathing.

To go home? Would he really just take me home? "Is there another soda for the road?" Samantha asked. She leaned toward the cooler with sluggish champagne-drugged movements. Moving awkwardly away from Skyler, Samantha tried to get out of Skyler's reach. Instead, he slid his hands slowly down her back.

"There should be a few cans left," Skyler said.

Samantha wiped dripping soda from her mouth. She wasn't sure of anything, except she needed to get away from this man. How could she do it? Slowly his body moved to hers. Her body—tense and rigid. Her mind—on high alert.

"Samantha," his soft strong voice pierced her. "I need you next to me. Let's spend a few quiet minutes together. We need to let the champagne settle a bit before we leave. I don't want your parents to suspect I got you drunk." Skyler lowered her onto the blanket, his hard, tanned body close to hers.

She stiffened, but she needed a nap. She needed to

shut her eyes, if only for a moment. Why had she drunk the champagne? Never again, she thought, as she tried to stay alert. Her mind raced, screaming. But her body bowed to sleep.

* * * *

Skyler waited a few minutes to ensure Samantha was asleep. "You and I are meant to be. We fit, you'll see that," he whispered, kissing her hair like she was a napping child. He was careful with her and lifted her onto himself—like he would with an infant. She lay in the crook of his arm, and—humming a lullaby—he stroked her soft dark curls.

Skyler loved the texture of her hair, the fresh soap scent of her warm flesh, her perspiration. It tasted good to him. He wanted her. He needed to touch her, inside. To feel her fully. But he would wait. She needed her strength. A nap would do them both good. He wanted her to remember her time with him.

The couple nestled on the blanket in silence, except for the gulls that swarmed and dipped, and then squawked and circled above them.

* * * *

The faces appeared, and Samantha was sure she'd made it to her room safely, without harm or encounter. The faces, still in pieces, floated in and out of her sight. But the dream was different this time. The pieces, always familiar, had parts she looked at every day. This time, they were her own.

Her brows, her high cheekbones, her eyes, her full lips. No ears. She didn't have ears, either. The pieces floated, and she tried to catch them. She couldn't. They floated onto the wheel. She saw a sign. She had never been able to read it before. It was at the top. The wheel of destiny. She squinted. She saw the figure of a woman. An old woman. Nana?

"Nana?" She called out. She tried to reach her, but she couldn't. She tripped, and her body fell forward. She was awake.

Where was she? Where was her bed? What was this scenery doing in her room? She lay confused, reality slowly filtering back, as she felt Skyler's arms around her tighten. "It's about time you woke up, sleepyhead."

She wondered how long she had dozed, her mind still muddled, perplexed by the sleep she had fought so hard against. Her dream seemed like it had taken place over a span of hours. Her eyes focused on the still beautiful scenery. The sun had only moved slightly.

"I have to get home. I don't feel well. My parents. They'll be worried."

"No. I told you they won't. I took care of that already. You have nothing to worry about," Skyler said, forcibly rolling her from her side to her back. "I have something that will make you feel better."

Samantha's eyes widened and uncontrollably filled with tears when his face was within inches of hers. "Please, I really have to go."

"Relax," he said in a soft hypnotic voice. "Relax."

Samantha's head pounded. She was alert, her body stiff. Her insides trembled. She knew it was time. She knew he would take her, out here, for all to see. What could she do? Helplessness set in.

Skyler didn't respond.

Samantha sobbed harder, but he didn't seem to care.

He reached into the cooler for something. Her eyes streamed tears, but were now locked on the clear blue water. She focused on the rippling effect of the water to calm her, to help her think her way out of this.

"Here, Sam. Take these. You'll feel better."

Samantha stared at him. "What?"

"Water and aspirin. I forgot what a lightweight you are when it comes to drinking. Aspirin," he repeated. "Take two. It always works. Trust me."

Samantha hated those two words. She didn't trust anyone these days—especially him. And she didn't want him continually asking her to do something she shouldn't and didn't want to do. She faced him through her tears and met his eyes. He seemed sincere. Slowly she took the aspirin and the bottle of water.

Skyler was silent as she put the aspirin in her mouth, one at a time, and drank the water in large gulps. Skyler again began to massage her neck, back and shoulders.

He was silent for a time and then again he whispered, in almost silent prayer, in tune with the rhythm of the massaging circles, "Relax… Relax… I'm here… You can trust me…"

Samantha, though confused, was comforted by his caring movements, his attentiveness, and his soothing voice. She felt almost foolish she had thought the worst of him and guilty she despised Skyler, and he was being so kind to her. His voice was soft and tranquilizing. She felt the need to sleep again. Her lids were heavy. She was so relaxed. He seemed to anticipate everything she felt, every move she wanted to make. She had never known anyone quite like Skyler. The perfect… the perfect… devil. That was it, she thought, relaxing into his trance. The perfect devil. That's who she was with. The devil, who didn't allow her to feel his evil.

* * * *

Skyler let her sleep as he quietly packed up their meal. He watched her. He loved watching his captured beauty. So unaware. So easily manipulated. So much needed to execute his plans. The shade from the tree had moved over them. He watched as the lines of shade devoured the sunlight that spilled across her body. Her cheeks had a natural pink glow, now red from the sun.

He watched the thin gold wire hoops dangle from her small ear lobes. He liked them on her. He took them. She wouldn't miss them. After today, she'd probably think she'd forgotten to put them on, or she'd lost them. Either way, he knew she'd never ask him about them, so he wouldn't ponder the question. He didn't have to. He cocked his head and smiled, folding them carefully into a white handkerchief he had pulled from his pocket.

* * * *

She stirred, startled again by the sleep she had taken. What was wrong with her? She made a pact with herself to remain alert, to stay distant from this man, this devil. She felt his hard body against her. His firm strong fingers, his muscular hands were on her. His soft mouth touched hers. She felt it, so natural—no. Her mind raced. Not natural. Yuk. Ugh.

He kissed her long and hard. He kissed her again, deeply this time, stroking her hair away from her face. Kissing her cheeks, her neck, and her mouth again and again. She looked up, her clear-blue eyes wide. Here it came. Here he was. Please God, no. No. Her mind raced, screaming in the depths of her inner reality. But no one could hear the screams except her own mind … and maybe God. Yes, that was it. God. Only God can help me fight the devil. God, help me please, silently she begged.

"Get up," he gently ordered. "I've packed, and as soon as we fold this blanket, we're ready. Come on, time to go."

Samantha gaped at him, stunned that a few kisses were all he wanted. Quickly she jumped to her feet and helped him fold the blanket. Shoes back on, she grabbed the blanket and the small cooler to ensure her hands were full. She walked toward the path leading up to the car. She didn't wait for Skyler to pick up his things and the picnic basket. She wanted to keep a safe distance from him.

"Hey, don't worry. We'll get you home on time," Skyler said, quickening his stride to catch up to her.

"I'm sure my parents are worried, and Emily was supposed to call this weekend. It got late so quickly." The lies flowed easily, believably, from her mouth.

Silence passed between them in the minutes it took to reach the car. Samantha felt relief and confusion. Again, he hadn't forced himself on her. Why? What was he doing? What did he really want? Hadn't he made himself clear weeks ago? A few kisses. That's all. Maybe that's all he needed—she hoped. She thanked God.

Samantha continued to ponder and watched the moving cars pass them. Maybe he didn't like her inexperience. Maybe she was as repulsive to him as she was to herself. That was fine with her. She should be grateful, and then stole a glance at his face. His eyes, from the side view, looked like speckled-green limestone. He had the longest lashes she had ever seen on a man. Without those heavy whiskers and thick brows, he could be a beautiful woman. Yikes. Then, clasping her hands, she reminded herself no woman would be as cruel as this man. This devil man.

Still, why didn't he want her?

"Samantha, I really had a nice time. I hope you did, too." He sounded normal.

Samantha looked out the window. She didn't want to look at him. She was so confused. Her mind. Her feelings. His voice. His presence. His actions. Nothing matched. Nothing made sense. She steadied her voice and narrowed her thoughts. "The view was beautiful. Thank you for sharing it with me."

He reached over and patted her hand.

When they pulled into the driveway, Samantha grabbed her bag and her purse and reached for the door handle. "Bye."

"Not so fast, sweetie. Tuesday's the Fourth. I want very much to take you to dinner and the fireworks. Pick you up at seven?" Skyler said, and then he winked at her with a wide grin. "Remember, if they ask, we went to the driving range and dinner at the Eatery."

Did she have a choice? She opened the car door, jumped out, and slammed it shut. She loved Fourth of July fireworks. She wouldn't let him spoil them. She'd be safe. Too many people would be around for him to even kiss her. She'd have a good time, because she wanted to.

The house was silent and empty. Her parents were still at the club. Good. With any luck at all, she wouldn't see them until morning. In her room she anticipated the solitude and serenity of a hot shower and her sheets. She peeked in her closet to see what she had to wear for the

Fourth of July and then jumped in the shower.

Just as she dozed off that night, the phone rang. Believing it to be her parents checking up on her, Samantha picked it up. "Hello?"

"You seem to be feeling better, love. That's the nicest greeting I've received in ages." Skyler said.

Samantha's heart sank immediately, and warm tears welled in her tired eyes. "Oh, it's you. I was just going to sleep." She wanted to explain to Skyler she had anticipated hearing one of her parents' voices. But she didn't dare, for fear he would take the liberty to come over, and he would never again believe her when she said she had to get home.

"I wanted to hear your voice before I go to sleep. I hope you had as nice a time as I did. I really think you are someone special, Samantha. I hope you know that." He sounded as sincere as a priest.

Samantha blinked in the silence that followed. She knew she had to respond, but his comments had frozen the connections between her mind and her mouth.

"Samantha, you have to know by now how much I care about you."

"Yes. I do," Samantha reluctantly admitted.

"Good. Just relax. Everything will be fine. I'll take care of everything. Pleasant dreams, love."

Samantha tossed and turned until her subconscious fluttered into dreams. The familiar faces, still in pieces, floated round and round. They felt friendly, but for the lost ears. Engrossed in finding ears and attaching them, frustrations engulfed her.

CHAPTER 10

Skyler was pleased with his day. Samantha had followed his instructions, and her parents were at ease with their friendship. He would be the friend she needed. Eventually she'd trust him completely, even learn to rely on him. His calls at night just before she fell asleep assured she'd dream of him. Controlling her mind, her body, her life was easy. She was weak to his power.

Everything was going as planned. He grabbed the slick book he'd checked out from the library a couple of weeks ago. *Hypnosis For Better Living*. He turned a page, and his cell interrupted. An unassigned number. He and the caller exchanged greetings.

"Mr. Castriano understands you had trouble with one of his girls," the deep voice said.

"Taken care of. Everything's fine," Skyler said, on the alert. He couldn't ask any questions, wondering what had been said, how they knew.

"You left loose ends. Mr. Castriano said to tell you the problem has been taken care of."

"But, there is no problem."

"He wanted you to know from now on there won't be any more. Next time you're to immediately inform him. He doesn't like to find out on his own. Mr. Castriano takes care of his friends."

When the cell went dead, Skyler tossed it on the table. What had the girl told them? Skyler closed the book, replaced it on his nightstand and thought about the girl refusing to deliver. There was no issue. She disappeared. Done deal.

CHAPTER 11

The next morning, Samantha lay in bed and took stock. What more could this devil take from her? She couldn't trust Skyler, but sometimes, she found herself fantasizing about him. The idea of that man having any positive qualities revolted her.

If only she could confide in her parents, in someone she could trust who would believe her. Trusting Skyler had been a mistake. But she didn't need to be shamed.

Samantha dressed for Sunday brunch, an Armstrong tradition. Served promptly at eleven o'clock in the breakfast room, it was mandated family time. With the twins in law school, Samantha had once enjoyed her time alone with her parents. Now it was almost unbearable.

Dressed, she applied enough makeup to hide the dark circles that announced her unsettled sleep. Her dreams felt real to her, and she saw them more and more clearly, even in her conscious hours.

She swiftly checked herself in the mirror, avoiding her face. She was certain, her parents, more self-absorbed of late, wouldn't notice the extra make-up or her fatigue.

* * * *

After they exchanged greetings and compliments, Samantha poured a glass of orange juice and sat. Her dad eyed her above his bifocals and asked about the golf lesson and if she liked the new clubs.

Travis folded his hands.

Samantha tried to convince him the clubs were fine, she was fine, everything was fine. She just wanted to eat and get out of there. And she didn't want to outright lie.

Mom prattled on about the weather and the doorbell bell.

The butler entered and said, "It's Mr. Marks, sir. In the foyer with something for you."

"I thought we didn't allow guests during family brunch." Samantha looked between her parents.

"Skyler has taken an interest in you. He's like family." Travis folded the Sunday paper and handed it to the butler. "Please ask Mr. Marks to join us, and then ask Gloria to set another place."

"Mom, may I be excused?" Samantha tried not to sound panicky.

"You need to finish eating. We can't be rude to our guest." Her mom recoated her lipstick.

Samantha braced herself. She not only had to repel the devil, but her own parents had become his thralls.

* * * *

Behind Dad, Skyler strolled into the breakfast room and sat in the vacant chair right beside Samantha. She caught his skeevy wink and looked away. She felt warm and gulped her orange juice.

"I've given Samantha's clubs and shoes to your doorman." He turned to Samantha. "We had such a good conversation, you forgot to grab them from my trunk. I discovered them this morning."

"I'm sorry, Mr. Marks. I was so tired, I forgot."

"Please call me Skyler." Skyler turned to Dad. "If that's okay with you."

"Of course." Dad motioned to Gloria to pour coffee for him and Skyler.

"There's nothing like a few buckets of balls to improve the swing. You'd be impressed with Samantha. Might even beat you at a round of golf." The men laughed. Samantha grimaced into her cup. But she didn't say anything.

Intently, she broke apart and buttered her blueberry muffin. Samantha surveyed the adults now engrossed in a conversation of their favorite golf ranges. They talked as if golf were the most important aspect of their lives. She knew peace of mind was important, being safe was important. Most of all, she knew getting away from Skyler was important—and necessary.

Samantha moved the food around her plate until the butler called her to the phone.

"May I be excused?" Samantha made her eyes silently

plead with her mother.

"I want to show your father the computer information."

"Sure, Mom," Samantha agreed, gratefully.

"Samantha, before you leave, I wondered if you'd like to join me on Tuesday for the fireworks? My brother and his girlfriend will be up for a few days from Michigan. You could talk with them about Michigan State," Skyler said. He flashed his white teeth at her then between her parents. "In fact, Anne and Travis you are welcome to join us."

"Whatever." Samantha rose, but her father's stern look prompted another response. "Thanks. Yes. Happy to join you," she said and then left the room.

Even though her father's study was off limits, Samantha chose to answer the call there because it was private.

"Hello?" she said into the house phone.

"Samantha. So excited to hear your voice."

"Emily? It's about time you called." Samantha was so relieved she sighed deeply, to release all of the bad air she'd breathed with Skyler next to her. She didn't realize, until she heard Emily's voice, just how much she missed her friend. She wished she'd confided in Emily before she'd left for to Europe. It would have to wait until she returned.

* * * *

Before leaving the study, Samantha pulled from her skirt pocket the list of legal phrases she'd copied. She'd folded and unfolded it so many times creases had worn into the paper. She stared at the leather-bound books she believed held the key to her liberation from Skyler. She'd find a way to unlock the knowledge from whatever book held it. She returned the paper to her pocket. It wouldn't be now. Footsteps outside the door announced someone approaching. So she slipped out the door.

"Why were you in your father's office?" her mother asked.

"Emily was on the phone. I'm going upstairs to email her." Samantha spoke quickly and upbeat.

"Of course, you'll see her before you leave for college."

"She gave me the date she's coming back. I want to make plans."

Her mom told her she and Dad would be going to look at some investment property.

When Samantha reached her room, she peered out the front windows. Skyler and her father stood in the drive-way talking. Her father's arms were flailing to accentuate whatever story he was telling. She recognized the smug look on Skyler's face. He was fake-listening, his hands hanging out of his pockets by his thumbs. She knew that mocking grin. Why didn't others see it? Grown-ups. They weren't as astute as they thought. She felt old, yet she felt so young, so naïve. She'd believed Skyler and fell into his trap. They all had. How could she foil his trap?

Samantha hated her parents passing her off to Skyler, for trusting him. They had no clue what he was capable of.

She retreated from her window and sat on her bed with the word list in front of her. Trying to find the missing link, she poured over the definitions. What had she missed?

Minutes turned to hours. She vacillated between reality and fantasy.

Afraid the sense of safety would again disappear, she didn't want to leave her bed. It was safe, comfortable, and hers. Serenity in solitude. Her Nana was here with her. The long Minnie Mouse arms crawled from one number to the next.

"Samantha? Are you in there? May I come in?"

Hearing her mother's concerned voice, she stiffened. She had fallen asleep. She tucked the paper under her and answered her mother.

Her mother pushed open the door. She had on a new pantsuit, perfect hair, and pristine makeup.

"Why are you hiding up here on such a nice day?"

Samantha rearranged the pillows against her headboard.

Her mom kissed the top of Samantha's head. "The grill's on. Dinner is just about to be served. We're having a wonderful salad, barbecued ribs, chicken, and your favorite: corn on the cob and diced potatoes."

Samantha studied her mother.

"Who's coming to dinner?" Samantha didn't trust even the smallest change in routine, especially after Skyler had joined them during their family-only brunch.

"No one, that I know of," her mom said. "Why do you ask that?"

"Sounds like a lot of food."

"What difference does that make? Your father asked for barbecue. Do you want Cook to make something else?"

"No. Whatever. I'll be right down." Samantha shrugged off her mother's kiss and attempted hug. She didn't want to be touched. It was as plain and simple as that; being left alone was good. Touching was bad.

Her mother closed the door behind her.

When will they ever treat me like an adult? "I feel like I'm two," Samantha muttered.

But Samantha launched herself into the bathroom and stared at the warm water splashing fiercely in the sink. The water mesmerized her, its intense sound rushing in her ears, clearing her mind, calming her fears. Samantha wrung out a facecloth. Exactly how she felt—like someone had wrung her into a lifeless rag. She couldn't look at herself. She hated seeing her face. She wanted to forget.

In the shower, she lost all concept of time. She felt no hunger. She only craved the solitude.

"Samantha? What are you doing in there?" Again, her mom pounded on the bathroom door. "Come out of there, or I'm coming in."

"Really, Mom, you're so dramatic. I told you I'd be down soon."

"Soon has passed dear. Dinner's on the table. You

should have been seated twenty minutes ago." Mom paused. "Are you feeling all right?" She opened the door.

"Yes. Quit asking me that and get out," Samantha said, uncoiling the towel from her wet hair.

"Sam, honey, I ask because I care. I see you suffering, and I don't know why. You're my only daughter. I always thought we could talk; we had each other in a house full of men. If it's college, stay home a year."

"You worry too much." Samantha stretched the sentence, each word enunciated. Catching her own tone, she gently added, "If you must know, I'm having my period. I'm having cramps, and I had a little accident." Her mother's face changed from concern to understanding: woman to woman. It had worked. Motherhood and womanhood, with the word *period*. It always works.

"Would you like a tray of food sent to your room?" her mother asked.

"Really? Yes. I need to toss on my nightshirt and crawl into bed," Samantha said meekly, with sincerity.

"Just this once, it'll be fine. Promise you'll eat everything. If you feel better, join us for dessert?" Mom gently kissed her. "Hope you feel better, dear."

Samantha winced. "Thanks, Mom."

* * * *

Samantha quickly readied herself and crawled into bed. She put her list of legal words into her pillowcase. The list, however indecipherable to her, was a comfort. She needed to keep it close. It was her insurance policy to finding her voice, to finding herself, and to finding freedom.

The butler brought her a tray, and she was happy to be alone. But the aroma of freshly barbecued animal flesh sickened her. Lies were always hard to swallow. She picked at the food and made an honest attempt at eating it. But after a few bites, she shredded the rest and flushed it down the toilet. Everything fit, but the bones and the corncob. She gulped the chocolate milk, to wash down the lump of guilt. She covered the emptied plate and set it out of sight.

Samantha couldn't sleep. She thought about the Fourth of July, and she remembered she had to find something to wear or go out and buy something. She didn't feel like shopping these days and had been complacent at best about letting her mother pick out her clothes whenever they did go. She didn't even bother to look in the fitting-room mirror, but simply judged by her mother's expression. What mother liked, Samantha bought. Usually her mother's taste was pretty good. She was always on top of fashion and was careful about Samantha dressing conservatively. Too conservative for Samantha's taste, usually. But lately, Samantha preferred it that way. Clothes weren't as important to her as when she was in high school, before everything. She couldn't think about it. She wouldn't think about it. She'd simply try to find something to wear in her massive closet.

Samantha pushed aside one hanger after the next.

Nothing seemed suitable. She couldn't bring herself to try anything on. Emily would tell her she was going through *the uglies*. They would've laughed and made hair and nail appointments and maybe scheduled a massage to cheer themselves up. Their mothers had passed on a pampering tradition they'd embraced.

Those days felt like a lifetime away. Samantha closed her closet door. She needed Emily. Only six more weeks until she returned. Emily would be there for her birthday party. Samantha would have to hold out until then. She couldn't trust anyone else.

Frustrated, Samantha again sat in bed, against the fluffy pillows, filing her nails so short her hands looked like those of a young boy. She didn't care. She didn't want to fuss with them anymore. The rhythmic scratching of the emery board against her nails calmed her. When would Skyler call? That voice. It was somehow relaxing, she had to admit, but why? Just a few days ago, it had frightened her. Even now she should be afraid, but she heard his words over and over: "Relax, relax." They soothed her.

Samantha closed her eyes, repeating the words. She wanted to relax. She needed to relax. She was in the safety and solitude of her own room. No one could harm her here. She repeated the words again. "Relax, relax..."

Relaxing on cue, now on the verge of sleep, she dreaded the pieces of faces. Dreams created illusions. The illusions kept flowing, funneling in all directions, pooling into a paralyzing confusion that led Samantha into a black sleep that was anything but contented.

She was alone. She didn't want to be alone. Where had they all gone? She looked, squinting to find the hidden details in the dark. Was this a new game? She turned slowly around and around. And then she felt it. His touch, warm against her arm. It was kind and gentle and protective.

No!

No one could touch her. She watched herself and shuddered, but he did touch her again. Cold. She felt isolated and so cold. Where had all the people gone? Where were the familiar parts, the parts she could make whole? The ears. Were the other parts somewhere with the missing ears?

She needed to be close to someone. She wanted to be touched, to be desired. Isn't that what every girl wanted? Shouldn't she want it, too? Seventeen, Glamour, Cosmopolitan. The cover girls rushed by her. They didn't stop to see her. They didn't stop to talk. They didn't notice her, not one bit, not at all. She was alone again. And then she felt it. The familiar touch. The warm voice. "Relax, relax..." And she felt warmed, like the sun was rising, but it remained dark. And in the darkness, the sun cast a shadow; a familiar shadow.

Relief. She wasn't alone. It was him. Her skin flushed warm, but with goosebumps. Her mind raced, trying to remember the bad things he represented; what he was.

She looked for another familiar face. But there was no one else, just him.

Skyler was there, smiling, staring as if looking right through her, as if he could feel all of her emotions and erase them all at once. Even the bad things he had done to her. She suddenly understood them; they had a purpose.

She looked closely at Skyler. Was he near or far? She couldn't tell. He was waving her toward him, and then he stopped. It was her turn. He wanted her to make the move toward him. Her choice. Samantha stood still, fear and pleasure ran together through her body. Which was which?

Skyler was the devil-man. She couldn't think fast enough to keep up with the beckoning glow of his speckled-green eyes. His perfect teeth flashed against his full lips and tanned, flawless skin. His eyes somehow captured her, made her like him more.

His eyes wanted her to want him. She hadn't actually seen her own full reflection in such a long time. She felt older and prettier. She felt confident and preened in his reflection of her. She had no other reflection. She was a woman in his eyes, an equal, an adult. No one else treated her like that. Had she misjudged him?

Wasn't what happened between them partially her fault? She shouldn't have been drinking. She'd led him on; she must have. And she was an adult now. This beautiful man couldn't really have hurt her. No wonder he got angry and blackmailed her. Was it blackmail or truth-telling?

He vanished.

Samantha looked for him. Around her, drifted flash-drives, computers, cell phones. Had he recorded her to protect her, to show her he cared? What did it all mean?

The faces reappeared, the familiar parts. But they were different—colder. The floating parts no longer smiled. The ears were still missing and the pieces were smaller than she had remembered. The mouths were too large, too stern. She didn't like them. She didn't want to play. She ran, but her feet didn't move. She couldn't get away. She willed herself to run.

"Samantha? Wake up, you're dreaming. Samantha? I'm right here," Mom said.

"Mom? What are you doing here? I didn't hear you." Samantha's vision was not focused. Mom was sitting on the edge of the bed?

"What in heaven's name were you dreaming about?"

"Was I dreaming? I don't remember." Samantha closed her eyes. "I don't know." Staying possum-still, she didn't respond to any further prodding from her mother. Samantha wanted to be alone. "I'm fine." Mom straightened the covers and left the room, closing the door quietly behind her.

Samantha opened her eyes in the darkness. She peered up at Minnie's fluorescent face. 11:47. Had she really slept so long? She tried to recall her nightmare. Piecing as much of the dream together as she could remember, Samantha rubbed her temples to ward off the pounding.

Samantha had never had trouble with headaches—until now.

She got up and retrieved the box with her new supply of sleeping pills, aspirin, and other assorted medication she had pilfered from her mother's medicine cabinet. Sleeping pills and something with codeine ought to do it. She swallowed the pills, but immediately realized they wouldn't stay down. Clenching the countertop, she closed her eyes until the nausea abated.

Her dream came flooding back. Skyler. What did he see in her? Why would he want an ugly teenage duckling?

Back in the safety of her own bed, she didn't want to dream. Her cell phone rang, and she answered it. As the medicine took a hold of her, she felt she was inside a stranger's body. She could cope that way. "Hullo."

"Hi, baby. You sound sexy. Were you thinking of me?"

She didn't want to admit she had been thinking about him, okay dreaming about him. She felt dull and heavy, but relaxed. "I was almost asleep."

"Alone, I hope." Skyler said, in his deep voice.

"Mmm," Samantha answered, barely hearing the question, relinquishing her body to sleep.

"Okay, baby. Sounds like you're tired. Like you need to relax. That's it. Just relax. I love it when you relax."

"Relax."

"See you Tuesday. Meanwhile, we'll meet in dreamland. I'll be in yours, like you're in mine."

The cell phone dropped to the floor.

CHAPTER 12

When she woke, Samantha purposed to have a better, stress-free day and bolstered herself with positive thoughts. She wouldn't let anything get to her. She'd be pleasant and smiling and happy. She'd make it through breakfast and then retreat to her room without any problem. She had to convince everyone she felt much better, so they would leave her alone. She'd have to eat and smile and laugh and talk.

Standing in the shower, doubt got the best of her and acting happy seemed an impossible. "Relax, relax." She lathered herself with mounds of soapy bubbles. They made her white and pure, and she smelled new, fresh, and clean. Unlike what she was. "Relax, relax."

Stepping into her familiar robe, she was pleased the steam-covered mirror hid her reflection. Still focused on relaxing, she dressed in a lightweight cotton sweater and a long denim skirt and then bounded down the stairs. Her hair was held back with a thick headband. She only had to act happy until she could be herself in seven weeks at Michigan State. Leaving for a new life would be a relief.

"You've decided to grace us with your presence." Her dad's voice was stern.

Samantha felt uncomfortable feeling her father study her from head to toe.

"I'm sorry I missed dinner." Samantha forced herself to brush a kiss on his cheek. She kept her lying eyes from meeting his.

"I want you to go for a physical. You're sick too often," he said. "You need a full check-up."

Pain seared through Samantha's temple. For a second, she couldn't see. If she went to a doctor, he'd tell about the abortion. She couldn't make her mouth work.

"If you don't call your mother's doctor first thing Monday, I will. He's a first-rate doctor."

"Give me a break. I feel fine." I won't be fine if I have to see a doctor.

"Samantha." His voice was strong.

Samantha looked at her plate. "Fine. But I want to see a woman doctor. Not a man." Samantha was surprised to hear her own voice use such an assertive tone.

Her parents' silence felt uncomfortable, and Samantha's mind floundered for a reprieve from their stares.

"I'll call," Samantha whispered. She felt like a scolded three-year-old.

"Fine, you do that. Anne, see that she does." Dad removed himself from the table, tossing his napkin onto his half-emptied plate.

Samantha didn't look up.

"Well, what did you want him to do?" Mom said. "Your father is very worried about you. We don't know what to do anymore. You don't eat. You have nightmares. You don't go out unless we force you. We don't know what's wrong."

Samantha wanted to cry. She wanted to tell her. Most of all, she wanted to feel something other than fear. She waited for emotion to filter through her body. But it didn't come. She heard only the pounding in her head. At least she could still feel pain. Samantha, lost in her own thoughts, stared blindly at her mother.

"You'll make that appointment. Dr. Sugars has a new partner, a woman. I don't recall her name. She's about thirty-five. I think you'll like her. In fact, I want to go with you."

"I'm too old to have you in with me. I'll call."

"I am going," Mom said.

Samantha didn't want to fight. "I see the doctor alone, or I'm not going."

"Only if we speak to the doctor together after your checkup. That's final, or I'll demand your father join us."

"Fine," Samantha said.

"Fine." Her mom picked up the carafe and sloshed coffee into her cup.

Stale-mate. They sat still in silence. Meanwhile, servants stepped in and out, clearing dishes, adding fresh coffee. Samantha ate, but only tasted distrust, betrayal, and dismay. "Relax, relax."

CHAPTER 13

The next day at breakfast, Samantha crept into the kitchen. "Cook, where is everyone?"

"You know your dad is at the office, and your mother, she ate her breakfast in the study this morning. Said she had some work to catch up on."

"I'm going to go talk to my mother."

"No, Miss Sam, I'm under orders to make you breakfast and watch you eat it. How about some coffee and juice to start?"

"Great," Samantha said sarcastically. It was an invisible slap in the face.

* * * *

Samantha found her mother in her office and sat in a plush chair facing the desk. "I'm sorry about yesterday," Samantha said. "I didn't mean to be a brat. Are you and Dad still mad at me?"

"No one is mad at you. We're worried about you." Her mother studied Samantha like an algebra problem. "If there was something really wrong, you'd tell us, wouldn't you?"

"Haven't I always told you everything? There's nothing wrong. Really. I'm fine, and I think it's because of the sleep I've had in the last few days. I even woke up hungry this morning, and ate a plateful. Ask Cook," Samantha said.

"I suspected as much. But I do expect you to keep the doctor's appointment. You can talk to your doctor about anything." She fisted her hands. "I mean if there's anything you aren't comfortable talking about with your father or me."

"I don't need to see any doctor. Besides, I'll need a doctor in Michigan, and I don't need two." Samantha tried to sound sincere and casual, but she couldn't help feeling nervous. Seeing her mother's disconcerted face, Samantha felt her breakfast thinking about coming back for visit.

"You have a point. The appointment is in one week. If you can convince your father, and if you feel good all week, I'll cancel it. If not, we go," her mom said.

Samantha nodded. That tone was not one that should be challenged.

Her mother continued. "And that includes eating. I want to see you eat good meals. And, an episode of illness means we walk into the doctor's office that same day. You'll not be in another state, far from home and sick. Understand?"

"I do. I'm fine." Samantha jumped to her feet and kissed her mother's cheek. "Thanks. I'll probably have a snack before lunch."

Skipping up the steps to her room, Samantha entered the solitude of her room and headed straight for the bathroom. Her breakfast was too much for her shrunken stomach. One look into the toilet, and she deposited her breakfast into the wet porcelain. Then she sprayed the room with disinfectant, brushed her teeth, and reapplied her lipstick. She couldn't take any chances. She had to look and act perfect. A perfect puppet controlled by three masters.

There was no room for what she wanted, for what she really felt. She resented being told where to go, what to eat, how to act. She'd be the master of this charade.

CHAPTER 14

That evening, turning in front of the mirror, Samantha was pleased with her appearance. In honor of the Fourth of July, she chose royal-blue shorts with a matching red, white, and blue polo shirt and flat white canvas shoes. She sported a wide red headband and bouncy curls. Her makeup was applied to perfection.

Samantha paid attention to every detail. She anticipated her parents' inspection: her mother would check her clothes, hair, and makeup; her father would check her mood, tone, and mannerisms.

He had put up a fight for her to keep the doctor appointment, but begrudgingly gave in after she and her mother convinced him she'd only had a virus, coupled with female problems. He told her he'd keep a careful eye on her.

Samantha understood her father would ask Skyler for a detailed report of their evening. She didn't want to give Skyler even the slightest opportunity to complain about her. She was even getting excited to meet Skyler's brother and his girlfriend. It would be fun to talk about

Michigan State and life in Michigan. She wouldn't be alone with Skyler, so why worry? To avoid the headache she anticipated, Samantha swallowed some pills. She slipped a few more into the little purse slung over her shoulder, just in case. Samantha rubbed her temples, repeating the words that had become second nature to her. "Relax, you can do this. You can pull it off. Relax, relax."

Samantha worried about the frequency of her headaches. They came out of nowhere and were getting more intense. Maybe, when she was on her own at Michigan State, she'd see a headache doctor who wouldn't need to check the rest of her. A Michigan doctor wouldn't know her family.

* * * *

It was almost eight when Skyler arrived, and he was waiting in the den with her dad.

Samantha entered the room, and it hushed.

"You look very patriotic." Skyler stood.

"Thanks," she said. She accepted his offered hand and shook it. "Sorry I wasn't downstairs when you arrived. I hope I haven't kept you waiting." She barely looked at him, but her voice was bubbly. Samantha averted her eyes and smiled widely at each of her parents.

Samantha felt her father's inspection. "Nonsense. Your delay gave me time to get the update on Skyler's big criminal case. You might like to watch it."

She saw the wishful thinking, that she might choose law over vet school, and didn't want to disappoint him. "I'm so busy planning for school, I'm not sure. Can I let you know later?"

The thought of watching Skyler left her cold, coating her arms with bumps like that of a freshly plucked chicken. How appropriate, she thought, the chicken-hearted becomes chicken-fleshed. She smiled at her own humor.

"Make the time. Skyler is a brilliant defense attorney. He's the kind of attorney every aspiring lawyer should have the opportunity to watch."

Samantha let her smile answer instead of her voice. She didn't know what to say, and nothing she could think of would solve her dilemma.

"I appreciate your confidence in me," Skyler said. "We had better get on our way. It won't be dark until around ten. And we're meeting my brother for dinner before the fireworks," Skyler said, he turned toward Samantha. "Ready?"

"Sure." Samantha kissed her dad. She really was the master of her charade.

* * * *

The ride to meet Tom and Darcey was pleasant enough. Samantha waited for Skyler to speak, to start a conversation, to look at her— anything. But he didn't. Samantha loved the silence between them, but hated it. The quiet gave her too much time to worry. The new Samantha needed to take control of the situation now. Right now, before she slipped back. "Radio?" she asked.

Skyler clicked on the radio, but remained lost in his own thoughts.

"Thanks," Samantha said. She had to think hard and find just the right thing to say. But what could she say? After a few more minutes, she asked, "Where are Tom and Darcey? Mom and Dad hoped to meet them."

Skyler didn't take his eyes from the road. "It would've been rude for me to bring people over without being invited, don't you agree?"

Not. "Of course, you're right."

Skyler still didn't look at her. "We're having lunch with your father tomorrow. I'm sure your father won't mind if you join us."

Without an invitation from my father? But she said, "Who is *us*? Tom, Darcey, you, and my father?"

"Exactly."

"I begin classes on my new computer. Dad wouldn't like it if I missed class to go out to lunch with the same group I saw the night before." Samantha tried to project an earnest tone. "My parents are strict about keeping commitments and following-through."

"I've received a few of those lectures myself," Skyler said with a half-smile. He finally turned to Samantha and winked. "He means well."

At least he looked at her, but she still hated that creepy

wink. "I've memorized that lecture," Samantha said.

* * * *

Skyler tipped the host for a better table on the upper patio. Samantha followed him outdoors, and they sat so close to the railing she felt like she was perched on the tail of the Big Dipper. He greeted almost every person they passed.

"How did you find this place?" Samantha asked. It was exquisite and unlike any place she'd ever been. The white linen tablecloth with the floral napkins and delicate centerpiece reminded her of home. She felt immediately comfortable, yet hesitant at the same time. They were confusing feelings for her, and she was unsure what to say. How young and weak she felt next to Skyler who was so worldly, so knowledgeable, so strong. So evil.

A mirror-image of Skyler stood next to him. "Hope you didn't wait too long."

"About time you two arrived." Skyler shook Tom's hand and kissed the cheek of a tanned, petite blue-eyed blonde attached to his arm.

Samantha barely listened to the introductions. Two devils a decade apart? A smile pasted on her face, she compared the brothers. Tom's blond curls looked like they should be pulled into a ponytail. His tan, his teeth, and his eyes were cookie cutter copies of Skyler's. He had the body of an outdoors person.

Listening to the brothers talk, she saw the real

differences, ones that relieved her. Tom was easygoing. He effortlessly made everyone around him feel comfortable, but Skyler often spoke with big words and had stiff mannerisms. Samantha had decided it was just lawyer-speak.

In the presence of Tom and Darcey, Samantha easily submerged her troubles. She almost forgot how much she hated Skyler. She loved listening to Tom and Darcey's stories about Michigan State, cross-country skiing, camping, and hiking.

Darcey was as much an outdoors person as Tom. Her natural beauty allowed her to be free of makeup, and her clothes had clean, simple lines that underscored her open personality. She didn't wear a bra and showed no self-consciousness about it. Her blonde hair was thick, straight, and waist-long. Samantha studied Darcey's fine features and lean body. She reminded Samantha of the flower children she'd seen in pictures from the sixties and seventies. Darcey wore a wide black neck-ribbon with a hanging gold peace sign. Samantha didn't know anyone who dressed like Darcey.

Samantha memorized every feature to begin her own transformation to college student. She needed a less conservative look than the clothes she and her mother had purchased so far.

Samantha marveled at how well Tom and Darcey understood each other. Samantha felt as if she had known them for a long time, and she loved the way they touched each other.

Samantha pushed her old self far away. Hiding the old Samantha felt safe, and she could forget her fears. The evening progressed with small-talk, laughter, and stories, and dinner quickly turned into dessert. Samantha let her subconscious take over and enjoyed the evening. She didn't think about the old Samantha. It felt right to feel safe and happy and to let her problems go. Relax, relax. She repeated the words, pushed her troubled-self deeper into her soul, into invisible caves. She locked all the unpleasantness in total darkness.

All too soon the evening was over, and they had to leave the restaurant. Samantha was disappointed the fireworks interfered with these precious moments. Inexplicably, she'd felt more during dinner than she had felt in a long time. She didn't want to explore the reasons; she just wanted to let it happen, whatever it was. She finally felt comfortable, and the circumstances felt right, normal, and natural. She wasn't going to jinx herself by over-examining the situation. She wanted so desperately to be happy. And, now, talking about her future, her college, her Michigan, she felt overwhelmingly relieved.

By the time they drove to the fireworks, Samantha looked at Skyler as she'd have at any other date. She wanted the feeling to last. She hadn't felt normal in so long. Somehow, this felt right. Everything was right.

Turning her head back to ensure Tom and Darcey were still following them, Samantha said, "Tom is really nice. I like Darcey, too. What did you think of her?"

"She seems to care about my brother. She must be the reason he chose Michigan State to earn his Master's."

"What do you mean?"

"She was only a first-term freshman when they met. Tom never talked about obtaining a Master's until recently." Skyler paused. "He only recently mentioned being serious with Darcey. Could be there's more to the story."

"Lawyers. You're all the same. That sounds just like something my father would say. Honestly, you are all too suspicious about everything."

"Not suspicious—careful. We are always on guard, so no one outmaneuvers us; so we are not blindsided. Is there anything wrong with that?"

"It's just a strange way to live, that's all." Samantha folded her arms, turned, and gazed out the window.

"It's the right way to live. If you attend law school, the first lesson you'll learn is CYA, or 'cover your ass.' Protect yourself, because you are the only one who can and who will. It's also the first lesson I teach my clients."

Samantha sighed.

"Haven't I taught you that much this summer?" Skyler turned off the engine and reached into the back seat for the blanket and cooler.

"I never thought about CYA," Samantha said. But *CYA* was about to be her new mantra.

＊ ＊ ＊ ＊

The fireworks were spectacular. Samantha watched Darcey settle back and nestle into Tom's shoulder in the darkness. The pair watched the blazing sky and intently whispered between the whistling of the firecrackers. They melded like one bronze art sculpture, posed for all time to be admired. Samantha didn't dare interrupt them. She enjoyed watching them more than she enjoyed the brilliance of the glowing sky.

Skyler stayed close enough to Samantha for her to feel his warm breath and to hear him whisper how beautiful she was. But Samantha barely noticed, lost in herself, lost in the sky, lost in the magic of the couple next to her. She longed to be a part of someone, to feel the closeness, the tenderness, the comfort. She longed to feel content. She wanted that more than anything. In the darkness she felt Skyler's hand rubbing her back and shoulders, slowly, gently. She relaxed and focused on the loving couple next to her. She felt part of them. She fixed her thoughts on them while Skyler's warm hands were on her.

Too soon, it was over. The finale sounded in their ears, and smoke from the bursting fireworks filled the nostrils of viewers below. Samantha felt warm and content. She basked under the multihued bursts and her pain seethed back penetrating into the depths of her most inner self burying the old Samantha. She felt cold and then warm.

Her body tingled. She felt reborn. She no longer remembered the hurt, the pain. She was untouched, fresh, alive. Fearless.

Hundreds of people stood up at once and retired happily to their cars. Samantha didn't object when Skyler placed her hand in his and lead her back to his car. She focused on Tom and Darcey paces ahead of them, their arms locked around each other's waist. Samantha, reverently silent, absorbed it all.

They hugged, said their good-byes and Samantha wistfully watched Tom and Darcey drive away after promises to keep in touch and that they would see her in the fall at Michigan State to show her around.

Samantha wished she could be Darcey, with a man like Tom—someone with a jovial personality who spoke freely and honestly, a tender man who was considerate of the female point of view and feelings. Maybe she'd find that man in Michigan. Maybe she could get to know Tom better.

"What are contemplating?" Skyler asked in an animated voice, resting his hand lightly on Samantha's thigh.

"Tom and Darcey make a nice couple."

"That they do."

"Where are we going? I promised I'd get home early."

"Your parents said they'll be out late, and they know you're safe with me. You know that too, don't you?" Skyler began to rub his hand up and down her thigh.

Samantha didn't respond. Her mind fluttered back to Tom and Darcey, sitting as one, watching the fireworks. She felt part of them.

"It's time. You know that, don't you?" Skyler stated.

Samantha's brows knitted, but she didn't respond. She didn't want to. She didn't want to think or move or feel. She didn't want to do anything that would break the magical spell Tom and Darcey cast upon her. Her eyes remained fixed on the road ahead.

Skyler exited onto a pebbled road that led to a dirt lane, Samantha's senses rose to high-alert. Caught, trapped in her own mind, unable to unleash the old Samantha, the new one took over. Samantha inhaled a deep soothing breath. She reassured herself. Calmness emerged and she was immediately comforted, when from the depths of her soul a familiar chant reverberated through her over and over, "Relax, Darcey, relax..."

Skyler maneuvered the dirt lane for a few minutes then pulled the car over into a clearing. He turned off the ignition and let the keys dangle. It was dark and quiet. Only the brilliant crescent moon lighted the ground.

Skyler grabbed Samantha and pulled her close. Putting his mouth over hers, he clenched her curls between his fingers, pulling her neck taut and her head back. Samantha held her breath, trying to grip her fear, trying to take control.

Within seconds she knew it was useless to fight and Samantha's inner strength gained control. She relaxed.

She reasoned with herself, found her inner power. There wasn't anything to fear. She was home. She was in her bedroom. She was in the comfort and solitude of her bathroom. As she took off her clothes, she felt herself step into the comfort of the water. She relished the hot pounding water. It felt good and clean and right and she remained in that clean place.

Until she emerged into somebody else. Darcey released herself, kissing him back deliciously. Running her hands around his face, her fingers through his long hair, the curls twirling around her fingers.

Skyler unlocked the door next to him and grabbed the blanket they'd used during the fireworks. He opened the passenger door and swiftly led Samantha to the smooth grassy clearing in front of the car. Skyler spread the blanket, clicked into Pandora on his cell and tossed it on the corner. He directed Samantha to sit on the soft plaid blanket. Within seconds, Skyler found his way around Samantha's body, memorizing each curve, slowly, gently parting soft supple crevices that moistened at his touch.

Samantha closed her eyes to keep the water from getting in them. Darcey reveled in his touch.

Samantha couldn't see his features clearly in the darkness, she only saw what the shadows allowed by the moon's glow. Samantha didn't feel his body against hers; she didn't feel his hot breath against her, only the steam from the shower. But Darcey did, she felt it all. Darcey took it all in, enjoying each of his fingers prodding every crevice, entering her body, moving within. Darcey took him deeper and deeper. Darcey moved with him and felt him grow inside her until he swelled into an explosion that left her body limp, her insides wet.

Tom was gentle with her. Darcey felt his muscular body against her slim, naked body, and the sweat that had pooled between her breasts and on her neck rolled off, as her chest rose and fell with each breath, in and out. She belonged to Tom. Darcey felt him touch her shoulder. Her eyes fluttered open feeling his body over hers. He was touching her gently, lightly lifting her, dressing her, slowly, carefully, as if she were a china doll that would break.

* * * *

The ride home was silent. Skyler held Samantha's hand with his right hand and drove with his left hand. He stroked each finger, and his thumb sensually rubbed her palm. Samantha was revolted by his touch relieved it was only her hand he touched.

Samantha wondered if her parents were home and how her computer class would be. She had to get up early. She pictured her closet and wondered what to wear to class.

Darcey felt Skyler's hand and wondered if he really liked her. If she had pleased him.

Pulling into the driveway, Skyler brushed a kiss on Samantha's cheek and she closed her eyes and held her breath. Darcey crept from the car and smiled at him.

"Sleep well, sweetie. I won't call tonight. I'll let you get your rest. You can dream about me without any interruption. We are made for each other. We'll talk tomorrow," Skyler said. He flashed a dazzling grin, his deep voice soft and lustful, winked and then pulled out of the driveway.

Samantha didn't hear him. She was alone in her dreams, searching through the blackness. Darcey returned a flirtatious smile and watched his car pull away.

After her shower, Samantha slipped into bed and into a disturbing dream. In her dream, she walked and walked. She turned her head from side to side, her eyes going round and round looking, searching. Why was she alone? Why had they left her? She looked down at her feet. There was a box. It was pretty and pink. The faces were gone. The parts were gone. She couldn't find them. There was only this box. She picked it up and held it. It comforted her, she felt herself roaming about in empty rooms of darkness. Darkness was everywhere. She couldn't see anything clearly except the box. Nor could she see any of the rooms she was in, but she knew she was wandering in rooms. The rooms had no doors, no windows, only entrances and exits. She wasn't scared, but she felt more alone. There was no longer safety in her dreams, only silence and darkness. A tear fell, traveling over her thick lashes, noticed only once it spilled onto her hand—the hand that held the box. She blinked.

She pulled the box open. A familiar tune and timeless words rang into the darkness: "Humpty Dumpty sat on a wall, Humpty Dumpty had a great fall, all the King's horses and all the King's men couldn't put Humpty together again." Samantha dropped the box.

* * * *

Morning startled Samantha. The brightness of the day filtered through her drapes and blinded her. She craved a shower. She didn't remember how she'd gotten home, how she'd gotten into her bed. The last thing she remembered was the blazing sky. She tried to retrace the evening and gave up.

She remembered she enjoyed being with Tom and his girlfriend. It was worth spending the time with Skyler just to meet them. Samantha was proud of herself. She had made it through her date with Skyler. She even enjoyed herself for the first time in a long time. Maybe could even learn to better tolerate, even like Skyler. He'd been a perfect gentleman to her. Maybe she had been wrong about him. Maybe he really was her friend, or could be her friend.

* * * *

Why couldn't she remember getting home? Maybe coffee would help. Looking at Minnie, she realized her parents would be waiting. She couldn't miss breakfast with them. She'd promised she'd be perfect. If she failed, it meant the doctor.

"Samantha, you look bright this morning. The evening must have gone well," her mom said.

Samantha was relieved she'd applied make-up, pulled her hair back with a cheerfully colored art-deco barrette, wore matching earrings and jewelry that complemented her colorful dress. Surely her parents could see the difference.

"My computer classes begin today. I want to be early to load any programs I might need. Skyler's brother told me I should learn to use a program that creates outlines."

"Buy only what you need. There are new programs developed every day."

"Oh, Mom, I know. Tom said it would really make a difference if I used a program that would put my class notes in order from the very first class. That's what he does to stay organized. Good idea, huh?" She poured milk into a bowl of cereal.

"Of course. If you need it, buy it. I think you should ask your instructor."

"How'd you like Tom?" Dad asked Samantha from behind his morning paper.

"He looks like Skyler, but they aren't alike. Much more easygoing. Very easy to talk to. I loved Darcey, his girlfriend. They told me all about MSU and college life."

"What's the girlfriend's last name?" Mom asked.

"I think it's—you know—can't believe it—I've

forgotten. I'm sure I'll think of it," Samantha said. Names filtered through, and she discarded them one by one. Shrugging, she decided not to give it any more thought.

"I'm having lunch with Tom and Skyler. You're welcome to join us."

"No thanks, Dad. Say *hello* for me," Samantha said, her mouth half full of cereal. "I've got to run. I'll be home for dinner." Samantha gulped the milk from the bowl picked up the oversized bag that held her computer and headed for the garage.

CHAPTER 15

Samantha loved the computer classes and stayed late, learning every function she could. It was easy. The computer was something she could submerge herself into for hours at a time. Now, stretched out on her bed. Her elbows dug deep into the comforter, where she'd been concentrating for hours typing on her computer. She'd made a to-do list that also contained every item she was taking to college. Working on her computer helped her escape. She set it on her bedside table

Exhausted, she slipped off her clothes, showered, and fell into bed. It would be easy to grab the computer and escape into it quickly, when her parents entered her room. Another masterful way to fool their watchful eyes. Lying-guilt no longer bothered her. Lying was easy. Eventually she'd master being perfect.

Closing her eyes, she quickly entered familiar blackness, but she felt uneasy and was confused. Her once-limber body stiffened. She felt awake, but was watching herself dream. Was that possible? She felt the uncomfortable presence of someone looming in the darkness.

She walked, ran, twirled. Then she sat down. For all of her movement, she still stood in the same place.

In the distance, the nursery-rhyme tune chimed in. The box. Where was the music box? She couldn't see it. The tune got louder and louder. She wanted out of the dream. Then she looked down. She saw her hands, wiggled her fingers and then pinched herself. Ouch. She must be awake. It wasn't a dream? The faces appeared, and some were familiar, others weren't. She looked closer. New parts, new features. Still no ears.

The music disappeared into ringing. Where was it coming from?

Startled, she blinked. Her cell phone was ringing. She touched the screen. 12:35. Samantha frowned and said, "Yes?"

"How about a friendly hello or a 'hi honey, I missed hearing your voice all day?' Is that too much to ask?" Skyler said.

"You woke me up."

"Aren't you even going to say you're sorry, and you've missed me?"

"Okay."

"Okay what?" Skyler said, his voice was forceful.

Samantha froze. She needed to be alone, unencumbered by the ever-present fear of Skyler. She wanted to hide, to sleep and never wake up. She tightly gripped the phone. She squinched her eyes closed and tried to push him out of her body, shield her mind. Another voice spoke into the darkness and answered Skyler.

"I missed you. I'm glad you called. When will I see you again?" the voice coming from Samantha said. It was vibrant and direct. It was soft and sensual, and she purred, as if she'd said them so many times before. She had said them many times before. She loved Tom. He was kind and gentle and fun and, best of all, he loved her, too, just the way she was.

"Get dressed and slip out and meet me. I'll park down the street about a block. Fifteen minutes. Are you game?"

"You're serious?" The voice dripped with love.

"Don't get caught. If you do, tell them you're taking a walk around the block." Skyler kissed the phone. Darcey jumped from her bed and peeked out into the hallway.

No one was there. She closed the door and dressed. Darcey smoothed her long locks, washed, and didn't bother with makeup. She didn't need any more color than what the sun had given her. Tom hated makeup. He wanted the natural woman who didn't fuss. She slipped on a summer jumper without the matching shirt underneath. The jumper barely covered her bra-free cleavage. Bare feet, pushed into thinly spiked heels, made the skirt on the jumper look shorter on her long legs. Dropping a house key into the jumper pocket, the Darcey-imposter slipped down the staircase, through the side door, and into the midnight air. She had an aura of extreme confidence.

Within minutes she arrived at the Jaguar and slid in.

"Glad you're here," Darcey whispered to Tom.

"Just for you," Skyler pulled the car from the curb and kept the lights off until they were another block away.

"Where are we going?" Darcey asked, staring at Tom's handsome features.

"It's a surprise," Skyler said. He rubbed his hand up and down Samantha's thigh, reaching higher and higher with each stroke until he found the top of her cotton panties and yanked them downward. No words were spoken in the moving car. With tacit understanding of what was before them, their eyes remained silent and focused on the road ahead.

A few miles later, Skyler turned off the car lights and then turned down a dark, deserted alley. Darcey watched silently. Skyler pulled over, turned off the engine, the keys still in the ignition.

"Push the knob so your seat goes back," Skyler ordered.

Samantha—the Darcey-imposter—was delighted when Tom was forthright. She opened her door, got out of the Jaguar, and let Skyler slide over from his seat into hers.

"Come on back in. Hurry up."

Darcey slid into the cramped seat onto Skyler's lap, facing him, her panties stuffed into her pocket, her heels thrown onto the back seat, her arms around his neck.

* * * *

Darcey stayed in the back seat and finished dressing

while Skyler drove. She felt great but didn't understand why tears dropped through her lashes. She felt lost but dared not speak. She loved being with Tom. He'd never treated her so roughly before. She felt tired and sore. Darcey looked up at Tom's reflection in the rearview mirror. She studied what she could see in the darkness. His beautiful face. In an instant, she was smiling again.

Darcey got out of the car a few houses away and entered the familiar house. She was glad she'd had a few minutes with Tom before he had to get back to his books. He must have been worried about his exams.

That must've been it, she decided. She hurried up the stairs of the sorority house quietly so as not to disturb the housemother.

CHAPTER 16

As the summer progressed, Samantha kept busy with her computer, shopping, and meticulously packing for college. She counted the days until her eighteenth birthday and Emily came home. Her parents were, much of the time, in Washington, planning fall fund-raisers. Her father spent the remainder of his time with his clients. Her mother spent all of her free time—or so it seemed—working on the Foundation for Women Candidates, and their never-ending candidate search.

Samantha didn't mind that her parents made themselves absent during her last summer at home. Since she'd turned fifteen, she'd been increasingly alone for longer periods of time.

Now, at times her parents seemed to forget they had a daughter, unless she was other than perfect.

Walks in the hot August sun and the smell of September's impending arrival helped her pass her time. She shied away from evening strolls. Until she was raped by Uncle Greg she enjoyed walking alone in the dark.

Now, she feared being alone in the darkness.

Yet somehow, in the past few weeks, she found herself frequently in the night air, walking as if she didn't have a care in the world. She wasn't sure if she should be thankful she was over her fear, or fearful she didn't remember how she got over it. A voice inside her told her not to be afraid of it, not to question it. So she didn't. Yet sometimes the night startled her. Sometimes she didn't remember having gone out, and those were the nights fear immobilized her once again.

Samantha worried about not remembering, but decided it was a result of stress. She vowed to take things more slowly, so she'd remember more, so dreams and reality wouldn't confuse her. She was ready and packed for college. She wanted to spend her time with Emily and working on her laptop.

One day, when making the bed, tucked between the headboard and the mattress, she'd found the worn paper she'd written on so many weeks before. She unfolded it carefully so the worn creases wouldn't separate. The list of words had become part of her permanent memory banks. But the definitions, still foreign, had not merged with the words, nor had they offered any solutions.

Samantha sat on the carpet. She smoothed the paper. At first, Skyler had terrified her, but he'd toned down his desire for her. She was tired of his calls. He kept close tabs on her life and what she did almost every minute. Happily, she would leave and be far away from him and all the negative things that had happened. She'd never have to deal with it again—any of it: the rape, the abortion, Skyler, her absent parents. She closed her eyes, crossed her fingers, and made a wish like she had when she was a child. When she was little, it had made her feel better. It was hard to feel anything now.

Samantha frowned as she explored her options. Silence usually comforted her. Today she felt disturbed by the silence. She felt like some unrecognizable voice was telling her to leave everything alone. To stop thinking. To stop searching. The voice, loud and haughty, called her from within. Her head ached. She crawled into bed and smacked a pillow over her face, holding it tightly against each ear. An inner voice, now wispy, didn't stop. It laughed at her. It called her a wimp, a child, a baby. Nothing quieted the voice. Samantha was losing control.

The dreams had now permeated her reality. She was sure she was going crazy. There wasn't a thing to do. No one would believe her. No one would really listen. She would be blamed, shamed, and punished.

Samantha sprang to her feet and headed to her mother's medicine cabinet. In her folks' bedroom, she felt a chill of loneliness and raw sadness rip through her. She felt homesick for her parents. Homesick in her own home, in their empty room.

She stared into the medicine cabinet—tubes and jars, vials and bottles. Lots of bottles. Clear ones, green ones, brown ones, white ones. Lots of orange plastic ones.

It had been reorganized—new bottles added, familiar ones gone.

Samantha lifted them, one by one, carefully replacing each exactly as she'd found it. Her mother suffered from migraines, so she'd have the right drug to cure headache pain. She was old enough not to need her parents. She was old enough to take care of herself and figure this out.

Finally, she found Xanax, Tylenol 3, Vicodin. What should she take? She held up the bottle, Tylenol 3. She swallowed two. Maybe she'd need more. She pocketed the bottle. The voice told Samantha that her mother would never miss it. She closed the cabinet and swiftly retreated to her room.

Back in her own room, Samantha returned the list of words to the caverns under her mattress. The inside voice laughed. Music encircled her. Where was it coming from? She sank into a state of numbness. Skyler's words engulfed her. CYA. Cover your own ass, protect yourself, stay a step ahead. She needed to pursue the words. Protection.

The nursery rhyme from the dream screamed, and it drowned out the laughter. The music box spun around, she couldn't catch it. She found herself staring into a long looking glass.

It reflected Darcey.

CHAPTER 17

The morning sunlight sent Samantha staggering to the blinds to close them. She'd slept almost ten hours, except for the interruption of Skyler's annoying call. Her mouth was dry, her throat sore. Her body felt tender and bruised. Had she fallen out of bed? Light-headed, she crawled back into her bed.

Samantha tried to piece together what could have made her so exhausted and feel so rotten. She heard movement. Her parents were up. They'd been gone so much during July and the first weeks in August that they must have given up the habit of waking her for breakfast. Were they off their kick of watching her eat?

Samantha felt too ill to worry about it. She didn't feel like eating. She couldn't go down. She'd make her excuses later.

What was it Skyler had said to her on the phone? Something about her birthday and his gift to her. She didn't want him to give her anything and told him exactly that. He insisted she'd love it, that it was something she wanted, but she just didn't know it yet. What did that mean? She didn't want to figure it out. She wanted him to disappear.

Had she fallen asleep while they were talking on the phone? Samantha became restless and went into the bathroom. A cleansing bath. She was too tired to stand in the shower. She turned the knobs, set the temperature, and over-poured bubble bath into the filling tub.

As she pulled off her pajamas, she felt a pool of wetness drop into her underwear. Her period wasn't due for a few days. Was it early? Was that possible on birth control pills? Looking into the cotton crotch of her panties, she felt the wetness. It had no color. It was clear. There was no reason for the liquid that made any sense to her. She smelled it. It smelled foreign to her. No, it smelled like, like sex? Had someone touched her in her sleep? How was this possible? It must be an infection. Had Skyler given her one? Did she get it from Greg? Samantha felt nauseated.

Quickly climbing into the bubbled water, she leaned her head back onto the plastic air pillow and closed her eyes. STD flashed in her mind. She'd read about them— and now she had one.

She couldn't tell anyone. She couldn't go to a doctor. She refused to tell Skyler. The thought of telling Skyler, of asking him, gave her goosebumps even in the heat of the water.

Samantha pushed away her thoughts. They weren't real to her. She didn't want them to be real. Relax, relax.

Samantha lay still in the water, letting her thoughts drift under, concentrating on planning her day. She picked up the gold bar of soap, she saw her severely wrinkled fingers, hurriedly finished.

Wrapped in her robe, Samantha was surprised at how much better she felt. She spent the next hour checking her underwear every fifteen minutes. There was no more wetness. A fluke. She buried her fears. What could she do about it anyway?

Her cell phone rang, and she glanced at the number.

"Emily," Samantha said. "I can't believe it's you."

"I got home a week early. I couldn't stay away another day. Everything was great, but I was more than ready to come home. Am I invited over, or do you want to meet me somewhere? I'm dying to see you."

"How about Maxine's? We can have lunch and talk, go shopping? Unless you spent all your money in Europe," Samantha teased. She felt renewed, and suddenly aware it was another beautiful day, and she'd soon be outside and part of it.

"Maxine's in half an hour," Emily said.

* * * *

Samantha applied her makeup and fixed her hair. She wore a blue peasant-blouse, matching long crinkled skirt, and white flat sandals, she'd selected to mask her inner turmoil. Downstairs, she found her mother in her study and told her she'd be spending the day with Emily.

∗ ∗ ∗ ∗

Samantha entered Maxine's restaurant and was surprised to find a grownup, sophisticated Emily—French twist, low-cut clingy dress, and matching pumps. From behind, Samantha tapped her arm.

"You look beyond fabulous," Samantha said. The girls hugged and sat.

To any stranger listening, the conversation would have been gibberish, yet they understood each other like twins.

Samantha was relieved Emily's down-to-earth core hadn't changed, despite her sophisticated appearance. Emily could be counted on, but could she be confided in? Before Samantha found her courage, they headed for the mall.

During the short drive, while Samantha followed in her own car, she practiced versions of how to explain everything, but it was tough. She turned the radio up to drown out a whispering voice inside her head. Why couldn't she shut that voice up? Why had it begun when she decided to tell Emily? Was it a warning from her inner core, or was it her fear of telling her best friend?

There it was again. It called her a weakling, a baby, a wimp. Tom was the only one she could trust.

Tom, she thought. Who is Tom? The only Tom she knew was Skyler's brother. She barely knew him. Then, just as quickly, the voice disappeared. Samantha parked next to Emily. Together, they strolled into the mall. She couldn't tell her friend now. Tomorrow. She'd tell her tomorrow.

* * * *

It was almost midnight when Samantha got home. Her parents had either gone to sleep or had gone out. Samantha didn't care to find out. She wanted to keep her day with Emily private and tossed her clothes carelessly onto the chair beside her dresser.

She went into the bathroom, found her prescription, uncapped it, popped two pills in her mouth, and then realized the bottle was nearly empty. Had she really gone through the prescription that fast?

The phone rang. She wished it would disappear.

"Hello?"

"Well, what is this? The traveler comes home. Was he interesting?" Skyler asked.

"What are you talking about?" Samantha mimicked his sarcasm.

"The man you were with all day. Was he as good as me?"

"I was with Emily."

"I thought she wasn't coming home for a few more days. I can check, you know."

"She came home early."

"Really? What did you do?"

"We met at Maxine's for lunch. Ate burgers and fries

and chocolate malts. We went shopping at the mall. When the stores closed, we ate dinner at TGIF I just got home." Samantha sputtered detail after detail. What she wore, what she bought, what time she did everything. She would never feel good about accounting to Skyler. She felt trapped, without choice. But she wouldn't let anything ruin the great day she'd had. Not even Skyler.

Samantha wished she could scream, instead she barely listened while Skyler bragged about his trial and how he would get Mr. Castriano who would owe him big—beyond money, blah, blah.

She sat on her bed, rested her cheek against a pillow, hit speaker, and murmured an occasional disinterested response. She tried to stay awake.

She fell into the darkness and smelled scented soap and expensive cologne. She saw a man. She didn't recognize him, but recognized the anger in his eyes. She ran from him when she saw him furiously rip off his t-shirt, and then his belt, tossing them off. He ran after her. Her head jerked back. He'd caught her. She froze.

"Roll over, bitch. You're just like the rest of them. You take from me, and you don't give me anything back." It was Skyler's voice. It was his face. She saw it clearly. She heard the harsh whisper and felt his weight against her. She dropped. He tore her clothes and climbed onto her nakedness.

Shaking, she followed his orders. She didn't dare refuse him. She promised God she'd be good if she could go home. He entered her. She cried out, "No, no, you're hurting me."

His fiery voice laughed. "Now tell me you love it. Now, bitch, right now. Tell me how you love it. Tell me how you don't want to live without me."

CHAPTER 18

At breakfast, Samantha tried to engage with her parents, but her petrifying dreams preoccupied her. They felt real.

"Emily cut her trip short? Did she say why?" Mom asked.

"We were so happy to see each other and catch up, I don't think she said. She looks so sophisticated and so much older. We went to the mall, and she helped me pick out a few new outfits for school."

"You girls shouldn't be in such a hurry to grow up. There's so much ahead of you," Mom said. She sipped her coffee while checking off names from some list. "You two could help with the League fundraiser."

"Oh, really," Samantha tried not to sound exasperated. "Where's Dad? Isn't he having breakfast with us?"

"He met Skyler early this morning. Something about new evidence. Prosecutor is giving Skyler a hard time allowing late evidence. He wanted your father there for backup."

"Oh."

She pushed the scrambled eggs and soggy toast around her plate. "Mom, could I be excused? I need to call Emily," Samantha said.

"You've hardly touched your breakfast. Have a few more bites, and then call Emily. Really, dear, you are still too thin for my liking."

"You worry too much. You've seen me eat lots of food. Pretty soon you'll have me outgrowing all my new clothes." Samantha popped an obligatory bite of eggs into her mouth, washed it down with the rest of her now-warm orange juice.

"Just promise me you girls will take time out to eat, whatever you decide to do."

"Yesterday, we ate out twice."

"Take some money from my wallet and treat Emily to a nice meal, or use the charge I gave you. Tell her it's my *welcome home* to her."

"Thanks. I'll let you know when we figure out what we're doing."

"You need a party dress—"

Samantha grinned at the thought of turning eighteen. She didn't want the party, but it was an Armstrong tradition to have a full family gathering, with friends and all the trimmings, to welcome her to adulthood.

She dialed Emily and committed herself to be sophisticated looking. But she'd still be herself. Emily and Darcey could help her. She remembered Tom down to the very last detail, she wanted to find someone like him, eventually.

* * * *

The next few days went quickly for Samantha. Not even Skyler's inquisitions could break the spell of happiness she felt from Emily's return.

Her brothers were expected to arrive in time for the party, and the house was buzzing with preparations. She slipped into her black spaghetti-strapped dress and satin pumps. It was time to go down. She could hear sounds of their guests. Had her brothers arrived? Surely they would've pounded on her door. They must be running late. It would be like the twins to make a splashy entrance. Even at their age, they still garnered all the attention they could get, and when they didn't get attention, they created a situation to divert it from others.

The dining room was packed with family and friends holding drinks. Waiters wove through the crowd offering specialty appetizers. She studied the crowd and realized just how much she'd missed being with welcoming people. In that brief interlude, she felt normal. She felt like it was Christmas morning and the past months were nonexistent. Her parents, aunts, uncles, and cousins, even her brothers were there. The twins raised their eyebrows at Samantha, pulled her between them, and kissed each cheek.

"Hey, Sammy-cat, you look great for such a baby." Taylor grinned. "Did you see the mountain on the gift table?"

Putting his arm around her shoulder, Tad said, "Our present isn't there. You know us; we didn't wrap it."

"But you'll love it," Taylor said.

"Tell me what it is, pleeeeaze." Samantha felt five again.

"What d'ya think?" Taylor looked between her and Tad.

"It's Sammy-cat's day; your wish is our command," Tad said. "Pull it out, Taylor."

Samantha only felt the presence of her brothers in the room. From the inside pocket of his suit jacket, Taylor pulled out a small box.

"Happy birthday," they said in unison. Tad added, "We thought you could use it at Michigan State and in law school or vet school. It's like the one dad uses at the firm."

"A digital recorder. This is really cool."

"That way you can save the battery on your phone," Tad said. "It will download into your computer or your phone. High tech."

"You can use it to relisten to class while you drive or study."

"It's perfect. Thank yous." Samantha hugged her brothers.

Samantha slipped the tiny recorder into a small drawer in the buffet. A waiter carrying a tray of champagne walked by. Without thinking about it, Samantha violated the no-drinking promise she'd made to herself.

Her father was about to make a toast in her honor. She vowed she'd dump it out after the toast and before she blew out the candles and sliced the cake.

She slid into place between her parents. A hundred champagne-filled crystal glasses raised in her honor. All eyes were focused on her father. She visualized her grandparents in the room, beaming at her and raised her eyes.

Dad cleared his throat and began. "Yesterday I held a tiny, pink baby girl in my arms; today we see a grown woman …"

He said so many kind things about her. Samantha looked around the room at the smiling faces, caring faces. She wondered if anyone could see through her, and then pangs of panic pulsated inside. She felt naked, sure the crowd knew she wasn't the innocent woman her father described. Not worthy of the elegant toast.

And then she saw the parts, the pieces from her dreams. They were here. They were whole. They were real. She no longer heard her father. She only saw the familiar features with their raised glasses and their artificial faces.

She saw Greg.

She dropped the crystal glass, and it shattered on the parquet floor. The room lost light.

And Skyler stepped into view. She forgot how to breathe.

Skyler got his arms around her and steered her to a

chair. The butler tended to the broken glass.

Samantha couldn't grasp the words she heard, who the people were. Slow motion set in around her. But—except for Skyler—no one seemed to notice her. Everyone was mesmerized by her father's speech, an excellent orator developed by years of trial work.

Her father finished, and everybody sipped champagne. She said thank-you and drank. She guzzled the remainder of the gold bubbly liquid and grabbed another from a passing tray. Skyler helped Samantha stand, and she smiled and shook the hands of family and friends, who'd formed a line in front of her. She barely uttered a word. The crowd sang, she sliced the cake, and Cook plated it. She nodded, smiled, and thank youed, over, and, over again. Finally, she stepped into an escape hatch—the foyer—while everyone returned to their individual conversations. But Greg and Skyler followed her into the foyer.

"I thought you'd never be alone," Skyler whispered. "You look wonderful. Happy birthday, my sweet." He handed her a small silver-wrapped box.

"I can't accept this," Samantha said, stuttering, unsure of how to react. She looked for a way to escape, maybe upstairs to her bedroom. People would hear if she made a fuss. And if the men followed her upstairs, she would freak-out.

"It's yours. You'll take it. You'll wear it every day. You'll think of me." Skyler spoke next to her ear through clenched teeth. His caviar breath nauseated her.

Samantha unwrapped the gift. Greg stood a few feet away on the other side of Skyler, silently observing, in paid-bodyguard position. She loathed Skyler for bringing him near her.

From the silver box, Samantha released a gold necklace. Skyler took it and clasped it around Samantha's neck.

"It's a broken heart, Samantha. See, it has an 'S' on it. Everyone will think it stands for Samantha, but we'll both know it stands for Skyler. I have one just like it, the other half—I'm your other half." Skyler whispered from behind her neck. "Greg knows that and won't bother you anymore. You and I are the halves that belong together."

Samantha glared at him. She wanted to shut him up. He'd promised her a special surprise on her birthday. Was it the necklace, or was it Greg? She wanted to run but was paralyzed.

"You don't have to say anything. It's your day, you should enjoy it. I brought your buddy Greg, so you remember to behave. Remember you are mine, and you'd better stay that way. If I find out you've even thought about being with one of those college guys, well then, there will be consequences. Greg wants another taste. We might just see how you enjoy two men."

The threat was clear. Samantha stood in mortified-mannequin-mode.

"I played your little recording to Greg. He won't

bother you again—unless you deserve it," Skyler whispered. "Happy birthday," he snickered in a sing-song voice.

The evil pair turned and walked away.

Anguished, Samantha saw everything around her melt away like a kaleidoscope of burning plastic. She stepped backward, fully intent on running up the stairs to her room and locking the door. Instead, a headache stymied her desire and her ability to leave. Inexplicably, she felt separated. Mystically, her wish came true. She could hear the others, but she couldn't see them. Samantha floated away, far away to her safe place, her private place.

She looked around uncertainly before settling in. The serenity in the silence of her room was magical; her bed, comfortable. Relax, she told herself. Relax.

Where is Tom? Darcey searched the room. She lifted a fresh glass of champagne from a silver tray. That was odd, Tom was just here talking with someone she didn't recognize. *He'd better not be cheating. Ha. Never.*

Darcey emptied the champagne glass and slipped toward Tom, another man, and an unknown girl. She strained to hear their conversation.

"So I hear you and Samantha have been doing quite a bit of shopping lately. Did you leave anything in town for the rest of us to buy?" Skyler asked, laughing.

"Just the big-ticket items we couldn't carry," Emily said. "Mostly things for college. Samantha and I have had a lot of fun these past two weeks."

"She's a lovely woman. I'm sure she'll do well in college. Her father tells me her major is pre-vet, but she is leaning toward pre-law." Skyler paused. "Can I bring you something to drink? Steal a tray of appetizers?" His voice was flirtatious. He stood too close to Emily.

Emily stepped back. It was clear she was uncomfortable. "No, thanks. I'm done. I've already eaten too much."

"Come now, there's always room for champagne," Skyler said in a low sensual voice, his lips almost touching her ear.

"Sam? Samantha," Emily called out.

Darcey swooped in and wrapped an arm around Tom's shoulder. "What are you whispering about over here? Telling secrets?"

Tom raised both hands as if he were surrendering to the sheriff. He and the other man suddenly felt the need to huddle.

"I think you'd better let me take you upstairs," the strange girl said. "You get a little outrageous when you drink. It always makes you strange." Her voice was filled with sisterly concern.

"I'm perfectly fine." Darcey searched the room, only to discover she'd lost sight of Tom and his companion. The strange girl pulled on Darcey's arm and moved her out of the foyer and up the stairs.

"No, I don't think you're fine. Come on, let's get out of here for a while. It's quiet upstairs." Clearly trying to avoid any attention, the girl grabbed Darcey's hand.

Not seeing Tom, Darcey shrugged and followed.

* * * *

Darcey closed her eyes in surrender, and Samantha slept soundly, except for the music box. She could hear it, but she couldn't find it; she couldn't close it to stop the sound. But she could hear the words that went with it. "Humpty Dumpty sat on a wall; Humpty Dumpty had a great fall; All the king's horses and all the king's men couldn't put Humpty together again." Who was chanting those words? She felt as if the words were coming from inside of her; yet her voice wasn't her own. Whose voice was it? Samantha tried to speak, to call out. No words came. The music was coming closer and louder. Samantha twirled. Still, she couldn't see the music box. The room spun.

"Samantha? Samantha?" the voice whispered. Samantha opened her eyes. She focused, confused. Why was Emily standing over her?

"How are you feeling?" Emily asked.

"What are you doing here? Why am I here? Is the party over?"

"I haven't been gone that long. Here, have some coffee." Emily sat on the edge of Samantha's bed.

"I feel okay." Samantha sipped the hot coffee.

"When I brought you up here, you weren't making any sense," Emily said. "You didn't even recognize me. You really shouldn't drink. Alcohol gets to you too quickly."

"I only had two, maybe three glasses of champagne. I didn't even finish them. Every time I set my glass down, some maid came along and took it. Besides, since when do you tell me not to drink? Who made you my mother?" Samantha said.

"I'm sorry. It's just, well, you weren't you; you scared me. You were saying strange things."

"Like what? I don't remember saying anything. In fact, I don't remember you coming up here with me." She was embarrassed to admit to Emily she didn't remember leaving the birthday party. The last thing she remembered was needing to escape from Greg and Skyler and her headache.

"You were talking about a boyfriend named Tom. You said you came to the party with him. Trust me, you weren't making any sense. You don't have a boyfriend you haven't told me about, do you?"

"You know I don't have a boyfriend. And, I can't think of anyone named Tom at my party. Oh my God, Emily, how long have I been up here? We've got to get downstairs." Samantha said, suddenly frantic. "Trust me, this is not good. My parents will kill me if they think I ditched my own birthday party. You don't know how they treated me all summer."

"You've told me. Don't worry, I'll cover for you. If they say anything, we'll tell them I wasn't feeling well."

"Thanks. Let's hope that works." Samantha rolled her eyes.

After descending the stairs, they immediately inserted themselves into a large conspicuous group. The party was so big, people were now spread throughout the house and into the backyard; no one had missed the girls. The Armstrongs, always the perfect hosts, kept their company entertained and well fed."

Soon the three siblings and Emily found their way to the game room with their cousins, a tradition at every family function. When people began to leave, Mom called the twins and Samantha, so they could stand united as a family and properly thank their departing guests. Samantha, Taylor, and Tad had always hated this part. After each guest stepped out of the house, one of the siblings smirked a soft rude comment that sent the trio into gales of laughter. It was a tradition the twins had begun and taught Samantha. It was private, it was fun, and it was theirs. They knew it was childish. When the house emptied, they retreated to the game room with Emily to begin their own celebration.

CHAPTER 19

The remaining August days blended one into the other. Samantha grew restless for her escape to freedom, to college. Even Emily couldn't keep her occupied and content at home. Samantha worried a lot. More often than not she'd find herself not remembering what had happened or would find herself dressed in clothes she didn't remember putting on. She blamed it on stress. There was no other rational explanation. She remembered important things. It was small things that escaped her. Unanswered questions threw her off-balance: *what time did she fall asleep? Why wasn't she at home when she told Emily she'd be? Why did her legs ache and cramp up like she'd been running? And when did she change her clothes?* Looming questions daunted her.

Samantha remembered Nana forgetting things. Nana had told her *'forgetfulness is the result of a busy mind'* and *'when people became preoccupied with life, small things slip through the brain, but big, important things would be there forever to be retrieved when they were most needed.'* Nana's words comforted her. They kept Nana close.

Samantha heard Nana asking her: '*Will you remember me when I'm gone?*'

Samantha repeated her response. "You'll never leave me."

And then one day she did. And, in an instant, Samantha was left alone, forever. But Nana's words, her voice, they were always with Samantha, and for that she was grateful.

Thank you Nana, she whispered and carefully packed a picture of Nana between her sweaters.

Samantha's headaches had increased, and she decided as soon as she had settled in her dorm room and her classes, she'd see a doctor. She'd be in Michigan for Labor Day—in four days. Classes began the last week in August, and she needed to get settled.

The last of her boxes packed and labeled. Plus an overnight bag. At the very bottom of the bag, underneath the padding, she hid the pills she'd pilfered from her parents' collection. Some of the prescriptions were outdated. She picked them from the trash bin next to her mother's nightstand. They'd never be missed.

Emily was about to pick her up. The girls had decided they would spend the last few days before college at Emily's summer home. Their parents would join them on Saturday, and Sunday they would be headed for college.

Samantha looked around her room, confident she wouldn't miss it once she was gone. Her brothers didn't miss anything from home except a few of the favorite dishes Cook spoiled them with. Samantha wouldn't miss anything.

The twins' stories about college and law school were exciting. She wished she'd had a chance to ask them questions about the words on her list. But she didn't. She couldn't. She felt guilty bugging them like her father did. Instead, they told stories about college parties and gave her advice on how to survive college.

When the twins left, the house felt empty. She knew her parents felt it, but Samantha was surprised how lonely she felt without them. Samantha never before felt that strongly about their departure. This time was different because all of their lives were changing; she wouldn't always be there when they came home, and they might not be home when she visited.

"Samantha? Are you up there? Are you ready?" Emily climbed the stairs.

"Get up here. I've just got one bag and my purse. Cook made us a basket. She wouldn't tell me what she packed, but she guaranteed me we'd like it. Cook said she packed our favorites, so we wouldn't want to stop along the way for fast food." Samantha smiled fondly as she repeated Cook's words, imitating her voice. "Never can tell who ya meet in them restaurants. Better you eat my food and stay on the road."

"That sounds like our Cook. I'll go with you to the kitchen to thank her," Emily said. "We won't tell her I stopped at the *Gas & Go* to buy junk food. She'll take it right out of the car."

Samantha loved the way Emily understood, not just her, but her family. "Shall we?" The phone rang.

"Are you going to answer that?" Emily asked as Samantha shut the door.

"It figures it would ring the minute we're leaving," Samantha said, talking more to herself and the phone than to Emily.

"Your father just told me you're leaving." Skyler's voice was angry. "And you'll be leaving for Michigan Sunday. When were you going to tell me?"

"I didn't think about it," Samantha whispered. Emily sat on the top step. Could she hear this embarrassing conversation? How would Samantha explain it?

"Clearly," Skyler said. "Who are you going with?"

"Emily and I are just about to leave."

"What did Emily say about the necklace you're wearing?"

"She saw it at my birthday party."

"You wouldn't dare leave home not wearing it."

"Emily's waiting. I have to go." She felt lightheaded.

"How many parties are you planning?"

"That's not why we're going."

"If there wasn't anything to hide, you wouldn't be sneaking off."

"I just forgot. It didn't seem important."

"Everything you do is important to me. I've made that

clear," Skyler said.

Samantha hesitated. Emily stared at her. Samantha began to sweat and felt a headache coming on. She closed her eyes and concentrated on getting Skyler off the phone.

"Yes, I'm sorry," Samantha said, in as calm a voice as she could find. "I'll call you when we get there." Before he could answer, she clicked off.

"Who was that?" Emily asked. "Are you seeing someone you haven't told me about?

"No. Let's get out of here. I swear, I'll tell you later. Please?"

She'd never hung up on him before.

* * * *

Skyler stared at the phone. He wanted to hunt her down right that moment, but he was in the last days of the Castriano trial. Final proofs next week, and closing arguments. He had to get Samantha out of his head long enough to deliver a brilliant closing argument. Skyler smiled. There were many ways to get ahead in this town. Samantha had skipped out on him when he needed her. She'd learn not to do that again. He'd teach her.

Skyler pictured Samantha dancing, flirting, and in the arms of another man. He unbuttoned his collar and loosened his tie. He couldn't concentrate. His mind envisioned her—her touch, her taste, her smell. He threw his papers across the desk. He dialed the summer house.

No answer.

She'd lied. He dialed again. And again. Surely the maids would answer if they were there. He hit redial.

Skyler dug a key from the back of his file drawer and used it to open the office safe. He pulled out a double-shot glass and a fresh bottle of Royal Crown Whiskey. Pouring one, then another, straight down his throat. He felt warm and relaxed. Using the small key, he opened a dark-cherry box. Skyler reviewed its contents. Samantha was his, and he had all the proof he needed to keep her his for a very long time.

He pulled out a thumb-drive. Next, he retrieved the labeled evidence bags. All memories of Samantha: strands of hair, an earring, broken fingernails, and the doctor's file.

Let her enjoy her childish weekend. Let her go to school. He'd teach her.

* * * *

During the long ride, the girls made their peace. Neither wanted to spoil their last weekend before college separated them, so both avoided talking about the phone call. They'd talk about it later.

They entered the long driveway leading to the beach house, and Emily broke the silence. "Yay, we're here. What should we do first?" Emily asked.

"Let's unpack, wash-up, then take a really long walk along the shore. We can walk and talk. Okay?" Samantha was certain Emily could hear her heart pounding. She needed to talk things over with Emily before she got it into her head to mention anything to her parents or anyone else.

"It's a plan. Let's have a sunset picnic." Emily grabbed up the bags, carried them to the door, and unlocked it. The phone was ringing. "Must be one of our parents. Likely upset we turned our cell phone ringers off for the drive."

"You'd think they didn't trust us to get here in one piece," Samantha said.

Emily picked up the receiver, expecting her mother to be on the other end. "You've got great timing. We just got here."

"That's strange," Emily said, replacing the receiver. "I guess whomever it was didn't like my comments. They hung up." She giggled. "Don't you find that hang-up just as we arrive a little strange?"

Samantha bet the caller was Skyler. He hadn't believed what she was doing; now he'd know. *Damn lucky I didn't answer it.* She followed Emily up the winding staircase. After they unpacked, Samantha made the excuse she'd forgotten her purse in the car. She made her way to the breakfast room, and called Skyler.

"I'm not available, please leave a message." Skyler's recorded voice.

"You asked me to call. We're here, and we're going for a walk. I hope you get this message. Bye."

"Samantha? Where are you?" Emily yelled down the staircase. "Let's get outside."

"Coming," said Samantha. "Just left my parents a message that we'd arrived and we'd be out for a while."

The pre-autumn weather was brisk near the water, although the sun gave no hint of relinquishing its control. "This feels so good." Samantha carried the picnic basket and cooler. She knew it was time to confide in Emily.

"Let's go over to the rock pile near the weeping willow and talk," Samantha said, trying to buy just a few more minutes.

Samantha knelt on the grassy area and spread a large blanket and Emily sat cross-legged facing Samantha.

She opened her mouth to speak and heard an unfamiliar rasp in her voice. How could she explain someone had stolen her—invaded her body and snatched her soul. She opened a bottle of soda, took a long swig, then tried again.

"You were right, Emily," Samantha began, avoiding direct eye contact with her. It was the only way she could maintain control enough to speak. "I was talking to a boy, but he's not a boy. I mean, he's a man." Samantha scanned Emily's face. "You know him. It was Skyler."

"Skyler Marks from the office? Why is he calling you?"

"He helped me out a few months ago, and now he, well, he doesn't want to see me get hurt, and so he keeps a close eye on me."

"Sam, that doesn't make sense. How did he help you? Do your parents know?"

"No. And you can't tell them. You can't tell anyone. You swore you wouldn't." Samantha grabbed Emily's arm.

"And I won't." Emily shook her arm free. "You know I won't tell. I can't believe you didn't tell me. This is why you were weird last spring."

Samantha nodded.

"Spill it. You know I'll help you."

Samantha said, "I was at the library later than I should've been, and it had gotten dark, really dark. My parents were supposed to call from Washington. I didn't want to miss their call and make them worry. So I…" Samantha hesitated. "I cut through the alley. And there he was. And he grabbed me. And—"

"Skyler grabbed you?" Emily whispered.

"Not Skyler. It was…" Samantha stopped and then hearing a familiar voice crying from somewhere deep inside, quickly continued. "I didn't see the man. He pinned me. I couldn't move. He was too big and heavy. I couldn't move. His belt was around my neck. It was hard to breathe. I couldn't move. I thought I was going to die. I might have passed out. He raped me." Samantha sobbed. She wrapped her arms around her waist, and rocked back and forth. She couldn't look at Emily, she couldn't tell her the name of the man or the threats Skyler and Greg had made at her birthday party.

"My God," Emily said. "Samantha, did you tell the police? Why didn't you tell your parents? Or me? We all would have helped you. Sam, you have to report it; give the police a description. What if he comes after you again or rapes someone else?"

"This is exactly why I didn't tell you." Samantha stood. Started slamming things back into the picnic basket. "I knew you'd take over and start—"

Emily took hold of Samantha's wrist. "Sam. It's okay. I will never tell anyone. Never."

"I know." Samantha sank onto the blanket next to Emily. "I'm sorry I didn't tell you, but I just couldn't. It was so awful. Too awful to believe. Too awful to talk about. It still is. I just want to go away to college and forget."

"I still don't understand what Skyler had to do with anything."

"He was there at the door in the morning. I looked so bad—bruised, and I was shaking, and I just sort of blurted it out."

"But Skyler is an attorney. Why didn't he take you to the police?"

"You don't understand. I was hysterical. I had taken a shower and cleaned off all the evidence. And he said it would be just my word against the attacker. He said my parents—the media would have had a field day with the story. I didn't want my parents to be disgraced."

"Samantha, this doesn't make any sense. Why would

they be upset with you? You were the victim."

"I took the shortcut through the alley. I wasn't supposed to be in the alley. They always told me to stay away from the alley. It was my fault."

Emily rubbed her face.

"I'm sorry," Samantha whispered.

"You have nothing to be sorry for. It wasn't your fault. But, you should have—I mean I wish you would have— told me. I would have found a way to help you."

"There wasn't anything anyone could have done." Samantha wiped her face. "It's over, and I just want to forget about it."

"Were you tested at least? Are you all right, really? What about AIDS?"

Samantha tried to calm herself, so she could reassure her friend.

"Yes. I had an AIDS test right after it happened, and I went for another one last week. Out of town. They say I'm fine. But I'm going to go for another in six months, just to make sure."

"Why is Skyler still calling you? What does he want?"

"He started calling and checking on me, and he even got me out of the house a few times at first, right after it happened. He got possessive." Samantha paused, studying her friend's face, and then added, "He's worried the guy will come back." Samantha was sad she couldn't tell her friend the whole truth. "But he's just too intense."

"Really? I got that from the tone of voice you used

when he called," Emily said.

Samantha turned up a corner of her mouth. "Yeah, I guess I was a little bitchy to him. Okay, a lot bitchy. But the guy deserves it. He won't leave me alone."

"Just tell him to leave you alone—or else." Emily waggled her fist in the air. "He knows all about stalking laws."

"I've tried to get through to him," Samantha said.

"Try harder. Try again."

"He just doesn't listen. It's the lawyer in him. Just like our fathers. They must teach it in law school. Skyler has his opinion, his side of the argument, his needs. He won't listen to me. What I think or want isn't important."

"We'll make him listen," Emily said defiantly.

"No, you can't. You promised. I don't want to make him mad. He really means well. Besides, we're leaving on Sunday for college. What's a few more days?"

"I won't tell anyone," Emily said. "Just swear you'll tell me everything. Swear you'll tell me if he doesn't leave you alone?"

"I swear, Emily; I'll tell you. Just please don't say anything to anyone. I just couldn't bear anyone else to know."

Samantha hadn't lied. She just hadn't told the whole truth. She couldn't tell her friend the rest; she was clear about that. She didn't want to put either one of them in any danger. She'd be gone in a few days, and then it wouldn't matter; it would be all over. It would all be behind her.

* * * *

Samantha and Emily talked the sun down and enjoyed the brilliance of the evening sky. They had so many things to catch up on. Real thoughts and dreams. Feelings they hadn't shared with anyone else; feelings they couldn't share with anyone else.

The magnificent sunset and serious conversation marked a new beginning for the girls. Tired, talked-out, in-sync with nature's silence, a stronger pact between them, they strolled up to the house. The lights had been turned on in every room.

CHAPTER 20

The trip to Michigan was the longest drive Samantha had ever made by herself. It boosted her confidence. Settled in the bottom bunk of the small dormitory bed, she looked at the initials carved into the hard wood over the years. She wondered who they were, what their lives were like now, and if their spirits would bring her luck.

Waking up Monday morning, she felt truly liberated. She tossed off her nightshirt and pulled on an oversized green-and-white football jersey her brothers had given her for Christmas. She wanted to shed the bad clutter of the past and start over.

The campus was beautiful. She was grateful she had a third-floor room. Not only did she have an expansive view of the grounds, but she already felt safe there.

It was a long hike to carry in all of her boxes, and she had a few more to carry up. Her room was at the end of the hall, more private than the others, and a bit larger. She yawned at the maze of boxes she'd piled into the small open area between furniture. Time to find her way to the cafeteria and a large mug of coffee.

Samantha felt lucky she was let in last night, since the dorm didn't officially open until this morning. The handsome Resident Assistant she had awoken just a few hours earlier, told her that traditionally the dorms didn't open until Monday morning, except for the RAs—as she learned they were called—since they had the task of settling everyone in. Fortunately, he already knew the room assignments for the entire dorm and was either too tired or too nice to turn her away.

Samantha would do something to thank him later for helping her unload most of her things. He was so kind, and she'd felt at ease the instant he spoke. John Scott. Even his name had a nice ring to it. It was simple, yet poetic.

Where was the RA for her floor? She stepped out of her room and looked down the long hallway, tucked her key into her back pocket, and headed out to search for the cafeteria.

It wasn't hard to find. She followed the aroma of food and the trail of people. Although everyone ignored her, she felt part of college and the dorm already. She didn't want to feel visible, or even be visible. She wanted to be left alone in her new cocoon to make her metamorphosis without criticism. So far, everything was as she'd imagined, as she had hoped. She grabbed a tray and filled it. Then she headed to the drink bar and grabbed orange juice and coffee.

It had been a long time since she'd actually thought favorably about eating. She sat and removed the heavy, glazed plates from the tray. A newspaper sat on the seat next to hers. *The State News.* How cool. The university had its own newspaper. She lifted it curiously and smelled its freshly inked pages.

Suddenly she felt a firm hand on her shoulder, and she stiffened. Every nerve froze.

"Hey, first you wake me out of a deep sleep, then you work me to death, and now you steal my paper? What's a guy to do with you?"

The deep voice frightened her until she placed the face and voice together. Samantha saw the Tootsie Roll-brown eyes of the Resident Assistant.

"John, you startled me. I didn't mean to take your paper. I mean, I didn't know it belonged to anyone. Where can I buy one?"

"You're fine. You look like you've seen a ghost. I didn't mean to break your concentration. I'm just kidding about the paper." John set his tray down across from hers. "The paper's free. The State News is delivered to every dorm early every day. This is the first one of the semester."

He was so casual. So confident.

"Can I join you?" he said.

"Sure. I'm actually glad you found me. You're the only one I know, and I hate to eat alone."

He took his seat. "Has your roommate arrived?"

"No. I'm eager to meet her."

"You'll make lots of friends. Would you like me to introduce you around?"

"No," Samantha said, with more force than she'd intended.

"I'm sorry. I didn't mean to imply you couldn't make friends on your own. I thought I could give you a head start. Sometimes it's not as easy to make friends as it should be," John said.

"I didn't mean to snap at you." Samantha paused. "If I meet too many people right away, I might not study."

"Oh, I get it. That's smart. Most freshmen don't think like that. Every term, I know people who are placed on academic probation. I admire your commitment." He coffee-toasted her.

Samantha liked John. He was so easygoing. He seemed trustworthy. Maybe after today, when the dorm was filled, she wouldn't ever see him again. Surely he had a lot of friends. She needed to be careful. She couldn't afford to be fooled again.

Lost in her own thoughts, she half-listened to John answer her question about the process of dropping and adding classes.

"Not hungry? Dorm food grows on you. If you want I'll show you a few restaurants where the food is good but cheap," John said.

"That'd be awesome," she said. "It's getting late, and I need to organize my room. My roommate will hate me if she sees my mess. Thanks for sitting with me."

John grinned. "Let me know if you need any more help moving boxes."

"I will," Samantha said. She flashed her best southern smile.

Samantha hadn't felt elated in months. It was an unusual feeling for her.

Back in her room, she kicked off her flats and flung herself onto the stiff bunk bed. Staring up, she laughed at the coils staring back at her and imagined stars hanging from them. This was her new world. With closed eyes she pictured John. She replayed John's strong, comforting voice with his Michigan accent.

She couldn't wait to tell Emily about him. Even if she never saw him again. She'd get out of bed in a few minutes.

Instead, she fell into a deep sleep. Samantha felt her body being lowered down, down, down, into quiet darkness. No faces, no music. Nothing in the darkness. It was still and peaceful.

The door flung open with a crash. She jerked up just as the second of her stacked boxes hit the floor. A small figure stood in center of the room.

"Oh, I'm sorry," the strange girl said. "Are you Samantha?"

"Yes. Melissa?" Samantha looked out the window. It was getting dark. How long had she slept? "Sorry I meant to finish unpacking before you arrived." Her new

Apple Watch showed 5:57 p.m.

"Everyone calls me Missy. I'm going to eat before I empty my car. Do you wanna join me?"

"Sure. Let me just wash up. It'll only take a second."

Missy already felt like someone Samantha could get along with. She wanted to learn more about her.

"Samantha?" Missy knocked on the bathroom door. "Phone call."

"Really?" It's probably Emily.

Missy handed Samantha the phone. Samantha took it into the bathroom. "Hello?"

"So, you finally made it." The hoarse, angry response made her shake so hard she was afraid she'd drop the phone.

"And you didn't call, didn't text. I've waited three days. Didn't you miss me?" Skyler sounded irate.

Samantha breathed deeply and tried to remain calm. She hadn't given anyone her dorm phone number. "I haven't called anyone."

"I had to call the campus operator to find you. You had no intention of giving me your number."

His cross-examination voice pierced her. "I didn't have time." She worried her new roommate might overhear.

"Don't lie. You didn't miss me, either. Maybe I should come up there and remind you of just how close we really are."

Samantha didn't want that. "Sorry. Really. I did miss you." She bit her lip.

"Save it. You're a liar. Every word: a lie. Who's with you in your room?"

"My roommate," Samantha whispered, then quickly added, "She answered the phone."

"And who else?"

"No one." Samantha's voice was void of emotion. Everything she'd felt earlier was gone, stolen. In one call, Skyler poisoned her happiness, her place, her new beginning.

"No cute men?"

John Scott's face flashed in her imagination. "No," Samantha said. Uncontrollable streams of tears rolled down her cheeks.

"Do not ever lie to me."

"I'm not."

"So where are you off to?"

"Dinner in the cafeteria, then unpacking with my roommate."

"I have ways to find out if you lie to me. Call you later. Be sure to answer the phone yourself." Skyler ended the call.

Samantha straightened up her hair and makeup. What would she say to Missy? Opening the door, she avoided Missy's face. But Melissa didn't even ask about the phone call. Walking side by side down the hallway with Missy, Samantha felt that old feeling of helplessness she'd run away from. Relieved she didn't have to speak, she listened to Melissa's chatter.

When they set their filled trays on the laminated cafeteria table and sat down, Melissa paused briefly. "You haven't said a word. Are you looking for someone?"

Geez. Samantha didn't want to explain John. At least not yet. "I was looking around to see where that laughing is coming from."

Missy looked around the large room. "I don't hear it. You must have really good hearing."

"You don't hear that? It's so loud, how can you not hear it? It sounds like it's at our table," Samantha said, turning around to be sure no one was standing behind her. Turning back to a perplexed Missy, Samantha decided not to pursue the issue. She picked up a carrot from her salad plate and bit into it, hard, hoping the crunching noise would drown out the laughing. It didn't. Samantha widened her eyes. Her ears were on alert. Her senses amplified. She twisted around again. No one was behind her.

And then the laughing disappeared. Had it ever been there? Was she going crazy? Samantha stared at Missy eating contently, smiling and nodding at everyone who passed their table.

Samantha picked at her food. She wished Missy would hurry. She didn't want to be rude and return to their room without alone.

"So, are you unpacked?" a deep voice said.

"Hi," Samantha said. John grinning with a full tray in his hands. Glad for the reprieve from her thoughts,

Samantha responded in kind to his friendly grin. "No, I was bad. I fell asleep."

"Can I join you?" John asked.

"Sure," Samantha said. She stiffened aware he'd chosen the chair next to her. Her heartbeat raced in reaction to his nearness.

"Hi, I'm John," he said, grinning at Missy.

"I'm Missy, Samantha's roommate."

Samantha felt her cheeks pink. "Sorry, I should have introduced you. You caught me off guard," Samantha said, her smile focused on John, intuitively sending Missy the clear message he was hers.

John's presence distracted the girls from learning more about each other and focused them on questions related to the dorm and the campus. John held their attention with stories and introduced them to several students who passed by their table. By the time they decided to get back to their room the cafeteria had emptied and tables were being cleared and set for breakfast.

Samantha looked at her watch and gasped. "Oh, my God. It can't be almost nine."

"What's the hurry? You don't have any homework yet," John said.

"I promised I'd call my parents. I haven't called them since I arrived. By now they've probably called the state police."

"You said you have brothers in school. I'm betting your parents know what it's like to settle into a dorm and meet new people. You'll see, they'll understand," John said.

"I've got to go. See you later," Samantha said barely listening to his response or noticing Missy following her rapid gait.

* * * *

Skyler sat at his desk. Just over three hours since he'd talked with Samantha. Where was she? He'd been more than clear. He rubbed his hands over his neck and dug his nails into his skull at his hairline in agitation. He pounded her number again. Continuous dead ringing in her room. Her voice mail on her cell. His eyes focused on the corner of the outline of the closing argument he had worked on for hours. What would keep her away from her phones for three hours? He'd see to it that never happened again. She was his. She owed him. He owned her.

A dark sinister smile emerged. It gave him private pleasure. What would her punishment be this time? He rubbed the day's thick stubble on his face with fierceness. His gold and silver Rolex watch clocked the passage of fifteen more minutes. Time to dial again.

* * * *

Samantha grabbed her key from her back pocket, fit it into the lock, and tensed hearing the phone ringing.

She knew who was at the other end of the line. Her chest felt heavy. Her heart beat fiercely. She began to perspire. Samantha dropped the key. Missy quickly bent down and picked it up.

"Are you all right? You look pale. Sit down with your head between your knees," Missy commanded. "I'll open the door."

In an instant both girls were in the room. Samantha plopped her body onto her bed. Missy answered the phone.

"Samantha, it's your mother," Missy said, walking the receiver over to the bed.

"Samantha, how are you, dear? How do you like it there?"

"It's great, Mom. I've been busy unpacking and meeting people. How did you get my number?"

"Why, Skyler, of course. He said you called the office and left the number with him earlier and you were fine. I'm sorry we weren't home when you called. It was such a beautiful day, your father finished early, and we spent the afternoon golfing."

"Oh," Samantha said. Damn him. She listened to her mother's chatter and mumbled an occasional bubbly response; why can't he leave me alone? He had no right to call them.

"Your mom sounds nice," Missy said.

Samantha got up from her bed and hung up the phone.

"You look like you're feeling better. I'm going down to my car to get my stuff."

"I'll come down with you and help."

"The way you look? No way. But if you're up to it maybe you could move a few of your boxes so I can move mine in here."

Samantha was relieved she had a few moments to herself. She needed to find a way to not jump every time the phone rang. She decided to change into her sweats and unpack. That would keep her mind occupied for a while.

The boxes felt heavier than when she and John loaded them into the room. She began filling the large chest of drawers with her clothing. The ring from the phone caused her to jump. Picking up the receiver, she anticipated her mother's voice again.

"Hi, Mom. Wha'd you forget to tell me?" Samantha said, dangling the phone between her ear and shoulder allowing her to unzip a black bulky suitcase.

"Wha'd you forget to tell me?" The deep voice responded.

"Oh. Sorry. I thought it was my mother calling again," Samantha said, taking a deep breath, closing her eyes and wishing she hadn't answered the phone.

"No, it's just me. Remember me?" Skyler said intensely. "I've been calling. "Where were you the past three hours?" He grilled her sternly. "And why isn't your cell phone on?"

"I told you we went to the cafeteria for dinner. I left

my cell in the room charging."

"Who is we?"

"Missy and . . ."

"Who else was there?" Skyler said, intentionally cutting her off.

"We got talking and didn't realize it had gotten so late."

"You mean you were flirting with the boys who sat at your table?"

"It was Missy and I," Samantha said.

"Did he ask you out?"

"Who?"

"Don't be coy with me. You know who, the guy who sat with you or was it the guy at the desk?" Skyler paused. "And who were you on the phone with all evening?"

"I wasn't on the phone, except with you and my mother. She said you gave her my number, and I had called you with it. Why did you do that?"

"First little girl, I don't answer to you. Second, your parents were worried. Instead of questioning me, you should thank me for relieving their worry. Now say it. Say thank you, Skyler. Thank you for taking care of me," Skyler said.

"Thank you," Samantha said begrudgingly, immediately feeling the bitter taste of those words.

"You aren't going to tell me who else called, are you? Someone else called. There's someone you haven't told me about," Skyler said.

"Nope. Nobody. I told you already. I can make someone up?" Samantha's voice slipped into sarcastic mode. At least he was miles and miles away. He couldn't touch her. He couldn't hurt her. Relax, relax, she told herself hearing his unrelenting voice.

"So what else?" Skyler said.

"What do you mean?" Samantha asked. Missy bounded through the door, breathless, dropping the large bulky load she had carried.

"Hi, Missy," Samantha turned and said. "Need help?" She hoped Skyler would get the idea she had to get off the phone.

"I take it your roommate returned from the car."

"Uh-huh."

"So tell me, what else is going on? What are your plans? What's on the agenda?"

"Nothing. Just school. You know unpacking, getting my schedule together, drops and adds, buying my books. The campus is so large, I have to carry a map with me. And, I'm going to buy a bike." Samantha tried to sound upbeat so Missy wouldn't notice her anxiety.

"If you do, make sure you buy a good lock. You'd better be careful walking around there, especially alone at night."

"I know. That's one thing you don't have to remind me of," Samantha said and bit her lip. She felt the sting in his words: *remember what happens in the dark.* The pain, the blood, the fear, fluttered to the surface.

"Pleasant dreams baby. I'll see you in them," Skyler said.

His voice was soft and sensual and she shivered.

"Bye," Samantha said and clanked the black receiver into its' silver cradle cutting the umbilical cord between them.

"Geez, you get a lot of calls. Was that your boyfriend?" Missy asked, briskly tossing school supplies into her desk.

"No, just a friend. Would you like me to help you with the next load?" Samantha asked, quickly changing the subject. "I have a few of my own left to unload."

"Let's go," Missy said, and turned out of the room.

"Right behind you. Gotta use the bathroom." Closed behind the bathroom door, her hands hard against the stool, she gurgled from the sudden inner surge. Samantha vomited. And then again and again. She reached up and flushed the evidence down. She watched, mesmerized by the swirl of the water that quickly disappeared and returned clear again. She wished everything were that simple.

Missy was on her next load by the time Samantha joined her. Fifteen minutes later they'd emptied their cars and two hours later they'd unpacked and arranged their rooms so they could walk without tripping.

A strong pizza aroma seeped into their room. Missy opened the door announcing she was on party patrol. She promised to return with party plans or pizza and beer. Samantha giggled, but didn't join her, instead, she broke down empty boxes. Punching her knuckles into the cardboard felt powerful. Dissuading Skyler would make her feel even more powerful, but how? One, two, three, she punched down another box. That's it she said out loud. "I'll reply in one to three words and he'll get bored with me."

CHAPTER 21

Lost in the maze of vine-covered brick buildings, Samantha lifted her heavy backpack from her shoulder and set it down onto the soft, leaf-littered grass. She sat next to the bag and studied the campus map she'd torn from the college class catalog. Her class was in a nearby building. Herds of students trailed around her in every direction. She relaunched her backpack, stood in the direction of Bessy Hall and within a few minutes stared at the vine covered building.

Once inside she climbed wide stone stairs. She immediately felt the presence of the millions of students who'd climbed the same steps before her and was elated. What was the fate all those people? She was excited to learn hers.

The building smelled freshly waxed. It was old and austere. Samantha easily found the classroom door that screamed 221 in bold block black numbers. She was early. A few students sat in the aged chairs facing the clean graphite board. Most held *The State News* and were uninterested in her sudden presence. Samantha decided she'd do the same since reading the school newspaper felt like a ritual. She chose a seat in the second row.

Anxious for class to begin she pulled out her textbook and began flipping through the chapters. The classroom was filling up. The room was small, the faces were unfamiliar but each gleaned anticipation like her own. Samantha was comfortable no one knew anything about her. A perfect way to hide from the rest of the world.

Samantha's gaze shot to the doorway when she heard the loud flicker of lights being turned on. John? John. What was John doing here? She studied him. He placed a tattered brown, overstuffed leather briefcase on the professor's desk then grabbed a long white piece of chalk from its front pouch. He turned, without acknowledging her or anyone else, toward the chalkboard and wrote a list of words. Before finishing, he scribbled his name, office hours, and the due date of the first assignment.

When the wall clock displayed exactly ten, John began class by calling roll. He called her name without acknowledgement he knew her. She was puzzled. He was a student. Why was he teaching? Why didn't he tell her he taught? Feverishly she jotted notes of the lecture and was soon consumed in his lecture and class discussion. Samantha was awed by the examples John presented of various writing techniques. She listened carefully as he read a story about what he did last summer. That was their first assignment—to be read in front of the class— five hundred words.

She frowned. It wasn't going to be easy to stay anonymous. Worse yet, she had nothing to write about last summer, certainly nothing she wanted to share in public.

When the class ended, Professor Scott put down the chalk, spanked his hands free from the dust, then watched the students collectively file out of the room. He grinned warmly at Samantha and she returned the smile.

"I can't believe you're my professor. I thought you were just a student getting your Master's degree," Samantha said. She stood at his table in the now-emptied classroom.

"You never asked. English Master's. I'm not really a professor; I'm a TA: teacher's assistant. Teaching helps pay my tuition and bills; being an RA lets me live in the dorm for free. I've been accepted to law school. I can begin in two years, but I'm on the waiting list to get in sooner. I need to save money, and as long as I'm still enrolled in school, I don't have to pay back my student loans. English has always been my first love and law my first interest, so I have the best of all worlds."

"I need to call you Professor from now on," Samantha said, fidgeting with her backpack, unsure of what to say next. She was impressed with John. She liked him more and more with each new facet he revealed. He was so together—not like anyone else she'd ever met in her age group. John laughed and Samantha noted his pronounced dimples. A woman would kill for dimples like that. *I can't believe he's my professor.*

"John will be fine. Professor is too formal. Each time a student refers to me as professor, I want to turn around and look to see who they're talking to. Can I walk back to the dorm with you?" he asked.

"I have another class. Natural Science, I think. Astronomy," Samantha said, her eyes focused on her schedule and map.

John's eyes focused on the map she held. "Two buildings down. Exit and make a left and you're there."

"Thank you. I can't wait until I learn my way around."

"It doesn't take long. See you later?" John said.

"Sure," Samantha said and turned toward the door.

"How about dinner?" he called after her.

"Dinner?" she asked, and twisted toward him.

"We both have to eat. I'll pick you up from your room, and we can eat at the cafeteria, or we can eat at one of the restaurants on Grand River. Your choice."

"Cafeteria," She said. Her anxious heartbeat seemed too loud. Had she just made a date, or was he just being friendly?

"Great. See you around 5:30. Okay?"

Samantha nodded and left for her next class. Thank goodness the building was near, she thought. She loved college, even if it was only her first day.

She thought back as she walked. First days in high school had been difficult and tense, until she figured out how many friends she had in each class, and which teachers she liked and hated. College was different. Everything was her choice. Her happiness did not depend on how well she fit in and how popular she was. No one even noticed what she wore. She took a deep breath excited for her next class.

* * * *

Samantha was elated. Her classes for the day were finished. The campus was beautiful and she was easily learning the campus, just like John said. She'd have lunch, buy the rest of her books, and study until John picked her up. Back in her dorm room, she pulled her books out of her backpack, lined them across her desk then heard the sound she now hated—the phone.

"Hello?" She said, momentarily distracted by the mess Missy had left strewn around the room.

"Where have you been?" Skyler's accusing voice demanded.

"Class. Where else?" Samantha said. Sarcasm dripped onto her words.

"I don't know. You tell me."

"I had English and Nat Sci. I came right back to the dorm to eat lunch, tackle my homework and then I have a few more books to buy."

"So, who'd you meet?"

"No one. It takes almost all the time I have in between classes to make it to the next building for class. This campus is huge. I need to buy a bike." Samantha's words sprinted from her mouth. She knew if she hesitated in her speaking, Skyler would become accusatory. She hated his calls. She hated his voice. She hated him.

"Do you miss me?" Skyler said.

Samantha felt nausea rising hearing his playful voice. She winced and grabbed her stomach. She visualized him winking at her. It gave her chills. She swallowed hard before responding, "Of course." Her faced winced feeling the bitter pill of his voice.

"I need your class schedule. I don't want to call when you're not in. I think your roommate dislikes me."

"She hates answering the wall phone. It's across the room."

"Give me her schedule, too."

"Okay." Samantha sighed. Agreeing was better than fighting or worrying he'd ask her parents.

"I'll call you tonight."

Samantha understood he intended to call her room, not her cell, and she'd better be there. What was she thinking when she agreed to dinner with John? How would she explain the urgency to return to her room? How could she explain Skyler's threats, demeaning comments, and that she was afraid of him?

Samantha hurried to the cafeteria. She had so many things to do, but she didn't dare miss lunch if dinner would be cut short. And, the promise to her mother that she'd send the punched meal card at the end of the month, to prove she was eating. The meal card had to get punched, regardless of what she ate. Claustrophobia infiltrated her from the anxiety of Skyler and her parents and she'd barely been on campus a week.

The plus was that John lived in the dorm. She didn't have to go far to see him. Having him as a friend was a comfort to her. She had to hide John from Skyler and Skyler from John.

Samantha spent the rest of the afternoon studying. Hearing her old clock Minnie, ding, she realized John was late. Maybe he wasn't coming. Samantha stiffened hearing the door open and relaxed at the sight of Missy clambering inside.

"Hi, Samantha. Are you going down to eat?"

"Soon. You?"

"Yeah. Join me. I've got to eat early because of my night class."

"No. I'm not really hungry. I'll see you after your class." Samantha breathed relief knowing Missy wouldn't be in the room when John picked her up. She didn't want her to know. What if Skyler asked Missy questions? She shuddered. Relax, relax, she chanted, taking deep breaths, reassuring herself everything would be all right; she'd find a way.

A knock on her door struck just when the wall phone began to ring. Oh God, her mind screamed, what now? In seconds, she answered the door with her fingers to her lips, indicating to John he needed to be silent.

"I'll just be a minute," she whispered. John sat at her

desk and waited.

Samantha picked up the receiver.

"Hi. I'm leaving the office and decided to check in. What's up?"

Skyler's voice was casual, but hearing it caused her heart to thump. She clutched the springy cord nervously. She tried to avoid John's studying eyes but kept returning to them.

"I'm on my way to the cafeteria to eat."

"With Missy?"

"She ate earlier. She has a night class." She mentally kicked herself for not lying, for not leading him to believe Missy was waiting for her in the cafeteria.

"So, you'll be alone all night? Who's coming to visit you while she's gone? Surely you've had offers?"

"I've got to study. I've already got tons of homework. You should see the syllabus I have from just two classes."

"Good, that'll keep you out of trouble. So, you still haven't told me."

"Haven't told you what?" Samantha asked. She'd forgotten what to defend herself against.

"C'mon, Samantha, you're playing games with me. You're just stalling for time."

"No. Really, I don't recall. Can't you just ask me again?" Samantha pleaded. Droplets of nervous sweat dripped into her bra. She prayed her new Spartan sweatshirt wouldn't reveal her leaky body and the steam that rose when Skyler's vexatious voice screamed into the receiver.

"Who are you eating with?" Skyler's impatience blared through the receiver.

"No one."

"I'll know if you're lying. I'm going to ask Missy."

"That's fine."

"Did she tell you I called earlier?"

"No."

"You said you saw her. How is it she didn't tell you?"

"I don't know, but she didn't." Samantha was suffocating, drowning in the murk of Skyler's questions and accusations. Would it ever end? She had to get off the phone.

"You tell Missy to give you your messages from now on. Sweet dreams, baby."

"Bye."

Samantha ignored John's tilted questioning head and grinned. "I'm ready."

"You don't like whomever your caller was very much, do you?" John asked gently. He didn't move.

"Why do you say that?" Samantha asked and motioned him out of her room so they could begin the walk to the cafeteria. She didn't want to risk any more phone calls in front of him.

"You were fidgeting with the cord the whole time you were talking. You had an expression on your face as if you were in pain," John said. "You were a nervous wreck, and I'd bet all the money I've saved for law school on that," John said. He stopped walking down the hall and frowned. "Do you have a boyfriend you haven't told me about?"

"No. That was just a family friend who works for my father and feels compelled to check up on me." Samantha started walking. "My parents go away a lot, and I think he got it into his head that he'd impress the boss through his daughter."

"Weird. But if you're okay with that and if that's all it is. Based on the expression on your face while you were talking to him he doesn't seem like a friend you want," John said.

* * * *

Skyler exited the firm angered by a picture of Samantha in the arms of another man was cemented in his core. Dejected and cheated upon his jaw tightened. She would pay for her illicit behavior. They were bound together. She was his. He would be pleasured by her as he pleased. She owed him.

A life for a life. He grinned. She'd learn that. His twisted face smiled back at him in his rear-view mirror while he waited at a long red light.

Hearing an engine racing beside him, Skyler turned curiously at the car stopped next to him. A pretty blonde combed her bobbed hair with her fingers. He met her gaze and winked at her, she flashed sparkling white teeth. Skyler thunderously revved his engine and mouthed "Take me on now." He was in the mood for a race. He'd win. His green Jag against her red Camaro. He had the greater horsepower, the greater control; and the greatest motivation.

Winning. It was all about winning. And he was a winner, he revved his engine, and when the light turned green, he floored the pedal and laughed at the Camaro many paces behind him. He might have to pull over and show her what he excels at best.

CHAPTER 22

Samantha awoke to now familiar sounds that seeped through the old dorm's thin walls: slamming doors, loud whispering voices, and alarms that dragged on for what seemed hours. She hated her early morning classes, despite only having an eight o'clock class Tuesdays and Thursdays. The morning dormitory noises confirmed Skyler was miles away, but his continued midnight calls and texts disturbed her sleep. She felt tired all the time. Today she needed to nap after lunch, she decided. Dragging herself out of her warm, soft sheets she glared into the mirror above the dresser. Dark circles. Stretching her sluggish body, she turned back at the unrumpled top bunk. She'd hated telling Missy her boyfriend couldn't sleep in their room. The result was that Missy spent most nights in her boyfriend's dorm. It gave her the creeps to even think about them sleeping together with her in the room.

Missy hadn't been happy, but had accepted it. She kept a packed duffle bag of toiletries and clothes that she traded out regularly. Her boyfriend's phone numbers were tacked on the message board next to the door with explicit orders to call her immediately if her parents phoned, and a list of excuses she could use followed.

Samantha loved looking out the large window in the tiny room while she stretched to wake up. The vibrant blush of maples and oaks erupted colors in the last days of warmth, pressing the sun exquisitely into each perfect leaf. The trees at home didn't change this soon. She was delighted Michigan was so different. She looked forward to the cold and snow. She craved change. She craved the unusual, the exciting, the new. Like the trees, she wanted to shed her problems, and by spring, be a whole new person.

Just as she threw her wool blazer over her shoulders and unlocked the door, the wall phone rang. Oh God— Skyler. Can't he leave me alone?

Samantha started through the door, but froze. She had to answer it. He wouldn't like it if she wasn't there. He'd accuse her of not having spent the night in her bed, even though he had called at midnight. Reluctantly, she answered the phone.

"Hi, Sam. Did you sleep well?"

Skyler's chipper voice caught her off guard. His voice was very different from the angry, accusatory one she heard last night.

"Yes. Fine. On my way to grab a cup of coffee and go to class," Samantha said. Her voice was hurried, trying to sound rushed.

"What are you doing this weekend?"

"This weekend?"

"Tom called and said he had extra tickets to the Michigan versus Michigan State game. He wants me to join him and Darcey. I thought you might join us."

"Football?"

"Of course."

"I'm not into sports. I've had too much homework."

"So you're refusing to go?" Skyler said sternly.

"I didn't think I—"

"Look, get your homework done if you have to stay up all night. I'll arrive late Friday night. I'm staying with Tom. We'll pick you up for breakfast." Skyler said.

"Fine," Samantha said meekly, hearing the gruff orders. He nerves chilled.

"Your parents are thrilled I'm going to see you. They expect a report. We won't disappoint them, right?" Skyler said.

Skyler's dark laugh before he hung up drummed a headache into Samantha. She moved her fingers inside the small zipped pocket in her backpack and fisted a few pills. She walked briskly into the cafeteria.

Samantha grabbed a gray cafeteria tray, a disposable coffee cup, a bottle of water, and a toasted bagel. Her ears were ringing, buzzing. A soft lull of noise. Her head began to throb. She untwisted the bottle of water and swallowed her pills. She heard laughter. Loud, shrill, irritating laughter. Where was it coming from? Who would make such a sound? She looked around and bit into her cream cheese covered warm bagel. The laughter scared her. It was too close to her, yet there wasn't anyone there at all.

Samantha wanted to run all the way to class, but her legs carried her back the solitude and safety of her quiet room.

Letting her backpack thud onto the floor, she vehemently tossed off her clothes. Perspiration leaked from every inch of her body. She craved another shower, yet she didn't feel stable enough to stand. The laughter faded when she opened the window for fresh air. She placed her bed sheets over her head and let the pills work.

Her mind floated. Behind closed eyes, Samantha studied the sea of blackness. She wanted to find a friendly face, she wanted to find John. But she couldn't see him. She followed the music and the sharp laughter. Silhouettes of faces were around her, hiding. She tried to capture the pieces to lay them side by side and fit them into a picture. Desperately she tried to make sense of what she saw. But, she couldn't. There were no ears. Where were the ears? Shadows spun and some looked familiar. Cold clammy strong fingers reached out and grabbed her shoulder. It caught her, grabbing her hair first. She ran and ran, but she didn't move. She was frozen; her body, her voice. She couldn't scream. She couldn't breathe. She began to shake as she felt it press against her.

Samantha awoke in terror, her body warm and moist,

her throat parched. She craved a drink, but she was too disorientated to get up. She clenched the sheets, slowly orienting herself to reality. Samantha existed on the fine line between reality and fantasy.

A few minutes later, she climbed out of her sheets and grabbed a diet cola from the inside door of the miniature refrigerator. Popping it open, she guzzled the cold liquid, barely stopping to breathe. It felt good. She wiped sticky drips from the corners of her mouth and released a loud belch. It was almost noon. Missing her morning classes was missing more than she wanted to. Vowing not to miss any more classes, no matter what, Samantha again heard the phone beckon. Fearfully, she answered it.

"Yes?"

"Why aren't you in class?"

"I took a nap. I'm not feeling well. I'm getting ready to go to my next class."

"Who is there with you?"

"No one."

"C'mon. You can tell me."

Samantha knew Skyler was angry. She didn't know how to make him stop. She answered each question, with more determination, until he let up. She knew he'd never believe her. She knew she had no choice but to answer him.

"I told you, I wasn't feeling well. I'm alone. I'm going to get something to eat and then go to class."

"Who are you walking with?"

"No one. I'm riding my new bike."

"I'm on my way to the office. Just won a not guilty verdict on all counts against Mr. Castriano who is now turning all his legal business to the firm. That should get me some real respect around the office."

"Congratulations," Samantha said.

"You're just like your father. You really don't care, do you?" Skyler growled.

"I do; he does, too. Dad always says how smart you are. I don't understand why you're upset," Samantha said. She was confused.

"You will understand very soon. I'll call you later."

Samantha plopped the receiver onto the silver wall holder as if it were poison. She couldn't get upset. She simply chanted relax, relax, took deep breaths then retreated the cloistered warm spray of the shower.

* * * *

Samantha sat through class watching slides of art and listening to the professor explain periods of art. The white rectangle of screen flashed Renoir, VanGogh, then countless other artists. She typed it all into her computer. The computer kept her organized. It was the only friend she had, except for John. He was a good friend. She feared each touch to her hand or her shoulder, and when he sat too close. She truly liked him but couldn't help it when he got too close and she cringed. She wanted things to be different.

The class bell rang, and streams of students poured out of the building. Everyone was so focused on themselves, no one cared about her. No one questioned her. But, she decided, it was time she found someone she could question about the law. But who, she wondered as she pedaled toward her dorm. If she declared her major as pre-law, maybe her counselor could give her a mentor or answer some questions.

Suddenly, hearing the hollow sound of scraping metal, Samantha was thrust forward. She flung over the handlebars and landed on the grass, confused, mangled into pain. And, blackness set in.

"Are you all right?" a concerned voice asked.

Samantha's eyes fluttered open. "What?" Samantha asked. She was confused, why was this dark eyed young man peering over her?

"Are you all right?" the voice repeated.

"I . . ." Samantha paused. She looked around. Her new emerald green bike was on the ground, tangled with an unfamiliar blue bike and her legs were between them. She lifted her right leg and the boy separated and lifted the bikes to free her.

"I'm sorry about your bike. I think they'll both be okay, though," he said. He set the bikes aside.

"Let's see if you can walk. Grab my arm."

Samantha put out her hand, fluttered her legs then straightened them before standing and shifting her weight onto them. She felt bruised, but she was stable. "I'm fine," Samantha said.

The dark eyed, auburn-haired student, with the long ponytail held her bike out for her and lifted her backpack toward her. "I think your backpack saved your fall."

"I'm sure I'll be black and blue in the morning," Samantha tried to laugh.

"You should go over to Olin Health Center and get those scrapes checked. Can I follow you there?"

"No," Samantha said alarmed. "I'm fine. Really, thanks."

"I feel terrible," he said. "I should've been paying more attention."

"No, it was my fault. I was distracted," Samantha said, with as much composure as she could find.

"Let's call it even," the man said, his voice still filled with concern.

"Thank you." Samantha secured her backpack then climbed onto the bike. "I've got to get studying." Her feet pushed the pedals and she sailed away.

A few minutes later Samantha was at the bike rack. She looked over her bike then locked it in, and headed for her room. She took off her blood-and-grass-stained clothes and threw them across the room onto the overflowing clothesbasket. Grabbing a few cotton balls from a glass jar and a small brown plastic bottle of hydrogen peroxide, she wiped over the scratches on her face and arms. It was too early to see any bruises, but from the aches and stiffness she already felt, she knew she'd be black and blue by morning. "Time for homework," she said out loud in the empty room. She organized her notes, read her next assignments in each class, then sent e-mails to her brothers and parents. It was almost time to meet John in the cafeteria.

Samantha slammed her books closed with a loud thud in the too silent room. She felt accomplished having been constructive.

Standing at the bathroom sink, she ran the water as warm as she could tolerate it and splashed it over her face. She switched to cold and began splashing. A loud pounding on her dorm room filtered in. She grabbed a towel, turned off the faucet and panicked the door would reveal an early arriving Skyler. It would be just like him to arrive a night early.

Unlatching the door to the beaming face of John, she forced herself to not fling her arms around him in appreciation.

"Hungry?"

"Famished. Sorry, I lost track of the time. I'll be ready in a minute."

"Are you limping?" John asked.

Samantha frowned seeing John's downcast eyes inspecting her legs. "I had a little bike accident and then sat too long at my desk studying."

John frowned. "What happened?"

"I was riding on the bike path and crashed into some

guy. To tell you the truth, I never saw him coming—I'm not even sure who was at fault. Thankfully we didn't break our bones or our bikes, we're just bruised."

"Were you checked at Olin Health Center?"

"No. I'm fine."

"You should get checked. You could have a hairline fracture. That leg seems too sore to just be bruised."

Samantha smiled and tried to stand straight. "I promise, if I feel worse or if it swells, I'll go in the morning."

"Your face is scratched and you have a bit of swelling. You might need a tetanus shot." He placed his right hand on Samantha's shoulder.

Samantha's body stiffened.

John removed his hand. "Will you sit down and let me look at your leg?" John placed his fingers softly under her chin, forcing her eyes to his.

"No. I'm fine, really. You can look later if I feel worse. Hell, I'll let you drive me to Olin if we can just go down and eat." Samantha laughed and stepped outside her room.

John stepped behind her.

The phone rang just as the door was about to close. "Do you want to get that?" John asked.

Samantha nodded and returned inside the room hoping it was her mother when she said hello.

"Hi. How was your bike ride to class?"

A fourth call today. Damn. Samantha bit the inside of her cheek then answered. "Class was fine. I'm on my way to eat dinner."

"I'm counting on you to be homework-free and with me at the game."

"Got it."

"Have you met anyone interesting?"

"No one."

"What's on the agenda tomorrow?"

"I have classes. I had a small bike accident after class today, so I might go to the student health center to get my leg x-rayed."

"Are you hurt?"

"A few bruises and scrapes, and my leg is a little stiff."

"Oh, so you just want to see those young physician residents. Isn't that true?"

"No. I never even thought about that. It didn't even enter my mind."

Skyler cut her off, his voice showing his agitation as he ran his words stiffly together. "I think you were flirting with the guy who hit you and the two of you were so distracted you crashed? You just had to flirt, didn't you."

"I didn't even notice there was another bike near me before we crashed."

"So, it was a guy. You hid that little factoid from me."

"I didn't, I—"

"And, you give him your phone number."

"No. It wasn't like that."

"Then why didn't you tell me about it right away? Why did I have to pry it from you?"

"You didn't; I just didn't think that—"

Skyler shouted into the phone in a crazed, ruthless voice, "You are lying. You are a liar."

"If you would quit cutting me off, I could explain—"

The phone clicked off cutting real fear into Samantha. He would arrive in thirty-six hours. Would he show his anger when they were with Tom and Darcey? Samantha met John's eyes and realized his stare was one of quiet disbelief.

"Who was that?" he asked softly.

"Skyler, the family friend I told you about." Samantha said lightly.

"More like family pest," John muttered.

"I'm hungry," Samantha said. She walked out of the room, motioned John to accompany her and then locked the door.

"Why don't you tell him to stop calling? He calls you every day. It's eerie. He's like your personal stalker. Something just isn't right about him."

"He works with my dad. I don't want to upset my parents, or I would." Samantha wished she could run into the bathroom and never come out.

"Friend? My God. I heard him screaming from across the room. Did he accuse you of causing the accident?" John's cheeks reddened. It was clear he wasn't just concerned but angered.

"My being hurt upset him. He'd warned me about the hazards of biking on campus."

"Samantha, he's not a friendly guy. I have a bad feeling about his motives." John's thick brows knitted. "You'd tell me if you were in trouble, wouldn't you?"

"Of course," Samantha said, and avoided John's stare. "If he gets out of control, I promise, I'll let you know." But could she? John absorbed her and imprinted his strength, loyalty, steadfastness and alliance into her.

CHAPTER 23

Samantha dressed slowly. She loathed Skyler's arrival. He was invading her safe space. She didn't want him touching anything in her room, touching her. Chills raced through her, chasing the burning heat she'd felt moments before. She closed her eyes, concentrated, breathed deeply. Just as she felt some relief, the door flung open and her heart jumped.

"Hi. You're up early," Missy said. "Jack's waiting for me in the cafeteria. Want to join us? I'm here to change for the game. Jack got us great tickets."

"Sorry, I can't join you. I'm going with friends. I haven't seen you for days. How are you?"

"Fine. You look awful. Who won the fight?" Missy asked.

"I got into a biking accident. I'm just bruised and scraped."

"I'm sorry I wasn't here to help you. By the way, that guy you know keeps calling. Seems like every time I run in to pick up a change of clothes he's calling. Can I hang up on him?"

"He's harmless. Friend of my dad's," Samantha said.

"He's rude. Never leaves his name, he just says, 'she knows' and then hangs up." She pointed to a clump of messages pinned into the bulletin board."

"Yeah, I saw them."

"His voice gives me the creeps. And he talks in phrases, almost riddles, instead of sentences."

"I don't like talking to him either."

"The way he talks reminds me of a southern Barnabas Collins. An ancient soap opera that was creepy. *Dark Shadows.* My mother owns every episode. She and my grandmother watched it back in the day. Ever seen it?"

"No. Not my kind of show," Samantha said. She was enjoying Missy's effervescence and the way she wove issues and rambled from one subject to another. It was hard not to like her. Samantha wished she could see more of her.

"This telephone creep isn't your boyfriend is he?"

"Ugh, no way."

"He acts like one. Still calling every night?"

"Yeah. Clearly overly protective."

"He's nosy, too. He asks me all sorts of questions about you. I don't answer them. I just say I haven't seen you. That is what I should say, isn't it?"

Samantha nodded. "That's the truth." Samantha paused. "What'd he ask?"

"Just stuff like: where is she; who's she dating ; who else calls—basic parental interrogation questioning. It's the ultimate mom inquisition." Missy grinned. "If I can get past my mother's questions, I can do it with your Skyler-dude." Missy grabbed her bag. "How do I look?"

"Beautiful. Sorry if I held you up."

"Don't be silly. What are roommates for? See you Sunday night. If my parents call before I get back—"

"Tell them you're at the library," Samantha said. They laughed and Missy bounced out of the room.

Samantha pulled her green Michigan State sweatshirt over a white turtleneck then donned matching sweatpants. They were, after all, attending a football game.

The bold knocking on the door told her Skyler was behind it. She swung the door open and stepped out, purse and jacket in hand. She needed to avoid inviting him inside.

"John?" Samantha tried not to sound surprised. "I'm leaving to go the game." Samantha studied his face, afraid he could hear the escalated pounding of her heart and the worry in her voice.

"Too early to leave. Join me for breakfast? Pleeeze…" John said, playfully.

"I can't. I already have breakfast plans." Samantha hated seeing John's face drop. "You know I like having breakfast with you." She wanted to be soaked up into John's strong brown eyes. She wanted to wrap herself around him and beg him to protect her, to wipe the slate clean. She felt the pounding of her heart migrate directly to her head, triggering instant distress. The pain was deep, sharp, and piercing. She rubbed her temples.

"Sam, it's me. You're not looking well. Do you need to go to Olin?"

"I'm fine."

"You don't look fine. Is something going on?"

Samantha groaned. "If I tell you, you need to leave. Promise?"

"Promise," John said.

"Skyler's in town. He and his brother Tom are picking me up for breakfast. We are going to tailgate parties, then the game. I don't want to go, but I have to."

"Then don't go. Tell him you have too much homework or something. You can't be forced to go."

"I can. I told you, he works for my dad. My parents expect me to be nice to him. He'll tell my parents if I don't go, who knows what he'll say."

"But that's not right. Call your parents and tell them you are behind in your studies."

Samantha knew she had to convince John to leave before Skyler arrived. She feared John's reaction. Rudely, she cut him off, fearing her own safety at the moment more than his hurt feelings. "There's nothing more to explain and you promised you'd leave."

"I'll be in my room most of the day," John said stiffly. "Later, when you can talk, I hope you trust me with the real story. I want to help."

Samantha ushered him away, then returned inside her room directly to the medicine cabinet. She swallowed two pills for her headache. She jumped hearing the locked door knob jiggle. Biting her cheek and taking a deep breath, she opened the door.

"Hey, Babe." Skyler said. He pushed passed her locked the door and stood in the middle of the room. He leaned forward and kissed her cheek, then squeezed her into him. "Give me a real hug like you're excited to see me."

"We'll be late. Where's Tom?" Samantha asked. Distracting Skyler with conversation was her only hope.

"Downstairs waiting with Darcey."

"Who's that?"

"Darcey? You know Darcey, Tom's girlfriend."

"Oh. Oh, yeah," Samantha said, puzzled she didn't remember Tom's girlfriend or ever having met her. She did remember he had a girlfriend. Who had told her? It must've been her mother; but when had they met? Oh well, I can't remember everything, she rationalized, shrugging it off.

"So, where's my hug?"

Reluctantly, Samantha put her arms around Skyler lightly, as if he were a stranger. Skyler squeezed her into him, kissing her tightly pursed lips. His tongue pried open her mouth, and penetrated her deeply.

"Wash off the lipstick off, Sam. You know I don't like it," Skyler ordered. "And get me a cloth as well. You'd better not have gotten any on me."

Quietly, Samantha followed his orders then returned with a half-wet, half dry facecloth.

He wiped his mouth and tossed the cloth onto her desk. "Let's go. There'll be lots of time for us later. Tom thinks I'm leaving tonight, but I'm leaving tomorrow," Skyler said, winking, before putting his arm around Samantha's now jacketed shoulder.

"We'll have a wonderful night together, I promise," Skyler whispered sensually in her ear as they left the room and headed for the car.

When they arrived at Tom's car, Samantha felt her headache getting worse, not better. Thankful she'd brought more pills, she decided she'd take another tablet at the restaurant.

"Hi, Samantha. It's great seeing you again," Tom said, smiling.

She climbed into the back seat with Skyler. "Thanks for inviting me. I know these game tickets were hard to get."

"You remember Darcey, don't you?" Tom said, as he put his arm around his girlfriend and pulled out into the road.

"Of course," Samantha said, gazing at the pretty girl she didn't remember. Perplexed, she tried to think of a question she could ask that would jog her memory about their previous encounter. Listening to their fun-loving conversation and easy laughter, she stared mindlessly at Darcey. Darcey had immediately recognized her. How could she have forgotten Darcey? Tom and Darcey talked and giggled like one working unit. Samantha could feel they were part of each other's flesh. Samantha remembered Tom, but not remembering someone as vibrant as Darcey, didn't make sense. Had she taken too much medicine that day and zoned out?

Samantha focused on Tom and Darcey, paying close attention to every word. The blaring radio interfered with some of their conversation but she picked up enough to know they were planning the rest of their weekend together. Samantha concentrated so intensely on the couple she failed to see Skyler move closer to her until he grabbed her hand. Weaving his fingers with hers, he used his thumb to caress her. She held her breath and tried not to wince. Skyler moved his free hand in between her thighs, slowly moving it up and down her sweatpants.

Samantha stiffened with fright. She sat rigid with a thin, artificial smile on her face. She couldn't make a sound, fearful Tom could see them in the rearview mirror. But Tom never checked the mirror. Tom was so focused on Darcey it was a wonder he found his way to the restaurant, she thought, dismayed his presence wasn't a deterrent to Skyler's behavior. Samantha was relieved when they pulled into the parking lot across from Harper's because Skyler finally removed his hands from her.

Before they were seated, Samantha excused herself and headed for the rest room. With a smile at Tom, Darcey followed her. Closing their respective stall doors, Samantha reached into her purse for her pill case and grabbed a white one with a number three on it. She hoped it worked faster than the pills she'd swallowed earlier. Quickly, she flushed, opened the stall door and went to the sink, washed her hands then cupped them to hold water. She sipped and swallowed the medicine.

"Headache?" Darcey asked, genuinely concerned.

"Yes. I didn't sleep well last night. I'm hoping it doesn't get any worse and ruin the game for me," Samantha said.

"Breakfast might help. Coffee and eggs—caffeine and protein always works for me. I'm really glad you were able to join us."

"Thank you for inviting me."

"Skyler adores you. He asked Tom to get four tickets for the game when we were there over the Fourth."

Samantha watched Darcey speak but felt she saw right through her. Her mind couldn't decipher if is she was really there, if she was real.

"That was nice of Tom." Samantha smiled appreciatively.

"Oh, it's a treat for us. Skyler paid for the tickets and sent us a gift certificate for a really expensive dinner. He's a great guy."

"My parents think so, too," Samantha said, matter-of-factly. She hoped to convey that Skyler was only her friend because of her parents.

"I know there is an age difference between you and Skyler, but I don't think age is important, do you?"

"Skyler is like an uncle to me. I haven't ever thought of him as anything else."

Darcey looked uncomfortable. "I'm sure I just misread things. He does treat you like family," she said.

Samantha nodded. She was too close to tears to use her voice.

"It's going to be a spectacular day," Darcey exclaimed happily. "I can feel it."

Samantha nodded and followed Darcey toward the now-seated men.

Breakfast was almost fun but for the presence of Skyler. Tom was so very different from him. Samantha remembered why she liked Tom when they first met during the summer. Samantha loved the way Tom smiled at her when she spoke. She found herself having jealous feelings toward Darcey and despite not remembering her, she liked her. Samantha had to restrain herself watching Tom touch Darcey. She was driven to slap her but restrained herself as if what she had to say was important. Despite being uncomfortable with most men, she enjoyed Tom. Maybe it was because he didn't want anything from her. He was just a nice person.

As they moved on to the governor's tailgate party, they all had to endure Skyler's bragging about how Mr. Castriano had finagled an invitation to the party for them, and it would be an opportunity to meet Michigan's governor. Samantha suspected the invitation had nothing to do with Mr. Castriano and everything to do with her parents and their Washington connections. They'd attended the governor's conference and ball, not Skyler. She also remembered her mother telling her they had made it a point to meet Michigan's governor since she was a positive role-model for Samantha. Surely her father had passed the invitation on to Skyler, not anyone else.

Samantha rolled her eyes contemptuously at Skyler's bragging. Too bad Emily wasn't here to pick up on it; they'd have had a good laugh. Samantha made a mental note to tell Emily about Skyler. Skyler was fraudulent in everything he said and did. It was more and more obvious to her. Why couldn't anyone else see it?

Samantha had never been to a tailgate party. She wasn't even sure what it was, but she found herself enjoying it. Looking out into the crowd, she could see a slow-moving sea of green and white. It was like being at an enormous high school pep rally. She began to feel the excitement of the upcoming game. She couldn't believe she ate two hotdogs and kept them down. Her headache for the most part was gone. Except for the slight ringing in her ears, she felt pretty good.

Samantha felt safe in the crowd, despite Skyler watching her every move. She tried not to talk to any men, but didn't want to be rude. Each male who said a word to her or glanced in her direction sparked notable anger in Skyler. Samantha didn't know what to do. Reminded of a childhood trick she and Emily used at the garden parties their parents forced them to attend, she wove in and out of the crowd and got lost in the flock.

Moments after deciding she lost Skyler, she bristled, feeling a sharp squeeze to her hand. She feared her tiny bones would tear from the joints of her knuckles and rip through her skin. She looked up through the unwanted tears brought out by instant pain. As she smelled his warm beer breath through the rough hostile voice she hated. She bit the inside of her cheek so hard she tasted blood. The pain she inflicted upon herself was better than the pain he inflicted. At least her own pain gave her some control of her body and mind.

"Going somewhere?" Skyler asked.

"Just looking around." Samantha whispered through the pain.

"From now on, you stay by my side. Is that clear?"

Samantha nodded and he released her fingers. Putting her hands together, she straightened her fingers and rubbed the pain away gently. She kept her hands hidden in her pockets while she followed Skyler through the crowd. Skyler, for the moment, was content linking his arm through hers. When they caught up to Tom and Darcey, it was game-time.

The tailgate space around the stadium was so crowded they almost missed kick-off. Their seats were on the fifty-yard line.

The game was more exciting than Samantha anticipated and she forgot her hand trauma and Skyler. She was hoarse from shouting and cheering. Michigan State won the game and they headed toward dinner.

Once at the restaurant, Samantha marveled at its atmosphere; it was like something Hemingway would have written about with its' eclectic decor. She wished Skyler was John. Samantha frowned, suddenly uncomfortable again.

"Is something wrong with your drink, Samantha?" Tom asked. "I can order a different bottle of champagne. I'm sure Skyler would love me to add it to his tab." Tom winked at Skyler, playfully jabbing his arm.

"Rub it in, why don't you, little brother," Skyler said laughingly, pretending to spar with Tom. Darcey rolled her eyes at the two of them.

"It's fine. It's just been a long day. All that screaming made me tired." Samantha loved the way Tom looked at her. She hated the way Darcey looked at him when he looked at her. Why did she have all of these growing negative feelings about Darcey? Samantha felt out of place again.

Samantha felt Skyler's eyes penetrating her. When dinner was served, the conversation dwindled and Samantha excused herself to the restroom. She went into the one-stalled brightly painted room and vomited. She tried to stop, but couldn't. Her stomach empty, she dragged a weak hand to the sink and washed her face, and brushed her teeth.

"Samantha, are you all right? The guys wanted me to

make sure you hadn't fallen asleep in here," Darcey said, stepping into the small room.

"I'm fine. I just felt a bit warm in there and wanted to brush my teeth and put cool water on my face."

"Oh. That's just the champagne. You don't drink much, do you?"

"No."

"You'll figure out what you like to drink and what you can tolerate."

"We'd better get back," Samantha said. "I'm sorry I took so long."

"No problem. It was time for me to get up anyway."

Samantha was glad she had thrown up her food. It gave her room for the dessert Skyler had ordered for her. She felt Skyler's eyes sear through her with every spoonful of chocolate mousse she swallowed.

"Well, thanks, you two. It's such a great night; I'm going to walk Samantha back to her dorm. I'll take a taxi back to your place."

"I'll drive you," Tom said.

"After all we ate, a walk will feel good," Skyler said. "You two stay here and spend some time alone. I'll tell them to put anything else you want on my tab," Skyler said. His tone was jovial but Samantha felt the additional force in his words and knew Tom wasn't to argue any further.

"Thanks, it was great seeing you again. I had fun." Samantha said to Tom and Darcey, while she donned her jacket.

Not listening to their good-byes, Samantha wished she could think of something to delay them, but nothing came. They stepped out onto the well-lit street. Samantha crossed her arms in front of her body and concentrated on the sidewalk.

Skyler whistled as he walked, his hands were hooked into his pant pockets by his thumbs. His whistling was annoying, but his silence was terrifying.

"What are you thinking about?" Skyler finally asked.

"I was just replaying the day."

"It was a great game," Skyler said. "But you just like those guys in their tight pants."

Samantha remained silent. She didn't feel like playing his word game. She'd only lose. Her mind raced for a topic she could quickly divert him with. "Does Tom live far from here?" she asked.

"No. Why? Do you plan on going to visit him?"

"Just wondered."

"I saw you staring at him. You like him, don't you? You'd like to try him out to see if he's better than me, wouldn't you?"

"No. I stared at him because he looks so much like you."

"We're brothers, of course we look alike; but we've grown more alike as we've gotten older. You didn't answer my question. You'd like to be with him, wouldn't you?"

"No. I don't want to be with anyone," Samantha said defiantly. That included him.

"Except me. Isn't that right, Samantha?"

Samantha echoed his words. "Yes, that's right."

"Good. Just so we understand each other."

"Well, here's my dorm. Thanks for the walk," Samantha said, dismissing him.

"No, no. You don't understand. We have a lot of work to do. We have to baptize that little bed of yours," Skyler said, pulling her toward him, pressing her hips to his.

Samantha felt his hardness. She stiffened, stunned by his brashness, and fearful of his locked hold. She stopped breathing to avoid his scent.

Skyler kissed her gently, then pulled away from her. He winked and rubbed his forefinger up and down the center then length of her palm.

"Men aren't allowed on our floor after midnight," she said, averting her eyes.

"Come on, Samantha. It's been a while since I've been in college, but nothing's changed. There were always women on the men's floor, and men on the women's floor. Twenty-four hours, seven days a week."

"What if Missy is there?"

"She told me she spends weekends with her boyfriend. Has that changed?"

"She stops by for clothes and other things."

"Then we'll deal with that. Don't worry, sweetie. I'll take care of you."

Samantha's headache grew once they reached the dorm entrance. She felt as if she might vomit, but she vowed she wouldn't; she needed to stall him. "Can I show you around the dorm?"

"I'm not interested in the dorm, just you."

Samantha began to breathe deeply. Her headache was impossible to bear. She began to weave toward her room despite trying to walk a straight line aligning herself with the wall. Each step was taken with certainty she was headed to fall off the cliff of doom.

"Would you like me to carry you?" Skyler laughed then wrapped his arm tightly around Samantha's tiny waist. "You need to learn how to hold your liquor."

Samantha no longer heard his voice. She was inside her head telling herself to relax—visualizing the safety of her room. She pushed out Skyler, ignoring his nearness and his impending invasion of her space.

"Where are your keys?" Skyler reached into Samantha's jacket pocket. "Never mind, I've got them."

Samantha tried her hardest to push away the panic with her first step into her room. She pictured herself alone and safe and forced Skyler to disappear. A gale of calm rushed over her. Where had Skyler gone?

She needed her bed. She needed sleep. "What are you talking about, Tom?" Darcey asked wearily.

"Very funny. You'll pay for that," Skyler said.

"What?" Samantha asked. She wondered why Tom's mouth was taut.

Slowly, Tom began to remove her clothing, kissing her, caressing her, playing with every inch of her body. Darcey returned his kisses. She moaned in pleasure feeling his fingers enters her most private sensual crevices then into the warmth of her soft delicate cavity.

Darcey studied Tom. He was handsome. The moonlight seeping through the open windows cast shadows on his strong athletic features, accentuating his intense robust face and the immense muscular bulges of his torso. Darcey enjoyed the rapture in Tom's eyes. She held his gaze, relaxed and allowed his body to be one with hers.

Gently he began. Moving slowly, carefully in and out, rubbing himself deeply inside her. Darcey smiled hearing Tom's words: "You're mine. All mine. Tell me you love it. Tell me you love it, right now."

Tom's words echoed in her head. She didn't comprehend them. She wasn't used to Tom treating her like this. She felt uncomfortable; she didn't like it. She remained silent.

"Bitch," Skyler said, pausing his movement in her. "You like it don't you?"

Darcey stared. There was something different about Tom, but she wasn't sure what. Suddenly, she felt pain as his hands fiercely pinned down her shoulders and put his lips to her, kissing her deeply. Without warning, almost growling, he took her bottom lip between his clenched teeth and gruffly said, "Didn't you hear me?"

Darcey, feeling pain, could only say, "Mmmm." She was unable to answer him with her lip still locked in his teeth.

Understanding she had given in, Skyler released her lip and listened to the meek response.

"Yes. You know that," Darcey said.

"I know what? C'mon baby, tell me."

"You're great. You're the best. No one could do what you do to me. You just get better and better," Darcey said, unblinking at Tom in the darkness, still wondering why he was being so rough with her.

Empowered with Samantha's answer, Skyler moved inside of her until his body felt full and fluid and ripe. As his eruption rushed forward, filling her, his knuckles clasped the mattress, eyes closed tightly; and a low, self-satisfied moan echoed in the silence.

Darcey felt the weight of Tom now, resting on her nakedness. She closed her eyes and warm drops fell. She loved Tom, didn't she? Why was she crying?

* * * *

Skyler left Samantha sleeping. He rummaged through her drawers, her closet then her bathroom for evidence of another man. Annoyed there wasn't anything he could use against her, he threw her hairbrush into the sink after removing a few strands of hair that he carefully sealed into a small, clear plastic bag he retrieved from his pocket. He returned to Samantha and stared hungrily at her. *There she is*, he whispered, *Sleeping Beauty; my Sleeping Beauty.*

Quietly, stepping under the warm spray of the shower, Skyler stretched before lathering himself. Physically he was refreshed, yet emotionally he was disappointed the alcohol knocked Samantha out so quickly. Maybe he shouldn't have pushed the walk. From now on, no alcohol. That would solve the problem, he thought, staring in the fogged mirror as he brushed his wet hair back and towel-dried himself. After all, he decided with a raised eyebrow, he wanted her to remember him clearly, not in a drunken blur.

He could have her repeatedly all night. He laughed out loud at that thought. Too bad he had to go to Tom's. He began to count how many times he could take Samantha in one full night. He'd have his chance, of that he was certain. Things would be very different next time, he vowed, as he straightened his clothes, tucked the sheets and comforter around his sleeping beauty, and quietly exited.

It was almost one. Still time to catch last call before taking a taxi, Skyler decided to walk down the brightly lit street toward the little bar near the restaurant they had dinner in. While he didn't remember its exact location, he could find it. He watched crowds of young female coeds everywhere, walking, laughing. They were vibrant, alive, full of energy.

Skyler stepped onto the dimly lit side street anxious to find his young prey in the bar below the street.

CHAPTER 24

Samantha awoke, Sunday morning startled by the dryness in her throat, the nausea in her stomach and the dull throbbing in her head. The familiar effects of too much alcohol. Her eyes closed tightly. Her breathing slowed to shallow puffs; she wished she could dissipate like vapor into thin air.

Snuggled beneath the warmth of her tangled sheets, she felt stiff and more like how she felt after the bicycle accident. The far recesses of her mind replayed the previous day with Skyler and Tom: breakfast, the tailgate, the game, dinner. What had happened after dinner? She remembered not feeling well. Skyler grabbed her to steady her, and then? Then, what? She couldn't remember. Had she blacked out? Samantha was frightened at the thought of a blackout. So many things had happened to her she couldn't remember.

Her stomach cramped, and she quickly sprang from the bed.

* * * *

When she stepped out of the shower into her fluffy pink robe, she felt soothed, except for a nagging she couldn't shrug off. Grabbing panties and a comfortable sweat suit, Samantha got dressed.

What's this? Samantha squinted her eyes on red and purple spots on her shoulder. Bruises. Small bruises. Where had they come from? There were five sets of oval bruises, some small, some larger. Fingerprints? Bite marks? She pulled her other shoulder toward the mirror. It was the same, five sets of oval bruises. Oh no. Samantha wanted to scream. She froze. She couldn't scream; there was no one to hear her. Even if they could hear, her mind raced, she couldn't let them hear.

A rush of panic set in. The reasons for the bruises escaped her. Instinctively, she knew they had something to do with Skyler. She must have blocked what happened. He'd told her he would show her a good time. Over and over again, he'd told her in detail what he wanted to do to her. How he would touch her, how she would like it, how she would beg for more.

Dressed, she grabbed a thermos bottle and headed toward the cafeteria. She needed coffee. A lot of fresh black coffee. She headed down the hallway. She heard a low sound. A real sound. The familiar laughter intruded on every thought, tainting her emotions with rising fear. It followed her to the cafeteria.

She returned to the room, thermos full without remembering having been in the eating area. She locked the door, sat on her bed, poured a cup of coffee, and drank. She didn't care that it burned her mouth, her throat.

She lay down, pillow over her head.

Before long she floated into lifeless slumber, where her terrifying thoughts became, for a time, extinguished.

* * * *

Skyler checked in at the airport and then clicked in Samantha's number. Phone to his ear, he sprinted to the gate. He had to hear Samantha's voice again before he departed. How was she doing with what had to be a miserable hangover? Smiling at his vision of what could have been, he thought it was too bad he'd had to go back to Tom's.

He listened to the unanswered ringing and hung up. She had to be there. He dialed again. He was tired; he hadn't had much sleep, and he'd had an early breakfast with Tom. Counting the rings, his annoyance grew. His hands trembled. Where was she? Where could she have gone? Had she faked her drunken state last night? There was no way she would be out this early; it wasn't possible. Hearing his flight called, he packed the phone, picked up his briefcase, and boarded.

* * * *

In the dorm, Sundays were relaxed. After ten, breakfast

became brunch served until two; dinner wasn't served at all. John and Samantha had a ritual of eating brunch together at eleven. John looked forward to his Sunday brunches with Samantha. It was the highlight of his week because it was usually when she was the most relaxed. He had never met anyone like her, and he had an unquenchable thirst to be with her, even if it was just as friends. He'd made it clear he wanted more. She'd made it clear she wasn't ready and couldn't handle more. Their mutually agreed upon pact was to take it a day at a time, no pressure, just good friends.

John checked his watch. She was late, and he was hungry. Could she have forgotten? Maybe she decided not to eat; he knew she didn't eat very much. Suddenly, it occurred to him, although he'd promised not to interfere with Skyler's visit, maybe something was wrong. Leaving his books open on the cafeteria table, John decided to check on her. Walking at a rapid pace to her room, he was there in minutes. He knocked. He knocked again, harder. No answer. Disappointed, he wrote her a note on the laminated Garfield board tacked to her door.

Returning to his books, he decided to have a quiet study brunch, but he barely tasted his food. He couldn't concentrate on his literature; thoughts of Samantha crept in. Maybe he should have insisted on meeting Skyler. He'd promised Samantha he wouldn't push, but his intuition told him something wasn't right.

* * * *

Missy walked into the darkened room. Was Samantha sick? It was almost six. She looked like hell. Had she slept all day? She quietly threw her clothes into her laundry bag and refilled her backpack. Should she wake Samantha? She grabbed a small mirror and placed it under Samantha's nose to make sure she was breathing. She bent over to hear her breathe. She felt her hands, they were warm. Deciding Samantha was in a deep sleep, she looked around the room. A stack of open books sat on Samantha's desk. Missy decided she must have some homework, and it was in Samantha's best interest to wake her up.

"Samantha? Samantha? Wake up. Don't you have to get up and finish your assignments for Monday?" Her voice got louder with each question. Then shaking Samantha's shoulder, Missy yelled. "Samantha?"

* * * *

Samantha inhaled deeply and then exhaled loudly. Yawning, she opened her eyes to see Missy, shaking her.

"What? What's wrong?" she asked.

"I thought you were dead or something."

"I had too much to drink."

"Yeah. I can't drink much either. But Jack gets some really great weed. You ought to try it. I can get you some, if you want."

"No. I don't smoke." Samantha said. "Oh, my God, I can't believe I slept so late. John's going to kill me." Samantha sprinted to the bathroom to freshen up.

"Why would he do that?" Missy asked. "Are you dating him?"

"No, nothing like that. I was supposed to meet him for brunch."

"Well, that explains the note on the door. Look," Missy said. She opened the door and read the note out loud: *"Sam, call me when you get in. Dinner? J."*

"I'd better call him," Samantha said.

"Gotta go. See you tomorrow," Missy said. "Remember, if my parents call—"

"You're at the library."

* * * *

Samantha looked around the cafeteria for John. He hadn't sounded very happy with her. What would she say? How could she explain why she had missed brunch and what happened yesterday with Skyler?

"Hey, Sam. You look great," John said.

"I'm really hungry; let's go over to Jersey Giant and share a sub. Then we can study, maybe go to the library." Samantha smiled ensuring there was no hint of anything negative that needed discussing. She wasn't clear-headed enough to know what—if anything—had happened anyway.

It wasn't a lie. She wasn't sure what to say to John.

She wished she could turn off her mother's stilted voice that wreaked havoc in her brain: "Men don't like bruised fruit." She wasn't just bruised; she was a little mangled, too. Would that matter to John? Would the truth affect their friendship, or would lies affect it more?

Samantha took a deep breath and told herself to relax. Walking next to John, she grabbed onto his arm trying to make him believe she was fine. The scent of his skin comforted her as much as it scared her.

Sitting at the table, subs open, Samantha sipped her cola.

John slowly stirred his coffee. "How was the game?"

"We won." Samantha bit into her sub.

"No kidding. I meant with Skyler. He did come in, didn't he?"

"Yes, he did. It was okay." She shrugged and took another bite.

"Nothing else?"

"Like what?" Samantha said, she tried to look innocent.

"Geez, Samantha, why are you playing games about this? I've been upset, worried about you, ever since you told me he was coming. I just want to know if everything—" John stopped.

Samantha intently pulled pieces of bread off the sub, to make it thinner. She knew what he wanted her to tell him. Samantha felt him staring, but she couldn't look at him; she couldn't face him.

Finally, after several minutes of silence, John spoke. "I'll help you with anything, but you need to trust me. I'm sorry you don't. I thought we were past that."

Guilt flooded through Samantha. "I do trust you. With my life." But she wasn't ready to talk. And she feared saying anything more. "It's me I don't trust."

CHAPTER 25

"Hey Samantha, who was that cute guy you were with Saturday night?" Jennifer asked, plopping her overloaded laundry basket on the empty washing machine.

"What?" Samantha asked, surprised.

"You know, the cute guy who was all over you? I walked David out and saw him unlock your room with your keys. You looked a little out of it." She giggled. "I'm not surprised you don't remember seeing us. We said *hello*."

"Sorry. We went to the game. I had too much to drink, and he brought me home," Samantha said. She avoided eye contact and pulled her wet clothes from the washer into the dryer.

"So, who is he?"

"Just a friend who flew in from home for the game."

"Must be a good friend to fly in just for the game. You're lucky Missy is always at her boyfriend's, so you never have to worry about kicking her out when you have a guy over."

"I didn't have a guy over, at least not like that; he

spent the night at his brother's apartment not with me," Samantha said, trying to convince herself and her floor mate.

"Right," Jennifer said. "Look, I don't care who you sleep with. No one here cares."

"Okay, but for the record. We're just friends. And, trust me, his looks are deceiving. I'd rather sleep with an ugly man than him," Samantha said. "So, who else saw us?"

Jennifer shrugged. "No one was around. Don't worry, I won't say anything. If you're still just friends, can you introduce me next time?"

Samantha turned on the dryer. "Sure. But, I guarantee, you'll be disappointed."

"No way," Jennifer yelled toward Samantha, who was headed out of the laundry room.

* * * *

Samantha entered her room to the ringing phone.

Minnie showed ten o'clock. Sam picked up the receiver. "Hello?"

"Well, it's about time. Where have you been?"

"Mostly in my room being sick. Studying and in the basement doing laundry."

"Not true. I called you from the airport. I called you when I arrived. I called you before I had dinner. Shall I go on? Or would you like to tell me the truth?" Skyler shouted.

"Stop it. Stop it." Moisture beaded on her body, and her breath quickened.

"Then stop lying to me."

"If you would just listen to me—"

"Listen to what? You haven't said anything."

Samantha collapsed on the floor and began again. "I woke up really early, and I got sick. I shouldn't have had any alcohol. You know it always makes me sick."

"Yeah, yeah. You still haven't said anything."

"I threw up a few times. I got the dry heaves. I brought coffee back to my room to study with but fell asleep. I had a really bad headache so I took Tylenol with codeine. It knocked me out. When I got up, I had something to eat—"

Skyler cut her off. "I'm still waiting. Who was with you?"

"I was alone all day."

"You're lying. Didn't you eat with anyone?"

"No, I—"

"You're lying. That's it, you're just a liar. I worried about you all day. I didn't hear from you, and you didn't answer the phone. How am I supposed to react when I don't hear from you? And just how many times do you think I'm going to call you? I really have enough pressure. I don't need your lies."

"I told you the truth. I must have slept through the phone calls. I've had terrible migraine headaches. If you don't believe me, you can ask Missy. She woke me up;

she told me I looked dead. And, you're the one who told me not to call you."

"Oh, I'll be asking Missy, all right. I told you not to call me at the office. But you could call me at home, or on my cellphone."

"I'll call," Samantha said, twisting her hair around her forefinger.

"Call me when you leave your room if you're going to be away, other than for class. Then we won't have any problems; if nothing is going on, then you won't have any problem doing that, will you?"

"Fine."

He clicked off.

Samantha remained on the floor for several minutes. She wanted him out of her life. She didn't want people to associate him with her. She wanted the lies to stop, no—she needed the lies to stop.

She began to look forward to seeing John on Saturday, instead of dreading it. It was time to get help, time to tell the truth, regardless of the consequences. Confiding in John was her only hope.

Looking at her empty laundry basket, she took a deep breath. Time to get her jeans from the dryer and finish her homework. She had to do well on the rest of her midterms. Four more days. Her schoolwork was the only thing keeping her sane at the moment. Well, she thought, turning the knob, that and John.

CHAPTER 26

Samantha and John strolled along the banks of the Red Cedar River, jumping on and off each large rock and in and out of every pile of fallen leaves. Like small children, avoiding the traveled paths, they explored and created their own. They knew, in time, they would find their chosen spot and, calling it their own, begin their personal journey.

In a cul-de-sac of trees, Samantha and John stopped, untied their jackets from around their waists, and spread them on the cold ground. Quietly, they sat facing the beauty of the river—their private nature center.

"Whatever the problem, I will help you," John said. "I promise, I will find a way."

Samantha felt the sincerity in his voice, but she had trusted once before. "You may hate me after what I tell you, and I won't blame you. I hate myself."

"Never," John said.

Samantha didn't look at him; she kept her eyes fixated on the grass. But, she finally managed to tell him about the rape. The first one.

When she finished, she met his eyes. His face was solemn but filled with compassion.

"I wasn't supposed to cut through the alley. He came out of nowhere. I didn't see him until it was too late." Samantha stopped. She composed herself, ignoring the tears rolling down her face. She gulped hard, tightly hugged her knees, and she rocked back and forth. "I tried, I really tried, but I couldn't breathe. I couldn't move." Samantha's voice trailed off, and she paused briefly, staring into the horror of a memory she had avoided for so long.

"I may have passed out for a minute or two. I don't remember. I wondered if I was alive. Then I saw blood—my blood—everywhere. My hands, my broken nails, torn clothes. I didn't feel any pain, but I couldn't stop shaking, and I remember running home. I felt like I had wings. Like I was in someone else's body. Like I was watching a movie."

Samantha paused to wipe her face. "I ran as fast as I could. No one was home. Cook, the maids, everyone was gone. I didn't know what to do; I showered. I threw away my clothes. I don't remember sleeping. In the morning, Skyler showed up and he helped me."

Samantha stopped and looked again at John, waiting for a reaction. She still saw compassion. He didn't need to respond; she felt his caring. "I trusted him. I thought he helped me."

"There's more." John held her hands. "I can handle it."

"Just when I thought everything was over, and I was ready to move forward, he told me he would tell everyone, everything, if I didn't have sex with him."

John stiffened. "The bastard."

"At first I thought he was joking, that I'd misunderstood, because I'd had a few drinks that night. Finally, I believed him," Samantha said.

John handed her a package of Kleenex from the pocket of his jacket. Samantha wiped her face and tried to compose herself. "He recorded the conversation of me telling him everything that morning. I don't know how he did it. He gave me a copy on a thumb-drive. I listened to it. He says he has other things, too. My parents wouldn't understand; they wouldn't believe me. They wouldn't like being in the newspapers."

"This is not your fault. You know that don't you?" John unzipped the side of his backpack and pulled out a large wide-mouthed thermos of cafe au lait, and poured them each a steamy cup.

Silently, they sipped, letting its warmth coat their insides.

Samantha appreciated John's sensitivity. She'd never felt as secure with anyone as she felt now with him. If only he could make her whole again. She met his gaze, and his tender smile immediately reassured her. He slid closer to her and wrapped a strong arm around her shoulder.

Samantha pulled out the familiar worn paper. Without

unfolding it, she handed it to John.

"What's this?" Slowly, he opened the tattered paper.

Samantha blinked at him in silence. Her rocking subsided as she watched him read the careworn words.

"I don't understand," he said.

"They're legal words. I need you to help me understand what they mean."

"What will that do?"

"It will help me get away from Skyler. He told me the law is on his side, that he isn't doing anything wrong, that blackmail for sex is legal, and that there's no law against it." Samantha found the rest of her words difficult to say out loud. Her mind raced, and her heart pounded. Rocking again, she blurted out the words she feared the most. "And, an illegal abortion is murder, and I will go to jail."

"The bastard is an idiot."

Samantha meticulously answered all of John's questions. Several silent minutes passed. She rested her head on his shoulder.

"Let's go," he said.

"Yeah, and you-know-who will be calling. I told him I'd be at the library for a few hours," Samantha said. "I'm sure he's already called ten times, trying to pinpoint my exact time of arrival."

"Samantha," John said. He turned toward her and held her by the shoulders. "You can't take his threats lightly. Blackmail for anything is illegal. There are laws against what he's doing. He knows that. He's very dangerous. Don't underestimate him. Act as naturally as you can. Don't tip him off in any way until we can figure out how to handle this. Promise me."

Samantha looked into his sincere face. "I promise." She understood the gravity of his words.

"Pinky swear," John said, offering her his curved pinky finger.

"Pinky swear." Samantha curled her pinky around his.

Silently they walked back to the dormitory. They climbed the stairs to the entry. "I'll walk you to your room," John said.

"No. I'm fine. I'll see you for dinner," Samantha said. "I need to pull the leaves out of my hair and get into some fresh clothes."

"One hour. Movie after dinner?" John asked. "I think we both need a diversion."

Samantha sighed. "How will I explain it?"

"Don't. After you talk to him, leave your phone off the hook.

Tomorrow, tell him you hung it up wrong."

Samantha felt lighter. "I haven't tried that before."

* * * *

Samantha returned to her room and with one foot in the shower, the phone rang. She grabbed a towel, then the phone. "Hello?"

"Well, well. What have you been doing? You sound

in too good a mood to have been at the library all afternoon," Skyler said.

"I am in a good mood. I got lots done at the library. After I eat dinner, I'm going to put all my notes on the computer and finish the first draft of my paper. I feel pretty good about that. I thought it would be a lot harder than it was."

"Well, good. I'm glad you are adjusting well. Now tell me who else was there?"

"Lots of people were at the library. I didn't know anyone, though."

"Then why were you there for so long?"

"I told you, research. You know how long it takes to do research."

"I know you were looking at all those muscle-bound college men. It's all right, you can tell me."

"I wasn't. I didn't." Samantha said, unsure of what else to say, remembering John's words. It kept going back and forth until Skyler demanded she tell him she loved him and put her on notice that he'd call an hour after dinner.

She hated Skyler, now more than ever. Confiding in John, hearing her own haunting words out loud, forced her to realize she'd been a fool to believe Skyler's lies. It was time for an exit plan. She was done with Skyler.

* * * *

When John arrived for dinner, he said, "You look wonderful." He pointed to the phone on the floor. No one could get through. "Hey, nice job on the phone." He closed the door behind them.

"I do know how to follow instructions," Samantha said.

* * * *

It was midnight when Samantha returned to her room. She switched on the light, threw her purse on top of the dresser, then kicked the receiver against the wall. She wasn't about to replace it. Knowing there couldn't be a call allowed her to feel more normal than she had in months. She finally began to believe that Skyler and the whole mess she was in would soon disappear forever.

Samantha slid into her sheets with the smile John had left her with. Dinner, movie, and a long stroll with John embedded a calm sense of normalcy. Trusting John was easy. She fell asleep easily contemplating taking her life back, sharing it with John, and never having to speak to Skyler again.

* * * *

John fell into his bed exhausted. He'd not anticipated Samantha's story. He wasn't sure about the existence of God, but he did believe there was a stronger force that kept the world evolving. He believed now was the time, if ever there was one, to ask God to show himself—by guiding him to help Samantha and protect her from further harm.

In the dark quiet, he pictured her innocent face and the cruel, immoral journey she'd traveled alone. He used his cell phone to Google attorneys, who handled criminal cases. He looked up the words he recalled from Samantha's list, then he researched the county prosecutor. In the morning he'd research Skyler. Operation: Get Skyler Arrested and Disbarred was underway, at least it would be when he finished.

CHAPTER 27

It had been a week since Samantha confessed everything to John, yet he hadn't approached the subject of what they would do. He just kept filling a notebook and asked her about every conversation she'd had with Skyler.

"What are you writing?" she said.

"I'll show you when I'm farther," John said. "Operation Free Sam, is what I'm calling it. OFS for short."

Samantha snorted. "You couldn't have thought of a better acronym?"

"What'dya mean? You'll know when I refer to 'oafs' I'm referring to OFS, but anyone listening with think I'm talking about an oaf, like maybe a bully. I thought it was pretty clever." He pointed pouty lips at Samantha and then broke into a smile.

"When you put it like that, I'll give you a few points for creativity." Samantha laughed.

"I've been researching, like nonstop, and I think I found something important," John said gently.

She nodded and waited.

"It is illegal to tap a phone, except under certain

circumstances, like when the police are involved."

Samantha stared.

"But you can record conversations on your own phone, as long as it is not for illegal purposes. Recordings can be used in court, and they can be given to the police for proof of a crime."

"Are you saying you want me to get proof?" Samantha rubbed her temples.

"Record what you can, but also make a diary of all your conversations with Skyler. If you can't do it word for word, do it as close as possible."

"I could I keep it on my computer."

"Yes, but make sure there is a password on your computer so no one has access and keep it backed up. Name the diary something that sounds like part of your research for one of the papers you've written. Don't tell anyone what you're doing."

"Who would I tell?" Samantha asked.

"Learn to use the record button on your iPhone. You can't afford to let him know you're documenting anything. So you need to be able to flick it on if he surprises you."

"I'll work on that but right now, I've got to get to class. So do you, professor," Samantha said. She couldn't handle anymore at the moment but didn't want to hurt John and his big plan by telling him she needed some space.

John got up from the table. "See you for dinner. Six o'clock."

"Sure." Samantha watched him leave the cafeteria.

Just as she put on her jacket, she heard Missy call her name from across the room.

"What's up?" Samantha asked. "I'm heading out. I've got class."

"I found the receiver on the floor and hung it up. Like ten seconds later your weird friend called. Like usual he asked a million questions."

"What did you say?" Samantha said.

"First, I told him you were in class because that's what your wall schedule said. Second, I told him our phone was broken." Missy grunted proudly. "Figured that wasn't a lie since I had to fix it by hanging it up."

Samantha giggled. "Thank you."

"He asks more questions than any parent I know," Missy said. Her face soured. "He's creepy. If you want to keep the phone off the hook, I'm all for it. I was sorry I answered it."

"You did great. Thank you." Samantha hugged Missy.

"You'd do the same for me," Missy said. "But from now on, I am not fixing the damn phone. It can stay off the hook."

* * * *

Samantha took her time walking to class in the brisk air enjoying the shock of cold with each snowflake that landed on her face and in her eyelashes. She needed to walk off the anxiety of Missy's conversation with Skyler. Her head throbbed. Missy's words about Skyler rambled around in her head. Her hearing became deaf to the sounds around her, except the laughter. It was back. It got louder with each step.

Samantha ran into the building. She found the bathroom. Dropping her backpack onto the floor, she turned on the faucet, cupped her hands under the cold water and splashed her face. She reached into the small pocket of her backpack for the pill bottle, popped off the lid, and took two red capsules along with a white-and-green one.

She sat, leaning her head against the overstuffed back pillow of the old couch in the restroom. The worn fabric smelled musty. She listened, suddenly remembering, wondering where the laughter was. It hadn't followed her into the building. It must have been the wind, she convinced herself. Twenty-five minutes until class began. By then the pills would begin their work. One thing was certain, she had to see a doctor; she needed more pills. How could she survive without them?

* * * *

Olin Health Center was lined with students. Samantha stood in line, student I.D. and credit card in hand. After checking in, she waited for almost an hour on a hard faux-leather couch, and read a magazine until a young nurse led her into a room and jotted notes in a file for the doctor.

"I've been having a lot of headaches—migraines. I

need something for them. They get so bad I faint and get nauseous. I hear things, too."

"You mean like ringing?"

"Yes, that's it," Samantha said, deciding not to mention the laughter or her occasional forgetfulness.

"Anything else?"

"No."

"Are you on any medication?"

"No. I mean, I use Excedrin for Migraines; but I think I need something stronger, because they just don't work anymore." She paused. "I'm taking birth control pills. I need a prescription for a refill for those, too."

"Did you think the birth control pills could be the cause of your headaches?"

"No."

"Well, I'll note it in your chart. The doctor might want to change your prescription or method of birth control. Anything else?"

Samantha shrugged then watched the nurse dismiss herself. She sat in the stark room, picking at her nail polish. Watching the flakes of polish fall onto her sweater and jeans, her heart pounded faster, and her anxiety grew.

"Hi there," said the white-jacketed man. "I hear you're suffering from headaches?" He handed the chart to the nurse, who shadowed him. The doctor waved a small lit flashlight into Samantha's eyes.

She nodded and blinked. "That light does not feel

good." She wished she had demanded a female doctor. Patiently, she listened to his lecture about college stress, the need to eat protein and good food, not drink too much alcohol, and then finally how underweight she was. He was a doctor who liked to listen to himself. Would he listen to her?

"I know you want something for your headaches. I believe you're suffering from migraines. I'll be giving you a diet to follow and some pills you should take every day that have been proven to provide relief. Also, I'll give you a prescription for new birth-control pills."

"What if I get a migraine?"

"I'm writing you a script for pain relief, but you should take it at the onset of a headache. Don't wait too long, or you will go into a full-blown migraine.

Samantha nodded. She wondered if she should've taken notes when he handed her four prescriptions.

"About birth control—are you sexually active?" He stopped writing and looked up.

"Well, not really. No."

"You either are, or you aren't. Have you been checked for sexually transmitted diseases, and have you had a pap smear this year?"

"Yes, my family doctor at home; but he wanted me to be checked by a doctor here and make sure the pills were the right dosage for me," Samantha said, lying. She didn't want him to touch her like that. Not a man. Not ever. She began to perspire profusely. The gray-haired doctor looked like he was considering something.

"Samantha? Are you feeling okay? Can you hear me?" the doctor said.

Samantha heard a loud ringing in her ears; she couldn't hear the words the doctor was saying. Suddenly, everything went black.

"Samantha? Samantha?"

She heard her name over and over again, and she smelled the ammonia. Fluttering her eyes open, she saw the doctor standing over her and felt the nurse checking her pulse.

"You fainted. You're okay. We're going to keep you here for a little while. Did you come here with someone?"

She shook her head.

"When was the last time you ate?"

So many questions. Samantha just wanted to leave. She wanted her prescriptions. She wanted her room. She wanted her bed. She answered the questions. She hoped her cooperation would be the key to her release. Samantha drank the carton of milk and ate the vending-machine sandwich that had been brought in.

"Are you feeling better?" the nurse asked.

"Yes. Can I go?"

"We called your roommate."

"How—?

"You listed her on your form. She's waiting in the hall. I'll bring her in."

"No. Wait. Please don't. I mean not until I'm ready to

leave. Please."

The nurse nodded. A few minutes later, the serious-faced doctor returned.

"I feel fine. Really. Can I go?" Samantha asked, trying to act chipper and alert.

"What happened here concerns me. I know students forget to eat; I see dozens every week, like you. Your body is giving you a warning, a message you need to treat it better. Do you understand?"

Samantha nodded.

After scheduling several tests and a follow-up appointment, he released her. Samantha didn't care about anything but the prescriptions she had in hand. She'd met her goal.

Missy listened as Samantha thanked her for coming so quickly and explained she'd fainted but was fine.

"I can't believe they didn't admit you."

"Doctor told me I need to eat more protein at breakfast and gave me a special diet for my headaches."

"Now that I'm here, why don't I stay? We can go to dinner together. I can meet Jack later; we're going to a movie and then to Harrison Roadhouse. You could join us, if you feel up to it. I really don't want to leave you alone."

"I'm meeting John for dinner, and I think I'll go to bed early," Samantha said, immediately regretting she'd let John's name slip out. "You should see Jack. You've done enough for me."

"John? You're seeing John, as in dating? Why haven't you told me? I thought you two were just friends."

"We are just friends. We get along really well." Samantha stopped walking and turned to face Missy. She gently touched her arm. "Please, don't tell anyone."

"You mean Skyler," Missy said. "Your secret is safe with me. Really. Don't worry. I haven't told him anything. Besides, I owe you for covering for me with my parents." She paused. "You and John should meet us at Harrison Roadhouse."

"Maybe. Let's just play it by ear, and if we decide to go, we'll find you there. I'll text you. Okay?"

* * * *

After dinner Samantha and John returned to the privacy of her room to discuss the Skyler issue.

John pulled her down beside him on the carpeted floor, their backs leaning against the bed. "I've done some research. And, I've talked to some people," he began.

Samantha gasped. "You promised. Oh my God, what have you done?"

"I didn't use your name," John said. He held her hand. "I mentioned a hypothetical situation and posed some questions to a couple of law professors."

"Is blackmail for sex illegal?"

He nodded. "Just like I told you. Rape is a felony, and an illegal abortion might cause the doctor to lose his license, and he could face criminal charges, as well. I need to know how far you are willing to go."

"Go?" Samantha began to panic.

"You want to be rid of Skyler and of being blackmailed and the rape, the whole mess, right?"

"Yes."

"The only way I can see any of those things happening, is to call Skyler's bluff and prosecute. He can lose his license to practice law and be prosecuted. You'll be free to move forward with control of your life."

"My parents—"

"For God's sake, your father is a lawyer. I'm sure he'll be the first to agree you need to get these guys."

"You don't know them," Samantha said.

"I know you. You are, hidden under all this, a fighter. Your parents gave that to you."

"But the family name . . ."

"If your family name is more important than you taking your life back, then I can't help you; nobody can."

"That's not what I'm saying."

"Then you are willing to go the distance?"

"I need this to be over. I will do whatever it takes," she said. John squeezed her hand. "You're right. You're right."

"Good. I have the name of a detective. He might want the FBI involved because there are two jurisdictions: Arkansas and Michigan; and I'm betting they will set up a sting operation to trap Skyler. We have to get enough unimpeachable evidence to make it stick."

"Unimpeachable—like what?"

"Michigan has very strong anti-stalking laws. That's what Skyler is doing to you, essentially; he stalks you through the phone. That's illegal. And the FBI can get a court order that allows wiretapping. The attorney I talked to said your case, the hypothetical case I asked about, would be one of those."

"Attorney? You said you talked to professors."

"Yes. The professors at MSU College of Law are also lawyers with great contacts. I have the name of a good criminal attorney and contacts in the Prosecutor's office and the FBI."

"When do we start?" Samantha asked.

The phone rang.

Grabbing her computer, she quickly switched it on then answered. "Hello?"

"Hi, sweetheart. I heard you weren't feeling well. What are you doing?"

"I just have a twenty-four hour bug. I'm just reading in bed."

"Alone?"

"Of course."

"No, really, who is in bed with you?"

"My text book."

"What book are you reading? Something that'll turn you on?"

"Homework. I hoped it would put me to sleep."

"Well then, I have perfect timing, once again. You can dream of me inside you, touching every part of you. You need me, we have something special together."

After the call John read the screen and grimaced. He promised to spend the next day with Samantha, and then left her to sleep.

* * * *

Stirring, Samantha felt summoned. But by whom? It was dark. Where was she? She couldn't focus. She moved her fingers, her arm, then her legs. She sprang up from her pillow, wide-eyed. She wasn't dreaming; she was awake. The phone. Damn. Samantha sighed loudly, crawling out from underneath her barely creased sheets.

"Hello?" Samantha said. She went to her desk and her awaiting computer.

"Hi, baby. I just had to hear your voice before I sleep. I need you here with me in these cold sheets. We'd warm them up. You know you have a great body, don't you? Such soft, sexy skin; it really turns me on. But you know that, don't you?"

"I was sleeping. What time is it?" Samantha looked up at Minnie.

"Two-fifteen."

"My clock says three-fifteen."

"Daylight savings. Turn your clock back. You lucky girl, see, you get to sleep in an extra hour. Do you know what I'd do with you in that extra hour? Do you?"

"I really have to get some sleep. Can we talk tomorrow?"

"No, damn it. Who is there with you?"

"No one."

"Well, then, tell me something nice. Tell me how you like my mouth all over you. Tell me how I feel inside you. Tell me how I'm the best lover you'll ever have. You know I am, don't you?" Skyler's voice was direct and sensual, clear and driven.

Samantha felt the underpinnings of pure evil, the devil's voice. Samantha stared at the keyboard while she typed his words. His breathing became labored, his words pulsating. Her head pounded with his rapid, breathy words. She felt herself drifting, floating, in and out of sleep.

"Take off your panties."

"I can't," Samantha whispered. Small rigid tremors pulsated through her.

"Now, Samantha. I want them off."

She closed her eyes and pictured herself in her bed, relaxed, sleeping. But in the darkness she heard laughter. Louder and louder. Her head pounded. She pushed hard on her temples. Sleep, she needed sleep … Relax, relax …

"Now, take your hand …"

Excited to hear Tom's voice, Darcey lay in the darkness and followed Tom's instructions.

CHAPTER 28

Standing in the Ingham County Prosecutor's office, Samantha mechanically shook the young attorney's hand. He fit the stark room perfectly with his pale blue eyes, freckled skin, and fiery red hair. She wasn't sure if she could trust the disconcerted prosecutor's stiff manner. He bent forward over the conference room table. "What can I help you with?"

"We have a problem we hope you can help with," John said.

"Prosecutor Kincaid," Samantha said. "It's really complicated, and, it's my problem. John came with me for moral support. Is everything I tell you confidential?"

"Absolutely. But to get everything right, I'd like to take notes and record our conversation, if that's okay."

Samantha nodded.

"What's on your mind?"

Samantha focused on the prosecutor's pen scribbling notes while she spoke. John remained silent, not interjecting until she reached the point in time when they had met. At that point, John explained the phone conversations he'd witnessed, the words on the computer he'd read, and the fear he saw growing on Samantha every day.

Assistant Prosecutor Kincaid stopped occasionally to ask questions, but for the most part, until the pair concluded their stories, he noted questions in the margins, without any hint of emotion or surprise.

"Without real proof, I can't help you. That is where law enforcement comes in," he said. "Working with detectives, a case can be built that leads to successful prosecution."

Samantha refused to cry. This long journey couldn't be stopped until it was over, regardless of the outcome. She had shown her cards. She needed them played out. She had boxed herself in and reality was about to take over.

John stood, with carefully outlined notes of their instructions. They shook hands with Mr. Kincaid. Samantha murmured grateful remarks and stared bleakly at the two men. How could they know how she felt, what she had been through? How could they understand she didn't want to prove her innocence and Skyler's guilt? She didn't want to prove anything; she just wanted it to all go away.

CHAPTER 29

Rebecca Smalley was anything but small Samantha decided as she entered the intimidating office. She studied the large-boned woman with the loose auburn bun pulled atop her head. Her fair skin and rosy cheeks suited her and completed the setting of the austere Victorian office.

Assistant Prosecutor Kincaid's intense regard for Rebecca Smalley rang in Samantha's ears. He distinguished her qualifications from other attorneys, who handled cases dealing with family and criminal matters. He'd said she had the keen ability to compile minuscule details into meaningful prosecutions or defenses. She was often hired by the police department and the Prosecutor's office on a variety of sensitive and complex high-profile cases.

Samantha pictured her father and how distraught he would be if he knew; how disappointed he would be she hadn't confided in him, that she didn't ask for his legal expertise to help her. But how could she ask him without evidence? How could she tell him about Greg and Skyler? How could she risk the disapproval in her parents' eyes or put her parents needlessly in the public eye? How could she explain the foolishness she felt every time she heard herself explain her situation?

"What can I do for you?" the attorney asked.

Samantha tried not to stare at the woman's cranberry red mouth. Too much lipstick, Samantha's mind ticked off.

She introduced herself and told the saga again. Finally, a woman to confide in, even if Samantha didn't know her very well.

✳ ✳ ✳ ✳

Rebecca Smalley listened and made notes. She had been molested as a child, and she relived it each time she listened to a client talk of forced intercourse. Rebecca worried she didn't appear compassionate because even after years of counseling, she never knew when she herself would be triggered. Helping clients, though, usually kept her grounded knowing that fighting back was their only real weapon to regain control and take back a piece of what was stolen from them.

She knew Samantha didn't lack financial resources, unlike many of her clients. Her sweater, skirt, and heels were designer label. Her pearl earrings and matching necklace looked real. And the long, wool London Fog coat hanging over the back of the chair next to her was superior quality and a limited edition.

"Did Prosecutor Kincaid tell you I don't come cheaply?"

"Yes. As I explained to him, money doesn't matter. I mean it does. You see, my father is a lawyer. We have money. I have money I put in a bank account for emergency use, and taking my life back is an emergency, but—"

"To represent you, I need to know everything, without hesitation. Is that clear?" Rebecca studied Samantha. "One lie means I relieve myself from representing you. That is not negotiable. Do you understand?"

"Yes. I need you to know that my father doesn't know any of this; no one does, except my roommate Missy, and she only knows bits and pieces. And, John, my friend from the dorm; he knows everything."

Samantha's tone got lower, desperate in her plea. "I don't want anyone else to know until there's enough proof against Skyler and Greg—"

"I'll proceed with the case as I see fit. If charges are issued, it will be impossible to keep the details shrouded, given the nature of the crimes involved. Are you prepared for that?"

Samantha blinked and pursed her lips. "Does that mean you'll represent me, Ms. Smalley?"

"Yes. Call me Rebecca. We'll work closely with Assistant Prosecutor Kincaid and pursue both criminal matters and civil claims. I'll draft a contract, which we will both sign. You'll pay me a large retainer. I'll give you an accounting of your retainer every month."

* * * *

Samantha felt comfortable this woman was on her side and handed her a ten-thousand-dollar check. It made everything not just real, but like it really mattered to someone—other than John. It mattered to an independent person, a woman who didn't dismiss another woman's feelings.

Samantha made notes of everything she needed to bring to their next meeting and advised Rebecca that Mr. Kincaid had set up a tentative meeting with an FBI agent at the end of the week. Rebecca nodded and wrote it in her book. Her secretary buzzed in, advising her of the arrival of her next appointment.

* * * *

Leaving the historic downtown office building, Samantha drew her coat closely around her. Snowflakes whirled around her, which she happily escaped when she got into her car.

She drove out onto Capitol Avenue to meet John for lunch, eager to tell him about Rebecca, despite the oncoming headache she felt stemming from the base of her neck.

Samantha hadn't seen so much snow outside of a glass Christmas snow globe. For the first time in months, she felt optimistic that a future without Skyler was possible.

CHAPTER 30

At the end of the week, Samantha stared at the man who'd entered Rebecca's office. She was no longer nervous. His intense aura captured her immediately. His confidence radiated success. If such a man was on her side, Samantha knew she had nothing to fear. His charisma was stronger than any she'd known: her father's, Skyler's. They didn't have the raw charm this silver-haired government advocate broadcast by his mere presence—and the investigation hadn't even begun.

"I've reviewed your file, met with the Assistant Prosecutor Kincaid, and read the transcripts of the phone calls you've transcribed on your computer. I want to help you. We want to get this guy. But I'll need to know everything. I'll also need the thumb-drive he gave you when he began blackmailing you," said Agent Everett Lloyd.

He pulled out a small leather-bound notepad. "I don't want you to touch it. I'd like to come to your room and take it from wherever you've hidden it. We'd like to see if there are any identifiable fingerprints, besides yours.

We'll need you to go to the police station and have a full set of fingerprints taken, as well. That is, if your attorney agrees."

"Agreed," Rebecca answered.

Carefully studying the agent, Samantha wondered if she could get him to look at her directly, eye to eye, despite his training that required him to avoid direct eye contact. It would be fun to try, Samantha mused.

"Just remember, it's not my client on trial," Rebecca cautioned.

"At this point, no one's on trial," Agent Lloyd responded dryly. "We all need to work together, Ms. Smalley, to find conviction evidence."

"I'll expect copies of everything," Rebecca said.

Samantha watched Rebecca and Agent Lloyd volley information like a game with a rule-book. They seemed more interested in one-upping each other than in her. She was thankful they were on her side, not against her.

"We'll need access to her room to do the wiretap once we get the court order."

"Disguised as the telephone repairman or whatever you use," Rebecca said.

"We are more than adequately trained to operate under the radar," Agent Lloyd said.

"Judge Claude will sign the wiretapping subpoena and order I've prepared," Rebecca said, handing Agent Lloyd a file. "My secretary is setting up a chamber meeting with the Judge this afternoon. Can you make it?"

"We would've taken care of that."

"I like to stay ahead of the curve." Rebecca folded her arms.

"Samantha, can you join us in case the judge wants to ask you any questions?" Agent Lloyd asked.

"Yes. Skipping my afternoon classes won't be a problem," Samantha said, looking between the dueling pair.

"Fine. Let's meet at one-thirty. We'll review the facts before we walk over to the courthouse," Agent Lloyd said.

Rebecca's secretary walked in unobtrusively and Rebecca grabbed the note she held out.

Rebecca immediately announced the emergency hearing inside the judge's chambers had been set for three o'clock.

"May I bring John with me?" Samantha asked, before turning to leave.

"He can't come inside with us since he has no real knowledge, other than hearing your end of the conversations with Skyler. If you need him there for moral support, that's fine, but we'll be there to help you. This is a long, complex legal process. John will have plenty of time to get involved," Rebecca said. Her voice was soft, like that of an older sister to Samantha instead of her lawyer.

Samantha nodded. It had begun.

CHAPTER 31

Weary of answering questions, Samantha leaned closely toward John. Between bites, she whispered the day's events at an isolated table in the corner of the cafeteria.

"The judge granted the wiretap order. We can't tell anyone, not even Missy," Samantha whispered. "Actually, they never said I could tell you."

John nodded. "How long will the wiretap be in place?"

"No idea. I guess until they get enough evidence, and they believe me."

"Did they tell you they don't believe you?" John put his silverware down. "I think that's important. Did they say they don't believe you?"

"Rebecca believes me, but she talked at length about evidence problems. Agent Lloyd hasn't said one way or the other. He just says he's there to help, to get to the truth. I trust him, but I have not one clue what he really thinks."

"The way FBI agents are trained, they're not supposed to let on how they feel or what they know. I bet by now they've looked up Skyler and Greg—and you, and your whole family, for that matter. They probably have files on each of you."

"Really?"

"Yeah. Haven't you noticed how formal he is, how he doesn't look anyone directly in the eyes, and that he takes notes on everything?"

"Yes, but how did you know if you haven't seen much of him?"

"They're all the same. FBI, CIA. Agents go through very specific training. What about Assistant Prosecutor Kincaid?"

"He seems skeptical like the first day we walked in. But, he did recommend Rebecca, and I really like her." Samantha became aware of John's easy smile, his kind expression, and the warmth emanating from his body. The realization she had nothing to give him for all his help and support saddened her.

"Did I say something to upset you?" John asked.

"I wish it were over. I wish I hadn't involved you."

"Look, if things were reversed, and I needed help, you'd be there for me, right?"

Samantha nodded.

"I want this to be over as much as you do. I told you we'd go the distance together. I meant it."

Samantha tried to deflect the discomfort she felt. "Skyler ordered me to come home for Thanksgiving break next week. I told him I planned to stay here and study. He had a fit."

"Are you still transcribing the conversations?"

"I think I should keep doing that even if they're tapped in."

"That way you could compare the accuracy of what you've written with what is recorded."

"I love the way you think," she said. "You're always thinking ahead. My father would admire that in you. You'll make a great attorney someday."

"Thanks," John said. "Would it bother you if I read what you've typed?"

Samantha shifted in her chair.

"Can I read the Thanksgiving conversation? I think you should tell Rebecca about it, if you haven't already."

Samantha ate salad and changed the conversation to upcoming concerts she wanted to see in the area. When they'd finished dinner and John consumed an over-filled bowl of soft-serve ice cream, he walked Samantha to her room. Without saying a word, they silently conceded it was time for Skyler's usual call. They entered her room, eyes on the phone.

"Rebecca was here to get the thumb-drive Skyler gave me. She was with another woman. I don't know her name. She looked really young. I got the idea she was an FBI Agent or one in training. It was really cool the way Rebecca handled herself. It was like watching CSI's Catherine Willows. She removed the thumb-drive from the bottom of my underwear drawer with tweezers and put it in a labeled evidence bag to give to Agent Lloyd."

"Have you ever listened to it?"

"No."

"He blackmails you with a recording, and you don't listen to it?"

"Yes. No. Truth is, I listened to the first few words. I recognized my voice. I couldn't listen to it any further once I began sobbing. It made me sick. Every time I thought about listening to the rest of it, I froze," Samantha said, the disappointment she felt in herself clung to every word.

"I'm sorry." John pulled her toward him.

Hearing the ominous ring, Samantha stiffened. She grabbed the phone and sat in front of her computer.

"Hello."

"Hi, honey. Your mother and I wondered how you were doing. Every time we call, you're out."

"Hi, Dad," Samantha said, relieved. "Where's Mom?"

"Right here, dear. We decided we'd each grab a phone. How are you? Are you eating?"

"I'm fine. I'm eating way more than I should."

"Listen, dear, Skyler said he called you a few days ago to see how you were doing, and something about you not coming home for Thanksgiving. Is that right?" Mom asked.

"My break isn't even a full week, and I have so much homework, I'd thought I'd stay here. It's too long a drive and too expensive to fly for just a few days."

"I want all my children home with me," Dad said. "We'll send you a plane ticket and be at the airport to pick you up. There's no homework you can't do at home. We have libraries, too."

"Fine, Dad," Samantha said.

John looked confused. Samantha felt her voice turn childlike, her sentences diminished into short responses. Single-handedly, they had the ability to turn her into gelatin.

"Parents," Samantha said, hanging up and shaking her head. She cradled the receiver. But it rang again.

"Who were you on the phone with?" Skyler demanded.

"My parents."

"I want to know, right now. What man were you talking to?"

"My father."

"I can check. I will check," Skyler said stiffly.

"Fine," Samantha responded, her eyes focused on the gray computer keys.

"Well, what did they want?"

"Me, home at Thanksgiving."

"So what's the question? You know you need to see me. You know you want my hands on those moist thighs of yours. I bet you're wet right now, aren't you, baby?"

Samantha bit her lip so hard she drew blood. She felt the gnawing pain at the base of her neck stem up through her head, toward her temples, in hard heavy throbs. Nausea gripped her with each word she typed.

John read the words flashing on the screen.

When she finally hung up, she flashed past John and into the bathroom. Samantha emerged fifteen minutes later in a fluffy, pink robe. She sat on her bed, staring at the wall, and brushing her hair briskly.

"Samantha, are you all right? Can I do anything for you?" John asked.

Samantha shook her head slowly, back and forth. She felt John's eyes, but she didn't know what to say and didn't feel like talking.

"Samantha." John turned on the small lamp on her dresser then switched off the ceiling light. "You need rest. I'm sorry if I pushed you." John took the hair brush, put it on her desk, and closed the door behind him.

Samantha crawled under her comforter. The drugs she'd taken in the bathroom had caused her head to feel light and her eyelids heavy. She was at peace, safe in her own world. She pictured John. Maybe he could join her over Thanksgiving. She needed a plan in place to keep safe.

CHAPTER 32

Samantha wiped her blackened fingers on the stiff paper towel Assistant Prosecutor Kincaid handed her, while a police officer delivered the finger-inked card downstairs.

"Now what?" Samantha asked, frowning at the Prosecutor's studious look.

"We wait. It won't be long before the prints are matched. Detective Spaulding has been assigned to work with Agent Lloyd. They'll be in contact with you or Ms. Smalley as soon as they know anything."

"Exactly what are they doing?"

"Your prints will be matched with any found. The computers will be checked for matches on any other print found. Arkansas has been contacted and should fax us Skyler Marks's fingerprints."

"Do they have them?" Samantha interrupted.

"All attorneys are fingerprinted before they are licensed. They'll be on file."

"Will they tell him? Will he know?" Samantha asked fearfully.

"No one will know," Assistant Prosecutor Kincaid said.

Samantha nodded but did not feel relieved.

"One other thing. They're transcribing the recording on the thumb drive. Your attorney will have a copy of the transcript as soon as we do. We'll go over the transcript with you. We may have more questions for you." Assistant Prosecutor Kincaid said.

Samantha barely heard him.

* * * *

Blue uniforms moved into action the second Samantha's body began to swirl downward. Assistant Prosecutor Kincaid grabbed Samantha, breaking her fall. He put her fallen body onto the floor carefully. An officer radioed for an ambulance, another checked for a pulse, and two others straightened the awkwardly twisted Samantha.

* * * *

Within minutes, her eyes fluttered and then opened. Why were several pairs of eyes staring at her? Was she dreaming? A knifelike pain stabbed through her. Her head hurt so much she had to close her eyes again. What had happened? Had she been in an accident? She tried to move, but was restrained.

"Samantha, lie still. We have an ambulance coming," Assistant Prosecutor Kincaid whispered. He pushed hair off her face, and an officer covered her with a gray wool blanket.

"I'm fine," Samantha said, trying to sit up. She felt too weak to stand on her own.

"They're here, Samantha. They'll take you to Sparrow Hospital. It's downtown, just a few miles way. I'll follow you in my car to make sure you're all right. Is there anyone I can call? John? Your parents?"

"No," Samantha protested fiercely. "Call anyone, and I won't go. Swear."

"Okay. No calls, I swear," Assistant Prosecutor Kincaid said.

* * * *

At Sparrow, the doctor said, "Severely underweight. I'd like to keep you here for observation tonight."

"It's not that I don't want to, I can't. I've missed too much school already."

"I'll be happy to contact the school, your professors, whomever," the doctor said. "You need to stay the night, maybe a few days. There are some tests I'd like to run before you leave, just to make sure there's nothing else going on."

Samantha didn't want to explain. She didn't want to fight. She just wanted out. Exasperated, she finally agreed. "Fine. I'll stay, but no one is to be called. I'm eighteen; I have my health insurance card in my purse, and I can sign the paperwork."

The doctor excused himself to write Samantha's orders. She motioned the prosecutor closer to her. "What about Skyler?"

"What about him?" he asked.

"What do I tell him when he asks why I didn't answer the phone? What will I tell him tomorrow? I can't tell him this. He won't believe me. He'll tell my parents," Samantha said, with closed eyes. Her head still pounded, even as her body began to relax from the shot the doctor had given her for her migraine.

"I'll call Agent Lloyd. We'll put a recording on your phone, saying the phone has been temporarily disconnected. I'm sure he can fix it with the phone company to say a phone line is down, if they are called. Would that make you feel better?"

Samantha sighed deeply, nodding her head. "And, John?"

"I'll explain. I'll tell him you're sleeping, and you'll call tomorrow. Will that work?"

Samantha tried to open her eyes, but she couldn't. Instead, she nodded slowly and waved him off.

"I'll stop by in the morning. Feel better," he said.

CHAPTER 33

Dr. Walker came in just as Samantha woke up. Samantha stirred and looked sleepily up at him.

"We need to discuss your health," he said.

But Samantha didn't respond. Instead, she pushed her breakfast tray away.

"Not eating?" Dr. Walker said.

"I'm nauseated, and I have a dull headache."

"How often do you have headaches?"

"Every few days, I guess. I don't always sleep well—studying and everything."

"Do you take anything for your headaches?"

"Olin Health Center doctor prescribed something called Pamelor. I'm supposed to take it every night, but sometimes I forget."

"What else?"

"Excedrin for Migraine and Fiorinal, sometimes with Codeine."

"Anything else?"

"No."

The doctor sighed. After asking a few more questions

about her headaches and writing down several notes, he closed the chart.

"I deal with thousands of college students every year. I know how tough it can be. I know instead of seeing a doctor, it's easier to take an old prescription or something from a friend. I got the results of the tests we ran on you yesterday. And the tests show you are using other drugs—a lot of other drugs. They have made your body toxic. I can only help you get healthy if you tell me exactly what it is you've been putting in your body."

Samantha nodded but stayed silent.

"Do you ever look at yourself? I mean really look at yourself?"

She blinked.

"Unless you eat better, you'll die. I'm not saying that to scare you. I'm simply stating facts. I'm going to put you on a diet. You'll eat several small meals a day. You might want to see someone, who will help you figure out why you don't eat."

She didn't respond.

"When you came in, your eyes were constricted, your blood pressure was extremely low, and you were lethargic. You were suffering from respiratory depression, which explains, in part, why you fainted. You have the same symptoms this morning, although to a lesser degree. You say you have a dull headache? That's common. It's rebounding—something that happens when you get addicted to a drug, take too many drugs, or the wrong combination of drugs. That's what's happening to you."

Samantha drank a glass of orange juice he handed her.

"I want to help you. But you have to want to help yourself." He stared at her.

"I . . ." Samantha wiped the flowing tears, then continued. "I began to get headaches several months ago. My parents worry too much, so I just went into their cabinet and took some of my mother's migraine medicine. She gets them—migraines, I mean—a lot. She has so much medicine I just took some labeled for headache. I guess I shouldn't have."

"Do you know the names of the drugs?"

"Tylenol 3, Percocet, Valium. Sometimes I take sleeping pills. I also take birth-control pills." Samantha said, almost whispering. "The doctor at Olin told me they can cause headaches."

"Well, that pretty much matches the toxicology drug-screen report. We checked your urine and blood for alcohol and narcotics. The combination of drugs you described accounts for your elevated liver function. The drugs you've mixed are very dangerous all together, especially when you don't eat or drink enough water."

Samantha shrugged, and he removed the empty glass of orange juice and replaced it with a Styrofoam cup of ice water.

"They're not just dangerous, but deadly. By playing doctor, you're playing with your life. If you mix alcohol with any of the drugs you've taken, there may not be a second chance."

* * * *

Kyle Kincaid entered his office with his usual breakfast—two extra frosted raspberry jelly donuts and an extra-large cappuccino. But today he didn't open the bag. Setting it on his desk, he reviewed his messages, grabbed his coffee and headed for the hospital.

Before entering Samantha's hospital room, he paused. He heard voices through the door. Peeking in, he saw the drawn curtain and decided she must be in with the doctor. Ugh, terrible timing. He headed toward the nurses' station and found a chair and aimed it so he had a clear view of Samantha's room. He hated the way hospitals smelled and the constant noise of the serving trays clattering down the hallway.

When he saw the doctor exit, Kyle approached and reminded Dr. Walker that he was the one who'd brought Samantha.

Dr. Walker said he couldn't give out information about her and stepped away.

Kyle went into Samantha's room and waved the little bag of donuts in front of her. "Lookin' good."

"Donuts? Is this a Prosecutor's bribe? I thought donuts were a police officers' thing." Samantha said.

"Donuts are a human thing. Especially these. Quality Dairy raspberry-filled. Best in Michigan." Kyle set down coffee cups and the waxed bag. "I thought you might like real food, even though you haven't been in that long. When are you getting out?"

"Soon, I hope. Can you take me to my car?" Samantha asked. "I'm sorry I've been so much trouble."

"Don't worry about it." He paused and bit into one of the donuts. "With doctors' clearance I'm happy to drive you. Can I ask what's wrong?"

"The doctor wants me to eat better—and I get migraine headaches like my mother. They'll do a CAT scan and release me."

"I'm happy you're all right," Kyle said, licking his sticky fingers and washing his donut down with coffee. "I've got to head back. Call me if you need a ride. I've got a hearing at two-thirty. Okay?"

"You didn't tell anyone did you? I mean that I'm here?"

"Like who?" he said.

"My parents for starters.

CHAPTER 34

Samantha sat on the couch in Rebecca Smalley's office. She studied her attorney's attire and wondered if her wardrobe was meant to be a power statement. Despite it being her office, Rebecca blended in like wallpaper with Agent Lloyd, Prosecutor Kincaid, and Detective Spaulding. They reviewed the files they'd brought with an occasional murmur and pointing of fingers. Samantha missed most of their hidden whispers. She was beyond curious about the contents of the files and what they had discovered.

"I'm sorry, hon," Rebecca said. "We'll be with you in a minute. Help yourself to a bagel and some cream cheese. You look a bit pale."

Samantha nodded, chose a swirled rye-and-white bagel and then coated it with butter and cream cheese, then swirls of jam. Three days in the hospital was enough. If it meant eating a bagel, she would choke one down. Nibbling her creation, she wondered what and how much they knew. What had Assistant Prosecutor Kincaid told them about her fainting? She felt the usual lump in her throat that was there whenever she ate. She tried to follow the doctor's orders and eat better, but it was difficult. She envisioned his concerned face, heard his serious voice at every meal. She didn't want to die. She would prove him wrong—she hoped. She took another bite.

"Samantha," Rebecca said, as the group moved toward her and began pouring coffee and grabbing bagels and donuts from the tray. "We have several things to discuss with you."

The group sat around the coffee table, files on their laps. Samantha knew these serious faces were on her side, but she felt as if she were somehow being negatively scrutinized. She felt the rampant beating of her heart, but felt some comfort that Rebecca was sitting next to her.

Detective Spaulding began. "We were not able to get good fingerprints. The taped conversation clearly tells your side of what happened to you; but it doesn't implicate Skyler Marks in any way, except that he had knowledge of a crime, which he failed to report, but had no legal obligation to report. He could use the argument of attorney-client privilege to get out of that, because he works for your father's firm, and under these circumstances, a logical argument could be made. And it could be confirmed by your requests to not tell anyone."

"Skyler was very good on the tape. He is an excellent trial attorney, and he certainly used those skills," Agent

Lloyd added.

Samantha listened carefully.

"But," Detective Spaulding continued, "We do have quite a file on Mr. Marks, thanks to Agent Lloyd."

Nervously, Samantha picked apart her bagel, focusing her anxiety on over-chewing the bagel.

"We've already targeted Mr. Marks because of a client he's been representing," Agent Lloyd said, now looking down at the name and photo in his file.

Samantha looked at the black-and-white photo he'd put in front of her, puzzled at what the shriveled man in the picture could have to do with her. Within seconds, she recognized him from the newspapers back home. She hadn't been able to hide her recognition or her surprise. So what did he have to do with her?

"You know who he is, don't you?"

Samantha looked from Agent Lloyd to Rebecca, who nodded at her to answer.

"Yes. His name is Castriano. I don't remember his first name. I've never met him. I've seen his picture in the newspaper at home."

"Did you know your father's firm—specifically, Skyler Marks—is representing him?"

"Skyler brags to me about him. He represented him in a trial he worked on most of the summer, and then this fall, he told me he'd get him off on some technicality, and then he did it. My father is always saying Skyler has a knack for finding technicalities," Samantha said. "What does any of that have to do with me? I don't know Mr. Castriano, except from the newspaper and what Skyler told me."

"We believe you can help us, if you're willing," Agent Lloyd said.

Samantha felt as if she were part of a play, and she had either lost her script or was on the wrong stage. She looked at Rebecca. "Is my father in trouble?"

"Gentlemen." Rebecca stood. "I'd like to go into the conference room with my client. Help yourself to more coffee. If you need anything, please don't hesitate to ask my secretary. She beckoned to Samantha, who put her plate down and followed the attorney.

* * * *

Safe behind the closed conference-room door, Samantha sat at the end of the table facing Rebecca.

"I don't understand," Samantha said. "Does this mean they want to get my father in trouble, and they're not going to help me?"

"It means they believe you. It means if we aren't able to get Greg Maston on rape, and Skyler Marks on stalking, blackmail, and whatever else we can think of, there's a chance we can at least put Mr. Marks behind bars for what he's been involved in with Castriano."

Samantha listened to Rebecca's outline of the process and rationale. She couldn't help but instinctively, fearfully, interrupt her.

"I think I understand, but I want it clear that my father didn't have anything to do with Mr. Castriano, and if he did, then can't there be some kind of deal?" Samantha clenched her fists. "Skyler told me more than several times he was upset my father didn't want him to take Castriano on as a client. I'll get him to say it on tape if that is what you need."

Rebecca suddenly seemed to get it. "Oh dear, no. They're not after your father, at least not as far as I know—not from anything I've seen in the file."

"Can you guarantee me? Because otherwise, I'm out."

"You are my client. Your interests are what I'm concerned with. Say the word, and I will call off any further talk of this Castriano person. I can't guarantee anything, but as long as Skyler Marks and Castriano are associated with your father's firm, everyone in your family could become a target. These are dangerous people."

Samantha nodded. "Okay. But please make all of them promise to keep my family out of it. Please, that's the only way. I can't handle anything else." Samantha's voice began strong and definite, but ended in a tearful screech. She hated that she lost control when she needed it most.

"I'll do my best," Rebecca said, then remained silent for a few minutes.

The silence allowed Samantha to compose herself. Samantha finally spoke. "Thank you for everything and for not pressuring me."

"There's one other thing you need to know before we go back in there," Rebecca said softly, placing her hand on Samantha's forearm. "You can't tell anyone about this. Not even your friend John."

Samantha frowned. Alone again.

"It's for everyone's safety. I will be here for whatever you need, twenty-four/seven. Do you understand?" Rebecca asked.

"Yes."

"Do you have any questions before we go back?"

"No," Samantha said and followed Rebecca back to the men. She made a silent pact with herself not to disclose the tapes she'd privately made of her conversations with Skyler. She couldn't handle anything else.

* * * *

By the time Samantha arrived back in her room, it was almost noon. She didn't feel the need for lunch; she had managed to eat her whole bagel. She hated that she also had Dr. Walker's voice infiltrating her own thoughts. It was just another thing she didn't control.

Grabbing the phone as it rang, she hoped she remembered all the instructions she'd been given over the course of the morning.

"How was your morning class?" Skyler asked.

"Fine. We got out a little early because the professor was leaving for Thanksgiving break and figured we all were, too. I was surprised."

"So when are you coming home? I'll pick you up from the airport."

"My parents are picking me up. They couldn't get me on a flight before tomorrow, so I'm leaving tomorrow morning—around ten, I think."

"What are you doing tonight? Any hot plans?"

"I'm packing."

"What else?"

"The dorm is really quiet. I think most everyone has gone home already."

"What else is going on, Sam?"

"I'm happy to be going home. It'll be nice to see everyone. Emily wrote and said she and her family are joining us for a pre-Thanksgiving dinner."

"Why are you suddenly so talkative?"

"Just excited to see my family."

"But me most of all. Right?"

"Right." She mindlessly answered Skyler's questions and concentrated on typing her usual script. It had become more than a habit. It had become a security blanket, a way of dealing with what was happening. She'd learned she could tuck Skyler away, tune him out, shut him off, and lock him out of her mind, while she concentrated on typing. She was amazed the wiretapped line sounded normal. She tried to remember the information she was supposed to solicit from Skyler. She tried to stay one step ahead of him to fit the questions naturally into the conversation.

"Am I invited to the pre-Thanksgiving dinner?" he asked.

"Ask my parents."

"No. That's your department."

"I'll try."

"You'll succeed."

"Are you still busy with your trial?"

"Which one?"

"The Castriano case."

"Don't you listen to anything I say? I told you a few weeks ago about that trial. Remember me telling you, as I had predicted, I got him off on a technicality?"

"Oh, yeah. Sorry. I don't remember how you did it, though. Remind me what happened?"

"I convinced the judge the evidence was tainted, and I had it thrown out. Winning my motion meant the prosecutor had no case."

"Was he happy? Mr. Castriano, I mean?"

"Of course."

"Did he—I mean, you said he was going to give you a bonus. Did you get what you wanted?"

"Mr. Castriano never goes back on his word. Why all the questions?" Skyler asked sternly. "You've never been interested before."

"College is opening my eyes, and I'm curious about what lawyers really do. I have to choose my classes for next term, and I wanted to jump ahead from the basics and take a pre-law class."

"What really brought this on?"

"I just told you. I mean, if you don't want to talk, like my dad, I'll just ask my professors." Being this assertive no longer came naturally to her.

"I've got to grab a quick sandwich and run over to court. I'll call you later, and I'll definitely see you tomorrow."

Hearing the sudden click wasn't unusual to Samantha. She was accustomed to his erratic behavior. She began packing her bag, hoping to finish before John stopped by. It looked as though Missy had been in their room earlier and had dropped off all of her books, leaving them piled high on her desk. Samantha scanned the pile and noticed a note next to it. *Sam—Happy Thanksgiving. See you next week. Missy.*

Not dealing with Missy was relief, Samantha thought, and finished packing.

When there was a knock on the door a few minutes later, she wasn't surprised to see John.

"Looks like you're packed," John said. "Can I take you to the airport tomorrow?"

"I'll take a cab. When are you going home?"

"In the morning around the time you leave. So, it's no problem to drop you off at the airport. It takes just over an hour to get to Saginaw."

"I'll need to be at the airport at eight." She studied him.

"You decide. Happy to take you whenever."

Samantha nodded.

"Since you're packed, let's go out for a few hours. You can leave your phone off the hook again."

"Okay, but, first, we've got to talk." Samantha sat on her desk chair, pulling Missy's chair out for John. "I met with Rebecca this morning. Actually, everyone was there. We're on to the next stage of my case. They've asked me to not discuss it with anyone." Samantha met John's wide eyes. "Including you."

"I don't understand. I'd like to help," John said.

"I know. They know that, too. They don't want any more people than need to be involved. I'm sorry," Samantha said.

"You have nothing to be sorry for. The professionals have to do it their way. I just want what's best for you."

"I know. I appreciate your help."

"I don't understand, but it's fine. It's your case," he said. "If you need me for anything at all, you promise you'll ask?"

"Yes. I swear," Samantha said, letting her southern drawl drag just enough to make him feel like the hero, who had rescued her and brought her to safety.

✳ ✳ ✳ ✳

Skyler looked at the clock on his nightstand. Eleven-thirty. Time to call Samantha. But the busy signal beeped over and over again. He continued to redial. Agitated, he called the operator, who informed him it was off the hook. Skyler slowly replaced his receiver, puzzled. She had left the phone off the hook. Where was she? How many times could she hang up the phone wrong? What was going on? Was she with someone else? He shoved his phone off the nightstand. Hearing it crash brought him back to the present and triggered more anger.

She had to be stopped. He would teach her a lesson about what it meant to lie, to cheat, to tease. He was in absolute control, not her. He would have her, or no one would, he vowed. He slipped on his jeans, shirt, and blazer. Tossing his keys into the air and catching them again, Skyler confidently whistled: "Ain't no mountain high enough to keep me away from you, babe ..." Then, getting into his Jaguar, he headed to his favorite bar for another *lucky night*.

CHAPTER 35

Samantha boarded the plane. Her anxious stomach and pounding head had become so normal, she'd automatically begun her day with medications, heeding the doctors warning and trying not to mix the wrong ones. She researched what she could on the internet. She was sure taking pills felt better than not taking them.

She made a conscious effort to eat because she now understood certain pills on an empty stomach could cause pain and nausea. She finally realized she felt better taking her medication with food, except when she had a migraine headache.

Grabbing a blanket and pillow before taking her seat next to the window, she hoped for sleep before having to deal with her parents and Skyler. The plane departed from the gate, she closed her eyes, and she drifted. A hushed evil laugh infiltrated her mind. Was it coming from the person next to her or behind her? She opened her eyes and looked around. The seat next to her was empty.

"Tom's mine," a voice whispered. "Keep your hands off him."

From the dormant recesses of her mind, Samantha felt a twinge of familiarity in the voice, in the laughter. But she didn't recognize anyone on the plane. The voice whispered fiercely, relentlessly laughing at her discomfort.

Maybe it was the drugs. The ringing in her ears. Her headache. Maybe the pain was getting to her. Maybe she took the wrong mixture of drugs.

She had to shut it all out; she didn't want to think about it. But the laughter continued. She pressed her head against the pillow as hard as she could and covered her other ear with her hand, but she couldn't rid herself of the voice, of the laughter.

Pushing the call button, Samantha asked the responding flight attendant for a glass of milk. He returned with a cold carton and a plastic cup, Samantha nodded her thanks then popped another pill into her mouth. It would help her sleep. It would rid her of the voices. It would make everything more tolerable; she didn't care what the doctor said.

Minutes later, everything went black and silent.

Samantha awoke to the flight attendant tapping her shoulder asking if she needed help getting off the plane.

Samantha declined, grabbed her things, and weaved off the plane to baggage claim into the waving arms of her mother.

"It's so good to see you. How was your flight?" her mom asked, and the family walked toward the baggage carousel.

Her dad echoed hello and planted a light kiss on her cheek.

"Fine, Mom. The noise on the plane gave me a headache, and just as I fell asleep, we landed," Samantha said groggily, hoping her mother wouldn't scrutinize her closely.

"Travis, why don't you bring the car around, while we get her suitcase? I think we need to get Samantha home for a real nap before dinner."

Samantha was relieved when her father pulled the car into the driveway and ordered her bags taken upstairs. Entering her room, she felt immediately guarded and exposed, rather than relieved. Why? She tore off her clothes and entered the safety of her shower, and then calm of her sheets.

* * * *

"Samantha?" Her mother called into the darkened room. "Your father and I are getting ready for dinner. Cook's made a special meal for you. We have guests joining us. Please dress appropriately." Her mother turned the light on before she pulled the door closed.

Samantha slipped out from the warmth of her bed. She'd had the dream again; she'd seen parts of people's faces. None of the faces were whole. She'd heard the laughter and the voices and the music box. She'd watched it all parade by her. She'd tried to cry out, but she'd lost her voice. What did it all mean? She sighed, pulled a dress from her closet, and opened her make-up case.

The pills. All this was happening because of the pills. Had she again combined the wrong ones? She finished her hair and make-up then opened her purse and pulled out two red pills. These would help her get through dinner and her still-pounding headache. When would she get relief from her dreams, from her headaches? She imagined a life without problems or migraines. She gulped down the capsules then pounded down the winding staircase as a sudden thought struck her. Had Agent Lloyd bugged her parents' phones, too? Would the investigators tell her? She heard echoes and headed toward them once she landed in the foyer. A few feet later, she entered the dining room and halted when she heard him.

"Well, well, well. The college coed returns home," Skyler said.

Thanks to you, Samantha snarled inwardly. She wished she could scream those words at him. Instead, she smiled with all the sweetness she could force from her depleted reserves.

"The twins won't arrive until late Tuesday evening. They couldn't miss any classes. I'm really proud of those boys," her dad boasted loudly, into the lull, nodding at Hyrum to pour the wine. He motioned everyone to be seated at the dining table.

Samantha couldn't concentrate on the dinner conversation. She felt she was in the room under remote control; someone pushed a button, and she responded, and in the interim, she lay dormant.

"May I be excused?" she finally asked her parents avoiding Skyler's piercing eyes.

"No dessert, dear?" Mom asked.

"I'm so tired I don't have the strength to eat it. Save me some?"

"All right, dear," Mom said. She put her cheek in the air, waiting for a kiss.

Samantha kissed her mother and then her father and said good-night.

"Nice seeing you again Mr. Marks," Samantha said.

"Very happy you're doing so well in school, Samantha. It was a pleasure seeing you. I hope I'll see you again before you leave." Skyler stood and shook her hand.

Samantha felt instant pain in his too-tight handshake grip. She knew Skyler was upset with her. Her body went cold and rigid the instant she heard the familiar tone in his voice, the slur in his words. She wished she could scream for the others to wake up and notice.

Once in her room, Samantha spent a lazy hour on the phone, catching up with Emily. When Emily inquired as to any developments regarding Skyler she shrugged it off saying school and distance had taken care of his interest in her. She worried Emily didn't believe her. She wondered why everyone was so blind to Skyler.

$$* * * *$$

Samantha awoke, immediately frightened, startled by a strong hand over her mouth. In seconds, her eyes focused on the face close to hers.

"It's me, Samantha. Don't scream. It's just me."

Samantha tried to relax, but he scared her. He wasn't supposed to be there, in her room. Skyler had now invaded her most private place; there was no place left to hide.

He removed his hand slowly, intimating with his sharp, deliberate movements that if she spoke up, gave him away, she would pay.

She remained silent. She had no voice with which to respond, and she had no kind voice, so silence suited her. She nodded in agreement with his terms.

"You are so beautiful, Samantha," Skyler whispered. He ran his hand through her hair, and clasped his fingers tightly around the thick clump of curls.

"Next time you'll stay in the room—whatever room we're in—as long as I'm there. It was naughty of you to leave the dinner table when I was there. You are to be with me. Do you understand?"

Samantha's eyes sprang wide. She clenched her hands tightly along the edges of her comforter hearing the sound of his loafers slipping off, the unbuckling of his belt, and the unzipping of his pants. Samantha focused on the ceiling. She couldn't watch; she knew what was coming.

Skyler crept between her sheets. Samantha slipped into a deep, peaceful sleep, where there was no danger, no threat, no violation. Darcey entertained Skyler exactly as he instructed.

CHAPTER 36

Wednesday evening, the night before Thanksgiving Day, Greg Maston sat quietly in the conference room of the firm's office, poring over the firm's accounting books, preparing the year-end report. He was confident his numbers were accurate. Travis Armstrong would arrive soon to review the figures before they were presented to the partners early Monday morning, after the busy holiday.

Greg didn't have family to spend Thanksgiving with. The break gave him time to concentrate. He stretched his legs in nervous anticipation of Travis's arrival. The stiffness in his back and legs made walking around the long conference table and placing a year-end report at each chair a welcome task. He didn't like working after hours and on weekends, but using the firm's office had benefits his home office didn't. He walked through the connecting door to Travis Armstrong's office toward the bar hid behind the movable panel.

Attorneys know how to live, Greg thought, making a small toasting gesture before he swallowed a double shot of Irish whiskey and poured another. His thirst satisfied, he closed the panel and turned the key to lock it again. The alcohol calmed his nerves. In the past few years, this daily ritual helped him maintain his composure, and he was able to accomplish more in shorter time frames.

The stillness of the office matched the lull in the nightly traffic noises. Greg hastened to finish his last notes and pack up his briefcase. He hoped for a very short review with Travis. He had a standing date at The Bishop's Pub and was anxious to take his seat by the television at the bar.

Bending over the extra copies of the report, he aligned them on the corner of his desk. He began to straighten his back and felt a sudden sharp pain. Confused, he turned to see what had happened. He reached his hand toward the razor-sharp pain. Had he run into something broken? His mind raced. He twisted back and saw the black gloved intruder, who'd struck him. Greg felt wetness on his shirt. Alarmed, he realized he was bleeding. Thick red blood was staining his shirt, spilling onto the floor.

His blood. It had to be. Yet, he felt no pain, only alarm and adrenaline. What happened? He wasn't aware of his breathing, of any movement. Time stood still. His body moved in slow motion, but his mind raced, questioning. His heart pounded imminent fear, sensing the intruder's animal instinct to hunt him down like prey, to finish the job. But he was strong, he rationalized. He could fight this attacker; he could survive.

He faced the darkly clad figure, but his leg caught the chair next to him. He lost his balance, reached up, just missed the table, and hit his head hard against its corner.

There wasn't any pain, but the gurgling noises must have been coming from him. The intruder jabbed repeatedly at his flesh. He peered through blood at his attacker. Then, his energy depleted, he felt his body release.

The office returned to silence. The lights clicked off.

* * * *

It was just before eight. The building had emptied, except for the plump, dark woman, who talked to herself while she unlocked the heavy-glass doors. She re-tied the scarf that held her unruly hair, while she performed her routine cleaning.

She opened each office door, flicking on each light switch she passed. Hearing the sound of keys, she turned.

"Good evening, Frieda," Travis Armstrong said. "Getting an early start, I see. How are you?"

"Fine, sir. I'm doing good these days. Gotta fit all my customers in." Frieda smiled broadly. "You're working late for a Wednesday. I thought you'd be home with your children enjoying the holiday."

"I have a little paperwork to review, and then, you're right, I'll be home for the duration."

"I miss seeing those fine young ones of yours."

"Thank you; we're proud of them," Travis said. "Have you seen Greg—Mr. Maston—anywhere? He's supposed to meet me here."

"No, sir. Maybe he's running late. You just run, run, run. I don't know how you all do it."

Frieda continued down the long hallway.

Travis heard the scream and darted from behind his desk toward the shrieks. He decided it was either a spider or that Frieda had hurt herself. He found her in the conference room. He examined her kneeling form to see where she was hurt, and then followed her gaze to the bloodied body of his friend. The stench of violence and coagulating blood on the arms of the chairs and edges of the tables made him weak. Blood seemed to be everywhere. He reached for Greg's wrist to find a pulse. But there was none.

* * * *

Minutes passed like hours after Travis's trembling 911 call brought ambulance, detectives, police, and a medical examiner to the crime scene. Hours passed while Travis sat in his office until he spoke to everyone who wanted to speak to him and all samples were collected, photos were taken, and questions were asked of him and Frieda. Police sealed the crime scene and the entire office.

Now motionless, Travis sat in his car, unable to drive. What the hell had happened? His mind exploded with emotion, with questions. How would he tell his family?

"Mr. Armstrong?" Detective Winston tapped on the

window. "Mr. Armstrong?"

"I'm sorry. Did you need something else?" Travis rolled down the window.

"Are you all right? Can I drive you home?"

"No. Thank you. I'll be fine."

"There's one other thing we'll need as soon as you can arrange it. We need a set of fingerprints of all of your employees and family, who have been in the office this week. Also a list of clients—anyone who's been in the office or has access to the office. The entry wasn't forced. More than likely the person who did this knew the victim."

"Prints from everyone? That'll take some time. I'll help any way I can; we all will. As to clients, there is confidentiality, and I can't release those names."

"The investigation will be much smoother with everyone's cooperation. We'll deal with the client issue. Hopefully, we'll find one good print from the assailant without having that battle. Can you arrange a time for us to meet individually with your staff?"

"Is tomorrow soon enough? I can't think about it tonight."

"That'll be fine. If you're sure you don't need a ride, I'll get back to the station. I really am sorry about your loss."

Travis nodded, no longer listening. He played the crime scene over in his mind. He couldn't bear to think the words, let alone say the words he needed to. There was no way to explain such a brutal crime.

"I'll call you in the morning," Travis called after the detective and slid the window slowly up.

When he got home, it was ten o'clock. Travis called his wife and daughter into his study. He poured a tall martini, drank it down, and then poured and drank another. Seeing Anne's questioning gaze, he poured one for her, refilled his glass, and then asked them to sit. Behind closed doors, they sat as a family.

"This can't wait until the twins arrive for this announcement. I just returned from my office where I found our accountant, Greg Maston brutally murdered."

Seconds later, the phone rang.

Within minutes, partners were at the door. The media positioned themselves on the front lawn. Travis called detectives, who agreed to show up, and Travis advised the reporters that once the detectives arrived, he would make a brief statement hoping the circus on the lawn would then exit.

Samantha couldn't watch. She couldn't listen. She had wished Greg dead, and now he was. She was relieved, even happy he was dead. And she felt guilty for feeling glad.

With an odd sense of calm, she struggled with a nagging suspicion she couldn't have been this lucky. Willing people dead wasn't anything more than wishful thinking, she rationalized; she wished that would happen to Skyler. There, she'd said it—maybe not out loud, but to herself. No crime in wishing.

"Samantha, you and your mother will join me for the statement. A united front. You two will stand to the back of me, one on each side," her father said gravely, but sternly intimating there would be no questions or discussion.

Travis summarized the night's events and relayed Detective Winston's instructions about fingerprints and interviews. He rested his eyes on his wife and daughter indicating they were also included in everything the firm was cooperating in.

* * * *

Samantha felt trapped hearing her father's orders. She pictured police finding her fingerprints all over the room. Her head pounded. Her breathing became uneven. Her father's voice began to fade; she heard ringing in its place. She listened harder and tried to focus, but she couldn't. Her flesh became moist, and her heart beat loudly in her ears. Samantha fell onto the plush white carpet. Her mind was blank, her body limp.

Travis rushed to her, picked her up, and moved her back onto the couch.

Anne grabbed a blanket from the back of a chair and placed it over her daughter. She leaned over her, stroking her cheeks, whispering, "Samantha, dear, it's your mother. Can you hear me?"

Samantha felt like a ton of bricks was on top of her. Her eyes fluttered open, she felt aghast as she saw her parents leaning over her, there with her mother's worried face and her father's stern one. My God, where am I? What happened?

"How are you feeling, dear?" Mom asked. "You fainted. We should have thought this might bother you. Should I call a doctor?"

Samantha's eyes grew wide, and her mind raced at the word *doctor*.

She shook her head. "I'm fine, really. I just pictured him the way dad described the scene and the blood," she lied, pausing long enough, her eyes downcast. "I'm sorry." She looked up and into her mother's eyes and then her father's. "I'm afraid I'll faint when you talk. Can I just go to bed?"

"Samantha, I'm sorry. You have nothing to be sorry about. I should've thought about the effect on you when I described the scene."

Samantha turned her focus from her father to her mother, who nodded. "You get yourself upstairs and into bed. I'll send Cook up with a glass of warm milk."

Samantha planted her feet firmly on the carpet, and made her way to her room, relieved to be alone.

Sadness overpowering her relief, Samantha swallowed a handful of colorful pills and slipped into her sheets. She wanted to relieve herself of the nagging migraine and sleep deeply. The pills would be her insurance she didn't dream.

By the time Cook brought her the large mug of warm

milk, Samantha was very relaxed. She barely had the strength to raise her head from the pillow. She drank the milk, while Cook's soft face watched her. Trying to cheer Samantha up, Cook told her the twins had arrived, and they'd been instructed not to disturb her, but they wished her a good night. Samantha nodded and closed her eyes.

CHAPTER 37

It had been less than twenty-four hours since the murder. Every employee of the firm was called in, fingerprinted, and questioned. No one had much to say except to express shock and sadness.

Thanksgiving dinner was subdued. Family and friends gathered. While cutting turkey, scooping mashed potatoes, piercing stuffing and salad the discussion turned back to Greg's murder no matter how much Samantha tried to change the subject.

She tried to show sorrow, instead of how thankful she was that God had used another's hand to strike her assailant dead. She stared at Skyler across the table from her and prayed he would be next. She hated the way he looked at her, as if she were being served on his plate. He winked at her every chance he had. She loathed his winking.

To Samantha's surprise, her mother clinked her water glass with a tablespoon and the table was immediately silenced. "We will not talk of tragedy at my holiday table when it's the first time in three months my family has been together." Anne looked around the table and her gaze ended at Travis. Samantha recognized her mother's silent stare that didn't just announce but ordered her father to agree and pick up his end of the entertaining.

Travis prided himself on being an exceptional host, but today he didn't feel like eating, entertaining, or celebrating. A man who had been like a brother to him, and one of his oldest friends, had been brutally murdered in his office. He felt responsible; he felt cheated.

Travis raised the champagne glass Hyrum had just refilled and pointed Hyrum to the emptied glasses on the table. "I'd like to make a toast." He waited until each glass was filled and raised. "Yesterday we lost a very good friend, who was as much a part of this family as everyone here today. It's important we remember who he was, not how he left us. Greg would want us to remember him fondly and enjoy this time together, as if he were here. Because, he is here. To Greg."

Glasses were raised, clinked, and emptied. Everyone, except Samantha, who excused herself. She ran up to her bedroom, and into the bathroom to release her dinner. Tears flowed freely as she brushed her teeth. She found her purse, grabbed one white tablet and one red capsule and swallowed them. Then she returned to the dining room.

The dinner conversation had shifted, and Samantha was grateful that by the time dessert was served, laughter and conversation kept Skyler focused on others.

When Hyrum entered, Samantha watched his body language and knew something was amiss. She followed her father out of the dining room and remained silent in the background.

"Happy Thanksgiving. Are you here with news?" Travis asked.

Detective Winston nodded. "I need to speak with your daughter, Samantha."

Samantha stepped forward surprised. "I'm right here," she said. Detective Winston stepped toward her. The two police officers accompanying him stood in front of the front door. Were they blocking it so she couldn't leave, she wondered? Why would they do that?

"I'm sorry, Samantha. This is a formal visit. We need you downtown," he turned back to Travis. "You may want to have an attorney present."

Travis looked stunned. He didn't believe what he was hearing.

"What?" Travis said. "Detective, surely, you don't believe Samantha had anything to do with Greg's murder?"

"You're welcome to come downtown with us. But I insist she come with us now."

"Not only is that absurd, but you've interrupted Thanksgiving dinner." Travis tried to keep the anger out of his voice.

"I'm sorry." He handed Travis a folded document. "I have a search warrant for your house."

Travis read the paper, alarm fell across his face. "We have guests. Could you at least be quiet and avoid the dining room? I'll steer them outside to our greenhouse. I'd like this as private as possible."

"We'll be careful not to disturb you or your guests, for now."

"Samantha," Travis spoke softly, putting his hand on her shoulder. "These gentlemen want to ask you a few more questions. They've asked us to go to the station with them. I'll follow in my car." Travis turned and spoke sternly to law enforcement. "I don't have to remind you she has counsel. No questioning without counsel."

"Are you representing her?" Detective Winston asked.

"That's right. Let's get on with this charade, so I can return to Thanksgiving dinner with my family."

Detective Winston raised an eyebrow at the officers, and Samantha followed his order to leave with the officers.

Samantha sat quietly in the back seat of the police car, heart pounding, mind racing. What was happening? The closed-in rear of the police car felt claustrophobic. She was grateful they didn't hand-cuff her. Her fear grew deeper with each passing minute. Why was she being taken to the station house?

* * * *

Hours passed. She sat alone in the beaten, dingy, conference room with the bottle of water she'd been given.

Where had everyone gone? Why wasn't anyone questioning her, if that's what they were there for? She chugged the water and tossed the empty bottle into the dented metal wastebasket. The noise echoed, a loud solitary thump, like the last beat of a heart. Her eyes darted toward the door that creaked open.

"Samantha, there's been some terrible mistake, but you're a suspect in Greg's murder," her father said.

Samantha felt her father study her reaction.

"That's insane. I haven't seen him since my birthday party. And, let's face it, I couldn't kill anyone." Samantha wilted, trembling with fright. She lay her head in her hands and rested it on the conference table.

"I know. I'll get you the best attorney I can. Skyler. Would you like that?"

"No. Not Skyler. Promise me," Samantha said desperately, her voice dry, her eyes wide and unblinking.

"Why in hell not? He has the highest criminal defense record in the county. You need the best."

"Not him. I won't talk to either of you if you force me. I'd rather go to jail."

"Skyler has been a friend to you," he frowned. "What exactly is your objection?"

"Promise, Dad. Promise me," Samantha said with a voice as forceful and desperate as she'd ever used.

"Fine, Samantha. I don't understand, but I'll promise. Maybe he can just consult?"

"No. Not one word. You promised. I want my own

attorney."

Travis stared. "Your own attorney? Have you called someone while you were waiting?"

"I hired an attorney at school. I want her."

"Hired her? Who?"

"Rebecca Smalley. She's a criminal lawyer in Michigan."

"Samantha, I don't know her or anything about her. A Michigan attorney can't practice here without special permission. You are in serious trouble. I want the best for you."

"I won't talk to anyone unless Rebecca is with me. I don't care how much trouble I'm in. I just don't care anymore." Samantha began to sob. It was all in slow motion; it wasn't happening.

"Fine, fine. You can have this Rebecca Smalley, but she'll have to work with an Arkansas attorney. We'll find you one together."

Samantha nodded. "I want an Arkansas attorney Rebecca likes."

"Whatever you say," Travis said with exasperated sigh.

"Can we go home?" Samantha asked her saddened father.

"No. They're holding you for questioning, and I suspect are bringing charges."

"That can't be. When can I go home?"

"If you are charged, they will have you arraigned by a judge and bond will be set. I'll pay whatever bond is set. I believe they will release you to me. It may take a few days, hopefully not longer. Do you understand?"

Samantha nodded.

Travis stood, opened the door, and Detective Winston entered. The men shook hands.

Winston sat a recording device center table and read Samantha her Miranda rights.

"Can this wait until my attorney arrives?" Samantha timidly asked.

"I thought your father is your attorney," Detective Winston said.

"I changed my mind. I don't want any attorney with my father's firm. That includes my father. I'm sorry," Samantha said nervously, hoping she didn't insult or hurt her father.

"That's your right. When you have an attorney, we'll continue with questions."

"Can I go?" Samantha asked anxiously.

"No. I'm sorry," he sighed. "Let's have an early understanding. You are being charged with the murder of Greg Maston. Meanwhile, we have the right to detain you for twenty-four hours while the prosecutor prepares the charges."

"You know she isn't going anywhere. Will you release her into my custody? I will be responsible."

"If the prosecutor agrees, with jail GPS tether, and you have an attorney within forty-eight hours. We don't want any unnecessary delay," Detective Winston paused. "This is a special favor to you. Don't make me regret it."

"Understood," Travis said, standing up simultaneously with Samantha.

* * * *

Tethered and finally outside, the silence between father and daughter was deafening. Neither had the energy to speak. Neither expected the other to understand their perspective or comprehend the reality of the impending disaster that was about to befall the family.

And neither had the courage to acknowledge the truth.

CHAPTER 38

The day after Samantha's arrest, Rebecca Smalley arrived at the Armstrong house just as afternoon tea was served.

Samantha stood on the landing of the staircase watching her parents introduce themselves. Pleasantries were exchanged. "Thank you for being here so quickly," Samantha said. She stepped off the landing and hugged Rebecca tightly.

"Would you like to talk privately with Samantha before meeting us for tea?" her father asked.

Rebecca nodded.

Samantha led Rebecca into her father's study and closed the doors. They sat at each end of the plaid couch. Samantha nervously stared at Rebecca, not knowing where to begin.

"Samantha, I need you to tell me everything that's happened since you came home. I brought my recorder. It is for my reference only, nothing else."

"I haven't told my parents anything about Greg or Skyler. I'm afraid to. I wanted to talk to you first. I don't know what to do. The police think I killed Greg."

Rebecca nodded.

Samantha, knew she had to say it: "I didn't, I swear."

Rebecca frowned.

Samantha gave her as much detail as she could remember about what she'd done the day Greg was murdered.

"Are you sure you were taking a nap when Greg was murdered?" Rebecca asked when she finished.

"Yes. I remember talking to Skyler; he called after dinner. I wasn't feeling well. I went upstairs, took something for my headache and lay on my bed. Just as I lay down, the phone rang, and it was him."

"Do you remember the conversation?" Rebecca asked.

Samantha recited the conversation, and then she faltered. Her mind blanked. She didn't recall how the conversation ended. "I must have fallen asleep while we were talking. I don't remember saying good-bye."

"That's fine, Samantha. The FBI should have it on tape. You haven't discussed any of this with anyone else, have you?"

"No."

"Not even Emily or John?"

"No. I even asked John not to call me at home, so he stays out of it. He's already done so much for me."

"I'll need to get those recordings or a transcript. They might help you, but understand we'll have to talk with the Assistant Prosecutor Kincaid and law enforcement to fill them in. Are you willing to do that?"

Samantha took in a deep, slow breath. "I'll do what I have to. I don't want my family hurt." Samantha whispered, her voice cracking as tears splashed through her lower lashes onto her cheeks. "You should've seen my father's face."

"I'll contact Agent Lloyd with the FBI. You bring in your father. I understand he's discussed your case briefly with the prosecutor. I'll get waived into this jurisdiction for this matter. We need to talk with your father. Are you ready to be honest with him? I'll be with you to help you through it."

Samantha nodded. She had to be ready to tell the truth; she was cornered. She couldn't spend her life in prison. She knew she didn't do it, but why couldn't she remember what happened after the phone call?

Samantha texted her father to join them. When he entered, he had a file in his hand with her name on it.

"Here are copies of the documents from the police file," Travis said bleakly to Rebecca.

"I appreciate that. Next time don't interfere. You and I both know, as Samantha's attorney, they'd have to show me the file," Rebecca said dryly. She took the file. "I can get waived in as you know, so you shouldn't need to hire anyone else to represent Samantha, but I leave that up to Samantha."

Samantha watched Rebecca read the file. She watched her father watch Rebecca. She was thankful no one watched her, and that her mother wasn't in the room with them.

After several minutes of jotting down what Samantha decided must have been notes, Rebecca closed the file.

"Samantha, are you aware of how Greg was murdered?" Rebecca inquired.

"Dad told me he was stabbed; that was also mentioned on the news."

"Do you know with what?"

"A knife, I guess. I don't know. Is that a trick question?" Samantha asked.

"Do you know how your fingerprints got on the murder weapon?"

"My prints? On the weapon?"

"There were two sets of prints, yours and Greg's."

"I didn't do it. How could there be prints? I swear, I wasn't there."

"I believe you. We'll get to the bottom of this. I just need you to answer a few more questions."

Samantha nodded, avoiding her father's eyes, amazed he wasn't participating in any of the questioning.

"You said the last time you saw Greg was at your birthday party. Do you remember what he wore?"

Samantha paused, puzzled at the question, not understanding the relationship between her birthday and the murder. "No. It was warm outside. I don't recall. Maybe a polo shirt and some khaki pants. That's how he usually dressed."

"Is it possible he was wearing a white shirt, the kind

he might wear to work?"

"I guess so. Why?"

"The police matched a hair sample from you with hairs found on Greg's body. There were a few hairs around a shirt button. They were stretched, like they were pulled out in a struggle."

"A hair sample from me? I didn't give them any of my hair."

"Maybe not, but when you went in for questioning, they knew about the fingerprints matching and, like most women with long hair, you shed a few hairs. They tested, and it was a match. They had taken hair samples from your hairbrush when they searched your room. The curious thing is that there were several strands of hair. One is from a third person."

Samantha stopped twisting her hair around her thumb and forefinger. "I swear, I wasn't there. I didn't do it."

"Samantha, just a few more questions, and then we'll discuss and analyze what we're working with—working against, rather. Assuming he was wearing the same shirt he wore to your birthday party, how close were you standing to Greg?"

"Not close. I wouldn't stand close to him. I couldn't," Samantha said slowly and emphatically. She focused so hard on her shoes, she could imagine her toes beneath the leather. She wished she could hide behind a curtain of leather, while she answered Rebecca's questions in front of her father. "I don't even recall speaking to him. He was with Skyler. I spoke to Skyler just for a few seconds."

Expressionless Travis piped in. "I can ask Skyler what he remembers."

Rebecca stared at Travis and then to Samantha's relief said, "Mr. Armstrong, I know you're concerned about your daughter and her welfare. However, she has asked me to represent her. She approved your presence. Please don't interrupt again."

Rebecca handed Samantha a photocopy of a black-and-white photograph of an earring. "Is this familiar to you?"

Samantha stared at the picture. "It looks like an earring I lost several months ago. It was one of my favorites."

"Do you have the mate to the one you lost?"

"No idea."

"Think. It's important. We might need to prove the earring they found is not yours."

Samantha wished she could remember. "I'll check my room."

"Do that this evening. If you find it, I want it. Don't give it to anyone else. I suspect they'd have found it in the search if it was in your room. Is it possible it's at school?"

"I don't know. It's real gold. I wouldn't have thrown it out after I lost the other one."

"Samantha, you're probably not going back to school, this term at least. I'll contact my partner, and she'll find whatever box or drawer you think it might be in. Will that be okay?"

"I'll call my roommate. She'll help." Samantha sighed. "Can you at least tell me where the earring was?"

"Under Greg's body. The police believe the earring was lost in the struggle."

"Then it can't be mine. I wasn't there. Besides, there must be thousands of earrings like the one in that picture," Samantha said, trying to reassure them and herself, as warm, fresh tears streamed down her face.

Rebecca and Travis nodded.

"Mr. Armstrong, I know you want to be involved in your daughter's case. I'll keep you apprised, with her approval. But it's imperative you don't discuss any—not even the smallest detail—with her mother, anyone in your firm, or anyone else."

"Of course," Travis said with a hint of sarcasm.

"Also," Rebecca said, returning the photocopy to the file, "I'll keep this file. There can be no copies of any part of your daughter's case in your firm's files or in your home files."

"What is going on, Ms. Smalley?"

"First we agree."

"Agreed."

"Samantha?" Rebecca looked toward Samantha.

Samantha saw the urging in her eyes. She felt sick. She wanted to slip into a crack, never to be heard from again. She tried to find her voice and a place to begin.

The lump in her throat returned, larger than it had ever been before. Never had she felt so insecure, so worthless, so dirty. Her voice quavered, barely audible. Finding the words was strenuous. The visualization was painful and exhausting.

Samantha told her dad what Greg had done and filled in as much of the detail as she could, taking long breathy pauses and uttering labored words that converted secrecy into exposure. Rebecca assisted by asking probing questions. The inevitable unmasking of her ordeal rendered Samantha unable to speak coherently at times. She felt the disapproving stare of her father.

When she broke down, her dad sat still.

"Let's give Samantha a break," Rebecca finally said. "Perhaps you'd like to update your wife. She'll need to know what's happening, but not every detail. We need as few people informed of the facts, and, that includes your wife. We can't afford to have any information leak. Agreed?"

Hearing her father's heavy footsteps when he left, Samantha's emotional paralysis was shaken.

* * * *

Rebecca followed Travis into the sitting room, where he poured himself a martini. Rebecca requested soda with a lime twist.

"Have you finished talking with Samantha?" Anne asked. She plucked the martini from her husband's grip and nearly finished it. The twins entered silently behind her.

"Please, call me Rebecca. Your daughter needs a break. She's resting."

"Travis?" Anne turned her body toward him.

"There are some things we need to discuss as a family. I don't want this to interfere with your school. Sunday, you'll both be on the plane. Understood?"

The twins frowned at one another and nodded. Anne sank into a stiff wing chair across from the couch where the twins perched. Travis freshened her drink and sat in the matching chair next to her.

CHAPTER 39

Agent Lloyd listened to the taped conversations, meticulously writing notes. Something wasn't right. Samantha's moods on the phone swung quicker than a jump-rope. Was she trying to set Skyler up? Sometimes she enjoyed Skyler's illicit suggestions, even followed along. Sometimes she was outwardly annoyed. Sometimes she was too timid to cross Skyler's orders. Was she that good an actress? He circled the note he wrote: behavior increasingly disjointed, disoriented, and dysfunctional. He dialed Rebecca Smalley's hotel room.

"Ms. Smalley?" Agent Lloyd said into the receiver, as a tired voice answered.

"Yes?"

"I need to meet with you as soon as possible."

"Agent Lloyd?"

"Yes, ma'am. I'm in Arkansas. I arrived a few days earlier than I planned. I'd really appreciate meeting with you as soon as possible."

"Can't this wait until morning?"

"I've been listening to the tapes we have on your client. They don't add up. You might be able to enlighten me."

* * * *

The police station was quiet for a Friday night. Rebecca found Agent Lloyd in an interrogation room behind stacks of papers, boxes of tapes, cold coffee cups and half-emptied diet-cola bottles. She placed a fresh cup of coffee and a custard donut in front of each of them, and then rifled through her massive briefcase for a notepad.

"Sugar to go along with my overdose of caffeine." Agent Lloyd lifted the donut from the bag.

Rebecca nodded. "Guess I should have brought you a sandwich. How long have you been at this?"

"Most of the day. I didn't want to stop. I've compiled a list of inconsistencies," Agent Lloyd explained, pushing his notepad in front of Rebecca.

Rebecca scanned the notes.

"Do you remember the boyfriend, John?" Agent Lloyd asked.

"Of course. What does he have to do with this?"

"Probably nothing. I've studied the typed transcripts, the record her boyfriend asked her to make. I remember Samantha saying the transcripts she'd made were just more of the same of what we now have."

"Yeah, I remember. What's your point?"

"I'm not sure," Agent Lloyd paused. "John suggests

she makes her own transcripts of every conversation as each conversation takes place. She follows his advice."

"And?"

"I'm assuming they're still together."

Rebecca nodded. "So?"

"I assume he never read the transcript he asked her to make; he respected her privacy. Read it. Then tell me what you think."

Rebecca flipped through the pages, closely scanning one after the other. Finally, she removed her glasses, sighed deeply, and shook her head.

"I guess I'd better have a talk with my client. Something's wrong."

"Want to shed some light on what you're thinking, counselor?"

"Speculation is a waste of time. But, you're right. We need to clear these discrepancies up."

"Want to know how I see it?"

"Sure."

"She was raped. It was brutal and traumatic. Skyler Marks comes along and helps her. Like a knight in shining armor, he takes care of everything. She feels better, maybe decides she can forget what happened, her life is back to normal. He took care of everything, like the servants she's been accustomed to all her life. Then she dismisses Skyler, relieves him of his duty to help her. He doesn't like to be treated like a dismissed servant after everything he's done, so he blackmails her for sex."

Rebecca nodded. "We know he's not the saint he pretends to be."

"Maybe your client without initially realizing it grew dependent, even addicted to him. Maybe she even recognizes the conflict within herself. But, she is clear that she now has a boyfriend, John, who Skyler is interfering with," Agent Lloyd stopped, waiting for any response.

"And?"

"Samantha Armstrong is an emotionally disturbed girl. I'm not saying she doesn't have reason to have emotional problems, but nonetheless, they are severe enough, even if we are able to get Skyler Marks, that in front of a jury nothing she says may be credible."

Rebecca sighed. "I hear what you're saying. After reading the transcripts, I understand your concerns. But, what this tells me is that I'm convinced, now, more than ever, there is more to all of this. I believe my client."

"I believe her disgust for Skyler Marks is genuine," Agent Lloyd said. "I also believe she hated Greg Maston."

"I promise you she's innocent of murdering Greg Maston."

"What I believe is there is much more to this whole story. The rape, the blackmail, the murder—all of it. We haven't even scratched the surface."

Rebecca tapped her pointer finger hard against the transcript. "Why have you shown me every transcript, except the one from the day of the murder?"

"You are smart Ms. Smalley. I saved the best for last."

Agent Lloyd pulled out a final transcript from underneath his pile of notepads and handed it to Rebecca.

"Has Detective Winston read this?" Rebecca asked.

"I wanted you to have first crack. Once the police read it, once they hear the tape, your client will be arrested and formally charged. They will have no choice."

"So you wanted to give me a head start? I thought you FBI guys always went by the book. Why are you helping us?"

"Because I know there's more to this case than what we have. I also realize that if your client is behind bars, we may lose Skyler Marks and blow the case we are building against Castriano—a case we've worked on for three years."

Rebecca pursed her lips. "His prized client."

"I've balanced the interest of justice and your client's interests."

"I'm impressed, Agent Lloyd. You made the right decision."

Rebecca tossed the transcript back in Agent Lloyd's pile and extended her hand in thanks.

When she reached the heavy metal door, he said, "My hunches are usually pretty accurate. Think about getting your client psychologically evaluated before the court orders it."

CHAPTER 40

Saturday morning arrived too early for Rebecca. Sleep came in small doses after her meeting with Agent Lloyd. Had she believed her client so completely she'd missed some sort of mental instability?

Assured the servants had retired to their duties after showing her to the breakfast table they'd prepared, Rebecca set down her fork. "We need to review a few details we've discussed previously."

Samantha tore a slice of toast into bite sized pieces and folded her hands. "What's up?"

"Tell me everything you did and that you remember, in detail, the day Greg Maston was murdered."

Samantha chewed on a bite of toast and shrugged. "Where do I begin?"

"From the second you woke up. I want to know every detail, regardless of how small and insignificant you think it is. Do you understand?" Rebecca set her iPhone on Record.

Hearing nothing, Rebecca tried a different tact. "Dreams. Dreams tell a lot. Do you recall what you were dreaming before you woke up?"

Samantha closed her eyes and released a sigh. "I don't remember dreaming, I barely remember going to sleep or waking up."

"Have you ever been known to sleep walk?"

"Walk in my sleep? No," Samantha covered her mouth with her hand. "Are you suggesting I killed him in my sleep? Is that even possible?" Samantha began to shake.

Rebecca stared at her client. She wished she could erase the terror she saw in her. What if Agent Lloyd's fears were right, and she had done it?

Trauma. Could the trauma of all she'd been through cause her to blackout? Could she really be that troubled? Concern compounded into questions. "We need to put everything together, compile every detail in order, so we can see what we are missing. I don't believe you are capable of murder."

Samantha wrapped her arms round her waist as if to comfort herself.

"Picture yourself in your room talking to Skyler. Try to remember the conversation. Begin there."

Samantha closed her eyes, then spoke. "I can see myself in the room, and it is dark. I was almost asleep when my cell rang. It was Skyler. I didn't want to talk to him, but I did. I had a bit of a headache, so while we spoke, I tiptoed to the bathroom and swallowed a few pills and returned to bed. I remember trying to make my voice slur like I was falling asleep, so he wouldn't keep me on the phone long."

"What time was that?"

"Just past eleven, I think. I'd finished a movie and clicked off the television just as the news began. Then the phone rang."

"What did you talk about?"

"He asked me about my day. Wanted every detail including who I talked to. When I hesitated, he started ranting about me lying." She bit her lip. "The usual questions he always asks."

Rebecca pulled out a file from her briefcase and set it next to the half-emptied plate in front of her. She began jotting notes.

"I remember that he talked about my skin, how soft it was. And my hair, how he loved the way my curls fell when we—" Samantha stopped.

"Keep going, Samantha. You're doing great," Rebecca said encouragingly.

"I can't. All I see is blackness. I don't remember anything else. I must have fallen asleep," Samantha said.

Samantha looked behind her. She looked around her.

"Did you drop something?" Rebecca asked seeing her client become distracted.

"Do you hear that laughter? Someone is coming."

Rebecca turned her head and held her breath. She heard nothing. "There isn't anyone here."

"Are you sure?" Samantha covered her ears with her hands.

"Samantha, do you feel all right?" Rebecca asked.

"Fine." A smile crossed Samantha's face.

"If you need to stop we can take a break."

Samantha shook her head *no*.

Rebecca proceeded. "I need you to read transcript of the wiretap of your conversation with Skyler. You have a good recollection of the conversation until the point where you believe you fell asleep. If you prefer, I'll read it to you."

Samantha pointed at Rebecca and she read the typed pages in front of her.

"Something is very wrong," Samantha said. "Stop reading. I didn't say those things. Someone got to the tapes. Someone is setting me up. I hate Skyler. I never have said those things," Samantha cried out. Her quaking hands hovered over her face. Her head shook from side to side.

Rebecca placed her hands over Samantha's. "That's fine, Samantha. That's what I wanted to know, what I needed to hear from you. Let's take a break and have dessert. Change the subject for a few minutes. It's almost eleven."

Samantha pushed her plate to the other side of her, and Rebeca placed clean plates in front of each of them.

Rebecca sliced them each a healthy piece of pound cake and piled on scoops of custard, strawberries, and whipped cream. After she poured fresh coffee and sipped, she stared at her client and waited until Samantha turned to face her.

"There's just one other thing, Samantha: I will need you to talk to a psychiatrist and to take a polygraph test. Are you willing to do that?"

"I'll do anything. But, why do I need a shrink and a polygraph? Do you think I'm crazy? Do you not believe me?"

"I think you are sane, and I believe you. I need to make sure your state of mind and truthfulness can't be questioned."

"A polygraph is a lie detector, right?"

"Yes. And polygraphs are not admissible in trial.

"If it can't be used in court, why bother?" Samantha paused then added. "What happens if I fail?"

"The polygraph will support your innocence and hopefully cause detectives to look elsewhere. You won't fail the one detectives see. Here's my proposal—understand it is the protocol I follow with my clients."

"Sounds okay," Samantha said hesitantly.

"I arrange a polygraph that you take without the knowledge of anyone except you and me. We go out of town to have it done. If you fail the polygraph test, we bury it, and there is no record of it, so nothing can be subpoenaed. Then we stall, and we don't agree to take one. On the basis it is inadmissible in trial. If you pass, we agree to have one taken at the State Police Headquarters. Do you understand?"

"You think I'll fail?"

"No. Innocent people fail them. They are not reliable, hence not admissible. The best evidence is your testimony. Understand?"

"I guess." Samantha stood and pressed a wall plate to let the staff know that the plates could be cleared.

Just as the table was cleared and fresh coffee, iced tea, and iced water were placed on a cart, near the table, the doorbell chimed. A moment later, Hyrum ushered Detective Winston and two female police officers into the study.

"Samantha Armstrong?" Detective Winston asked.

Rebecca answered, annoyed at his formality. "You know who she is. You know I am representing her. What's this about?"

The group placed themselves around Samantha.

"Samantha Armstrong, you are under arrest for the murder of Greg Maston," Detective Winston said while one burly female officer cuffed Samantha's wrists behind her back, and the other patted her down. "You have the right to remain silent ..."

* * * *

Knowing Samantha would be placed in receiving at the jail and processed, Rebecca followed Detective Winston downtown to police headquarters. They met in a small conference room. "Is arresting my client really necessary?" Rebecca asked. "She has no criminal history, no access to firearms, is not dangerous, and has a stable home, where she could be monitored."

"I've asked Assistant Prosecutor Hiller to join us."

Rebecca shook his hand and sat in a chair across the table from the men.

"Your client may not be a danger to anyone else, but she was lethal to Greg Maston. It's necessary, it's the law, and you know that, Counselor."

"Innocent until proven guilty beyond a reasonable doubt, and you two know that. Why arrest her now? I want to see just what evidence you think you have." Rebecca tapped impatient nails on the marred oak table.

"We have a witness placing Samantha outside the crime scene in a car owned by her father at the time of the murder," Detective Winston's said, sarcasm abounding. "We'd love to hear your client's explanation of that, in light of the previous evidence you've both had an opportunity to review."

"I want everything you have. I'll be at her arraignment. And at all times you have contact with her or want to question her," Rebecca said. "And what makes you think her father didn't drive his car, or someone else who had access to it?"

* * * *

At the jail, Samantha was escorted to an attorney-client private meeting room near a block of cells. She was dressed in a gray jumpsuit with big black letters on the back announcing she was now part of the county jail.

"On my way here I contacted a bondsman. I'll be at your arraignment, and I will ask for a bond with jail tether, so you can stay at your parents' house."

"They can do that?"

Rebecca nodded. "*Will* the judge do that? That's the real issue. You'll likely be arraigned in the morning, but it could be a few days before we're able to appear before the judge assigned to hear the Preliminary Exam."

Samantha placed her face in her hands.

Rebecca felt sympathy studying her despondent client.

"Can you really help me?" Samantha asked.

Rebecca outlined the legal process, explaining they would waive the Probable Cause hearing, so that she would immediately be bound over to the judge, who would ultimately hear the jury trial. "It will speed things up. I'm looking to get a dismissal or get this to trial sooner than later."

"Meanwhile I'm stuck in this cage?"

"We will keep you busy during visiting hours and in between when I'm not reviewing evidence I'll be with you. I need you to eat and sleep, so you remain calm and clear-headed. Can you do that?"

Samantha whimpered out a 'yes,' and Rebecca knocked on the door. The guard unlocked the door.

Rebecca tried her hardest to seem optimistic when Samantha's eyes met hers before she followed the guard down the hall to her cell.

Rebecca heard a dull thud behind her and turned back.

Samantha lay on the cold cement floor.

Rebecca rushed forward and screamed, "Call 911. She needs a doctor, now."

Uniforms surrounded Samantha quickly and help was radioed out. Raising Samantha's limp wrist, Rebecca was relieved to find a faint pulse.

EMS arrived minutes later, but to Rebecca it felt like hours.

Guided by jail security, she stood back and watched Samantha lifted onto a gurney and wheeled out toward an awaiting ambulance.

Rebecca ran out of the jail to her parked vehicle and sped toward the police-escorted ambulance to St. Mary's Hospital emergency room.

* * * *

Four hours later, after receiving permission to speak with Samantha's treating doctor, Rebecca was allowed to follow her out of emergency and into her room on the third floor.

"How are you feeling?" Rebecca said. She studied the grim expression of her young client. The dark circles underneath Samantha's naturally vibrant eyes caused Rebecca to hesitate before pressing Samantha with questions.

Samantha tightly clasped the white sheet and blankets

covering her.

"Your doctor said you fainted, and you'll be fine," Rebecca said. "They want to keep you here a few days and make sure you eat properly, your bloodwork is completed, and neurology has examined you. You are seriously underweight. They want you to get your strength back before they release you."

Samantha nodded.

"In the meantime, you should know there's a guard posted outside your door. I've left a message with Hyrum. He's trying to locate your parents. I'll stay until they arrive. Do you understand?" Rebecca reached for her hand squeezed it and felt Samantha relax into sleep. The medicine from the dripping the IV bag had taken hold.

Rebecca was anxious to review the newly obtained evidence.

CHAPTER 41

"How's Samantha?" Detective Winston asked, but didn't wait for an answer. He handed Rebecca a file and moved toward his office door. "Your copy of everything I have. A copy was scanned to the prosecutor's office. I've got something to attend to. There's a private room across the hall from my office."

Rebecca opened a bottle of water she'd pulled from her oversized bag that served as both purse and brief-case, and found the witness statement she was looking for.

"This doesn't make any sense," she said aloud in the empty room. She reread the statement looking for something behind the words. She began to make a trail of notes.

Samantha, or someone who looks like her, was in a car that may or may not be hers.

The license plate is seen, or is just known to be part of the Armstrong fleet?

Assume it was Samantha in her car.

Assume she drove to the office and waited for Greg Maston.

She parked the car and waited in front of the building, so she can make a quick exit.

She waited until she was certain Greg is absorbed in his work and won't notice her.

She knows the schedule of the office because of her father.

She enters after the firm's employees are gone and before the cleaning staff arrives.

How would she know for sure everyone in the office is gone?

After eight Wednesday night would anyone answer the phone if she called?

How would she know the schedule of the cleaning crew?

Why would she be so brazen as to park in front of the building?

Rebecca flipped over the statement then printed then circled:

Samantha is seen in the passenger's seat. Not the driver's seat.

Why does someone driving a Saab slide into the

passenger seat?

"They don't," Rebecca answered her last question out loud. "This witness must be discredited." She highlighted the point.

Rebecca eyed the photograph of the murder weapon under the witness statement. She pulled the photo to within inches of her nose. Three initials were engraved at the end of the handle. MAS. Could that be from her family set of steak knives? The first three initials of Samantha's name reversed; coincidence? The use of a knife was personal, but it was an odd weapon for a frail woman like Samantha to use. Rape was a personal crime, but was she capable of such a violent and personal retaliation?

She noted on her pad that the only fingerprints found on the weapon were Samantha's.

The next photograph was of the earring. Samantha hadn't yet found the matching one for her. She pulled a quarter from her wallet and sat it on the picture inside the earring. She recalled Detective Winston saying the earring was under the body and likely fell off during the struggle. Would it still have maintained such a perfectly round shape? A delicately looped earring especially one of fine quality would have been bent out of shape. She underscored that note on her pad and surrounded it with question marks.

The door opened, and Detective Winston popped his

head in. "Any questions? I'm almost finished and can sit with you soon, if you want to discuss anything."

Rebecca shook her head. "Can I see the reports on any hair, nail, and tissue samples?"

"We send out anything that requires DNA studies. I don't know how backed up they are. I'll get an update to you this week."

$$* * * *$$

Samantha opened heavy eyes lids to a full bladder and nauseated stomach. The IV in her arm hurt, and she decided it was taped too tightly to her skin. She pressed the call button hanging on the silver rail. How long had she been asleep? A nurse appeared in the doorway.

"How are you feeling?" the nurse asked. She lifted Samantha's wrist.

Samantha watched the nurse chart every bodily function. "My arm is sore, I have a headache. I need to use the bathroom." She gazed around the room. "Is there anyone waiting outside for me?"

She shook her head. I only saw the guard, but I just came on shift. You'll feel better after you've had something to eat. I'll help you to the bathroom, but you'll need to fill a bedpan."

While they tended to that, Samantha half-listened to the nurse's instructions.

"You won't be able to receive or make any outside phone calls. I'm not sure if you're allowed visitors. I don't think so."

"I have to make a phone call. Can you make it for me?"

"I need to tell your doctor you're awake. Ask him about phone calls." She snapped her chart closed and hung it on the wall.

"When will he be here?" Samantha asked.

"I don't know. In the meantime, here's the remote control to the television. Dinner will arrive soon. Looks like they've ordered you a high-protein meal."

Samantha watched the too-cheerful nurse exit and closed her eyes. How had things gotten so far out of hand? Where were her parents? Rebecca? Why suddenly had Skyler virtually disappeared from her? She slipped down inside her sheets until her head was covered. Clenching her sheets tightly between her fingers, she pictured her bedroom at home. She pretended she was there, alone and safe.

No. Her room was no longer safe. Why wasn't it safe? She tried to remember. She couldn't. Nana. Nana's room was safe. She could picture herself there, sitting with Nana, holding her yarn, listening to her stories, smelling the lilac-water scent she always wore.

Samantha drifted, as her thoughts calmed her immediate fears. She was safe in the arms of Nana, protected in their private cocoon. She relaxed. She was floating, calmly, peacefully. Without warning, Nana, her room, her safety, all disappeared. She was there in the darkness, standing, turning slowly around. Looking at the familiar pieces of faces, listening to the evil laughter and the music box. The music was soft, low and familiar. Eyes and ears; mouths and noses, were now together. Who did they belong to? Did they fit together? She put her hands over her ears, trying to concentrate and shield herself from the laughter, the music.

* * * *

Dr. Evans entered his patient's room and grabbed the chart. He noted that she was covered in her sheets and scribbled notes, while he listened to her mumbling. How could such a beautiful and privileged young girl have turned her whole life into a nightmare? He ordered something stronger to calm her, noting that the intravenous valium he'd ordered had not served its purpose. He called her name. "Samantha. Samantha, you're fine. Everything is all right. You are safe. It's okay to wake up. Samantha? Can you come up from inside the sheets? Samantha?"

After a long minute of calling out to her, Samantha opened her eyes and emerged from the sheets. She gasped.

"You're fine. Nightmare?" He gave her a few seconds to focus. "I'm Dr. Evans. I hope the rest of your stay here is less frightening than your dream. Do you remember it?"

"No. I don't," Samantha said, her eyes darted over his

right shoulder.

"There isn't anyone else in the room. Do you need something?" he asked and waited.

"A phone. I'd like to call my parents."

"I see," he said and closed the chart. He sat on the edge of her bed.

"I'm sorry. That's not up to me. The police detective said no visitors other than your family and attorneys, and no outside phone calls," Dr. Evans said. "I have your parents' number in the chart. I'll tell them you want to see them. But you make a promise to me you'll eat your complete tray of food. I hear the food cart down the hall now. You need to gain a few pounds before I release you."

"You mean incarcerate me."

"You eat, and we'll see how long I can keep you here," he paused. "Deal?"

* * * *

The familiar aroma of mashed potatoes and gravy neared, and Samantha looked up, expecting the door to reveal another starched uniform.

"Look at the treat I've got," Rebecca placed the tray on the swiveled desk next to Samantha's bed.

"Actually, I'd have cooked for you myself, but you've kept me too busy to spend any time in the kitchen," Rebecca joked.

Samantha tried to smile, but she was not in a mood to laugh or talk. "I want to go home."

"Working on just that," Rebecca said.

"Why can't I have a phone?" Samantha asked. "Have you spoken to my family? Have you asked the judge to set me free?"

"Your job right now is to eat. I'm trying to keep you out of jail, but only you can get yourself out of the hospital," Rebecca said, mirroring Samantha's stubborn tone.

Samantha painstakingly dissected and ate her meal, one tiny morsel at a time. Rebecca uncapped a large coffee she'd walked in with and eyed every bite.

"Samantha," Rebecca said, "I've spoken to your family a few times since we were at the jail. They're up to date, and they will be here soon."

Samantha was confounded. "They know I'm in the hospital, and no one is here?"

"Samantha, everyone is working nonstop on your case. Your parents know you are safe in the hospital, and the goal is to keep you here or at home, not jail."

"But I'm still being charged with the murder of my rapist," Samantha said. "Nothing has really changed. Just because there are no steel bars, doesn't mean there aren't any."

"I get it. So let me update you." Rebecca sat her coffee down and pulled out a pad from her bag and read. "I'm prepping to file motions and hopefully have the case against you dismissed. I'll be contacting your roommate. I need her information. I've a list she needs to overnight to us. I can pay her for her time."

"She'll help. Sure. But, why do you have to do all this? Don't you believe me? Doesn't anyone believe me?"

"Everyone believes you, Samantha. Especially me. Things don't add up, and I'm going to make sure they see that." Rebeca leaned in. "There's one thing I'm certain of after reviewing the evidence file that Detective Winston gave me."

"What is that?"

"There's much more going on here than anyone knows, and you somehow are in the center of it. I want to know why."

"Like what?"

"You and I are going to figure that out." Rebecca took a long sip of her coffee. "And about your family, blame me. I asked them to go about everything as a family and act as if this weren't happening. Your brothers want to assist with your defense. I've declined their help—at least openly. Your father can't work on your case except at home. I trust no one he works with."

"Exactly what are you saying?" Samantha's voice cracked.

"Your parents have been asked to keep Skyler occupied and out of town—too busy to read newspapers or make calls, too interested to want to return to Arkansas."

"Skyler knows I'm home."

"And your father told him you have a terrible flu and not to contact you if he wanted to continue to work for him. I think he made it sound more like a joke than a threat, but your father was convinced he wouldn't call you. Your parents asked Skyler to meet them in Washington under the guise of merging law firms."

"Dad knows people that I know Skyler wants to be introduced to." Samantha nodded. "What does Skyler have to do with my being charged with Greg's murder?"

"We're not sure. He was the last person you talked to before the murder and the first person you spoke with after the murder," Rebecca said. "That does not sit well with me."

Samantha rubbed her temples slowly.

"Samantha, you need to rest. I'll call the nurse," Rebecca said, moving the table away from her and seating herself next to Samantha on the bed. "I know you're upset. Believe me, we're making progress. I need you to agree to do something for me."

Looking at the seriousness of her attorney's face, she stiffened. "Okay, what?"

"The transcripts of the tapes. We've read them. We read the transcripts you and John made on your computer. The conversations are curious, but consistent. Do you understand?"

Samantha shook her head. "No." She tried to concentrate on what Rebecca was proposing.

"What you've said you remember, doesn't make sense with the contents of the transcripts."

"I'm not lying. I told you everything I recall."

"That's why I need you to talk with a psychiatrist and

agree to hypnosis. Are you comfortable with that?"

"You think I'm crazy?" Samantha asked.

"I need to explore every aspect of the case and avoid any surprise that could be thrown at us. Understand?"

Samantha didn't respond. A frowning nurse entered, and measured and weighed the now-cold food and liquids on her forgotten tray.

"How do you feel?" the nurse asked.

"Tired," Samantha responded. "May I have something to sleep?"

"I'll talk to your doctor. There is a note that the toxicology report from the lab must be reviewed before any further medication is administered. Are you allergic to anything?"

"No," Samantha said.

"I'll call the doctor," The nurse said, adjusting the drip of the newly changed IV bag, before drawing the curtains and turning off the lights.

"I have calls to make," Rebecca said. "While you rest think about every event and how you would place each into a timeline."

CHAPTER 42

On Monday morning, a District Judge and court reporter arraigned Samantha in her hospital room by special arrangement and request by the FBI. Rebecca was grateful to Agent Lloyd. The paperwork was completed, and filed back at the courthouse, and the case was bound over to the Trial Court, assigned to Judge Bingham.

At four o'clock, an emergency conference was held in Judge Bingham's chambers with Rebecca, Detective Winston, and Prosecutor Hiller present, and on the speaker phone: Assistant Prosecutor Kyle Kincaid and FBI Agent Lloyd from Michigan.

"I've reviewed the files," the Judge said. "You'll all need to file your various motions with accompanying briefs before I make any decisions. I don't even have a file, and I'm not clear if you all even have the police report."

Rebecca interjected herself as soon as she heard the judge pause. "Your Honor, if we may be heard on bond. Jail is not a place for an eighteen-year-old."

"Age has little bearing on this. Murder is a very serious

charge. I'll hear arguments on bond after I receive a bond report from Pretrial Services, and you notice it up for hearing," the Trial Court judge said.

"Safety in the jail is a concern. And," Rebecca said. All eyes on her, she proceeded. "I will be filing a Competency Motion."

"From what I've seen, she is able to assist you and understand what is happening. Do you mean at the time of the crime?" Prosecutor Hiller asked.

"I want all bases covered," Rebecca said. "My client is not guilty of any crime, but she was raped, and I do not know the emotional effect that has had on her."

Judge Bingham cleared his throat. "This matter is too early on for me to make any rulings that stick. Is that understood?"

"Yes, your Honor," the group said in unison.

"I'd also like to remind you that my review of the evidence, as well as anything additional either side may present today, is no indication as to whether the evidence will or will not be admissible in trial or how I will rule on any motions you all file."

Judge Bingham looked at each person in the group individually. "I understand Assistant Prosecutor Kincaid from Michigan is part of this meeting by consent of all parties because of another situation that affects defendant and may or may not be related to the murder file. Is that your understanding, Mr. Kincaid?"

"Yes, Your Honor," Mr. Kincaid said. "Aggravated

stalking and extortion, at a minimum."

"I'd like to hear from our Prosecutor's office, Mr. Hiller?" Judge Bingham folded his hands on his substantial dark oak desk.

"Thank you, Your Honor. This case is about a brutally murdered man. The evidence from the crime scene points to defendant, Samantha Armstrong. Fingerprints from the furniture and the murder weapon matched defendant's. Hair matching defendant was found tangled on a button of the victim's shirt, affixed as if in a struggle. Nail and tissue samples haven't returned yet from the lab, but we anticipate they will conclusively place defendant at the crime scene. An earring found under the victim belongs to defendant."

"Allegedly belongs to Ms. Armstrong," Rebecca chimed in.

Prosecutor Hiller cocked his head at her and proceeded. "We have a witness who identified the defendant in her car, in front of the building where the victim was found, at the approximate time of the murder."

"Anything else Mr. Hiller?" Judge Bingham crossed his arms over his chest.

Flipping a page of his legal pad, Prosecutor Hiller continued. "The victim worked for defendant's father as an accountant to the law firm. As to motive, the victim allegedly raped defendant last spring.

"No alleged about the rape of my client," Rebecca said sternly.

"It's a rape defendant failed to report. It is our contention defendant wanted revenge by carefully planning and subsequently taking the life of the victim," Prosecutor Hiller said, scanning his notes briefly before completing his summary. "Samantha Armstrong should remain behind bars."

Judge Bingham jotted a few notes on the pad in front of him, and then asked the defense to speak.

"Your Honor," Rebecca began. "What Mr. Hiller says is only one interpretation. There are many pieces of this case that don't match the crime and can exclude my client. Despite the evidence against Samantha Armstrong, she didn't commit, nor is she capable of committing, murder. Samantha hired me and reported to Mr. Kincaid in Michigan, asking for assistance in resolving a problem she was having with a man, who had been blackmailing and stalking her. She chose not to take the law into her own hands, rather used the law to her advantage. The FBI assigned Agent Lloyd to assist me."

"That's a bit unusual," Judge Bingham's brows were raised, and his eyes locked with Rebecca.

"I know we are not on the record, but I have to object. There is no evidence in the file regarding blackmail, extortion, or stalking. This court has no jurisdiction in Michigan," Prosecutor Hiller stated.

"What is your response to the signed statement of the witness, who claims to have seen defendant outside the office building?" Judge Bingham asked.

Rebecca felt his curiosity and respected his impartial demeanor and candor. "From the statement of the witness, it's not clear she saw the license plate of the car or any identifying mark on it. Furthermore, she has not yet identified her in a lineup."

The judge sighed. "Anything else?"

Rebecca nodded. "Additionally, the witness doesn't state she ever saw anyone leave the car, enter or exit the building."

"Mr. Hiller?"

"Your Honor, all the evidence, including what this witness says, points directly to defendant. The witness places her at or near the crime scene, and defendant, in her statement to police, states she was asleep, home all evening when, in fact, she was out."

"I've heard enough." The judge dismissed them. "We'll be on the record in ten minutes. My clerk will let you in the courtroom."

✳ ✳ ✳ ✳

"All rise. The Honorable William Samuel Bingham presiding." The law clerk's voice boomed into the courtroom. A few onlookers and attorneys filled the back.

The attorneys waived Samantha's appearance, argued the bond motion, answered the judge's questions, and sat at counsel table.

"After careful review of this matter, including the fact that defendant is currently hospitalized and of fragile health, bail is set in the amount of two-hundred-fifty-thousand dollars cash/surety. Defendant cannot leave the state, and she may be released to the custody of her father under house arrest. She can only leave for medical care, to consult with her attorney, and for court. I understand Mr. Armstrong has agreed to take responsibility for his daughter. Is that correct, Mr. Armstrong?"

Travis Armstrong approached from the rear of the court and stood at the attorney's podium. When he received a nod from the judge, he stated his name and then answered. "Yes, it is, Your Honor, thank you," Travis said. "She will be supervised at all times."

"Furthermore, I order defendant to undergo psychiatric evaluations for competency and criminal responsibility of defendant—"

Travis Armstrong, still standing at the podium interrupted. "Your honor, if I may address that?"

"You may proceed."

"As this Court knows, the Forensic center is running months behind causing cases to be delayed. I am happy to pay for Independent Psychological Evaluations with whomever counsel and you agree to. It will save time and costs to the county."

"Any objection?" The judge waited. "Hearing no objection, you all have three days to submit a name, otherwise I will choose one. Pretrial is set for Tuesday, January 8th. That's all for the record." The judge's clerk handed him the next file of the day.

* * * *

Travis Armstrong drove to the bail bondsman's office and posted bail for his daughter. He was preoccupied, wondering what had transpired in the judge's chambers. He felt uneasy knowing that people he knew, as well as complete strangers, had access to information about the Armstrong family, the law firm, and his daughter's future that he had been denied access to.

The more he tried to understand the reasons for his limited access, the more he didn't understand. So far, despite objections to being excluded, Samantha's attorney had handled her case properly. His legal mind still nagged at him.

Travis dialed his home, but the moment he heard Anne's sad voice, he wished he could hang up. But he explained the judge's orders and gave her instructions for the household. Only as many servants as absolutely necessary were to work. Cook and Hyrum were the only servants, who would deal with Samantha, once she was home from the hospital; they were to keep their eyes on her and report everything to him and Anne. No one was to talk of the pending trial or the charges; any servant caught talking to anyone outside the house was to be dismissed immediately. Media was to be kept outside the property boundaries. The twins were to be kept informed, but were to remain in school.

* * * *

Travis grabbed his messages from his secretary. Flipping through them, he called back, "Hold all calls. Buzz me when Ms. Smalley arrives."

Stepping into his office, Travis spotted Skyler at the bar pouring himself a double shot of whiskey. "A little early to be drinking, don't you think?" Travis asked. He tucked away his emotions while Skyler tucked back the whisky bottle into its cupboard.

"I'm sorry for everything you and your family are going through. I wish there were something I could do. Maybe I could go over her file with you and assist in her defense," Skyler said. He drained his glass and sat it on a coffee table.

"Thank you. We decided as a family that it was best to place Samantha's defense in the hands of someone not affiliated with us," Travis said, meeting Skyler's stare, trying to read his reaction.

Skyler rubbed his jaw, but said nothing.

"The doctors advised me she needs uninterrupted rest. Only immediate family is allowed contact."

"I'll just call her and give her my regards—"

Travis cut him off, sharply.

"She's not allowed any phone calls, newspapers, or news programs. She'll be in restricted seclusion."

"Surely she'll want to talk to me. Surely you can make an exception," Skyler pressed on politely. "I've grown fond of her, of your whole family. She's become like the little sister I never had."

"I won't go against doctor's orders. Surely you

understand," Travis said, so softly Skyler had to strain to hear his words.

Skyler sighed. "Sure. I'm here for whatever you need."

"Thank you. I understand congratulations are in order. You picked up several promising clients. The firm is proud of you." Travis forced a smile.

"I hope someday to make partner. I want to make you proud." Skyler grinned.

Second only to the devil. How could he be so two-faced, so evil? Travis felt such loathing it was hard not to show it. He wished Skyler were dead, too.

Turning toward the door, as if he were about to exit, Skyler hesitated. "One other thing. The midday news report said the bail hearing for Samantha was virtually behind closed doors, in judges' chambers. Why weren't arguments heard on the record?"

"Why are you surprised by that? You've done the same many times. Arguments were made to preserve the record for appeal. The in-chambers discussion was solely to protect Samantha's mental health and safety."

"What's this about her safety? Why is that suddenly an issue?" Skyler pressed.

"The real murderer is still out there."

"Travis, aren't you taking this a bit too far? I mean, whoever murdered Greg wouldn't want to see her harmed, just convicted." Skyler said.

"No," Travis stated pedantically. "The way I see it is that things would be cleaner if the suspect were dead and the investigation dropped. I won't risk that the real murderer might hurt Samantha."

Skyler nodded. "Got it." He walked out and closed the door quietly behind him.

Travis turned toward his window. What did Skyler know? Why was Skyler so desperate in his desire to see Samantha? Travis turned toward his desk, grabbed a notepad, and wrote down their conversation exactly as he remembered it. Rebecca Smalley would be interested. He tore his scribbling from the pad and sealed it in an envelope and printed her name on it.

* * * *

Seated in his office, Skyler dialed a familiar number, then counted the rings. One, two, three, four.

"Hello?" Margaret said.

"Hi there," Skyler said in his most playful voice. "How are you? It's been so long since you called—"

"Skyler? Is that you?"

"Yeah, babe. Did you miss me?"

"You know I did; but as I recall, it was you who was supposed to call."

"Now, now. You know what a busy caseload I have. You need to join me for dinner tonight."

"I have to work. I'm just on my way to the hospital right now. I'm off duty at eight."

"Great. Say a late dinner. I'll pick you up around nine?"

"Fine. I'll see you then."

"Mags—"

"Margaret."

"Mags, since you're going to the hospital, could you find out the room a friend of mine is in and whether or not she's allowed to have flowers?"

"One of your other girlfriends?"

"No, of course not. It's the daughter of my boss, Samantha Armstrong. I'd ask the family for the room number, but they've asked we don't send anything. I'd like to anyway. She's a good kid, suffering from anorexia, and I just want to show we're all rooting for her."

"Sure, no problem. I've really got to run."

"Thanks, sweet thing. I owe you," Skyler said softly, before quietly hanging up.

* * * *

When Rebecca entered his office, Travis was relieved. After coffee was poured and polite conversation dwindled, they turned to Samantha's defense.

"Samantha's doctors think she is quite ill," Travis said. "She has anorexia, probably brought on by the trauma of the rape and murder. She is also very anemic.

"The doctors don't want me, or any of us, interfering at this point. They said they need a few days where she isn't pressured by the trial. They're afraid she could go into herself. They also said she has severe nightmares. I thought you should know right away."

"No surprise. Thank you for sharing," Rebecca said.

"I've grown very fond of your daughter. I'll spend the next few days researching her case. I'd just like to check in with her so she doesn't worry, if that's all right."

"Anything to alleviate her worry. If that's possible." Travis scratched his ear.

Rebecca nodded. "Samantha needs her strength for trial. I've spent considerable time reviewing every tiny detail of the murder. I've found questionable areas, but not, at this point, enough to definitely prove someone else is the murderer."

"Can I help? For God's sake, I am her father." Travis folded his hands.

"Right now, focus on supporting your daughter. I know where you are, and I'll let you know if I need your help in any way."

"I've placed a private security guard at her door. He'll keep a log of everyone who visits or inquiries about Samantha. He reports to me daily and will pass those reports on to you," Travis said.

"Do you remember the day they first took Samantha in for questioning and conducted the search of your home and the surrounding premises?"

"Of course. You don't forget an intrusion like that. I'd never realized what my clients have been through, until the moment I saw my own possessions being touched and viewed by perfect strangers."

"Do you remember the search of the garage?" Rebecca asked.

"Yes. Why?"

"A witness placed your daughter in a red Saab, like the one you own, outside your office building, at the approximate time of the murder. Was she there with you? Did she drive you to the office in the Saab?"

"No. I wasn't scheduled to go in until later to meet Greg, to review the firm financials. I was at home all day until I found Greg, later that evening. Samantha was in her room most of the day as far as I know. I wasn't aware that anyone drove the Saab that day."

"The witness positively identified a picture of Samantha seated in the passenger side of the car," Rebecca said.

"The passenger side?" Travis looked confused. "Samantha loves to drive the Saab. If she had taken it, she would be the driver, not the passenger."

"I'd like to take a look at the car," Rebecca said.

"Of course. I'll advise Hyrum, and he'll let you in."

"Please don't let anyone touch the car. I need to see it like the police left it. Has anyone driven it since the search?"

"I don't think it's been touched at all. Hyrum would know. He has the task of maintaining the cars and their keys," Travis said.

* * * *

Samantha disliked the IV flowing into her veins. She didn't like being pressured to eat. She hated knowing that each bit she ate and each she failed to eat was measured and noted. Most of all, she didn't like anyone touching her body, peering at her.

She stared at the phone that was just connected. Her father was her only caller; her mother her only visitor. Had anyone told Emily she was in the hospital? Surely Emily would stop by, if she knew. And John. She missed him. Did he miss her? It was strange to have relied on him so heavily over the past few months and then not to speak to him at all.

Samantha feared Skyler would find out about John. They'd agreed to keep their contact minimal, but what was the real harm? Should she risk it? She knew there was a tap on the phone. She didn't care. She had nothing to hide. Except that she wanted to scream that she was happy about the murder of her rapist. "Turnabout is fair play," she said out loud in the silent room. "He murdered me inside; he deserved to be murdered." She shuddered, letting the words spill. She pulled the sheets tightly around her, chilled from hearing her own icy voice.

The connected phone both comforted and haunted her. Would Skyler call? Would he whisper his sick, twisted, controlling words to her? Would he touch her when no one was looking? Samantha felt instantly nauseated. Her head pounded, and the familiar pain crawled forward from the base of her neck. She pressed the buzzer.

A nurse with a painted smile and a stethoscope

hanging around her neck appeared. "How are we feeling today?"

"We?" She closed her eyes. "I have a terrible headache, and I'm nauseated. Can you give me something?"

The nurse smiled, scanned the chart, and muttered something about calling the doctor, and left. Minutes later she returned, stuck a needle into the IV bag, then increased the drip. "You'll feel better soon. I'll dim the lights, so you can rest."

Within moments, Samantha nodded off into a deep, silent sleep. She awoke to the clattering food trays and the smell that preceded their arrival. She sat up and noticed a beautifully wrapped bouquet of flowers next to her bed. She reached for the sealed envelope taped to it and freed it. Ripping into it, she read the typed words twice before letting the white card fall onto her lap.

"Silence is golden."

She tore at the tissue-covered vase and gasped. A dozen perfectly shaped golden roses surrounded one black rose.

Her heart quickened.

It became difficult to catch her breath.

Paralyzed, she stared at the ominous black center. She knew. Her body became clammy. Skyler. His message was clear. He knew she'd revealed their secrets.

What could she do? The trays moved closer to her room. She slipped out of bed stepping onto the cold floor, careful not to pull or tangle her IV line. She placed the ominous vase behind the colorful array of flowers, plants, and balloons that had collected on the shelf facing her bed. Confident it couldn't be easily seen, she tucked the card inside one of the novels her mother had dropped off earlier. She slipped back into bed, smoothed the sheets, and tried to calm herself. She had to tell Rebecca. Surely she could make him stop.

CHAPTER 43

Rebecca arrived at the Armstrong home just as breakfast was served. But it was clear to Rebecca that neither had expected to be joined for breakfast, so their eyes didn't waver from the paper as Hyrum entered.

"Sir. Madam. Shall I have another place set for breakfast?"

Anne spoke first. "Yes, Hyrum. Please have Cook bring another place setting."

Hyrum pulled out a chair for Rebecca, poured her a cup of coffee, and set a plate of lemon muffins in front of her.

"I'm sorry to intrude on your breakfast," Rebecca said. "I spent the evening making a chart of the evidence and the positive and negative aspects of the case. To ease your mind, things are falling into place."

"Then you'll be able to tell us more about our daughter's case?" Travis asked.

"Not yet. Too many pieces, at least the way I've placed them, must remain confidential until I know more."

"Travis?" Anne asked loudly, clacking her empty

coffee cup onto its saucer.

"Defense strategy. Is Samantha in danger?" Travis asked.

When she saw the raw emotion on the faces of Samantha's parents, Rebecca said, "*Danger* may be too strong a word. I think you all could be in danger, so less is more at this point."

"Worst-case scenario." Travis pointed his fork at Rebecca.

"Being an attorney, you know we have to be concerned about that. We have to be concerned with the safety of everyone involved.

"Could Hyrum show me to the garage?" Rebecca asked.

"Of course," Travis said. "Anne, stay put."

Anne stared at the trio as they left the room.

* * * *

Once Rebecca, Travis, and Hyrum were inside the garage, Hyrum took the cover off the shiny red Saab.

"Hyrum, has this car been touched since the police searched it?"

"No, except that I covered it after they left."

"Do you keep track of the mileage, a log for home and work for tax purposes?" Rebecca knew she was hoping for too much.

"No, Ma'am." Hyrum stood mannequin-like and waited.

"Did Samantha drive the Saab during Thanksgiving

432

vacation?" Travis asked.

"Yes, sir."

"Did she drive it the day Greg Maston was murdered?"

"Not that I'm aware of, sir."

"How can you be sure?" Travis studied Hyrum.

"The car spent most of that day getting its winter tune up."

"Where did it spend the rest of the day?" Rebecca asked, while she opened the glove compartment.

"Except for the time it was with the mechanic, the Saab was in this garage. The mechanic picked it up and dropped it off here. No one else, including Samantha, took the Saab out of the garage, not even for a spin around the block. You see sir, I had the keys. I forgot to put them on the hook," Hyrum said. "I'm sorry, sir. Will there be anything else?"

"Hyrum, I could kiss you for keeping the keys," Travis said.

Hyrum blushed and bowed his head.

"This Saab is spotless. It still smells brand new," Rebecca said with a sigh. She reached into her bag. "I've brought a camera. I'll let you both know when I'm finished," Rebecca said. She climbed into the driver's seat after texting an update to Agent Lloyd.

* * * *

At the hospital, Rebecca found Samantha in a restless sleep.

"Samantha?" Rebecca asked.

Rebecca hit record on the app in her phone and placed it as close to Samantha's mouth as possible without touching her. Several minutes later, Samantha rolled over and began to wake up. Rebecca clasped the phone when Samantha's eyes fluttered open.

"Hi. How long have you been here?" Samantha asked groggily.

"Just arrived." Rebecca smiled.

"All I do is sleep and eat. They keep giving me some drug that makes me tired. They told me I would be going through withdrawal from my headache medication. So far, I just sleep," Samantha said. "Did you find out anything?"

"First, can you tell me what you were dreaming about?" Rebecca asked.

"Faces I don't recognize bobbing around music. When everything went black, I woke up and saw you. I've had the same dream before."

"Dreams can be important. Your brain may be trying to remember something it tucked away because of the trauma—"

"Like to protect me it made me forget?"

"Exactly. You could remember something that could help us. I'll leave a writing pad with you. I want you to write down your dreams, no matter how silly or insignificant. Can you do that?"

"Sure."

"Samantha." Rebecca waited until Samantha met her eyes. "Who is Darcey?"

"I don't know a Darcey."

"Are you sure? You called out her name in your dream just before you woke up."

Samantha shook her head. "Have you found anything that will help me?"

"There are many holes in the evidence they have. Key pieces do not align. Is there anything you can remember about that day? Anything at all you haven't told us?" Rebecca asked.

"No. But, I . . ." Samantha paused. Her eyes focused on the bouquet of flowers. "I got this," she said. She pulled a card from her pillowcase and handed it to Rebecca.

Rebecca read it.

"The flowers arrived when I was sleeping. I didn't dare ask anyone who delivered them. They might ask why I want to know."

Rebecca placed her fingers over her mouth. She examined the roses after Samantha nodded. Was there an eavesdropping device? After a few minutes she was satisfied there wasn't. "Tell me what you think the note means?"

With downcast eyes, Samantha said, "I know it's Skyler. He always told me if I told anyone anything he would hurt me and my family. I know it's a warning I'd better be quiet."

"Do you mind if I keep the note and flowers?" Rebecca asked.

"No. I wanted to throw them out, but I knew you'd want to see them," Samantha said.

"Hey, Sam," Emily briskly walked toward Samantha's bed and placed a stack of magazines on her bedside table. "Your dad gave me special permission to see you."

"Emily, it's so good to see you," Samantha said. The girls hugged.

Rebecca introduced herself and left.

* * * *

Rebecca pulled out her computer, downloaded the pictures she'd taken, and ordered large prints: a color set and a black and white set from a nearby Walgreens. They were ready by the time she arrived on site, and she grabbed an oversized package of red licorice and paid for it with the photographs. She ripped open the licorice and pulled a few out of the bag. She stuffed the tail ends into her mouth then sat in her car, motor running, and unleashed the prints.

"Damnation," she said. "Not a damn thing." In her rearview mirror she spotted a Starbucks and aimed toward a spot.

In a few minutes she was seated, licorice, Venti Cappuccino, and photographs spread out in front of her across the large table she'd chosen.

She traded her licorice for a pen, numbered the back of the pictures, reviewed each one, and made notes. Free association had worked for her in the past.

She stared at a full color shot of the Saab, next a similar view, except it was black-and-white photography.

"Buying a new car?" a young man asked from the next table.

"No," Rebecca said, disinterested in a conversation.

"Oh," the man rambled on. "I'm getting a new vehicle. I've been renting different ones to get the feel of how they handle. I haven't found one I both like and can afford. I'd love to have a beautiful red Saab like the one in your pictures." He sighed wistfully and opened what Rebecca recognized was a chemistry text book.

"That's it," she whispered to herself, gulping her coffee, and grabbing another stash of licorice. "I've been looking for something that's not in the pictures."

CHAPTER 44

Agent Lloyd's instincts sharpened as he turned the corner several car-lengths behind the green Jaguar. He wasn't worried when it disappeared into the night; it was easily found. He passed the dark alley and saw the Jag had pulled in behind a black limousine.

Agent Lloyd turned off his lights and parked his car. After making a few notes, he radioed in the lighted license plate number of the limousine and a few minutes later he received verification it was owned by Castriano.

Fifteen minutes later Skyler returned to his car, shoved a thick white envelope into his breast pocket, and climbed into the low bucket seat. He reversed his Jaguar into the street. The limousine pulled forward out of the other side of the alley with only its parking lights on.

"Interesting," Agent Lloyd said.

* * * *

Skyler grinned. He wanted to celebrate. Too bad Samantha had to go and mess things up. She was off limits for the time being, but she was still under his thumb, and she knew it. Dialing his car phone, he reached a meek voice that was filled with confusion.

"Hey babe, want to come out and play?"

"Skyler . . .?"

"Mags baby, you don't seem happy to hear from me."

"Margaret. And, except for the name mangling, I'm happy to hear from you. But, honestly, I'm surprised—it's so late." She turned her alarm clock to face her.

"Midnight. What happened: you change into a pumpkin? We can play Halloween if that's what you want. Be ready. Fifteen minutes." Skyler clicked off. "I always win." Victor, he thought grinning to himself. I should've been named after the thing I love. "Victory." he said out loud, raising his right hand triumphantly and stepping on the gas.

* * * *

Agent Lloyd parked his car in the lot facing the nurse's apartment. He suspected it was a nurse who'd placed the flowers in Samantha's room, and Margaret Parks had been the only nurse on the guard's list, who didn't have a direct purpose for being in Samantha's room. When she'd been questioned with the rest of the hospital staff, she claimed to have placed an extra blanket on Samantha's bed because she was responding to a request for another blanket and must have confused the rooms.

Agent Lloyd asked her why she assisted a patient, who

wasn't on her floor. She insisted she'd stopped upstairs to see a friend. When she heard a patient buzzing the unattended nurses' desk, she answered it. Her prints, she explained, had been found on the vase of the flowers because she'd watered the flowers when she was in the room.

Agent Lloyd tuned in the radio and grabbed the silver thermos he'd belted into the passenger seat next to a small cooler. He'd been on too many cases to sit out the night on an empty stomach. That was for rookies. He bit into the smaller part of his hearty submarine sandwich. He didn't mind waiting.

* * * *

In Margaret's apartment, Skyler said, "Hey babe, you look great. Come here and take off that robe."

Margaret did as she was told. She knew better than to resist. The bruises had faded, but the pain lingered. She knew better than to refuse him again. She'd learned her lesson when she refused to deliver a second present to his friend. She didn't want his anger to resurface. The fight had been her fault. Realistically, he'd expect her to do it again. Fright embodied her after the FBI agent questioned her. She was too scared to tell Skyler about the FBI and to tell the FBI about Skyler.

She let her robe fall to the floor without taking her eyes from his. The minute she lay on the bed he grabbed a handful of hair from the nape of her neck, yanked her into him, then kissed her deeply.

"So you did miss me," he whispered.

"Mmm." Margaret winced breathing in his whiskey breath and powerful cologne. She paired her movements with Skyler's. Her body was on the alert. Why did she agree to allow him in her apartment? She screamed at herself. She opened her eyes into his. He was so handsome—almost too attractive. Her intellect blurred when his body melted into hers.

"See how much I missed you?" Skyler said, thrusting his hips against hers.

* * * *

Agent Lloyd reviewed his notes while he waited. He condensed them, page by page, into an organized, itemized list. Then he began a list of questions. As minutes faded into hours, he matched the two lists. Had his team found the rental car yet? Did Skyler have anything to do with the murder? If so, what? What was missing? What was inconsistent?

Doodling one question after the next, he remained occupied until his eyes captured Skyler's slinking shadow emerge from the apartment building into his Jaguar. Seconds after Skyler pulled onto the street, Agent Lloyd crept behind him.

CHAPTER 45

"Hey Missy, heard from Samantha lately?" John asked, setting a full tray next to her empty one.

"You're lucky you got food; I thought they closed the cafeteria half an hour ago."

"I've got pull. Resident assistants are allowed to raid the kitchen after hours," John said, scooping up a mouthful of lettuce leaves drenched in French dressing.

"Have *you* heard from her?" Missy asked.

"A few texts initially. But not lately. I want to call." John looked into Missy's watchful eyes. "But she told me not to."

"I know; me too. I'm worried about her. Her attorney asked me to send a box of things to her—weird things— and I haven't heard anything since."

"Weird things? Like what?" John set his silverware down.

"The contents of her junk drawer in her dresser and in her desk, hairbrushes, a jewelry box and makeup bag," Missy said. "Strange combination."

"She's coming back as far as you know, right?"

"No idea. Last weekend I received a check with a note from her mom. She asked me to pack and ship all Samantha's belongings home, but not to let anyone know."

"I won't say anything," he said in a serious and disappointed tone. "I'm betting she isn't coming back."

She patted his shoulder and got up. "I'll let you know if I hear anything."

John watched her leave the cafeteria and reread Samantha's last text.

John,

I wish I could see you. I'm still in the hospital, thinking the worst. Policemen are outside my door. Newspapers, television, and radio must be bad because I'm not allowed access to any. Thank you for believing me.

Skyler sent me black roses. I'm not supposed to tell anyone. I'm scared. Rebecca has a lot of people working my case.

This hospital food is worse than dorm food.

I understand if you want to forget me. I read the book you sent me every day. I focus on the phrase you highlighted, "Nothing real can be threatened." I want to believe that.

Missing you

John missed her blue eyes and the long, thick, curly mane that flowed around her face and down her tiny frame. She was so beautiful. He couldn't get her out of his mind. He was encouraged that she'd been reading the *Book of Miracles* he'd sent. She needed a miracle.

He'd promised himself to send a card, a letter, books, whatever he could conjure to distract Samantha. Rebecca had kept her promise and made sure they were able to communicate by text on a limited access cell and delivered to her whatever he sent.

CHAPTER 46

Samantha stared at the plastic clothing bags dangling from her mother's fingers. She didn't care what she wore to the trial. She didn't want to go. She hadn't done anything wrong, yet she was charged with murder. Pulling her right out of a hospital bed and whisking her into a courtroom, she felt like a rag doll.

Tired of being questioned and reviewing evidence, tired of being told the hospital was better than a jail cell.

"I picked up a few new outfits. Whatever you don't like, I'll send back," her mom chirped. "Can I help you try them on?"

"No, Mom," Samantha said. She felt certain her mother's shopping excursion was an excuse to check for weight gain.

"Fine."

Samantha waited while her mother hung up the clothes and pounded questions impatiently. "Have you heard anything about the trial? Will the case be dismissed? Is it still set to begin on Thursday?"

"Thursday, yes," her mom said, straightening the

bed covers.

"I didn't do it, Mom. This shouldn't be happening."

"I know, dear."

A laugh-track from within her head ran on and on. She tried to ignore it. Pictures of dripping clotting blood appeared before her.

"Samantha? You're so pale," Mom said. She leaned over and placed a hand on Samantha's head.

"I'm fine, Mom." Samantha removed her mother's hand from her forehead.

Mom frowned. "Your brothers will visit later." She sighed. "Can I send something with them for you?" She fluffed Samantha's pillows and sat in a chair.

"A cake with a silver file in it?" Samantha said sarcastically.

"There's that sense of humor I love." Mom half smiled. "Think positively."

"I'm tired of being locked up in here."

"You're not behind bars."

"I miss my friends and school."

"You need to make the best of things and follow doctor's orders."

"And attorney's orders and psychiatrists' orders and hospital rules, and, and, and. There's a forever-list."

"It'll be over soon. I promise." Mom stood and brushed a kiss on Samantha's forehead. "I'll be back later. Try on your new clothes in the meantime, and let me know." Mom swiftly vanished into the stark hallway.

Samantha was glad to be alone.

* * * *

Anne pushed the elevator button to the second floor and stepped out when it opened. She followed the room numbers until she found the doctors' suites. She scanned the list and found Chief Psychiatrist, Charles Levanstein, M.D. She popped two white pills into her mouth, stepped back to the cold water fountain behind her, then pushed open the office door, and gave her appointment time to the receptionist.

Within a few minutes she was called back to Dr. Levanstein's office.

"Your daughter signed a release giving me permission to speak with you," the doctor said. "I want you to know that Samantha wants to get better, and her attitude seems to be improving."

"Is she past the danger zone?"

"That's always difficult to determine. Her trauma causes her to have triggers," he said. "Her sleep pattern is irregular. She suffers from harrowing nightmares."

"Everyone has nightmares, don't they?"

"The rape and the murder activated deep-seated anxiety. Much of which is to be expected."

"I hear a *but*." Anne frowned seeing Dr. Levanstein flip open a thick file.

"Let me explain. Your daughter's dreams don't follow any particular pattern, however, she talks in her sleep and calls out the same words. Have you ever heard her talk in her sleep?"

"She's always woken up easily. I've never heard her talking in her sleep. Actually, that's not true, when she was an infant she would laugh in her sleep," Anne said. "What kind of words has she been calling out?"

"Samantha has asked me not to discuss that. I must follow her wishes."

"But I am her mother. I have a right."

"She is eighteen. My first responsibility is to doctor/patient relationship. Surely you understand that?"

Anne drew a deep breath. She knew he was right, and she hated it. "Can I trust you'll tell me what I need to know as a parent to help my child?"

"Of course. What can you tell me about your daughter's relationship with the woman she refers to as Nana?"

"Her grandmother? She loved her more than anyone. She spent a lot of time with Nana when she was a little girl. I was sometimes jealous of their relationship, but I've always been grateful Samantha had Nana when she was growing up. Is there something in particular you're looking for?"

"Did she sing Samantha a special song, or play her a particular piece of music?" Dr. Levanstein asked. "Or give her a musical instrument, or perhaps a music box?"

Anne shook her head at each suggestion. Then held up an interjection finger. "She received a music box for her fifth birthday."

"Does she still have it?"

Anne closed her eyes. "Samantha set it on her dresser. It's been there for years." When had she seen it last?

"Is it still there?"

"No idea. I don't know the last time I saw it. Can you talk with Samantha, maybe give her something so she's not nervous during the trial? She's very moody. I'm worried."

"How would you define very moody?"

"She's irritable and sulky. Sometimes I hear her mumbling to herself. Other times, she is unusually aggressive in her speech. I think she's going to break from the stress."

"With everything that has happened, all that is fairly normal."

"She's different." Anne leaned forward. "It's like she's transformed into someone else. I try to ignore it; after all she's been through; she's entitled to some outlet. Can she testify at the trial? It's coming up in a few days, and I'm not sure she's up to it."

"I believe she will be able to stand trial. At this point, she's eating better, and I have no solid proof she is unable to testify."

"Are you sure?" Anne asked, surprised.

"No. I'm not sure, but I believe there is a chance, at the trial, when she is confronted by the prosecutor, and questioned about the murder, her reaction may open a window that will allow me to put the pieces together to begin to really heal her."

"So you're using her as a guinea pig? The trial as some kind of experimental treatment? I thought you were the best. I thought you were trying to help her. You could cause permanent damage if she's not ready to stand trial."

"She's willing to take that risk. We have discussed the options."

"And I have nothing to say about your approach?"

"I'd hoped you'd trust me to do what you and your daughter have hired me to do, and that is to help her heal herself."

Anne didn't want to listen any more as Dr. Levanstein explained his rationale. She was tired of feeling left out of her daughter's life and out of the worst thing that had ever happened to her and to their family. She needed fresh air. She needed to be out of the small office and the smell of hospitals. Swiftly grabbing her purse, she fled from the office, thinking only of the safety of her home.

CHAPTER 47

In the courtroom, Anne and Travis Armstrong sat numbly behind a wooden railing that separated them from Samantha and her attorney.

Samantha felt like a perfectly shaped plastic doll with no other purpose than to be stared at and played with by other people. The uncomfortable chair in the box to the left of the judge's bench made her heart race. She wasn't just too close to the judge, she was too close to the twelve jurors, who would decide her fate.

She saw her parents and her brothers with heavy books on their laps in the front row and knew they were studying for the bar exam during breaks. She guessed her brothers were already prepared for their exam, and the books were used to zone out instead of answer questions about how her trial was going. She understood that feeling very well. She shifted her gaze to her attorney.

Stillness surrounded Samantha except for the booming questions that kept firing at her. And she remembered the worst days of her life. Court viewers watched and leaned forward, while she confronted her darkest days. She answered each question and tried to mask the fear, the pain. She was certain each spectator knew she heard the laughter, the voice, the one harming her and controlling her. The untold truth was her only hope of salvation.

Prosecutor Hiller motioned to his assistant to turn off the recording. The voices went dead and silence filled the tape. "Samantha, you previously testified this recording was made by Skyler Marks, and he gave it to you later, is that correct?"

"Yes."

"Can you tell this court why you never reported the rape to the police?"

"Skyler—Mr. Marks—told me I had washed away the evidence, and no one would believe me."

"Did he force you or coerce you into not reporting the rape?"

"No."

"Then I ask you again, why didn't you report the rape?"

"Objection," Rebecca called out. "Counsel is badgering the witness. She is not on trial for not reporting a rape."

"Your Honor, I believe the issue of the rape is critical to the case and goes to the Defendant's state of mind, credibility, and motive."

"Overruled. Please answer the question," Judge Bingham instructed Samantha.

"Thank you, Your Honor."

Samantha stared harder at Rebecca. Taking in a deep breath, she began. "I was afraid no one would believe me."

"It's true that you had the recording, and that could be some evidence, why not come forward then?"

"I thought it was too late. I took a shower. I was too embarrassed. I knew I'd let my parents down. I was scared." Her voice trailed.

"Did you love Greg Maston?"

Samantha lowered her eyes. She didn't want to answer; she didn't want to picture him. She had loved him. She now hated him. "Yes, but—"

The prosecutor cut her off, rushing in with another question. "It is true, isn't it that at the time you had sexual intercourse with Greg Maston, you loved him?"

Samantha's shoulders dropped, and so did her voice. "Yes, but—"

"And you failed to report that act of love as one of rape, isn't that correct?"

"Yes."

"Objection, mischaracterization of the evidence," Rebecca called out.

"Ms. Smalley, I'll give you latitude during your redirect. Your client already answered the question. Mr. Hiller, tread lightly."

"Yes, Your Honor," he said and stepped toward Samantha. "Could that have been because you enjoyed it, because it was something you had thought about, and you had wanted—to have sexual intercourse with someone you love like Greg Maston?"

"Objection. Counsel continues to badger the witness and is demeaning her," Rebecca called out.

"Sustained."

Prosecutor Hiller glanced at his notes. Flipping the page on the notepad in front of him, he began again. "Samantha, you testified under oath that you were raped by Greg Maston, and yet you want this jury to believe you didn't murder him. Is that right?"

"Yes."

"And you also want the jury to believe you had no reason to murder him, to want him dead, even though he allegedly committed a heinous crime against you. Is that also correct?"

"Yes."

"And because he raped you, it's true you wished he were dead?"

"Objection," Rebecca called out. "Speculation, there is no evidence of anything remotely close. Prosecution is again putting words into defendant's mouth."

"Sustained. Please rephrase the question," Judge Bingham said, almost disinterestedly, scratching notes on his pad.

"Thank you, Your Honor. Did you ever wish Greg Maston had been punished for his alleged crime against you?"

"At first, I—"

"Please, Ms. Armstrong, just answer the question, yes or no," Prosecutor Hiller said evenly, and the wide-eyed jury visibly edged forward in their seats.

"Yes."

"Thank you." Prosecutor Hiller said unleashing a slow deliberate smile. "You testified you knew your phones were being tapped by the Federal Bureau of Investigation. And we heard Agent Lloyd testify about the authenticity of the tapes entered into evidence. Is that correct?"

"Yes."

"Your Honor, I would like to play a few minutes of the FBI recording on the date of Greg Maston's murder, just prior to the approximate time of his death."

"You may. It's been introduced into evidence." The serious-faced judge paused, his eyes on Samantha's attorneys.

"Thank you, Your Honor," Prosecutor Hiller said. All eyes focused on him as he clicked a button on his computer, and the sound began."

Samantha felt uncomfortable. The voices—her own and Skyler's—echoed into conversation. But the words didn't fit. Her ears burned, her mind flooded with questions, and her nerves were jolted with fear. The voice was hers, but the words were not. The Prosecutor stopped the tape, staring at her. Her cheeks warmed, and her head pounded. Pain climbed up from the root of her neck.

"You testified earlier you didn't leave your house the night Greg Maston was murdered. Is that correct?"

"Yes. I went to sleep. I slept in my bed all evening. I wasn't feeling well."

"But you did in fact leave, didn't you?"

"No. I was sleeping."

The prosecutor turned the tape on again and Samantha shrank further into her chair hearing Skyler's voice ask her to meet him down the street, but when a soft, sexy, playful voice that sounded like her own, agreed, her back arched and her neck stiffened. She could never say those words to Skyler or anyone else. She'd never spoken to any man like that.

The voice inside her was laughing loudly. It grew. It swelled into gales of laughter. Her head pounded, and she covered her ears. She couldn't listen. It wasn't true. It wasn't true. Fury shrieked inside her. The pain she felt was now so piercing it numbed her into darkness.

Words began falling uncontrollably from her mouth. "I don't understand your problem," the sultry, sophisticated northern voice began loudly. "There is nothing wrong with me going out with my boyfriend. Tom and I have been dating for so long we're practically married."

A gasp filled the room and then immediately hushed. The prosecutor spread his hands out like he was silencing a symphony. The judge lifted his gavel. The onlooking crowd silenced. The jury visibly leaned forward in their chairs.

"Who is Tom?"

"My boyfriend."

"What is his first and last name?"

"Thomas Steven Marks. Everyone calls him Tom."

"What is your name?"

"Darcey."

"What is your last name?"

Darcey stared in silence. The prosecutor repeated the question, to no avail. Fearful he would lose the momentum, he continued, disregarding her non-responsiveness. Rebecca stood up at counsel table, but said nothing.

"Darcey, tell me where Samantha has gone."

"Samantha? She's a wimp. She can't handle anything."

"So you handle it for her?"

"Yes, that's right."

"Where is she?"

"Sleeping. She's always sleeping."

"Can you wake her up?" Prosecutor Hiller continued in the silence. "Please. I need to talk with Samantha. I need to make sure she is okay."

"Samantha's fine. I take care of her."

"Is that what you did the night Greg Maston was murdered? Did you take care of her by murdering him in cold blood?"

"Me? No, I didn't murder anyone."

"You were there. The night of the murder. You met Tom. You drove Samantha's car and met Tom, and then you murdered Greg. Did Tom help you?"

"I didn't murder Greg. I didn't drive Samantha's car. Tom was parked down the street. I met him. I walked. I always walk to meet him. We didn't want to wake anyone up," Darcey said, her tone filled with annoyance.

"Do you remember the color of the car?"

"Red. Fire engine red."

"What kind of car was it?" he demanded.

"It was a Saab."

"Are you sure?"

"Yes."

"Did you see the license plate?"

"No," she said.

"Are you sure?"

"Yes."

"Do you remember anything else about the car?"

"There was a sticker in the bottom corner of the windshield on my side."

"The passenger side or the driver side?"

"I said my side. I was in the passenger seat."

"What did it say?"

"I don't remember. I could see through it, except for where it had a letter and a number on it. I couldn't read the small printing on the bottom. It was dark."

"What else do you remember?"

"Nothing. I didn't murder anyone, especially for the wimp."

"Thank you for answering my questions. Can you bring back Samantha? I really need to speak with her."

Silence fell upon the startled crowd. Moments passed in hushed suspense until the meek voice returned.

"Sleeping. I told you I was sleeping, and I didn't leave all night."

"Your Honor," Rebecca interrupted, "May we approach the bench?"

"You may," said the judge with a wrinkled forehead, watching the group intensely.

"I am claiming surprise at my client's mental condition. Not one of the psychiatric experts found a multiple personality. I request a mistrial or at least a recess at this time," Rebecca whispered.

"Continuance, to talk with your client?" Judge Bingham scratched his ear.

"No, Your Honor. I believe we can continue with the rest of the evidence without our client."

"The jurors may be tainted by this display, don't you think?" Judge Bingham stared at both counsel.

"The People may consider *Guilty by Reason of Insanity*."

"You won't need to, but I will argue *Not Guilty by Reason of Insanity* and ask for dismissal if necessary," Rebecca said. "I'd like the opportunity to have her evaluated based on this newly discovered information."

"Any objection from the Prosecutor?"

"No objection. It's important we make certain she's not faking to avoid life behind bars."

"That's inaccurate," Rebecca chimed in.

"While this is highly unusual, I will agree that as long as this matter proceeds, and you don't waste this court's time. We will adjourn for two days."

CHAPTER 48

"Doctor, there's no history of mental illness in either my husband's family or my own." Anne paced while she spoke. "Samantha's problems were brought on by her circumstances, and she will get over it. She has strong genes."

"Samantha has made great progress. What concerns me is that she was so distraught that she created a second personality, the one that calls herself Darcey, to cope."

"Samantha has had the best of everything, including the love of her whole family."

"Love does not fix the depth of this pain, and because of this trial there aren't the years of therapy it might take to oust Darcey and find Samantha."

"I'm a good mother. How did this happen? Samantha has had the best of everything."

Dr. Levanstein stared at Anne, jotting notes as he listened and watched her. "This has little, if anything to do with parenting skills. Treatment and recovery takes time. More time than two days."

* * * *

When Judge Bingham took the bench and the jury filed in, the courtroom hushed.

Prosecutor Hiller called Melanie Harper to the stand.

"Miss Harper do you recall the evening of Wednesday, November 23rd of last year?"

"Yes."

"How is it you recall that date?"

"I was walking toward my sister's alterations shop. We were meeting for dinner at the nearby restaurant. When she wasn't there, I left my car in the restaurant parking lot and walked to her shop to help her close up."

"About what time was that?"

"Around seven-thirty. I remember that because I asked to have our seven-thirty reservations changed to eight."

"Are you familiar with the Armstrong law firm?"

"Yes."

"How is that?"

"My sister and I often pass by the Armstrong's office building when we meet downtown for lunch or dinner. It's across from my sister's shop. Also, a few years ago the firm helped us settle our grandparents' estate and set up family trusts."

"Do you know Samantha Armstrong?"

"Yes."

"How is it you know her?"

"I think everyone in town knows the Armstrong

family."

"Objection, non-responsive to the question," Rebecca called out, not looking up from the notepad she was scribbling on.

"Sustained. Please, Miss Harper, answer the question."

"Sorry. I don't know her exactly. I recognize her from pictures in her father's law firm. There are a lot of family pictures. I like to look at pictures. When I was in the waiting room or conference room, I'd always look at the photos, and I'd ask about them. I also recall seeing Samantha in the newspaper, her graduation photo."

Prosecutor Hiller interrupted. "Aside from photographs, have you ever seen Samantha Armstrong in person?"

"Yes."

"Tell us when the last time you saw Samantha Armstrong was."

"It was the only time I saw her. It was that night, when my sister and I had dinner. She was sitting in a beautiful red Saab. The car was running. I remember thinking it must be nice not to have to worry about saving money and being able to run the engine for such a long time."

"What do you mean when you say for such a long time?"

"Well she was parked there in front of the building, with the engine running, for several minutes. She was parked when I met my sister and when we walked to the restaurant."

"Can you estimate the time frame?" Prosecutor Hiller repeated.

"Maybe twenty or twenty-five minutes."

"Then, you saw her twice. Once going to meet your sister and once going to the restaurant with your sister."

"Yes."

"Did you see her get out of the car?"

"No."

"Did you see anyone with her?"

"No."

"Did you see the license plate number of the car?"

"On the way back to the restaurant we were walking toward the car. My sister was closest to the car, but we were talking, and her head was facing me. The plate was in my view."

"Are you in the habit of noticing license plates?" "No, but this one was easy to remember."

"How's that?"

"It had a catchy number."

"What was the plate number, exactly as you remember it?"

"A-U-T-O-4," Melanie spelled out slowly, looking confidently and steadily at the jury, just as she'd been instructed.

"I'm handing you pre-marked Exhibit 22. What is it I am showing to you?"

"A picture of the license plate from the Saab."

"Thank you Miss Harper, I have no further questions

at this time."

"Defense Counsel, do you wish to examine this witness?"

Rebecca rose, grabbed a pen and paper, and walked to the podium.

"Miss Harper, it's fair to say that at seven-thirty and eight o'clock at night on that November day it was quite dark?"

"Yes, but there were street lights on."

"Did the person in the Saab have a light on in the car?"

"No."

"Was the car parked under a street light?"

"No."

"Was the car parked near a street light?"

"No."

"Aside from a few pictures, you've never seen Samantha Armstrong in person, until that night?"

"Yes."

"And when you saw her, you saw her in a dark car on a dark street on a dark winter evening. Is that correct?"

"Yes."

"And you claim without a doubt, you saw Samantha Armstrong?"

"Yes."

"Miss Harper, you didn't see the woman's eyes?"

"Yes, I did."

"Really? Sitting here today, you can't tell the jury what color eyes you saw, can you?"

"No, I can't."

"And you don't know if she was wearing earrings?"

"No."

"You also don't know whether or not she wearing makeup?"

"I don't know."

"Then you cannot absolutely, without a doubt, be certain it was Samantha Armstrong you saw, correct?"

"I . . . I . . ." Melanie Harper stuttered. Her focus was immediately on the prosecutor.

"Isn't it true you just assumed it was Samantha Armstrong because of the location of the car in front of the Armstrong offices?"

Melanie's hands clenched the arms of the witness chair so hard her knuckles turned white. "Yes."

"I have no further questions." Rebecca returned to counsel table.

Judge Bingham recessed the Court for lunch.

* * * *

Travis and his sons approached Rebecca, while the courtroom cleared.

"We're going to the hospital to meet Anne. She's waiting for news of Samantha's latest psyc evals with a prominent psychiatrist and psychologist."

Rebecca nodded. "How is Samantha taking all of this?" she asked.

"Refusing to eat. Anne is distraught she can't hear

the testimony. She asked me to bring her what she calls 'Rebecca's interpretation' of the morning."

Rebecca smiled. "It's going better today. What do you think?"

"You poked a hole in the Prosecutor's assertion Samantha was in her car outside the scene of the crime. I've been watching the jury—"

Rebecca cut Travis off. "The jury, doesn't have all of the facts, and you know things aren't always what they seem."

"I'll remain worried until my daughter is not in danger of prison. We're in the middle of a trial that will determine the rest of my daughter's life, and we are still piecing together information and looking for evidence. How is that supposed to comfort me?" Travis said sternly.

"There is much more. Embrace your faith in Samantha. We'll put the real murderer behind bars." Agent Lloyd's voice was stern. "I wouldn't be assigned here if there was confidence local law enforcement got this right."

Before Travis could respond, Rebecca interjected. "We have a few leads. I can't promise anything, but I truly believe this is winnable, and Samantha will be going home with you to stay."

"Rebecca, we both know if Samantha is found *not guilty by reason of insanity*, she will be institutionalized. I can't bear the thought of that." Travis sighed.

Rebecca paused. "I'm hoping for dismissal or a finding of not guilty and final closure of this."

CHAPTER 49

Skyler wasn't allowed to be a spectator at the trial. He'd been subpoenaed by both prosecution and the defense. When the initial newspaper accounts didn't mention his name in connection with the trial, he'd been elated. But pangs of panic rose when he was called as a witness. For her sake, he hoped Samantha had played it smart and believed his threats.

He was convinced no one would believe he'd done anything wrong—after he explained she'd repeatedly begged to have sex with him.

He'd fallen for her. Age didn't matter. She was a consenting eighteen-year-old adult. Their consensual relationship was not a crime. How could he have anticipated the woman he'd known since she'd been a girl had mental problems and a strong motive to kill her rapist?

Leaning against the bedroom bureau, Skyler cracked his knuckles and stared at his cellphone. Damn her for not finding a way to call him. Each passing day without hearing her voice stoked his anger. How dare she challenge him after he'd been such a good friend to her?

How dare she not creatively find a way to reach him?

Shaking with outrage at his isolation from Samantha, he chugged a cold beer and then another. Samantha needed to feel his angry breath against her. That would send a stronger message than the note and flowers.

Inevitably the trial would end, and then he could visit her in prison. If he couldn't have her, no one would. He cracked his knuckles again, laughed at the sound, and then twisted open another beer.

* * * *

The only thing Samantha was sure of about the past three weeks was that time was passing. Isolated, she was painfully aware of the time she'd lost and the danger of being locked up for life. She grated the stolen plastic spoon against the cement floor and formed it into a spear. She felt safer.

Samantha wished the forensic wing in the hospital where she'd been transported allowed news, any up-to-date information. But with every inquiry she received the same information-less smile.

She flipped through the stack of text books John had forwarded from her classes. She flipped through the pamphlet he'd stuck in her art history book that explained Michigan State University's policy on receiving college credit by taking an examination. She plucked out an adult coloring book from the varied selection he'd included. Coloring kept her mind occupied, and her stress-level in-check. She'd reread the letter he'd included with the books so many times the words spoke to her from memory.

She'd become a master at anticipating the nurses sneaking in and out of her room; the choppy start-and-stop gait of her doctor; the hollow high heels of her mother; the brisk, heavy walk of her father; Emily's apprehensive, soft footsteps. The twins' energetic voices that announced them before she could hear their walk.

She felt neatly tucked away, a hostage amid dull captivity. She also felt wholly exposed outside of herself. She couldn't pull the two feelings together, nor could she eliminate one or the other. She didn't remember what normal felt like.

Looking up just before the door opened, she heard the hypnotic voice of her psychiatrist. Samantha sighed. She was tired of the mild-mannered man and his questions.

"Good afternoon. Haven't you been out of bed, yet?"

"No reason to get out of bed," Samantha said, eyes downcast, nervous hands clenching one another.

"Of course, there is. We need to get you healthy and home. How do you feel about that?" the monotone voice asked, as he closed the silver metal chart and opened his notebook.

"I don't have any choice over anything. Every time I turn around, someone is asking me questions," Samantha said, annoyed at his stern face. She wanted to ask about her competency status, but was afraid to hear the answer.

"Have you thought about going home?"

"I think about it a lot."

"What do you think about?"

"I think about my room, my clothes, my enormous bed filled with stuffed animals, my comfortable furniture, my wallpaper, my pictures."

"What else do you see?"

"My Minnie Mouse clock that my Nana gave it to me when I was really little. And the music box she left me when she died. We listened to it together, before she—" Samantha stopped. She refused to say *died*. "I miss touching it. I miss hearing it play."

"Obviously, you like your room. What else can you tell me about it?"

"It makes me happy."

"You talked on your phone quite a bit, isn't that right?"

"So?"

"A few moments ago you gave me a very detailed description of your room, but you didn't mention anything about a phone in your room. You mentioned everything, but your phone."

"So?" Samantha said, she began jiggling her right foot.

"You didn't mention it. It's important to talk about the reasons why."

Samantha was tired. She didn't want to answer any more questions. She didn't want to talk anymore. She didn't want to see him. She closed her eyes and sighed.

"What are you talking to her for? She always fell asleep

on the phone, if you really want to know."

"Darcey?"

"Of course. The wimp is asleep again. When things get tough, she calls on me."

"And she needed to call on you a lot, didn't she?"

"Yes. Sometimes she needed me a lot."

"What times were those?"

"You know, times when he wanted her. But it wasn't really her he wanted, it was me. He was my boyfriend."

"Who was your boyfriend?"

"Tom."

"Tom who? Do you know his last name?"

"Marks."

"Think. You are confused. Take your time. Picture him, listen to his voice. Hear his voice. Can you do that?"

"Of course."

"Then it isn't Tom Marks you are seeing, is it?"

Jolted, Samantha awakened. She felt clammy, sweat-drenched. The onset of truth: a parallel vision, clear and true, evoking an almost hypnotic awakening. "Skyler. I think, it was Skyler," Samantha cried. Strong warm tears streamed down her face, dropping into her lap.

"Can you tell me your name?"

Samantha paused. Was there someone else in the room? She rolled her eyes around the room. Had the voice come out of her? Whose voice was it? Samantha felt the psychiatrist piercing her. Suddenly, she was uncomfortable.

"My name? My name is Samantha Armstrong." Moments passed. The quiet startled her. Suddenly, she felt her facial muscles loosen, as confusion turned to understanding. "I didn't do it. Did I?" Samantha whispered.

"What do you believe?"

"I didn't do it."

"You are sure?"

"Yes."

"Had you ever considered murdering Greg Maston?" The doctor pointed his pen at her.

"I couldn't commit murder. I didn't murder Greg," Samantha paced her words slowly, thinking out loud, feeling a flood of genuine relief.

In the ensuing silence, panicked, she watched the doctor's hands quickly scribble notes.

"Could I have done it without remembering it, without knowing it?" Samantha held her breath.

"You tell me."

CHAPTER 50

Judge Bingham ordered the next witness to be called, and Prosecutor Hiller rose. He wished Samantha were well enough to retake the stand. But she wasn't. Everyone agreed to proceed with the trial anyway. There was no reason to wait. The evidence clearly pointed to Samantha Armstrong. He figured her lawyers thought so, too, or they would have pushed for a continuance, or better yet, mistrial.

"The prosecution calls Skyler Marks to the stand."

Skyler grinned boyishly as he was being sworn in. He carried an aura of success and confidently took his seat.

Prosecutor Hiller hoped he could undermine the high opinion Skyler had of himself. Sitting coolly in his freshly pressed powder-blue Brooks Brother shirt with its white collar neatly tacked in 18-karat gold, Skyler smiled and folded his hands. It was apparent to Prosecutor Hiller that Skyler would have the jury eating his words like hungry deer eat corn.

"Could you tell us how you know Samantha Armstrong?" Prosecutor Hiller asked from the podium, his body language casual and friendly, his tone congenial. He had to ask questions that would either make his case against Samantha or break his case against her. He was ready for the truth. As prosecutor, the truth was his first priority. Justice would follow.

"I've known her and her family for approximately eight years. I'm currently employed by her father and have met Samantha on several occasions, both socially and work-related."

"Samantha Armstrong confided in you that she'd been raped by Greg Maston?"

"Yes."

"Can you tell us how it is she came to confide in you?"

"I stopped by the Armstrong house to check on a matter with Travis Armstrong and found Samantha alone. I wasn't aware her parents had gone to Washington until then."

"What, if anything, made you concerned about her at that time?" the prosecutor asked.

"She was disheveled—bruised, incoherent. She was rambling."

"What, if anything, did you do?"

"I tried to calm her down and offered to help her."

"Were you successful?" the prosecutor asked.

"I think so."

"How do you know that?" the prosecutor asked.

"I asked very simple questions. Samantha just sort of nodded at first. I could see how upset she was. I was patient. Eventually she calmed down. I was able then to ask more detailed questions."

"What kinds of questions?"

"Where were her parents? Did she need anything to drink? How was she feeling? Did she need a doctor? Could I bring her anything? Where had she been last night? Who was with her? How did she get home?" Skyler paused before adding, "Things like that."

"Did there come a point when she explained in detail what had happened to her?" the prosecutor asked.

"Yes, after a lot of prodding, Samantha explained she'd been raped by a man that looked like Uncle Greg."

"Uncle Greg? What was your understanding of who that was?"

"She told me it was Greg Maston. That he had raped her."

"What happened next?"

"I asked her if she went to the hospital or called the police. We talked for a long time about the need to report the rape. She said no. I repeatedly advised her she should call the police—immediately, not later. I offered to make the call for her and to take her to a hospital."

"What was her response?" the prosecutor asked.

"She told me she had taken a shower, and she didn't want anyone to know about the rape. She really had it quite planned out."

"Could you explain what you mean by that?"

"She had everything planned, down to the little details

to include getting an AIDS test and pregnancy test in another town."

"What was your understanding of why she wanted to go out of town?"

"She didn't want her parents to know."

"What was your response?"

"In her state of mind, I respected her wishes."

"You're aware we have the recording you made that same morning, are you not?"

"Yes."

"Why did you make that recording?"

"For the police—in the event she decided to report it. I gave the recording to her when it became apparent she was sticking to her decision not to report the rape."

"Why didn't you tell Samantha you were taping her?"

"Actually, I was so concerned about Samantha I forgot I had turned the recorder on. The record was for her benefit. She wasn't thinking clearly."

"Then why did you tell us she had a clear plan?" the prosecutor asked.

"Samantha has a high capacity for self-preservation."

"Did you at any time have a sexual relationship with Samantha?"

"I like Samantha. Her family has been good to me."

"Did you at any time have a sexual relationship with Samantha?"

"She just wouldn't leave me alone. She interpreted my being nice to her as my wanting to have a different kind of relationship with her."

"Did you have a sexual relationship with her, or not?"

"I tried not to, but we became very close, and I finally gave in."

"When was that?"

"When I visited her in Michigan."

"Prior to your visit in Michigan, you didn't have sex with Samantha Armstrong?"

"Objection, as to the relevance of this line of questioning," Rebecca interjected.

"Counsel?" Judge Bingham asked, peering over his bifocals at Prosecutor Hiller.

"Your Honor," Prosecutor Hiller argued, "it is important to understand the relationship of Ms. Armstrong and Mr. Marks, which directly impacted her state of mind and shows her motive in the murder of Mr. Maston."

"Overruled. However, the relevance had better come to light soon. I will only let you go so far."

"Thank you, Your Honor," Prosecutor Hiller responded. "During the time you spent with Samantha, did you learn anything about her relationship with Greg Maston?"

"I learned that when Greg Maston raped Samantha, it was likely not the first time. I believe he raped her multiple times during her life."

"She became comfortable enough with you to disclose that?"

Skyler looked into the jury box. "Yes, she opened up, so I thought she was getting over it."

"To your knowledge, did she ever discuss her relationship with Greg Maston or the alleged rape with anyone else?"

"Only me, at least that's what I was led to believe."

"Did you find it strange she didn't discuss the rape with anyone else?"

"No. We discussed it many times. I don't think she felt the need. It was too painful. She was comfortable with me."

"Did she at any time tell you she intended to kill Greg Maston?"

"No."

"Did you ever see any behavior that might indicate she was mentally disturbed over the alleged rape?"

"Objection. Not qualified to make that assessment," Rebecca called out.

"Sustained."

"Did Samantha ever talk with you about Greg Maston, beyond statements about the rape and that she hated him?"

"After the first few months, she never mentioned his name, and neither did I. I knew it bothered her. I knew he had hurt her. I was trying to help her, trying to protect her."

"Did you see Samantha Armstrong when she came home from college for Thanksgiving?"

"Yes, I did."

"Could you explain the contact you had with Samantha

Armstrong during that time?"

"I had dinner at her house with her family the night she came home from college. And we spoke regularly on the phone. She visited the office to see her father. We spoke in the conference room while she waited for him. They were going to lunch. The next time I saw her was at her parents' house for Thanksgiving dinner."

"When Samantha Armstrong came home for Thanksgiving break, she and her father met for lunch. Is that correct, to the best of your recollection?"

"I believe so."

"Do you know where they went?"

"As far as I know MacArthur Station; it's close to our offices."

"Have you ever eaten there?"

"Many times."

"I'm holding up for you a knife that has been identified and marked into evidence. Prior to today, have you ever seen a knife like this one?"

"Mmm." Skyler bent his neck, leaned forward, and studied the knife the prosecutor held in gloved hands.

"I can't place it. Looks like a common steak knife," Skyler said. "They all look the same to me."

"Have you ever taken Samantha to MacArthur Station?"

"Yes," Skyler said.

"Now, let's think back to the evening of the murder. Did you see Samantha that evening?"

"No idea. That was several months ago."

"Did you talk to her then?"

"It's possible. We spoke almost every day during that time."

"Did she seem upset to you at any time?"

"Not that I recall. Except maybe when I called, and she was napping when she had a migraine. She was usually groggy from taking one drug or another, at least that's what she would say."

"What kind of drugs?"

"I'm not sure which medicines. I don't think I ever really asked."

"Did she say anything on the day of the murder about Greg Maston?"

"Not that I recall, but if his name had been mentioned, I'd have remembered."

"Did she seem upset or aggravated on that day at any time?"

"Objection. Witness said he doesn't recall that day specifically," Rebecca called out.

"Overruled. I'll give you latitude on cross-examination," Judge Bingham said in a flat voice, peering over his reading glasses, before again focusing on the notes filling his pad.

"Thank you, Your Honor," Prosecutor Hiller said, and then repeated the question.

"No. She was too groggy for me to tell."

"Too groggy to drive a car?"

"I'm not sure."

"Too groggy to commit murder?"

"Objection. These questions are speculation. Move to strike," Rebecca said.

"Sustained. So struck. Move on. You may proceed."

"Do you know what kind of car Samantha Armstrong usually drives?"

"A red Saab."

"Do you know the license plate of that car?"

"Yes."

"Isn't it odd to know someone else's license plate number?"

"No."

"Can you tell us how it is you know Samantha Armstrong's license plate?"

"All the Armstrong cars have the same license plate, except for the number. They all have A-U-T-O and then the number, depending on the car. Travis Armstrong's limousine is AUTO 1, and his Mercedes he drives every day is AUTO 2. Anne Armstrong has AUTO 3—it's a champagne-colored Corvette. And the children have cars, AUTO 4—the red Saab Samantha usually drives, and then the twins have AUTO 5 and AUTO 6, which I believe they took to law school with them."

"What kind of cars do the twins drive?"

"I don't remember. I haven't seen their cars since they went away to school."

"Did Samantha Armstrong take a car to Michigan?"

"I'm not sure."

"Have you seen Samantha Armstrong drive her Saab with the license plate A-U-T-O-4."

"Yes."

"Did you see her drive the red Saab during Thanksgiving break, before Greg Maston was murdered?"

"Yes. It's the only car I've ever seen her drive."

"Your Honor, I have no further questions. I reserve the right to redirect and recall Mr. Marks," Prosecutor Hiller said, flipping through his notes.

"Does the defense wish to cross-examine the witness?" Judge Bingham asked.

"Yes, Your Honor," Rebecca said, walking toward the witness stand as she unfolded and read the note Agent Lloyd handed her.

I have a hunch. Stall for time. Tell the judge you are ill if you have to. Buy some time. I may be gone an hour or a day. I'll be in touch. Text me if you need anything.

"Ms. Smalley? Are you ready to continue or do you need a recess?" Judge Bingham asked.

"I'm sorry, Your Honor. I am ready to proceed at this time." She turned to Skyler. "Mr. Marks, you testified Samantha Armstrong was sure Greg Maston raped her, is that correct?"

"Yes."

"And you also testified Samantha Armstrong told you

everything about Greg Maston and the rape, and she didn't tell anyone else about it, is that also correct?"

"Yes."

"She never told you Greg Maston tried to contact her after the alleged rape?"

"No."

"She never told you she saw him or that he was at her home several times after the rape?"

"No."

"If they spoke, and if they saw each other, and she didn't tell you, you would have to agree she didn't tell you everything?"

Skyler remained silent, smiling smugly. "She would've told me."

"Just before Samantha left for college, she had an eighteenth-birthday party. Is that correct?"

"Yes."

"You know that because you were there, isn't that correct?"

"Yes."

"Isn't it also true Greg Maston was among the guests?"

"Yes. I believe he was there."

"In fact you spoke with him?"

"Yes."

"And there was a time at that birthday party when you and Greg Maston spoke with Samantha?"

"I don't recall."

"Let me read to you from a sworn statement Samantha

made to police."

"Greg, wished me happy birthday. I walked away. Shortly after that Greg and Skyler came over to me and spoke. I excused myself with a headache and went upstairs to my room. I fell asleep and the next thing I remember, Emily, my best friend, was knocking at my door telling me to go downstairs; people were looking for me."

"So it is fair to say you and Greg Maston spoke with Samantha Armstrong at her birthday party?"

"Yes."

"Did you arrive at the party with Greg Maston?"

"No."

"But you did arrange to meet Greg Maston at her party?"

"No."

"You knew that Greg Maston was considered to be part of the law firm?"

"Yes."

"And that he would attend any party the whole firm was invited to, including Samantha's birthday party?"

"Yes, he usually attended firm functions, but I didn't keep track of him."

"That is interesting, considering your interest and concern for Samantha. If, in fact, you believed she had been raped by Greg Maston, you would've been concerned about his attendance at her party. True?"

"If I'd thought about it, yes; but I didn't. In retrospect, I would have done things differently," Skyler said solemnly.

"In fact you did see Samantha Armstrong talking alone, directly with Greg Maston on the night of her party?"

"I don't recall."

"Shall I reread Samantha's deposition?"

"No. I'm not sure why my recollection of them talking is important."

"You practice criminal law, Mr. Marks, don't you?"

"Yes."

"Would you say over the years you have developed a keen sense for detail?"

"Yes," Skyler said proudly.

"Then you would agree that not remembering Samantha and Greg standing, talking with you at her birthday party, is rather convenient?"

"Objection. Your Honor, argumentative, and, he has repeatedly said he doesn't remember," Prosecutor Hiller stated.

Rebecca plodded right over him, pretending not to hear, not waiting for the judge. "And, it is also true that the only reason you recorded Samantha is to later blackmail her and cause such fear in her she would become your puppet?" She didn't wait for an answer but saw the judge lift his gavel. "It's also true that when it comes to Samantha Armstrong, you are as much of a sexual predator as Greg Maston." And the gavel banged.

"Counsel Smalley, control yourself or you will leave by way of the jail. Sustained as to the last three questions."

"I apologize to the court and the jury. Your Honor," Rebecca responded, and then glanced at her wristwatch knowing the empty chair next to her was still empty, "I withdraw the questions." She paged through her questions even though she was confident in her questioning. *Buy time* kept flitting through her. Where was Agent Lloyd? "Mr. Marks, you've eaten at MacArthur Station with Samantha Armstrong?"

"Yes. Like I said, it's close to our office." He smiled toward the jury.

"In fact you and she dined there several times?"

"Yes, over the summer to talk about college. She asked me for advice."

"Seems you gave a lot of advice. Please stick to yes/no answers." Rebecca met his stare and then turned toward the judge, silently daring him to veer and face the wrath of the judge.

Rebecca held a stack of white receipts up. "In fact you dined with her at MacArthur Station over a dozen times during the summer?"

"Yes."

"Offer Defense Exhibit A, fourteen receipts from MacArthur station, previously provided to the People."

"Any Objection?" Judge Bingham stared at the prosecutor.

Prosecutor Hiller stood. "None."

"Admitted. You may proceed."

"Did you ever see Samantha Armstrong take anything that didn't belong to her from any restaurant?"

"No."

"No salt and pepper shakers?"

"No."

"No ashtrays?"

"No."

"Did you ever have to ask for another steak knife because one was missing?"

"Not that I recall."

"Samantha often didn't carry a purse, or she carried a small bag that she kept her cell phone in?"

"I don't recall."

"But you do know that anything Samantha carried would be too small to place a steak knife into?"

"I don't recall."

"And in fact, you had intercourse with her after every dinner, so if she had hidden a knife on her body, you would have seen it, isn't that right?"

"Anything is possible."

"Yes or no?"

Prosecutor Hiller jumped up. "Objection, calls for speculation."

"Counsel you opened the door on direct. Overruled."

"Yes."

Looking up from her notes toward the separating rail, she saw Agent Lloyd now seated at counsel table looking anxious. She nodded back at him. She had a few more questions to ask.

"It's fair to also say the first time you made Samantha aware of the recording was when you used it to blackmail her?"

"No. I'm not even sure what you are referring to."

"Just to be clear, you are denying under oath, using the recording, knowing that she didn't want her family to know about the rape, to force and coerce Samantha to succumb to you."

"We were in a relationship."

"A sexual relationship you knew Samantha would never enter into, except for your blackmail, isn't that correct?"

"No."

"Your Honor, may I have a moment to confer with co-counsel?" Rebecca asked.

"Two minutes. We are off the record."

The courtroom was silent, but all eyes focused on them, while Agent Lloyd whispered, "I've stumbled on startling evidence. We need a recess. Ask for two days?"

"Monday?" Rebecca asked, and he nodded. She stood. "Your Honor may counsel approach?" At the side-bar, she explained because of Samantha's condition, they needed the week-end.

Judge Bingham recessed the case until Monday, instructing Skyler not to talk about his testimony with anyone and to appear as the first witness.

CHAPTER 51

Monday morning the courtroom was much like it had been when they'd adjourned. Media scattered, the jury reseated, Skyler in the witness chair and re-sworn, and Rebecca continued cross-examination.

"It's true that you have been a passenger in Samantha Armstrong's red Saab?"

"Yes."

"It's also true that you were not in Samantha Armstrong's Saab at any time on the day Greg Maston was murdered?"

"Yes."

"I'm handing you a receipt from Classic Rent-A-Car Company." Rebecca handed Skyler the pink sheet after showing it to the prosecutor and handing him a white copy. "I've marked it as Defense Exhibit S."

"The car was rented by T. S. Mark."

"So?"

"According to the receipt, a red Saab was rented."

"So?" he shrugged.

"The date of the rental of the red Saab is the day before

the murder of Greg Maston?"

"Yes."

"It's also true the return date is the same as the date of the murder?"

"Yes."

"Objection. I've let this go on long enough," Prosecutor Hiller stated. "Defense Counsel has not established the relevancy of this receipt, nor has she laid a proper foundation as to its authenticity."

"Your Honor," Rebecca said, "I understand the prosecutor's concerns. With a little latitude in a moment, it will quickly become relevant. I'm still laying foundation."

"Overruled. This is cross, but I warn you my patience has a limit."

"Thank you, Your Honor," Rebecca turned toward Skyler. "I'm handing you proposed Exhibit R, do you recognize it?"

"Yes."

"It's an accurate picture of the license plate on your dark green Jaguar?"

"Yes."

"In fact, it's a specialized plate that reads: F-U-N-4-M-E."

"Yes. It was a gift from a client when I purchased my car."

"It's also true that you drove your Jaguar just outside the city limits the day before the murder of Greg Maston?"

"I don't recall."

"Objection, relevancy."

"Counsel, I have to agree. Where are you going with this?" Judge Bingham stared at Rebecca over his reading glasses.

"Your Honor, it will become evident within a few minutes, if I am allowed to proceed."

The judge sighed. "A few minutes is all you have. You may proceed."

"Thank you, Your Honor." Rebecca stepped away from the podium and closer to the witness box. "Isn't it true you rented the red Saab mentioned in the receipt?"

"Why would I rent a car?" Skyler said.

"I'm asking the questions. You are answering them, so let me ask again. Did you rent the Saab in the receipt?"

"My name is not T.S. Mark."

"Yes or no?"

"No."

"You have a brother, don't you?"

"Yes."

"He is younger than you?"

"Yes."

"And his name is Thomas Steven Marks?"

"Yes, but I don't know what he has to do with any of this."

"Does your brother look like you?"

"We are brothers. Yes, we resemble each other."

"So much so, you have been told by many people that

you look like twins. Is that a fair statement?"

"Yes."

"Your brother lives in Michigan. Is that correct?"

"Yes."

"Was he in Arkansas for Thanksgiving?"

"Yes."

"Did he need a rental car?"

"No idea what my brother did or didn't do."

"Isn't it, in fact, true your brother drove a rented red Saab on his drive from Michigan to Arkansas for Thanksgiving? And he rented it because after meeting Samantha and learning how much she loved her Saab, he wanted to drive one?"

"No idea. My brother doesn't have anything to do with this."

"Not directly, except that it was you, who rented the car for him using his credit card; isn't that true?"

"Yeeess."

"And the salesperson used his initials and then missed the "s" on Marks because that is how you read his name as he typed it into the computer. Isn't that correct?"

"No idea what the salesperson did or didn't do."

Rebecca pressed on, ignoring Skyler's editorializing.

"Is it fair to say you did, in fact, drive that rented red Saab during the two days before Greg Maston was murdered?"

"Not—"

"Yes or no?"

"I'm not—"

"In fact, before you answer that question, you may want to consider the fact I have a sworn statement from the cab driver, who remembers driving you to the rental agency. And in proposed Exhibit U, I have the original log the cab driver kept and turned into his company for the specific day you rented the Saab. The cab driver, Mr. Nate Williams, is willing to testify as to the authenticity of each document."

Rebecca stepped back and handed the prosecutor both the sworn statement and the log book. "Your Honor," Rebecca said, "once Counsel is finished reviewing the statement and the log, I would request they be entered into evidence under the business records exception in the interest of time."

"I have no objection to counsel referring to the documents at this time. I will likely stipulate if I'm satisfied by the testimony of Mr. Williams."

"Ms. Smalley you may proceed with that understanding," the judge said.

"Mr. Marks, again I ask, you, in fact, rented the red Saab indicated in the receipt?"

"I've rented many different cars over the years for my brother as a favor. I may have rented it and dropped it off to him, so he had a car when he was home, and never gave it another thought. It's been several months. My memory is not clear."

"And, in fact, you borrowed the Saab from your

brother during the time Greg Maston was murdered?"

"I have my own car I like to drive."

"Are you familiar with a business by the name of The Key Maker?"

"Yes."

"In fact, The Key Maker is located about two blocks from your home?"

"I've never counted."

"I am handing you a receipt from The Key Maker."

"It is in fact your receipt?"

"Don't recall."

"Let me help you. You had two keys made. Car keys—a door key and an engine key, Saab keys."

"I occasionally have keys made because I'm so busy I have a tendency to misplace my keys."

"Isn't it true that your Jaguar has keyless entry?"

"Yes."

"And it's also true that the car keys noted in this receipt were for the rented Saab?"

"No idea." He shrugged and smirked.

"The salesman will testify he recalls cutting the keys for you and that it is your receipt. Now, would you like to answer the question again?"

"I don't remember. I've made several sets of keys over the past years for cars I own and cars I rent. It is expensive to replace lost keys to rental cars, when the rental car company replaces them. I anticipate and avoid problems."

Rebecca paused and postured herself as close to the jury and the witness as she dared. "You would agree there is no reason to make a copy of rental car keys for a vehicle you are not driving?"

"No. In fact, I disagree. My brother has a habit of locking his keys in the car, just like me."

"Well, I thought of that, so I spoke with your brother. Would you be surprised that, according to your brother, Tom, he has never locked his keys in any car? In fact, he was unaware you had a set of car keys to his rental car."

"I don't tell him everything. I didn't want to make him feel bad; he doesn't like to admit he is forgetful."

"I see," Rebecca said, with intended skepticism in her voice. "So, it is fair to say you had, and kept, a set of spare keys to the rental car."

"I don't recall."

"Your Honor, may Agent Lloyd assist me with a demonstration?"

"Yes."

"Thank you, Your Honor."

"Agent Lloyd is holding up a license plate. Please read it for the Court?"

"A-U-T-O-4."

"Counsel Smalley is now holding up a second license plate. Could you read it for the Court as well?"

"Where did you ...? That's my license plate."

"In fact, it is your license plate. It was removed from your Jaguar by court order this morning after you arrived. Could you read it for the Court?"

"F-U-N-4-M-E."

"Thank you. Agent Lloyd is holding up another license plate. Please read that one as well."

"A-U-T-O-4."

"Thank you."

"Attorney Smalley is now holding up both license plates that read A-U-T-O-4. But there is one difference between the two, isn't there? Can you tell the Court what it is?"

"Objection, Your Honor," Prosecutor Hiller said. "While this has been entertaining, I fail to see where counsel is going with this."

"Counsel?" Judge Bingham asked, his tone clearly ordering a response.

"If the witness is allowed to answer the question, I believe the Court will understand the relevance of the license plates and the line of questioning."

"You may proceed."

Rebecca turned toward Skyler, being careful not to interfere with the jury's view of the twin license plates.

"Do you see a difference between the license plates?"

Skyler stared at the two plates for a moment before answering. "There appears to be a spacing difference. More space between the *O* and the *4* in the one she is holding in her right hand, than in the one in her left hand."

"Exactly right." Agent Lloyd approached with a bottle

of turpentine and a rag. All eyes were on him as he took the one without the space between the *O* and the *4* and carefully removed paint from around the *4*. Prosecutor Hiller didn't object as he watched the show.

"I present the new version of the plate. The cleaner, real license plate. Could you read it for the Court?"

"This is absurd." Skyler responded defiantly.

"Please read it."

"F-U-N-4-M-E."

"Thank you," Rebecca said, taking a file from Agent Lloyd. "I have in my hand an analysis from the FBI crime laboratory. It details an analysis of paint scrapings taken from your license plate."

"Is that a question?" Skyler said, smugness abounding.

"I also have in my hand a receipt from Hank's Hardware, Exhibit V. The receipt lists the mixture that exactly matches the license plate. Also," Rebecca said, "a search warrant was authorized and executed this morning on your garage. This can of paint was discovered. A sample has been taken to the FBI Crime Laboratory for comparison with the report from your license plate."

"A uniformed police officer approached holding a can of paint in gloved hands. Rebecca pointed at the can. "I ask that the paint can, Exhibit W, and Exhibit V be admitted into evidence."

"Without objection," the judge's voice boomed. "Admitted."

"It's true that not only did you drive the rented Saab

on the day of Greg Maston's murder, you attached the plate to cause the Saab to look exactly like the one driven by Samantha Armstrong?"

"That's absurd." Skyler turned toward Judge Bingham. "Your Honor, do I really have to put up with this harassment? I haven't been charged with anything. I'm not on trial here."

"The Clerk will remove the jury," Judge Bingham said and turned to his law clerk.

"All rise," the law clerk boomed out, and everyone stood while the jury exited.

When the jury door closed behind them the judge folded his hands. "You may be seated." Judge Bingham turned toward Skyler. "Mr. Marks, please answer the questions—unless you would like to take a brief recess, so the prosecutor can consider charging you with obstruction of justice. Or, perhaps you wish to consult with an attorney?"

Skyler said nothing.

"Counsel, you may proceed, but let's get to the relevancy of your line of questioning."

"Thank you, Your Honor. If the Court would bear with me just a moment." Rebecca stepped closer to the witness box. "Mr. Marks, it's fair to say you picked up Samantha in the red Saab after you placed the altered license plate on it?"

Skyler stared without responding.

"In fact, you then drove her to your office and left her

in the running rented Saab?"

Silence.

"You then entered the office and murdered Greg Maston?"

"Objection," Prosecutor Hiller called out. "Counsel has no proof; the scenario is purely speculation, and these questions are compound." His hands washed over his face. "We claim surprise."

"Surprise?" The judge raised his brows and waited.

Prosecutor Hiller said, "We ask that any such evidence be turned over to our offices immediately or that you hold counsel in contempt."

"Your Honor, all the evidence we have has been turned over to the police department and logged into evidence. We have also presented it—or will present it—here, today, in this courtroom. No further questions of Mr. Marks." Rebecca sat at counsel table.

"Your Honor we are ready for the jury." Prosecutor Hiller waited. "No redirect."

Addressing Skyler, the judge said, "Sir, you are released from subpoena. You may stay in the courtroom if you wish, but you don't have to. Don't discuss your testimony with any other witness."

Judge Bingham waited until Skyler stepped down and was seated in the back of the courtroom. "Counsel, do you have further proofs you wish to offer?"

"Yes, Your Honor," Rebecca said.

"Counsel, please approach."

Prosecutor Hiller and Rebecca leaned over the edge of the judge's bench to hear his whispered voice.

The judge leaned forward, one hand over the tip of his now-muted microphone. "I caution counsel, you may proceed, but without speculation. The only one on trial is Ms. Armstrong."

"Your Honor, may I have an opportunity to consult with opposing counsel? An Offer of Proof outside the presence of the jury may be appropriate if we can't agree." Rebecca spoke to the judge, but her focus was on the prosecutor.

"Clue me in on the topic?" Judge Bingham asked with slitted eyes.

Rebecca half-grinned. "I can almost guarantee you'll like the outcome."

CHAPTER 52

After the two sides conferred, everyone took their places in the courtroom again.

"Counsel, you may proceed with the Offer of Proof. Let's not keep the jury waiting too long," Judge Bingham said.

"The People call Agent Everett Lloyd," Prosecutor Hiller announced, and Agent Lloyd took the witness stand.

"Agent Lloyd, can you tell this court when you became involved with or interested in defendant Samantha Armstrong?"

"Samantha Armstrong filed a report in regard to an alleged rape of her by Greg Maston," Agent Lloyd said.

"Why would the FBI get involved in a local case of alleged rape?" asked the prosecutor.

"There's an ongoing investigation by the FBI of Skyler Marks."

"How is Skyler Marks involved in the alleged rape of Samantha Armstrong by Greg Maston?"

"There was an allegation against Mr. Marks in a

scheme to blackmail Samantha Armstrong for sexual favors in regard to the alleged rape by Greg Maston."

"Did your investigation include the alleged rape?"

"Somewhat. There was no actual physical evidence other than a recording of Samantha Armstrong confiding in Skyler Marks."

"Yet your investigation continued, please explain why." Prosecutor Hiller prodded.

"Samantha Armstrong was being stalked by Mr. Marks, and it became apparent their relationship was not consensual."

"What did you do, if anything?"

Agent Lloyd said, "Pursuant to a federal warrant, the phones of Samantha Armstrong and Skyler Marks were tapped."

"What, if anything, was the result?"

"Conversations reflected curious behavior on both the part of Samantha Armstrong and Skyler Marks."

"Could you explain, for the record, what you found curious?"

"Yes." He pulled out a handful of paperwork from a file he'd brought up to the witness box. "I keep a notepad for each case I work on."

He opened the file. "This notepad contains my notes during my investigation of Mr. Marks and the alleged rape of Miss Armstrong by Greg Maston. I want to be accurate, so I brought it to refer to."

"Thank you. Please define what you mean by curious

behavior," the prosecutor said.

"Yes. Samantha Armstrong was very reluctant to talk with Skyler Marks, yet there were times she enjoyed talking with him," the agent said.

"While that behavior is curious, it isn't illegal, is it?"

"No. But I became intrigued," Agent Lloyd said.

"By what?"

"Samantha Armstrong was recently hospitalized, and the pieces began to fall together when we spoke with her doctors."

"What pieces began to fall together?" asked the prosecutor.

"Samantha suffers from dissociative identity disorder, formerly called: multiple personality disorder. It was likely brought on by a serious trauma—in her case, it was deemed she'd also suffered post-traumatic stress disorder."

"Is this your conclusion?"

"No, it is from our behavioral experts and was confirmed by her treating physicians."

"What is your understanding of that?"

"When things become too much for her to handle, she has a second personality that takes over," Agent Lloyd said.

"A second personality?"

"The tapes obtained under the federal warrants show that Samantha began referring to Skyler Marks as Tom."

"Mistakenly?"

"No," Agent Lloyd said. "We discovered Skyler Marks has a brother, Tom, whom Samantha Armstrong is fond of. Tom Marks has a girlfriend by the name of Darcey."

"What, if anything, does Darcey have to do with Samantha?" asked the prosecutor.

"Under hypnosis, Samantha Armstrong's second personality responds to the name of Darcey, and in fact, talks about Tom."

"When you say second personality, what exactly do you mean?"

"Samantha Armstrong is one personality. Darcey is another."

"Your honor, I have People's proposed Exhibit 33. I have carefully marked portions of the recording with corresponding transcripts of Samantha Armstrong's and these transitions. Also, proposed Exhibit 34 is the chain-of-custody log of these recordings."

The computer turned on. Voices captured the full attention of the listeners. The first recording, a pause, and then the second recording, and finally the third. The utterances were similar. Skyler's prompting sexual comments. Samantha turning into Darcey, following Skyler's lead.

Travis kept his eyes closed.

Skyler's eyes shifted toward the door.

"Your Honor," the prosecutor said. "I call Dr. Wilhelmina Martins as a further *Offer of Proof*. Defense Counsel Smalley has agreed to postpone cross-examination of all *Offers of Proof* witnesses until I've concluded."

"That's correct," Rebecca called out.

Lively whispers buzzed through the courtroom for several seconds before the Judge banged his gavel, forcing immediate silence.

"You may proceed." Judge Bingham set the gavel next to his hand.

Rebecca placed a clean page in front of herself. She forced herself not to turn around again to see the last vestiges of Skyler's smug look crumble. It would be unseemly.

"Dr. Martins, can you tell this court how you are involved in the case against Samantha Armstrong?" Prosecutor Hiller said.

"I am the independent psychiatrist appointed by the Court to review the mental state of Samantha Armstrong."

"Were you aware that two other psychiatrists reviewed Samantha Armstrong's case?"

"Yes, I've reviewed the notes and conferred with her own psychiatrist, Dr. Levanstein, and the one requested by the prosecution, Dr. Ty."

"Were you able to reach a conclusion or make a diagnosis?" asked the prosecutor.

"Yes. After approximately sixty hours evaluating this case," the doctor said.

"Could you share that with us?"

"Samantha Armstrong has suffered a number of traumas resulting in her suffering and recovering from medical conditions. Those include prescription-drug abuse, hypoglycemia, anorexia, and migraine headaches. Additionally, she suffers from PTSD or post-traumatic-stress-disorder as a result of sexual assault. Her brain went into a type of recovery mode resulting in the development of a personality that enabled her to deal with and control what she couldn't handle as Samantha."

"Before we get into the specifics of what you just stated, can you tell this court if you believe Samantha Armstrong is able to stand trial?"

"I don't believe Samantha Armstrong can, at this time, stand trial, due to both her mental and physical conditions."

"Yet she was found competent to stand trial, and here we are. How do you explain that?"

"It is very difficult to diagnose dissociative identity disorder. It takes special training, which I have," the doctor said.

"Can someone with this diagnosis knowingly commit murder?"

"Anyone, under the right circumstances, can kill."

"I'll rephrase," the prosecutor said. "Are there markers you would have noted if she was violent?"

"Yes."

"Did you find any of those markers in Samantha's testing?" the prosecutor said.

"No. The PTSD was induced as a result of being deeply and continuously hurt in a way that made her feel without hope. She was and is afraid for her safety."

"Based on your treatment and testing of Samantha Armstrong," the prosecutor pressed, "are there indicators, from what you learned that she committed the murder of Greg Maston?"

"No. She simply was too fearful to be near him for any reason. This innate fear means that she couldn't have emotionally handled being close enough to him to murder him."

"But you did say she also suffers from a multiple personality. Could her other personality have committed the murder?"

"That is possible, but not probable."

"Could you explain what that means?"

"The second personality is stronger than Samantha, but it is not a dangerous or culpable personality. It is a sexual, flirtatious personality—a personality type that is not usually thought of as one with a profile that includes homicidal tendencies."

"Meaning what?"

"It is unlikely either personality murdered Greg Maston."

"Your Honor, may we approach?" Rebecca asked.

The judge nodded. "You may."

"Your Honor, I move to dismiss the charges against Miss Samantha Armstrong. The People have elicited reasonable doubt in their own case."

"Counsel, I don't believe there are sufficient grounds for dismissal, but I will listen to your argument." He pulled off his bifocals and rubbed his eyes.

"Please make your arguments on the record," Judge Bingham said and both counsel stepped back to their respective tables.

"Although perhaps premature, I move for Direct Verdict in favor of my client because it is clear the People cannot meet their burden of proof," Rebecca said.

"Your Honor." Prosecutor Hiller nodded. "Agent Lloyd—on a hunch and on behalf of the FBI—requested samples of evidence from this case be sent to FBI labs to confirm the authenticity and physical makeup of the evidence law enforcement collected at the crime scene. We proceeded to trial not expecting the results that were brought by messenger to me this morning just before we proceeded. I concur with counsel's motion, but ask for dismissal myself as the People cannot proceed."

Rebecca turned to the back of the courtroom.

Skyler stood and turned toward the door. Uniformed officers, who'd sat on each side of the door, now stood on each side of Skyler.

"Before I rule, may I be advised of those findings?" Judge Bingham asked, folding his hands patiently on his desk, as an official copy of the report was handed to him and then Rebecca.

The prosecutor read: "The strands of hair which

matched Samantha's DNA didn't match the hair color she had used on her hair for a Halloween party a few weeks before the murder, signifying the strands were from a previous date. An additional strand of hair found on the buttons of the shirt on Greg Maston's body indicate there is the possibility of a third person in the room."

Prosecutor Hiller paused, allowing the silent Judge to contemplate the information.

"The third set of hair samples has been matched and identified as having come from a Ms. Melissa Senger, Samantha's dormitory roommate at Michigan State University. There is no evidence to support Ms. Senger traveled outside Michigan at or during the time of the murder of Greg Maston. Nor is there any evidence to support she had any knowledge or relationship of any kind with the victim. Furthermore, we can find no evidence or information Greg Maston has ever been to Michigan; yet there were strands of hair belonging to Miss Senger present at the crime scene. Ms. Senger is available to testify and verify our findings. DNA testing of the hair found and that of one taken from Ms. Senger are conclusively a match. I offer this forensic science laboratory report into evidence and to support the motion of dismissal of the case against Ms. Armstrong," Prosecutor Hiller finished.

He accepted the DNA report from his assistant's hand and walked a copy to the bench and then to defense counsel.

"You may proceed," Judge Bingham said to Prosecutor Hiller.

"The second piece of evidence involves broken fingernails. The results also arrived at our office this morning. The torn fingernails, believed to be Ms. Armstrong's, were tested as to their age and were found to have dried to the point of being broken off at least six months before the murder. The age of the nails and the time of the murder don't match. Additionally, there were scrapings of skin found under those nails that have conclusively been found to be from the body of Mr. Maston, and which have been previously offered by the prosecution and accepted into evidence.

"Counsel, am I to understand you proceeded to trial without all of the evidence?"

"Your honor, we had no reason to believe that additional testing was needed, and when we finally sent it, we did not think it important to wait. We claim surprise and apologize to this Court, Ms. Armstrong, and her family."

Judge Bingham raised a brow and pondered.

"We now believe due to these tests, which determined the age of the fingernails, they were planted after the murder, and the scrapings were intentionally placed on them." Prosecutor Hiller paused. "In other words, it is now our belief, while Ms. Armstrong is probably guilty of not using good judgment, that is all she is guilty of. Someone tried to frame her for a murder she did not commit."

The hush in the courtroom was complete. Not a rustle of clothing or as much as a cough, could be heard. All eyes focused on Judge Bingham, who flipped over page after page of the reports he was just provided.

Judge Bingham pounded the gavel. "Case dismissed with prejudice. Counsel will join me in my jury room to thank and dismiss the very patient jury."

"One other thing," Prosecutor Hiller said, his voice raised above the hum in the courtroom.

Judge Bingham sighed. "Yes?"

"I move this court to order Skyler Marks be placed under arrest for obstruction of justice, and blackmail, for starters. He is a flight risk."

Courtroom onlookers hushed and turned toward Skyler.

"No reason to involve me," Skyler said.

"Officers, take Mr. Marks into custody—temporarily at least," Judge Bingham said. "We are off the record."

Cameras zoomed in on Skyler, and then around the room, capturing shocked faces of onlookers at Skyler Marks being handcuffed.

Travis sat stone-faced.

The gavel released its final bang.

Tears filled Travis Armstrong's eyes as he hugged his sons.

Cameras flashed.

CHAPTER 53

The courtroom had emptied, and the surprised jurors departed. Rebecca and Agent Lloyd entered the attorneys' lounge with Prosecutor Hiller, who shut the door behind them.

"Thank you for your help," Rebecca said, looking at Agent Lloyd and Prosecutor Hiller.

"We don't have enough evidence to convict Skyler Marks or anyone else of Greg Maston's murder," the Prosecutor said.

"Skyler Marks may have bigger problems than rape or murder charges. He may have crossed the line with the Castriano family," Agent Lloyd said matter-of-factly, pulling out a second notebook.

Hands were shaken. *Thank yous* echoed. Rebecca and Agent Lloyd grinned.

"Good thing you two aren't a permanent team; you might put me out of business," Prosecutor Hiller said.

"Thank you for agreeing to such an odd presentation of evidence. Your professional courtesy was much appreciated," Rebecca said.

"Don't thank me; thank Agent Lloyd. He presented me with quite a different picture than the evidence from the crime scene showed. I wasn't authorized to release any knowledge of that evidence for fear of tainting the FBI operation."

"What?" Rebecca gaped at Agent Lloyd and then Prosecutor Hiller. "Are you two going to fill me in?"

"Well, that all depends on whether you two will stick around to help us prosecute the real murderer," Prosecutor Hiller said.

"You've got my full attention," Rebecca said. "But there's one question I've got to ask. If you knew Samantha didn't murder Greg Maston, why'd you put her at risk of being convicted?"

"She was never in real danger," Agent Lloyd said. "We weren't sure she didn't murder Greg Maston, given her state of mind, until I spent a few weeks following Skyler Marks. He has some interesting friends and some bad habits. She was safer in custody."

"Then why not arrest him?" Rebecca asked, not hiding her surprise.

"We had to let him think he had gotten away with framing Samantha for murder. We hoped he would lead us to the rest of what we needed to convict him."

"Hmm," Rebecca murmured. "You wanted him to feel comfortable enough to make mistakes, but scared enough after he'd taken the stand, he'd have to dispose of any links between himself, the murder, Samantha, and the Castriano family."

"Very good," Agent Lloyd said.

"What specifically were you looking for?" Rebecca asked.

"For starters, the head of a human-trafficking ring where hundreds of young people have been sold, and that included illegal abortions. Several young women from this county alone have been found dead or sterile. There were also a series of young women who have been brutally beaten to death that led to Skyler or people he associates with. There have been a few lengthy sting operations against the Castriano family that were foiled by Skyler, an over-ambitious vindictive attorney, who took shortcuts, despite his brilliant legal mind, and who bought one too many cops." Agent Lloyd was out of breath at the end of his statement of Skyler's offenses and illegal connections. His voice was as matter-of-fact as if he were ordering hamburgers.

"All of that led to Skyler Marks?" Rebecca whispered in disbelief.

"Yes," Agent Lloyd said.

"Why Samantha?" she asked.

"Lust, greed, control, stolen innocence, the profile on Skyler Marks is endless. Our team had quite an interesting time putting his profile together. We are looking for hidden offshore bank accounts, which will likely show deposits from payoffs for a variety of crimes," Agent Lloyd said.

"Is there enough to detain Skyler?"

"Yes, but we are after more. If he is able to post bond, we'll follow him. We are tailing the Castriano thugs. When we impounded Skyler's car for the license plates, we decided to check it for samples. A lot of interesting things were found, including in the inner tire tubes. Two were filled with cocaine, two with cash. The boys found a smorgasbord of samples from the trunk that may resolve a number of crimes."

"How did you ever think of looking inside the tires?" Rebecca asked.

"We didn't. One of the police mechanics pulling apart the Jaguar just happened to comment on what a nice car it was, and how it was a shame the owner didn't do a better job matching the tires."

"So the guy has different tires. That's not a crime."

"You're right. Except, in this case, why would you drive with two worn tires and two new tires? Skyler Marks had enough money to replace all four tires. His Jaguar was in pristine condition except for those two tires. Criminals always make a mistake, have a 'tell,' and the tires were his. The wear on the tires would have given him a poor ride. It just didn't make sense."

"Tires? Wow."

"I also recalled a Texas border case we had a few months ago. A lot of drug trafficking occurs inside tires. We pulled in the canines; they went crazy. We opened the tires. Bull's-eye."

"Remarkable." Rebecca shook her head.

"We think the merchandise in the tires belongs to Mr. Castriano. He won't be happy Skyler didn't deliver. Skyler might feel safer in custody."

"There's more isn't there?" Rebecca asked.

Agent Lloyd nodded. "We believe Skyler has hidden significant sums of money he hasn't yet wired out of the country. We're looking for clues that might give us a hint to the hiding places."

"The money, if there is any, could be buried in his backyard," Rebecca said.

"True, except we found a key, and the boys are checking airport lockers for a match. We're convinced once we find the locker, we'll find large bills suitably packaged for traveling. You know, a million dollars fits nicely in a flight bag, if it's in the right denominations."

"You seem to have it all figured out," Rebecca said.

"Not yet, but we're close."

"Should I worry about the Samantha's safety?" Rebecca frowned.

"We need to leave her in the hospital to make sure she's healed, and that it's safe for her to be out." Agent Lloyd paused. "Castriano will want to know where his drugs and money are before he erases Skyler. We'll have Skyler Marks so closely monitored in and out of jail that we can hear him unbutton his shirt."

"None of that protects my client."

"We'll provide protection as long as we can. We're

close. The last thing we want is for her to be hurt or for millions of hidden dollars to appear as bond money or bribe money for the release of Skyler Marks or Castriano and his clan. Worse yet, those millions can be spent paying their slimy lawyers and keeping us in litigation for years. No offense intended counsel—you earned your keep," Agent Lloyd said, placing a friendly hand on Rebecca's shoulder.

"I'd like nothing more than to see Skyler behind bars. Thanks for sharing," Rebecca said. "I guess we all should be glad you are on our side."

"We have been at least two steps ahead all the way," Agent Lloyd said with confidence.

CHAPTER 54

Samantha looked delicate and beautiful, like a miniature pink rosebud atop a thin stalk, about to bloom. She sat motionless in her new pink-and-white robe, with a box of raspberry croissants on her lap. She gazed out onto the small, but well-groomed, lawn of the hospital, grateful her physician had made arrangements for her to use the staff deck every afternoon. Samantha, cocooned in thoughts she was glad were her own, wondered why her mother was so distracted.

"Why are you so fidgety?" Samantha finally asked her mother, not able to take another series of fingernail taps against the Plexiglas patio table.

"No reason." Mom sipped her coffee. "I think we should take a family vacation together, put all this behind us. You've looked so much better these past few weeks. You've been through so much." Her mom kept looking toward the balcony door.

"Mom, I'm fine. Please don't worry."

Her mom sighed again.

"You did it again. You only sigh when you're upset.

What's wrong?" Samantha asked, suspicious she wouldn't be told the truth, regardless of how many questions she asked her mother. So many things had happened; so much lost time.

"Nothing. You're being silly. I'm anxious to get you home," her mom said, focusing on her coffee cup.

Samantha drank her strawberry milkshake and tugged her croissant apart. The fresh air gave her hope she would get well. Her daily outdoor time had conditioned her to look forward to her meals. Most of her headaches had stopped, and she had survived the withdrawal of the concoction of drugs she'd been living on.

The nightmares, the dreams, and the voices, still puzzled her, but she was working through them with her psychiatrist, and they were fading. She didn't mind the voices inside her. She'd spent so much time alone, she actually began to feel better knowing they were there, and she wasn't alone.

She accepted that the voices and dreams would disappear. Once her psychologist had explained that she'd created them as a defense mechanism, as a way of coping, she had faith she would return to normal.

Samantha learned to do as she was told. It was her only way back home, back to school, back to John. It was Samantha's turn to sigh with each thought that provoked another question.

She was sure that no one would ever hurt her this deeply again. She promised herself that much.

"There's nothing to worry about, Samantha. Everything is fine," her mom said.

Her dad walked out onto the deck. "How are my two beautiful women?" he asked, planting a kiss on each of their foreheads and sat between them.

"Where are the twins?" her mom asked.

"Can we go back to your room for a few minutes? The twins are there waiting for us," Dad said. "We've got some things to discuss."

Mom stood, grabbed her purse and sweater.

Samantha was intrigued, but stayed in her chair.

"Come on, sweetheart. We can come back outside this evening if you want," her mom said.

"I'm not moving until I know what's going on. People are always whispering and talking as if I'm not here. I want to know. If something happened, you need to tell me now." Samantha shifted her gaze from one parent to the other and then back again, still making no motion to leave. She felt her newly gained power.

"Samantha, honey, you're right. But we need to talk in your room. Would you like to walk, or can I push you in your wheelchair?" her dad said.

"Whatever. But, I'm walking. I've been pushed around too much," Samantha said.

The walk back to her room felt long and strained. Samantha felt uneasy walking in the awkward, silent shadows of her parents. As they neared her room, she sensed the stares of the nurses. Something was wrong.

She was immediately frightened.

"Stop," Samantha said in a low voice, her teeth grinding together. "I want to know right now. What's wrong? I can feel it. Everyone's staring at me."

"Sweetheart, it's not that anything is wrong. It's finally right again," her dad said. He placed his hands on her shoulders firmly.

Samantha stiffened. She didn't like the touch of any man, not even her father. She looked to her mother. But she looked as confused as Samantha felt. "I don't understand."

Dad interrupted, opening the door to Samantha's room. "We'll let Rebecca explain. She's inside waiting with a few of your friends."

Samantha tiptoed into her room, slowly, cautiously, curiously. Within seconds, the curtain was pulled from around her bed. A chorus of voices echoed, "Surprise."

Samantha teared up, not understanding. She pulled her robe tightly around her body. Rebecca clacked her heels toward her and stopped just short of touching noses with her. Samantha stepped back, uncertain.

"We've done it. You are free. This afternoon, all of the charges were dropped, permanently," Rebecca said.

Samantha looked around the room and then back at Rebecca in disbelief. "Over? Where is Skyler?" She stepped backward. "He'll come for me. I'm not safe."

"It's over," said the twins in unison.

Her father nodded.

"No more worries about courtrooms or Skyler. He has much bigger things to worry about than finding you," Rebecca said. "Agent Lloyd will keep him busy for years, maybe a lifetime."

"We've brought you a cake with a file in it, just in case," Taylor joked.

"A chocolate file, I bet," Samantha said.

"We've saved the best for last," Rebecca said and then opened the door, revealing Agent Lloyd and John.

"Samantha, I've missed you." John wrapped his arms around her.

She shuddered. "How did you know to come?" Samantha whispered to him and hugged him back for a second, then pulled away.

John wrapped his little finger around hers. "I never forget a pinkie swear." He squeezed her.

"Samantha," Rebecca said. "I asked John to fly down for the end of the trial. Your parents agreed, and Emily and Agent Lloyd made the arrangements."

"Thank you all so much," Samantha said, unable to control tears. She turned and hugged Emily. Everyone was happy. But she felt discontented, unsure why. She hoped Rebecca would fill in the details later, but was curious about why there wasn't any talk about taking her home. The conversation died with the beginning of the jingling dinner trays down the hallway.

"I can be packed in a few minutes," Samantha said. She stared into the faces of the crowd in her room.

"Samantha." Rebecca pulled her aside from John and from Emily. "I'll be staying till Saturday. We'll have a chance to go over everything. I hear you'll be home by the end of the week, and I'll see you there."

"So, I'm not going home?" Samantha looked over her attorney's shoulder toward her parents. They were nodding.

"We'll pick you up when the doctor releases you," her mom said.

Rebecca squeezed her shoulder. "Spend some time with John. Have a good evening." She gave Samantha a reassuring hug and whispered, "You're finally free and safe."

Samantha nodded slowly and then watched Rebecca walk out of the room followed by Agent Lloyd and her family.

$*\ *\ *\ *$

"You've got a good friend in Emily," John said, when they were finally alone. "Hey, that tray doesn't look bad for hospital food. We've had worse in the dorm."

Samantha laughed, feeling no time had passed between them since they were last together. "Emily is a good friend; like a sister to me. I'm glad you two get along."

"I'll tell you what, as soon as you're released, we'll go out to dinner anywhere you want and then see a movie."

"I'd love it, but," Samantha hesitated, afraid to go on.

"Is there a problem?" John asked.

Samantha sighed, breathing deeply, trying to calm herself. "It's hard for me—being with a man. Being touched, even on the shoulder by my father's hand. My psychiatrist says eventually, in my own time I will get over that. I have no idea when."

"I understand," he said. "We have all the time in the world. Let's make a deal, okay?"

"What kind of deal?" Samantha asked, suspicious of any deal with a man.

"We'll start our relationship over in the fall at Michigan State. We'll go as slow as you want. You can knock on my window in the middle of the night. I'll help you unpack, hell, I'll unpack for you, while you eat a rainbow of soft serve."

Samantha laughed. "That's a huge commitment."

"Take all the time you need to adjust, to feel normal. But I promise you'll feel no evil with me or ever again. I will always be there for you in a good way."

Samantha smiled, remembering the day they'd met. She nodded. "Deal."

"Deal?" John said, and gave her the "pinky swear" sign.

Samantha held out her pinky and joined it with his. For the first time in months, she was beginning to feel there was hope, real hope, she'd be normal again.

CHAPTER 55

nxious to see the doorknob turn and reveal John's handsome figure, Samantha lay on her bed and watched. It had been great these past few months. It was a time of new beginnings and happy endings. John was nearing completion of his master's, and she was redoing her first term of college. They were a year older, but she was many years wiser, and John was happier.

She stroked the wooden box Nana had given her long ago and flipped open its meticulously polished lid. She inspected every crevice flipping it over faster and faster, testing her memory about the markings on each side. When she accidently dropped it, she gasped.

The music box rolled across the carpet. She retrieved it and put it on her desk. Hearing a clank, her heart sank. The bottom separated from the box. Desperately, Samantha tried to fit the bottom back into the box. She had to make it whole again, perfect again. She inspected it more closely. Why wasn't it fitting?

She studied the inside of the box. Why were there cotton balls stuffed inside the box? Slowly, she pulled at the cotton hoping that if she removed just a little, she could reinsert the bottom.

She pushed aside the cotton, and she found three small keys. What were they doing inside Nana's music box? How long had they been there? Nana must have wanted her to find the keys, to find what they went to, to give her a last present, a final memory.

She was comforted by that thought. Nana had given her something she could think about in the silence and serenity of her room.

Quietly, reverently, she placed them back inside their hiding place, inside the exquisite music box. Eventually they fit. With the cotton snugly wrapped around them, the keys were protected. The box was protected, and the base was returned to seal the box as if it had never been separated.

Samantha listened to the music box and chanted the nursery rhyme to the tune: *Humpty Dumpty sat on a wall, Humpty Dumpty had a great fall, all the King's horses and all of his men couldn't put Humpty together again.*

Samantha climbed onto the bed, drifted, and pictured John kissing her into reality. He had promised to take it slow with her, and he had. It was easy to want him, easy to care about him. During all those months in the hospital, she'd memorized every detail of his face.

When sleep finally consumed her, John's face came to her, and as quickly as she neared him, he was replaced with the faces in the shadows of her dreams. The pieces of the faces whole and recognizable. She saw him first: Greg Maston. Lying there. Face down. Covered in blood. Blood, oozing from everywhere. It was so red.

Skyler. Where was Skyler? He had caused this. Not her. He should pay. Not her. She watched herself moving coldly about the room.

She heard laughter and voices. The music box was playing, but she didn't see it. She tried to piece every-thing together.

The familiar voice, the one that liked to direct her and laugh at her, began. Samantha shivered, recognizing it, easily deciphering it from the rest. It called her weak. It had told her she couldn't have any man until she'd gotten rid of the man who hurt her. Samantha knew the voice was right, and it left her without choice.

Tom. Her handsome Tom appeared out of the dark-ness to rescue her. He saved her from the faces, from the mean voices. His image calmed her. He took care of her. He always did. He said he always would.

She turned. A baby was crying in the background. She tried to find it; she wanted to help it. The crying came from so many directions, but never the one she chose. And then, it too, stopped. Blood began to spurt from the walls around her, and then disappeared. She blinked in horror. The rest of the voices came. The faces, too. They began to laugh and chant—until the body rolled over. And she saw his face, calm, peaceful. Dead.

The voice. It was there again. Loudly but calmly. It mesmerized her, again chanting she had been brave and rational and right. Darcey's voice was right and true and strong. Darcey had helped her face up to what she'd needed to do. Darcey and Tom were helping her build a new life.

Samantha awoke with the quiet knock to see her dormitory door open. The music box, safely beside her, was silent. She reached up and placed it carefully on her desk to avoid dropping it again.

Sleepy-eyed Samantha blinked approvingly toward her handsome, confident John, who stepped into the room toward her. She was fine. She was cured. She slipped her hand away from the crumpled and badly worn legal words that had remained inside her personal pillowcase through all those changes of linen, for over a year because she hadn't let anyone touch her pillow.

She no longer needed the law. She no longer needed anyone, except John. And she needed sleep. She needed to not be triggered into her past pain. Would her inner nightmare ever end?

Samantha stared into his handsome face. Maybe one day he would help her find the answer to the puzzle of the keys. But then again, maybe not. Either way, she was confident with John, she'd feel no evil.